Prairie Cinderella

Vinnie Ream and the Gilded Age

By Joan Koster

Book 3 in the Forgotten Women Series

Tidal Waters Press

NEW YORK

e-Book edition ISBN 978-1-959318-17-0
Paperback edition ISBN 978-1-959318-18-7

Cover design by 100Covers
Book design by Kristin Campbell

This is a work of fiction. While some characters and circumstances portrayed by the author are based on real people and historical fact, references to real people, events, establishments, organizations, or locales are only intended to provide a sense of authenticity and are used fictitiously. All other characters and all incidents and dialogue are drawn from the author's imagination and are not to be considered real. In all other respects, any resemblance to persons living or dead is entirely coincidental.

Dedication

To my husband, Harold,
whose love of history has inspired my own.

To the Reader

Based on a True Story—Sort Of . . .

This is a work of both historical fact and historical imaginings. The majority of characters you will meet lived and worked in the late nineteenth century. Many have well-documented lives; some do not.

From the existing writings, diaries, letters, magazines, court documents, and news reports, I have conjured their lives as best I can. In particular, the inner thoughts, feelings, and motivations of Vinnie Ream, Cornelius Boudinot, Richard Hoxie, and their compatriots in this narrative are entirely imagined. My story does, however, abide by the generally known facts and events in Vinnie's life, and I have sometimes quoted from her diaries and letters.

If you wish to know more, a listing of the historical personages found in this novel and a discussion of the background research can be found in the Author Notes at the back.

Part 1
1861 to 1863

"The smartest politician of them all."

Mark Twain

"How Miss Vinnie Ream Got into the Capitol—and Won't Be
Turned Out."
The Chicago Republican, February 19, 1868

Chapter 1

MAY 1861

FORT SMITH, ARKANSAS

Fort Smith is the hottest it's ever been, but the oppressive air doesn't stop my feet from churning up the dirt and pebbles. I can't believe what I've heard.

I kick harder as if mere feet could stomp the coming disaster deep into the earth. Sweat pours down my neck and gathers in my armpits. My cotton dress tangles around my legs. My hair tumbles from the pins Mary inserted so carefully this morning. I stick to the shady side of the road. It helps little. Nothing will cool the burning betrayal inside me.

It's only half mile from Pa's real estate office to the boarding house. It feels like a thousand.

I arrive out of breath and in an unladylike disarray, sure to set Ma's tongue to lashing. I don't care. My world is crashing down around me.

Ma is hanging the wash in the yard like it's an ordinary day. Sheets drip onto the dry dirt. Chickens scratch for bugs. The sun beats down.

I skid to a halt in front of her. "We're leaving Fort Smith?" I see by the pinch in her lip that it's true.

My mother wipes her hands on her apron and uses the sweet-talking tone I can't abide, the one that works so well on Pa. "Calm yourself. You're sixteen, not a child. Arkansas has seceded from the Union. There's going to be a war."

All my hot fury flames out. "But why all the way to Washington City? Going there is what *you* want, not Pa. He loves the wild prairie. You're the one who hates it here. You just want to wear fashionable clothes and hobnob with politicians' wives."

Ma swipes the hair off her sweaty brow, her sun-crinkled face sufficient reproof against my accusation. "My days of being a fine lady are long gone, child. Not that I ever was one. Society ladies don't raise three children in a log cabin on the edge of the wilderness with a husband off exploring uncharted territory." She casts me a smile that hides all sorts of truths. "We are leaving because we can't stay here, Vinnie. Your pa's ill. He's been promised a position in the War Department—a desk job. He can't ride all day in the saddle, doing government land surveys anymore."

There's truth in what she says, but not enough to cool my anger. "Why didn't you tell me? I had to hear it from the shoeshine boy."

Ma hangs up another sheet. "We knew you'd react like this—totally unreasonable."

I stop bouncing my foot and straighten my posture. "Can't Bobbie do the mapping for Pa?"

"Your brother has no hankering for it, and you know it. He'd rather challenge his Cherokee buddies to a horse race or sit listening to the tribal elders' stories."

I pull a wet sheet from the basket and throw it over the line. "Fine, I'll do the surveys and say Bob did them."

Ma wags her finger at me. "That there notion is another reason we are going to Washington. Lord knows I've tried to wipe the tomboy out of you. Look at you. I sacrificed my savings to send you and Mary to that female academy. Lied about your age so you could acquire some social graces. What would Major Rollins say if he saw you looking like some country bumpkin? You've been raised to be a well-behaved young lady. You're not one of these native savages."

My heart does a little twist—not all the natives are savages. There is one . . . but that is an argument for another time.

I clench my fists, gather all my resentment, and spew it out. "I won't go. You can't make me. Not now. Not ever. I need space. I need air. I need to be with my friends."

"What you *need* is exposure to polite society where your singing and art are appreciated, not wasted on the local bucks nosing around after you girls. Just think. You and Mary will have a chance to marry fine gentlemen."

"Mary, maybe. Not me."

Ma's chin juts out. "Of course you will marry, Vinnie."

"I will never marry a snooty Easterner. *Never.*" I spin around and race to the paddock, whistle for my calico pony, leap onto his bare back, and dash to the gate. Our old coonhound, Thunder, expects a lark and runs after us, ears flapping, his once strong bay, a low grumble. I slow and wait for the old guy to catch up.

Ma shouts after me, "Miss Lavinia Ellen Ream. You get back here right quick. I swore you were too old at sixteen to switch. I see I was wrong."

No longer listening, I spur my pony down the lane, fleeing to my secret place, far from scolding mothers and impending doom.

In minutes, the last of the town's buildings lies behind. I lengthen the reins and give my pony his head. Racer needs little guidance. He knows the way.

We cross the wagon train tracks, head into the rolling hills, and follow the familiar deer path down to the Arkansas River's edge. My bower lies mere inches from the lapping current, the lower leaves mud-stained from the spring floods.

I tether Racer and crawl under the fronds. It's cooler here. My dress is already filthy, so I plop down on the muddy bank, yank off my boots and stockings, then trail my feet in the cool shallows.

Thunder arrives panting and settles into the damp earth beside me. Running my hand down his neck, I pinch off stray burrs. For years, he was Pa's faithful companion, trekking behind him as he crisscrossed the unknown western lands, fording rivers, sleeping rough, parleying with the Indians, and putting Iowa and Kansas on the map. I pat his head. The old hound's frontier-stomping days are long over. Soon, mine and Pa's will be, too.

I scoop up a handful of river clay, roll it in my palm, then smash it flat again and again. I refuse to be uprooted from the prairie I love and taken to the most corrupt city in the land.

With my fingers, I reshape the clay into a ball, work in eye sockets, a strong nose, and broad lips, then, using my fingernail, I etch in his long, flowing hair. Cornelius Boudinot—the handsomest and smartest man I know—my sister Mary's heartthrob.

I set the sculpture down and gaze up at the sky. Poor Mary. What must she be feeling, having to leave him behind? If Boudy were mine, nothing would stop me from staying here with him—if he were to ask.

But he hasn't asked.

I shake my head. And if he did, I'd have to refuse. He can't be mine. He's Mary's. He's been courting her for months and months. And I would never hurt my sister. I love her too much.

Chapter 2

MAY 1861

FORT SMITH, ARKANSAS

Our last day in Fort Smith comes way too soon. Through my bedroom's open window, harnesses jingle. Horses snort. Trunks *thud*. Pa grunts and groans as he and my brother load all our possessions into the wagon.

With a huff, I plop down on the bare mattress and peer around the room I've shared with my sister for the past three years. The room lies empty, curtains down, the quilts and rag rugs packed. Despite my arguments, we are leaving.

I scrunch my nose at my sister. We usually agree on everything, but for the last three days, she's quashed every idea I've had to keep us here, where we belong. I try again. "You truly want to leave?"

"Yes." She opens the lid of the battered trunk that crossed the ocean with our Scottish grandmother and will ferry our belongings far from the frontier where we've grown up.

I fall back on the mattress, my temples pounding, and broach the one argument I have avoided. "What about Boudy?"

She whirls around and glares at me. "What about him?"

I jerk my head up. I am not used to such a sharp tone. "You could marry him." I should stop there, but I don't. "I would if he were my beau."

Mary fists her hands. "Oh, Vinnie. Elias Cornelius Boudinot isn't going to marry me. He's a man with ambitions. A lawyer with a future. Why would a rising member of the Cherokee tribe hitch himself to a debt-ridden white man's daughter?"

"But you spent all that time with him."

"Arguing politics, singing duets together, and writing bad poetry is not love. Nor a basis for marriage. So, forget Boudy and get packing."

But I can't forget him. It was me he kissed that night in the stable. Me he declared he loved.

I glance at Mary's drawn-in posture. She looks like an old woman, not a young girl of twenty. She doesn't want to leave him. I can tell.

We have never had secrets between us, but for her sake, that kiss must be kept buried deep inside, no matter how much I long to let it out. I gnaw the inside of my cheek.

"Vinnie, stop daydreaming." My sister's voice cuts through my thoughts. "We've got to get over these Fort Smith buddies of Bob's who've been hanging around." She carefully folds up a stocking. "This is our grand opportunity. In the city, we'll be able to attract the finest, richest, most well-educated gentlemen in the land to be our husbands." There is no joy in her voice.

I roll over onto my stomach. "That's what Ma says. But Boudy is better than any of them. You know that."

Mary turns away and tucks up another stocking, but she can't hide the tears trickling down her cheek. She throws the ball of stocking in the trunk. "You know nothing about men, especially that one."

My heart pinches. I've hurt her. It was a mistake to badger her about Boudy.

Moving to her side, I throw my arms around her and inhale her lavender scent. "Sorry. I'm sure you and Ma are right."

She forces a smile. "You might not remember our trip to the Capital when you were five, but I do. I can't wait to get back there. You'll change your mind when you see how grand it is. Just think, we will be able to go to balls, ride in carriages, and be courted the way we should. So, stop delaying and move along."

It is fruitless to argue more. I'm not brave enough to stay behind on my own. And war *is* coming. Though why Washington City will be safer than Fort Smith, I have no idea.

I stare at the dresses hanging on the pegs and picture our looming future. "Why bother packing this stuff? Everything we own will be out of style in the city."

Mary huffs. "It will be a long while before we can afford any new finery. You planning to parade around the capital in your unmentionables?"

"I don't want to parade around that foul pit at all. I want to stay here in the West. The war won't affect us. We're not politicians, us Reams. We're explorers."

"Don't be ridiculous. We're anti-slavery Northerners. All those so-called friends of yours will turn on us once the shooting starts."

Gritting my teeth, I tug my workaday dress over my head and don the garb of the young lady I am supposed to be. Atop my chemise and stays goes the detested cage crinoline, the cotton over-petticoat, followed by my second-best dress. I hook the bodice to the skirt and button up the front. Last is the confining, starched white collar. I pinch it closed with my tiny pearl pin, a gift from my closest friend from Christian Female College, Elizabeth Rollins.

I face my sister. "Is this how we will attract those paragons of yours?" I hold out the yellow gingham skirt with its frayed hem and twirl. "Wearing these oh-so-fashionable garments?"

Mary peers down at her own washed-out calico. "We do need new clothes." Her mouth twists. "Once Pa has the mapping position, we'll be able to have something more stylish made."

For Mary's sake, I hope so.

Footsteps pound up the stairs.

"Ready with that trunk?" Bob bounds into the room, at twenty-three, all bone and muscle, and overflowing energy. "Pa's waiting. And Ma's fuming."

Mary scoops up her straw hat and sets it atop her neatly parted, buckeye-brown hair. "I'm packed, but Vinnie hasn't even started."

"Figures. I swear Vee is some waif Pa found on one of his mapping surveys and toted home in his saddlebag. Look at her—too dark eyes, too wild black hair. Never on time and always in the way."

The little piece of me that believes Bob's teasing twinges. I straighten up. "I am, too, a Ream. And I'm way more reliable than you, brother." I yank my few dresses from their pegs and squash them into the space remaining in the trunk. "Where have you been these past two days while we scrubbed and cleaned?"

"Off to Indian Territory. On man's business."

"*Man's business*? More like betting on horse races."

"No. Way more important stuff is going on, brat. There's a war brewing, in case you didn't notice. The Confederacy is enlisting men for the army."

"For sure, I noticed." I jam in the last flannel petticoat and slam the lid down. "It's why we're trekking across the country so Pa can make maps for a *War* Department."

Bob hefts the trunk onto his shoulder. "Be thankful you won't be going to the poorhouse. Pa needs that job. The real estate business has gone flat broke, what with the war coming and all."

Mary shifts to the side to let him pass. "I'm sure the conflict won't last long."

My brother throws back his head and laughs. "Beyond a doubt, the South will win its freedom from the Union in no time. Those wimps up north will never take up arms against their fellow countrymen."

Mary jerks up her chin. "They'd better. Slavery is an abomination. I will never forget seeing those poor women and children in shackles, being herded like animals. It would be ungodly to introduce the practice to the new territories." With a pinch-faced glare at Bob, she heads out the door and down the stairs.

I place my girlish straw hat atop my out-of-control curls and seize the ribbons. "You're wrong, Bob. The North will fight. Wait and see."

He readjusts the trunk on his shoulder. "Bah. Not when the Indians rise up against them, too."

I tug on the bonnet ties. "The Indians? What are you talking about?"

"The Southern Cherokee voted to fight for the Confederacy last night."

The ribbons fall from my hands. "Was Boudy there?"

"Of course. He gave a great speech about all the ways Washington has cheated the tribe and gone back on their promises."

Despite the early morning cool, I flush hot. "I don't believe you. Boudy would have told us he was going to side with the South when he last visited."

"You think he'd support the North after what the feds did to his Cherokee kin?"

My skin prickles. Bob's right. Boudy's mother might have been white, and he might have grown up in Connecticut, but members of his family died on the forced march to Indian Territory. His father was assassinated for signing the treaty.

"I know he has his reasons. I just wish . . ."

"What?"

"Did he give you a message for me?" With a gulp, I correct myself, "For Mary?"

"Nope. Why should he? He's got way more important things to think about than silly girls." Bob slides the trunk higher on his shoulder. "Now get a move on if you don't want to be left behind." With that, he turns and thumps down the stairs.

I stare at his disappearing back and fight back tears. Boudy will be risking his life in battle, and for the wrong side.

"Vinnie." Pa's voice resounds from the yard below. "We're leaving."

I survey the bare room to make sure I haven't forgotten anything. Oh, yes. I lift the loose floorboard beneath the bedstead and pluck out the clay head of Boudy.

Mary is right. I don't know men at all, especially this one. I should smash it to pieces, but I can't. I thrust it back between the floorboards, then bound down the stairs. Time to forget about Boudy. Time to face the coming future.

Half an hour later, our wagon halts at the dock. I gaze up at the giant paddle wheeler. Our itinerary has been drilled into my head the whole way here. First, the steamer will ferry us to the port of Napoleon on the Mississippi. From there, we will take a bigger steamship north, up the Ole Miss to Cincinnati, then another along the Ohio River to Pittsburgh, where we'll at last catch the train to the Capital. Over a thousand miles. Almost two weeks on the road. I can barely conceive of it.

Lifting the brim of my straw hat, I peer up the rows of cabin windows. The trip will be hellish. All Papa could afford is one measly cabin for all of us. How will I survive living in close quarters with my family for the next two weeks or so? Already, my sister is on my case.

Mary nudges me in the arm with her elbow again. "Get moving. No more of this pigheadedness. We're getting on that boat."

She stomps up the gangway ahead of me. I wrinkle my nose at her back, then gather up my precious guitar and music folio and follow her. At the top of the gangplank, I slow and gaze upriver toward my beloved hills and grasslands. How will I live confined in a city far from the prairie I love?

I shift the folio beneath my arm. Ma is right about one thing—I'm more likely to find fame and fortune in Washington City than out here on the frontier.

Music and art are my great loves. And I have the talent. My art teacher said so, and Pa's old friend, Major Rollins, has even arranged for my painting of Martha Washington to be put on display in the main hall at the school. Maybe, despite the anger balled tighter than a chigger in my chest, leaving Fort Smith and Boudy is the best thing that could happen.

I look back at the dock. The crowd has thinned. The wagons have been unloaded. Behind me, the steam boilers rumble. The ship's horn whoops. We'll be leaving in minutes. Turning my back on the river, I wend my way along a deck crowded with fellow townsfolk also fleeing the war and sweat-drenched slaves hefting bales of smoky-sweet tobacco and white fluffy cotton.

Ahead, angry voices rise over the churning of the engine. It sounds like Ma. I hurry forward, only to smash into Bob.

"Always in the way, brat," he hisses as he shoves me aside, knocking me off balance. Down I go. My guitar hits the deck and clangs in its case. My folio opens, and sheet music and pencil sketches fly in every direction.

Ma, hard on Bob's heels, glances at me but keeps going. "You get right back here, young man. You are *not* staying behind."

Bob jerks his head over his shoulder but doesn't slow his footsteps. "Pa said I could stay. I'll come on a later boat. I promise." Then he leaps down the gangplank and is gone in a flash.

Ma calls after him, "You stay safe. And don't you dare hie off to be a soldier."

I press my lips together. Knowing my brother, that's exactly what he'll do the minute the steamship leaves the dock.

I scramble to my feet, only to come face-to-face with my mother.

She glares at me. "Look at you. You are the clumsiest creature ever."

"But Bob—"

"Don't you blame your brother for your failings. Make yourself proper—gentlemen are watching. Then gather up all these papers."

I look down. In the melee, my annoying hoop skirt has hiked up, revealing my bare limbs. I tug the dress down and use my tiniest voice. "Sorry."

"Don't try that little-girl tone on me. How will we face our fellow travelers after such a display? In fact, consider yourself confined to the cabin till we reach the Mississippi." She punctuates her decision with a sharp nod. "Yes, that would be for the best. Mary can bring you your meals. You can do the cleaning and mending while pondering the errors of your ways."

My head pounds. I won't survive trapped in an airless cabin. "Ma, you can't lock me up."

"Of course, I can." Her voice trembles. The skin beneath her left eye quivers. She gazes off toward the dock. I can see the tears in her eyes, put there by my brother's desertion.

It is not me she's angry with, and I love her too much to add to her burdens. So, for once, I do not sass back.

Instead, I bend my neck. "Okay, fine."

Later, I'll appeal to Pa. He'll get Ma to relent. Bob might be my mother's favorite, but I'm my father's.

Chapter 3

JUNE 1861

WASHINGTON CITY

Mary and I cling to each other as we bump over the ruts of New Jersey Avenue. We have arrived in the capital, and I already hate it.

The hub of the Union is ten times hotter than Fort Smith, the air heavy with swampy damp and foul odors. Volunteer militia with ill-trimmed beards and dirt-stained uniforms shout lewd comments as we pass. Women in hoops, three times as wide as our country versions, avert their eyes. Fine gentlemen in toplofty hats laugh and jeer. Beside me, my sister sits like a statue, her back rigid, her chin tight. All her excitement at arriving in the city has been eaten away by the reality of our situation.

We are no fine ladies. After fourteen days on steamboats and almost forty-eight hours on the train, we look like the penniless, bedraggled refugees we are. But there is nothing we can do about it.

To distract her, I point at the building looming ahead. "That's got to be the Capitol. Looks like the pictures in our book at school."

"Stop pointing." Mary tips her head down. "Everyone's gawking at us already."

But I can't help myself. I've never seen such a grand edifice in my life.

I squint against the glare of the sun bouncing off the white façade. "It's just like the ancient Greek temples I sketched in art class. The capitals on the columns are Corinthian, I think." I poke out my lower lip. "Too bad the dome isn't finished."

Mary squeezes my arm. "Shush, Vinnie. One would think you want the whole world leering at us."

"Pah, Mary." I lean further out of the wagon to get a better view. "I hope our house is nearby. I can't wait to climb those gleaming marble steps, stand under the portico, and roam its halls. I bet it's just full of artwork." I swivel and yell over the stack of trunks to where Pa and Ma sit crowded in with the driver. "Are we close yet?"

Ma glares back at me. "Child. For the ten-thousandth time, set yourself quiet."

My father lifts his country straw and wipes his brow. "It's right fine, Lavinia. After all the wailing about leaving Fort Smith, I'm glad to see her happy to be here."

A couple passing by casts sour looks in our direction.

Mary hunches back against the trunks. "Bad enough we look like hayseeds. Do we have to act uncouth, too?" She yanks the brim of her hat down even further. "Why couldn't Pa have rented a closed coach?"

"There's no money left."

Mary lets the burr of frustration slip into her voice. "Don't I know it? We have a lot of work ahead of us. Unpacking. Cleaning. Getting ready to take in boarders. Until Pa gets the promised position in the War Department, we'll be living on what rent we can bring in."

That litany of hated tasks is enough to sweep away any excitement I have about being here.

I settle back and gaze at the passing scene, my spirits sinking lower and lower. We pass rows of houses, cheek by jowl in the hot sun, with no space between them, no grass, no trees, no air. How will I survive in such a place?

The livery wagon turns left and, a few minutes later, stops in front of a three-story clapboard house. I swallow a groan. The building surely dates to the Revolution, and the years haven't been kind. Standing alone on an empty section of the street, the house is the same unidentifiable brown as the bare dirt surrounding it. Not a blade of grass or flowering bush softens its unwelcoming appearance.

"We gave up our spacious Fort Smith house for this place?" I clamber off the back of the livery wagon and stare at our new home.

Pa, who always finds some good in the worst of situations, joins me. His shoulders droop. "I'm sorry, Vinnie. I know this is not where you wish to be, but I'm sure you will find lots to explore once we settle in. And with our antislavery views, we'll be safer here."

All but Bob. But I keep that to myself, put my hand in his, and squeeze. "I know."

Ma directs the driver to unload the trunks, grabs a carpet bag, and strides up the steps. She opens the front door and waves us inside. "Move along, girls. No one said this would be easy. Looks like we have a passel of scrubbing ahead."

I close my eyes, count to ten, then follow her in.

A month later, there's been no change in our circumstances. I wring out the mop and frown at the worn stone floor in the kitchen. I've done my part, but all the mopping in the world will not bring boarders to our door. We may be walking distance to the Capitol, but our location is too isolated from the political hubbub. Even the gaslights do not come this far. Across the way, cornfields stretch to the north. Untended pigs, geese, and goats wander the street and tear up our attempt at a garden at will.

If we don't get some boarders soon, Pa might have to shoot one of the annoying beasts so we don't starve. But tonight, Ma has made braised beef stew from a cheap cut of meat. It has been simmering on the stove all day to tenderize it, and the scent is making my stomach growl.

I lift the lid and inhale the rich aroma of the cloves and port wine that give Ma's stew its distinctive flavor. "Yum."

My sister flies into the kitchen. "Pa says a possible boarder has come."

Ma looks up from rolling out the biscuit dough. "Who?"

Mary tips her head toward the parlor. "Some stranger Major Rollins has brought. Pa has invited them to dinner."

Ma grins. "Smart man. Best way to land a boarder is to fill his belly with good food. So, get to work, girls. Mary, get that spiced pickle we made last week. Vinnie, finish cutting out these biscuits."

I stamp out a row of biscuit rounds using one of Ma's porcelain teacups, chipped from the trip East, and place the rounds in the cast iron pan. "I wonder if the congressman has any news of Bob?"

Ma bangs down the wooden spoon. "Don't mention your brother. I will not let Bob's foolish behavior affect our relationship with the major. We owe him too much."

Mary wraps her arms around Ma's waist. "Don't worry. Bob will show up any day now. He's just enjoying some freedom before heading east."

I pinch my lips together. I don't think so. My brother might hate slavery as much as we do, but his heart lies with Boudy and his Cherokee friends. But I dare not say anything. Everyone is on edge as it is.

Ma breaks free of Mary's hug and places the pan on the stove. "Vinnie, take the men some lemonade and tell them the meal will be on the table in ten minutes, soon as the biscuits are done."

I tear off the apron, fill three glasses, and place them on a tray. At the parlor door, I halt, hoping to catch some of the man-talk before they see me.

"It's the best I could do," Major Rollins says.

"No, that's fine, James. Half-time at the War Department will tide us over."

Rollins presses his palms together. "The work should increase with the war buildup. I'm sure they will give you more hours in no time. Meanwhile"—he turns toward me—"would you consider having one or both of your girls take a job at the post office? Their staff has been decimated by the sneaky dealings of that Confederate traitor, Postmaster General Reagan. The Southern sympathizers he lured away didn't just leave; they took the ledgers, documents, and maps. Lincoln's new postmaster appointee, Montgomery Blair, needs help to turn things around. Can't let those traitors stop the mails, you know."

I can barely breathe. A government job would bring in good money. Far more than Ma can make doing rich folks' laundry. And anything would be better than the daily drudgery and being under Ma's thumb all day long.

Pa leans back in his chair and fingers his beard. "I don't know. Mother is hoping our young ladies will find good men to wed."

Good men? I think not.

I step into the room.

The major looks toward me and winks. "The work would be no hardship for your bright angels. If my family were in Washington, I'd let my own daughters take the positions. The General Post Office is one of our most elegant buildings—tidy and expertly run now Blair is in charge." He grins at me. "You interested, Vinnie? They pay the same wage to women as they do men."

I tip my chin, as if considering, though earning a man's wages is motivation enough. "Sounds like a great opportunity, Major Rollins."

Pa wags his finger at me. "That's my girl. Always ready to jump into something new." He gives me a sad smile. "You know your ma will be none too pleased. She may say no, child."

I bow my head. Ma *will* say no. That's a surety. She insists our virtue be well-guarded. Still, a full-time job is the answer to my prayers. If I work, I can help Ma and Pa get on their feet again. With more money coming in, Mary could dress better and be more likely to forget Boudy and find her dream man.

"And Vinnie, I haven't forgotten your interest in art." Rollins tips his head toward the foppish stranger sitting beside him, adorned in an overabundant mustache and curls every woman would envy. "Meet the renowned painter, George Healy. Here from Chicago to deliver his painting of President Lincoln. I thought he could take a room with your folks for his stay."

George Healy. Even I have heard of his artistic accomplishments. He has painted queens, princes, and so many presidents. And now he sits beneath my schoolgirl drawing of the Parthenon, pinned up to hide a stain on the wallpaper. I should flee upstairs and bury myself under my covers. But I have never been that shy.

I balance the tray of lemonade and curtsey as best I can. "Most honored to make your acquaintance."

"Let's have some of that lemonade." Pa waves me over, and I pass out the glasses. When I reach Healy, I don the smile Ma calls my little flirt, the one that got me into trouble back in Fort Smith. "It is an honor to meet you, sir."

Healy takes a sip from his glass. "James has told me wonderful things about your talent, Miss Ream. I understand your portrait of Martha Washington now hangs at Christian Female College. And I see by this fine drawing you have a keenness of eye and a competent understanding of perspective."

I blink at the compliment and tuck it away to examine later for truth or flattery.

"Miss Ream is also a gifted musician," Rollins says. "Composed the college anthem. She must give us a Spanish serenade on her guitar before we leave."

Pa's eyes light up, and off he goes into his embarrass-me story mode. "Gifted? Why, back in Madison, I used to take this little girl every day to the widow woman in the next settlement so she could practice on her pianoforte. Weren't many of them in Wisconsin back in the 40s. In no time, our Vinnie was playing Chopin and more. Couldn't afford a piano ourselves. Bought her a guitar from a peddler when she was eight. Taught herself and a bunch of others, including the Menominee chief. I swear she can play better than that Madame de Goni, who was all the talk a few years back. And such an ear. Whistle a tune once, and she can pluck it straight out. Always said she'll perform for presidents one day. Wait and see. Soon, she'll be entertaining the highest folk here in the city."

Pa only says those things out of love for me. Still, I cringe at the exaggerated praise. His long-winded tales were fine out in the wilderness where people count time by seasons, but surely, Major Rollins, in his newly elected position as U.S. Representative from Missouri, has more to do this day, and Healy cares little for my schoolgirl tricks.

I tap Pa's shoulder. "I need to help Ma fetch dinner. Please escort our guests into the dining room." After a curtsey to Rollins and Healy, I rush back into the kitchen.

Ma is ladling the stew into our best serving bowl. "Hurry," I yell. "Pa's telling stories." I gather up the butter and the sterling salt cellar. At least we have one fine piece to display alongside Grandmother MacDonald's silver candlesticks.

Mary dumps the biscuits into a basket. "Oh no. In a minute, he will be jabbering about how Ma chased away a pack of threatening warriors by waving peacock feathers at them."

Ma picks up the stew pot. "Dear man always exaggerates. They were the most well-mannered gentlemen. I gave them the feathers as a gift. Sure do miss those plumes, though. Came all the way from Scotland in Mother's trunk. Now let's get this dinner served." She shoves the door open with her hip, and Mary and I follow behind.

By the time everyone's plates are full and grace said, my silly childhood escapades are long forgotten. I take a bite of my biscuit and look around the table.

Worn away by his troubling bouts of fever and the failure of his real estate business, my father is a frail wisp of the former tough-skinned explorer who mapped most of Nebraska, Iowa, Kansas, and the Indian Territory. My mother's face is creased with worry about our future in a city that has been less than welcoming. And my poor sister looks dull and subdued in what was once her fanciest dress.

We are at the lowest point in our lives. There's no way my sister can make inroads into high society so she can forget

Boudy and find her rich gentleman unless the family's fortunes are reversed.

I smile at Major Rollins. That post office position would be a godsend, for sure. What will I have to do to get it?

Chapter 4

AUGUST 1861

THE REAMS, NO. 325 NORTH B STREET, WASHINGTON

CITY

I look around the scrubbed-clean but still dreary parlor. The house needs so much work. Our clothing requires so much updating. Forbidden from taking the post office job, the best I've come up with is making officers' epaulets for a nickel apiece. I undo another thread. Enough to cover our food if I can figure out how to construct them. Who knew such elegant military decorations were stuffed with old cardboard?

Across the way, Mary is untwisting the gold cording from the sample and glaring at me. We've been tearing the dratted things apart for three days now and earning nothing.

I drop the epaulet into my lap. Nothing is working out as planned. With Healy gone, we are without boarders again. Pa's promised full-time position in the War Department has not yet materialized, and his half-time pay isn't enough to support us.

Not that it matters. Pa has taken to bed with one of his bouts of ague, and Ma is too tied up nursing him to take in more washing to keep us fed.

A loud knock on the door sends me running. With Pa sick abed, I've been tasked with keeping the noise down.

The boy on the stoop hands me a telegraph. I take it with a shaking hand. Nothing good ever arrives by wire—I scan it quickly—and this news is the worst.

I pinch the thin paper between my fingers. I want to yell. I want to scream. I would crumble up and burn it if I dared. But I can't. My parents need to know.

With dread in every step, I climb the stairs to the bedroom where Ma sits, sponging my father's fevered forehead.

"What is it, Vinnie?"

"A telegram from Bob."

My mother wrings out the cloth and extends her hand.

My poor mother. She doesn't deserve this on top of our empty boarding house and Pa's bout of illness. The news will break her heart. But there's no way to make it sweet. I pass her the missive.

She reads it silently, then fists her hands. "Noooo. That brother of yours has joined the 10th Company of the Arkansas battalion." She presses the hellish message against her chest, her face paler than I've ever seen it. "My foolish, foolish boy."

Pa lifts his head from the bolster. "Bob'll be all right, Lavinia. He's tough. A brilliant shot."

She glares at him. "You should have tied that boy to the wagon when he refused to come east. I worried every day you spent roaming the backcountry with him at your side. But facing floods, whirlwinds, and renegade warriors is nothing compared to going into a battle where everyone is trying to kill you—and for the wrong cause."

Pa's head falls back. "Look, Bob's no child. At twenty-three, I was on my own, earning a living."

She purses her lips. "Exactly. He ought to be here, landing a government job. Keeping us from starving. With so many enlisting, there are plenty of vacancies."

"We are not going to starve." Pa struggles to sit up. "I can work. I'll be better in the morning."

Ma grimaces. "Lie down." She slaps the wet cloth back on his brow. "You can barely lift your head. No way you'll be able to walk to the War Department and stand for hours over a drawing board tomorrow."

This is my opportunity. I clasp my hands behind my back and hold myself as straight as I can at a mere five feet. "Mary and I can help. We can take those post office jobs Congressman Rollins mentioned."

Color returns to Ma's face. "I told you no. Young ladies do not work in public. My daughters will not demean themselves by rubbing shoulders with people off the street. At least singing engagements expose you to a higher class of people."

I take a breath. "But Ma, despite the major and Reverend Hall's recommendations, Mary and I have had no requests. The rout at Bull Run frightened the city into a ghost town. Everyone who can has fled north, fearful of a rebel takeover. Those still here are in no mood for our music."

"Then stay home and help me with the washing. There's always laundry to be done."

"But we could earn so much more. They are paying women the same salary as men."

The skin beneath her eye twitches. "I can't bear the idea of it. How will you marry well after lowering yourselves so?"

"If we do not take those post office jobs, we won't have to worry about marrying at all. We'll be dead of hunger."

"Don't be melodramatic, child. We have resources. You'll never go hungry."

"Listen, Lavinia"—Pa lays his hand on her arm—"Major Rollins would never have mentioned the position if he thought it would damage Mary's and Vinnie's reputations."

If ever there was a time for my oft-criticized outspokenness, it's now. "We no longer have a choice, Ma. Bob is not going to help us. We must help ourselves. Look, if you won't allow both Mary and me to work, let me. I'm not of marriageable age, and it will only be temporary until Pa is on his feet again."

Ma lets out a long breath, then rises and swamps me in a hug. "Oh, Vinnie, I hate to ask you to make such a sacrifice."

"She'll be fine, Lavinia." Pa winks at me. "Our little girl has dealt with far worse characters than a bunch of city clerks. She can handle herself no matter where she is. And like she says, it will be only until I get full-time work."

Ma releases me. "I am not happy about it, but all right." She swipes her teary eyes with her sleeve. "Washington City was so elegant when we visited back in 1852. I thought, with a good job for you, our fortunes would rise and the girls would marry better than those wild men sniffing around them. But I was wrong. This war has spoiled everything. We should have gone to Ohio and joined my parents on their farm."

Pa rolls his head on the sweat-stained pillow. "I'm no farmer, Lavinia. Never was. And I haven't the strength for that work anymore. If I were the man I used to be, I'd be fighting for the Union, not sitting in an office."

She lifts his hand and rubs the leathery palm. "I know. But Ohio would have been nearer to Bobbie. Our boy could die out there all alone with us so far away."

I want to shout at her that Bob is a traitor. That he disobeyed Pa and is risking his life to preserve the horrors of slavery. That he doesn't deserve her worry and love. But how can I? I love him, too. My big brother may have teased and disparaged me growing up, but he has always been my hero. He taught me to ride, shoot, and never to fear anything.

I pat Ma on the shoulder. "Don't fret. I'm sure we'll figure a way to get letters across the lines. In fact, that is the best reason in the world for me to work at the post office."

My mother curls her fingers into mine and pulls me in for a hug. "You are so young to take so much on yourself."

"I only look young." I rest my cheek against her breast and inhale the familiar scent of starch and soap. "It will be fine. You'll see."

My mother rubs my back. "My dear child, always so full of hope."

I stand. "What I'm hoping right now is that the positions have not been filled." I pull away. "I'd better write Major Rollins at once."

I rush out of the bedroom and smack into Mary.

She rebalances the stack of laundry in her arms. "Vinnie? What's happened?"

"Bob joined the Rebels."

The linens tumble to the floor. "Oh. Ma must be devastated. I must go to her."

I bend down to help her gather up the sheets.

She lays a hand on my arm. "And Boudy?"

I toss the sheets at her and lash out, furious that the man I thought I loved could wreak such havoc on my family. That my brother could be so foolish as to follow him. I suck in a harsh breath. "*That traitor*. How could you even think of him at this moment? He's the reason Bob could die out there on some distant battlefield, gunned down by the very soldiers marching up and down our street. And for what? Friendship? What kind of friend puts our brother in front of cannon fire?"

"Sometimes you can be so hateful. You know I care about him." Mary wads up the linens and rushes down the hall.

I reach out to her. But she is gone, taking her recriminations with her.

I head down the stairs and grab my summer straw hat. Already, this war is tearing us apart. How will my family survive this crisis?

Then I remember I am going to work for the post office, and tendrils of excitement curl through me like rays of sunlight. Maybe Washington City won't be too bad after all.

Soon, we will have money coming in. Soon, Mary will have a new beau and forget Boudy. I touch my lips. If only I could forget him, too.

Chapter 5

GENERAL POST OFFICE, WASHINGTON CITY

Summer hangs on, hot, heavy, and malodorous, the stench of Washington Canal curling into every corner of the city, even up the elegant thoroughfare and into the halls of the General Post Office where I wait outside Postmaster General Blair's office. I fan myself with my hat and pray the position is still open. Government jobs are ripe plums quickly eaten by hungry political hacks.

I watch a fly crawl up the wall and tap my foot. I didn't expect Postmaster Blair to usher me right in without an appointment. But still, it doesn't excuse him for making me stand for over an hour, especially if the answer is a no. My best cotton dress is sweat-soaked, and my enthusiasm for the position has dissipated. All I want to do is find out if there's a job and leave. Except for a hustling messenger, no one has come in or out since I was admonished by Blair's shallow-cheeked clerk to wait in the hall.

At last, the door pops open. The clerk brandishes Rollins' recommendation in my face, then crushes it into a ball and tosses it from hand to hand. "Nothing for you."

The man's voice is too full of glee, and his treatment of a congressman's letter too foolhardy to be trusted.

Enough is enough. I slip under his arm, dash through the antechamber, and burst into Blair's private office. A dignified man with a carefully combed beard glances up. "Who in the world are you?"

The clerk elbows past. "This beggar girl thinks she can get a job at the post office."

I glare him. "I am not a beggar, sir. I graduated at the top of my class at Christian Female College in Missouri." I turn my full attention to Blair. "And I have a letter of recommendation from Congressman Rollins, which your clerk has crumpled up in his fist."

Blair wags his finger. "Let me see it, Hargrave."

The officious man smooths out the creases as best he can, then hands it over. "It's not real, sir. How could it be? Look at her. She's—"

"A dear friend of Congressman Rollins, it seems," Blair interrupts, holding up his palms as if to push the man and his lies away. "Leave us."

Hargrave stalks out, disgust crimping his lips.

"Miss Ream, I am so sorry. No young lady should be treated thus. Please sit."

I wiggle my way into the huge, upholstered chair facing the desk. My feet do not touch the floor, and I'm tempted to give them a swing, but I don't. Hands folded in my lap the way Madame Brusset taught us in etiquette class, I work hard to remove any trace of a Southern accent. Ma would be proud. "I'm here about the post office job. I hope it is still open. I know I look young, but I am hard-working and capable."

"Your apparent youth is no excuse for my clerk to treat you so cavalierly. How old are you?"

"Sixteen, sir."

The postmaster brushes his hair from his eyes. He is just as hot as I am, and I feel sorry for him in his woolen suit and tight collar. I picture the buckskins my father wore when out mapping. Frontier garb is so much more comfortable. Frontier folk are so much more welcoming. Homesickness sweeps over me. But I tuck it away and concentrate on winning this job.

He leans back in his chair and tugs his beard. "I do have a few positions vacant."

My hope soars. "I would be most honored to work for you. I am a fast learner. I kept the files at my father's real estate office before coming here."

"Unfortunately, you won't be under me. The only department head willing to even consider a female hire is Alexander Zevely, the third postmaster general. He runs the dead letter office. They have been inundated with mail from the Southern states, and we have no way to deliver it. Rollins writes that your geography is top-notch. You'll be a big help sorting it out and returning it to the senders."

My hands unclasp. "We're not delivering mail from the South?"

He flips his hand. "Can't accept Confederate postage, can we?" He jots down a note and offers it to me. "You can start Monday."

I mumble my thanks and clutch the note to my chest, my mind a whirl. No mail from the South? How will we hear from Bob? I open my mouth to ask, then close it. I can't risk losing this job by admitting I have a traitorous brother. Not now, when knowing the inner workings of the mail system is more important than ever.

Six months later, I'm still no closer to communicating with Bob nor in making a dent in the pile of unidentifiable letters that greet me every day. I sigh and select the next envelope. Inside, I find a carte de visite with *"love you"* scrawled on the back.

The only clue is the soldier's face peering back at me. He has the look of an unsophisticated farm boy. It is there, in the way he slouches to one side and clenches his jaw, as if embarrassed by the camera lens. I bring my loupe to my eye and search for any insignia on his uniform, but the symbols lie hidden in the folds of his too-large jacket, and not enough shows to identify his unit's regimentals.

I hold the image to the light, but no new clues appear. The chair he sits in is unremarkable. The blankness behind him is a photographer's canvas. If I were to guess, it was taken by one of the itinerant photographers who follow the troops, lugging a wagonload of equipment from battlefield to battlefield.

Relegating the card to the tray of photos to be tossed into the fire bin is like sending him to an early death if this soldier isn't dead already. From Virginia to Arkansas, the battlefields are strewn with boys like this one.

Somewhere, a mother, sister, or girlfriend desperately waits for this image of their loved one, and I have no way to help them. I shove the box away. No more than I can help my family get word across the battle lines to my brother. My attempt to feign Southern sympathies and get information from my former school friends has been met with silence.

My heart heavy, I reach for the next one. It has been like that today—one failure after another.

"Vinnie?" My co-worker, Emma, puts a hand on my arm. "Another lost soul?"

Dear, kind, quiet Emma. All the girls in the dead letter department have become close over the last year, working side by side in the airless balcony where the women clerks have been ensconced. But Emma understands that the job is more than simply sorting pieces of paper to me. Failure pulls on her heart, too.

I slump in my chair. "There are so many."

"Not for lack of trying. You identify the highest percentage of the unreadable ones. That's why Zevely assigned you to the photographs."

"But not all." I flip through the cartes de visite to be destroyed. Young. Old. Bearded. Cherubic. "Surely, someone would recognize these faces if we could only display them to the public."

Emma tips her head like a bird spotting a seed. "Why, that's it, Vinnie. We could hang them in the entrance to the main post office for all to view."

I sit up. "What a brilliant idea. You must tell Postmaster Zevely."

Emma wraps her arms around herself and shakes her entire body in one big no. "No way. I can never tell where Zevely is looking with those crooked eyes of his. And I hate walking past the vultures below. You're the brave one here. Go and ask him if we can."

I don't like meeting with Alexander Zevely any more than Emma does. It didn't go well the last time I took on a mission for the female clerks and requested more ventilation. Despite my well-reasoned argument, we are still suffocating in the balcony. He might be only the third-level Postmaster General, but Zevely is firmly in charge. Like all men, he thinks the women assigned to him give the dead letter office a disreputable air. No wheedling or protest on our part has convinced him otherwise, and after that encounter, he believes me to be the troublemaker in the group.

Still, Emma's idea is too good to abandon.

I tiptoe down the spiral staircase from the hot, airless balcony and enjoy the cool breeze blowing through the first-floor windows. I stop on the bottom step and tug down the bag-like smock we are required to wear—supposedly to keep our dresses free of ink but which are surely designed to hide our femaleness. Not that it works.

Now to face my fellow workers. In one sense, Zevely is right to be worried. However, it's not the female clerks that are disreputable; it's the male. Walking across the sorting floor is like navigating a field of prairie thistles.

I draw in my skirts and head directly for his office. Heads pop up as I pass. The men stop opening letters, halt making notations. Wayward hands brush against me. Under-the-breath rude comments trail after me.

You would think they'd never seen a woman the way these men behave. Nothing protects us from their unsavory leers. They're free to ogle and use obscene epithets to their hearts' content, whereas we female clerks are forbidden to open any envelopes on the off chance we might come across something unfit for our delicate eyes.

At Zevely's door, I knock, then wait for his grunt. And wait. Finally, the door swings open, and one of the younger male employees strides out. He yanks on a curl as he passes.

I soothe my irritation by tracking the miscreant back to his station. Tomorrow, Mr. Curl-Puller just might find a lovely worm or two in his tray. Not so ladylike of me, I know, but oh so satisfying.

Still, such offense by a gentleman deserves more than a handful of worms.

I step into the Zevely's office and form my lips into a smile, both girlish and solemn. It works well on Pa. It might be a winning combination today.

The postmaster taps his fingers along the edge of the desk. "Miss Ream, what is today's complaint?"

"You need to speak to the men about how they treat us ladies. I'm here because some of the girls refuse to come talk to you because of how humiliating it is to walk between the rows."

He huffs. "Miss Ream." His shoulders sag. "If I had my way, you would not be here to be trifled with at all."

I firm my stance. "Women are not the problem. It's the caliber of men you hire."

"We've been over this before, you and I. My preference would be to hire clerical men of highest regard and moral standing. But there's a war on, in case you didn't notice. I hire whomever I can."

"But . . ."

He raises his hand. "I hired you and the other girls, didn't I? Stay home if you don't like working here at men's wages."

I shouldn't argue with him, but I can't help myself. "If we women stayed home, you would be returning a lot less mail. Our presence here and our observational skills are key in deciphering the most obscurely addressed items."

"I can't deny you do excellent work, Miss Ream. You are an asset to the department." He scowls deeper. "There's your compliment. Now, is there anything else to disturb my day?"

He knows me too well.

I cross my hands over my heart for dramatic effect. "It breaks our hearts to throw away the carte de visite portraits we can't identify. We had the idea of putting them on display in the lobby of the post office. So many people go through Washington; surely some would be identified?"

Zevely raises his chin. "You want to hang up the ones we can't return? The Congress that funds this office will think we aren't good at our jobs."

"It's better to burn them? Let the sender believe his loved one received his missive—possibly his last?"

"Yes. Now get back to work, Miss Ream."

Heartless man. I press a clenched fist against my mouth to keep from saying that out loud, spin on my heel, and carry the bad news back to my friends.

It takes us a week to devise a plan to make Zevely change his mind. And today's the day.

Emma hands me another carte de visite, and I pin it to the board.

"Vinnie, are you sure this is a good idea?"

Of course, I'm not sure. Risking my job is a foolish thing to do. I'm putting the whole family at risk. But it's too late to stop. All around me, my coworkers are busy; some making a banner to hang over our display of lost portraits, and others creating numbered lists of the cards so images can be claimed. We might be sneaking about the post office after work and breaking every rule of decorum there is, but it is the most excitement we've had in weeks.

I give Emma a big smile and pray it hides my fear. "It's a good idea. Zevely will forgive us when he sees the public's response."

"But he specifically said no." Emma visibly shivers. It might be a hot box during the day, but after dark, the place turns into a tomb.

"He only said no to me. I will be the one losing my position." I pin on another card and hope I am not being prophetic. "Even if people do not recognize the men in the display, seeing all the photographs en masse will help them understand better who is defending our Union. How can anyone look into all these young men's eyes and not be moved? Maybe there will be more cries to end the war."

Emma clasps the locket around her neck. "If only that were true. I look for a letter from Peter every day, and when I get one, it feels like an iron has lifted from my chest. I am so glad he's guarding supply trains right now and not fighting on the front line." Her smile wilts. "Oh, I'm so sorry. I forgot. Your brother. Have you heard anything yet?"

I scoop up the next card. "Nothing. He could be dead, Emma. His unit was at Pea Ridge. A major defeat, according to the newspapers. And I know Bob. He would have wanted to be first up whatever hill they were attacking. We're hoping one of our friends will be able to pass a letter through the lines. But we have tried before." My fingers loosen on the photo. "My mother cries day and night."

Emma slips the carte de visite from my grasp. "Go home. Comfort your family. The rest of us can finish the displays and put them in the lobby. The big to-do will be when Zevely sees them in the morning. You won't want to miss that."

"No, I won't. I've invited Major Rollins and his friends, Congressman Yates and Voorhees, and asked them to bring their compatriots to our grand opening."

Emma slaps her hand to her mouth. "You didn't."

"If I've learned nothing else living here in Washington, it's that the right political pressure inserted at just the right point can be magical."

I turn and pretend to admire the finished boards. Now I just have to hope I've chosen the right point and the right politicians.

Chapter 6

SEPTEMBER 1863

THE CAPITOL, WASHINGTON CITY

The carte de visite display is a grand success. I rush to the Capitol. I can't wait to thank the major for his support. Of course, Zevely, once he saw the public acclamation, took all the credit.

I sidle my way inside Congressman Rollins' office, past the teasing clerks, the disgruntled job seekers, and a big man with a face like an angry bear, his eyes narrowed and his eyebrows questioning. He and Major Rollins are arguing over Rollins' new railroad bill. I will have to wait my turn to ask my question.

As usual, no one pays me a bit of mind. I seize a stack of papers and focus on choosing the right portfolio in which to file them. The major loves when I do little odd jobs for him, and I love hearing all the behind-the-scenes hubbub. It's much more interesting than listening to Ma and Mary lament the war, their lives, and the unrelenting work of running a boarding house. Besides, it's one way I can repay him for his assistance in finding me my job.

My salary has been a lifesaver. Everything keeps getting more expensive because of the war profiteers. Despite having three boarders, Mary has had to take a half-time position in the land office, and she hates rubbing shoulders with ordinary folk as if we are not the same.

Ma's constant laments about Bob have even driven Pa away. Downplaying his recurring fevers and rheumatism, he has taken a surveying assignment in Kansas. He has been gone for over a month. He promised to get word of Bob. But I miss him so. He is the kind voice, the wise voice, the loving voice that keeps the family together.

"Vinnie, come meet Senator Browning."

The long-faced bear of a man turns his attention to me. I wipe my hands on my skirt and step toward him. He is the first senator I have ever met.

"Orville, this is Miss Vinnie Ream. She is the true originator of the display of cartes de visite in the lobby of the General Post Office."

"Quite impressive, young lady. The President has told me it was an act of generous kindness to reach out to the public that way. Even if only a few of the images find their way to their loved ones, it is an opportunity for the viewer, stranger or not, to honor the sacrifice of each one."

"The President?" My pulse flutters beneath my collar. I drop my gaze. "I would think he would be too busy with the war to notice such a small thing."

"The soldiers fighting for our cause are always his concern. He feels for everyone."

"Orville is a close friend of the President." Rollins grins at me. "Besides her work in the dead letter office, Miss Ream is very active on the war's behalf. She volunteers in the hospitals. And she has given numerous concerts to raise money for the Union cause."

Senator Browning's meaty lips turn up into a smile. The smile changes his face from harsh to jovial. "You are to be commended. You are just what this country needs."

My face flames, and I curtsy. "I do my best. We all do our best. The display was a group effort by the female clerks I work with."

"And she's modest, I see," Browning adds.

Rollins laughs. "When it is in her interest. Vinnie once sent me a petition signed by every girl in her class at Christian Female College, including my own two daughters, asking me to get her teachers to excuse her from class so she could attend a weekend dance off campus."

My face heats. "I was very young. It was not one of my best ideas."

Rollins winks. "It worked."

Browning nods. "Nothing wrong with asking for what you want. You may not always succeed, but you never know unless you try. And it helps greatly if you sweeten the pot." He turns to Rollins. "Speaking of which, Illinois is going to need more benefit from this railroad proposal of yours if you want my vote."

And they are off arguing again, and I slink back to my corner.

I pick up a letter from one of Rollins' constituents. People request favors from him all the time. My family has asked for favors. Is it as simple as that? Be brave enough to ask and have something to offer in return?

I finger the remaining letters in the pile. We owe the major so much. Filing a few papers for him occasionally is too little repayment. I need to do more. But what?

The job seekers clear out. Senator Browning puts on a top hat as tall as Lincoln's and takes his leave. A messenger boy runs in and out, dropping off a missive.

Rollins studies the note, then looks up. "Vinnie, I must go to Clark Mills' studio. Would you like to come along?"

"The studio of Clark Mills? The artist who is casting the Statue of Freedom for the top of the Capitol?"

He waves the note. "Yes. He's sent word he's finished the medallion I ordered." Rollins sets his hat on his head. "I would like to have him make one of you, too."

A little shiver wings through me. "Me? But why?"

"You are going to be famous one day."

I scuff my foot. "Thank you for the compliment . . . but . . ."
He dips his head. "We'll see. Now, come along."

Clark Mills' studio on the Bladensburg Road at the Maryland border looks like an octagonal layer cake. It starts with brick, topped with crenellations on the bottom, a wooden superstructure above, and a cupola at the top. When I step inside, I see why. The space soars upward. Plenty of room for displaying tall sculptures.

I don't know where to look first. The place hums with activity. Shelves weighed down with busts and plaster casts of heads line the walls. Groups of visitors look at the display of medallions hanging at the front. Two men, too young for soldiering, bring out examples of work to show potential customers. The major points out Clark Mills, a pale-eyed man with dark hair and large, calloused hands. Fittingly, he stands in the center, surveying it all.

He rushes to greet Rollins and signals one of the boys to fetch Rollins' medallion.

While they talk, I wander from sculpture to sculpture. The work is strong and masculine. Mills has a penchant for emphasizing those features that carry a person's character. A stately chin. A heavy-lidded eye. A jowly neck.

I move to the shelves and study the disembodied limbs and heads. A hollow-eyed skull peers out at me. A chill meanders down my spine. I wonder whose it was. Not a soldier, I hope, though it is still a reminder of the men dying all around us while the wealthy customers here memorialize themselves in stone.

A rustle behind me pulls me from my morbid thoughts. It is the older boy. Tall, broad-shouldered, clay smeared across his apron. I give him a polite smile.

He sneers. "You lost, little girl?"

My smile sinks away. He reminds me of my brother's friends, all full of themselves, ready to belittle anyone who looks weak. But I'm not weak. And besides, I will never be here again. I let my pouty-little-sister repartee spill from my tongue.

"Miss Ream to you. I am the artist prodigy that Congressman Rollins has taken under his wing." I toss my head back and pretend to be a fine lady, a world-renowned sculptress, not a poor frontier girl wearing one of her only two good dresses.

The youth laughs. "*Prodigy?*" He points to a clay-smeared worktable in an alcove at the back, probably used to explore possible ideas with customers. "Prove it."

Stupid me. I should have expected that. How often have I had to defend the crazy exaggerations I've claimed? It was why Boudy was attracted to me, not Mary.

All his foolish taunts echo in my head. *You can ride bareback? You can climb up on the roof and walk along the ridge? You can play Mozart on the guitar? You can make my heart break with a song? Show me.*

So, I did.

All those times, I'd been confident. But I haven't touched clay since Fort Smith.

I approach the table slowly, hoping the major is finished. But he is looking at busts and gabbing with Mills. I've been quite forgotten, the perpetual lot of women and girls, when in the domains of men. The youth with the dark eyebrows and icy blue stare smirks at me. He is sure I will demur.

He digs a lump of clay from the bin under the table and plops it on the smooth wood surface. "There you are. Nice and fresh."

I step up and inhale the earthy aroma, that special mix of damp and rotting soil that only fine clay has. I am transported back to Wisconsin and the shore of Lake Mendota, where my Winnebago friends and I fashioned thick-walled clay pots to put our treasures in—a speckled bird's egg, a tiny pinecone, or a shiny, white river pebble.

I tip my chin a little higher and push my finger into the clay, then study the impression. The clay has been finely sifted, probably by this young fellow. I pick the lump up and heft the weight of it in my hand. It is perfect—damp and free of contaminants.

The boy harumphs. "You're really going to do this? What about your dress?"

My dress? I can't return home covered in clay. I look around and spy what I need. "How about that apron?"

His mouth twists into a silent laugh. "It will never fit."

I look up at him from under my eyelashes, the way Mary would. "You can hike it up."

He fetches the apron, obviously made for someone his size, and I let him move uncomfortably close and tie it behind my neck. I help him fold the cloth up at the waist as he knots it at the back.

He really is too near, his body warm against mine. His hands brush me lightly just on the edge of impropriety.

I feel every touch. He's young, but one day, he will be a charmer.

But not mine. He is too full of himself and too judgmental.

He leans in and whispers in my ear, "My name's Fisk. I'm Mills' best apprentice, and I know good sculpture when I see it. Now, let's see what you can do with your *prodigious* talent."

I rub my palms down the rough canvas of the apron. "What do you want me to make?"

He glances around. "How about the chief over there?"

It is the standard Easterner idea of what an Indian chief looks like—hawk nose, cheekbones sharp as razors, a mass of feathers in his headdress, like the one on the new pennies.

Real Indians don't look like that. I picture my friend the poet, John Rollin Ridge, with his rounded cheeks and soft eyes. An educated gentleman who would welcome you into his home and feed you food he could little spare, along with a poem. This boy and the people here would never accept a sculpture of that kind of Indian. Any more than they would accept Boudy as one of them, despite his green-gray eyes, pale gold skin, and law degree.

And they would be right not to. Boudy is nothing like these people. He is full of jealousy, anger, and resentment, able to wound and kill a man without a flinch. And he kisses with a passion that lanky city boys will never attain. He is a man who knows he might die in the next hour, or the next day, or the next month, merely because of his heritage. Torn from his culture as a boy, he wants it all now, from the tattoos around his neck and the silver earrings in his ears to the Bowie knife that never leaves his side. He has hurt me and my family without a qualm. And it is why I must bury my desire for him.

But I can create this sculpture for him and his people. A memorial to his tribe's devastation, and to the love for him that I'm unable to cast out, not even for my beloved sister's sake or his traitorous decision to fight for the South.

I nod at my challenger and form the clay into a ball. My overseer stares at me. I stop and give him a wide-eyed look. "Nothing better to do but watch me, Fisk?"

He grunts. "Watching you will be delightful."

I want to tell him to leave me alone, but I recognize that superior look. He's a stubborn boy on the cusp of manhood. He won't listen to me, so it is no use showing even that much weakness.

"Then watch," I say and work my fingers into the clay.

I shape the ball into the skull that underlies our mortal skin, turning it this way and that. Learning the clay. Relearning the pressure my fingers must exert. Inhaling the dry dust that coats my hands and wafts up around me.

I take special care at the start. Like the base of a round bowl, if the foundation is off, so will be the finished work. I tuck, pull, and pinch. I dampen my fingers and dab on little bits here and there. Bold eyes fill in the sockets. A strong nose for a proud man forms in the center. I work the cheekbones high, but more rounded than the model on the shelf. I think of the native men I have known and add fullness to the set of the mouth and the shape of the jaw. Finally, I insert a touch of Boudy's threat of a smile.

I apply more clay for the hair, braiding three coils into a braid. Using a fine-edged knife, I etch in texture, feathers, and more detail. Then I hold my creation in my palm and stare at the face I have created. It is not as alive as I would like, but it will have to do.

"You finished?"

I jump. I'd forgotten where I was. Forgotten about my judge. I cup the head in my hands. No bigger than a large apple, it lacks dignity and importance. It needs something more.

"No, not yet." I survey the shelves and find a bust to copy. I take more clay and form the neck and build out the top of the shoulders as a support. With the knife tip, I mark out the tribal tattoos and show a little of the beaded neckplate Cherokee men wear.

I stop. It is still not right. My paeon to the tribes looks stiff and lost. I want to cry. I can hear Boudy now. "Is that what you think of us? That we are stuffed pigeons for white men to shoot?"

I take a risk and twist the neck, turning the head up and a bit to the side, smearing the detail I had worked so hard on but giving my chief some life.

A smattering of applause fills the room.

What have I missed? Has Clark Mills just wowed some customers?

I turn around. The major and Mills smile down at me.

"For a moment there, I thought you were going to destroy it." Mills picks up my Indian chief, toylike in his large hands.

Rollins nods. "I told you she has talent."

Mills pinches his beard. "I'm impressed. To work on such a small scale and yet endow the piece with a unique personality is always a major challenge for a sculptor. She took a chance, twisting the head that way."

Rollins touches the braid. "This is not a typical Indian head. Is this someone you know, Vinnie?"

I shrug, suddenly aware of the clay splattering my hands and arms, my wayward curls loose from their pins. "I sort of . . . uh . . . combined several of my friends together."

Apprentice boy stares at me. "You have friends who are Indians?"

Rollins nods. "Miss Ream is from out West. Grew up on the frontier. She can ride a horse bareback like an Indian brave."

The boy's eyes widen. I can see the hunger for adventure that has scooped up so many like him and tossed them into bloody battle. "What's it like out there?"

I want to melt into the water bucket or turn into one of the lumps of clay sitting on the table. I don't want to be known as a wild Westerner to the greatest sculptor in Washington. I don't want this boy tempted to enlist and leave Mills' wondrous foundry, where the Statue of Freedom is being cast.

Mills rescues me. "Would you like to study under me? Learn to work larger on a wire framework?"

"What?" The boy's mouth hangs open. "She's just a little girl."

I'm equally surprised. I *am* just a little girl, a bit of nothing.

The major puffs himself up and defends me with the same vigor as if I were his daughter. "Miss Ream is a top-performing graduate of Christian College. A fine artist—I have portraits she painted of my daughters displayed in my home. And not only is she an accomplished painter, but she is also an exemplary musician. She performs on her guitar all over the city and in the hospitals."

"Well, grand things often come in a small package." Mills eyes the boy. "You can't deny Miss Ream has talent. And there are women sculptors."

"But . . . a woman in the studio?"

"You have a problem with that, son? Afraid you can't work alongside Miss Ream and treat her like the lady she is?"

His cheeks turn scarlet red. "Of course not, Father. She would be most welcome."

"Why, thank you." I dip a little curtsy, then look at the boy again. He's Mills's *son*? What must he think of me? Not that it matters.

I force myself to stand a little straighter. Mills has just praised me and offered instruction in the fine art of sculpture. It is like my most impossible dream has been placed before me on a crystal platter, and all I need do is say yes to partake of the feast.

The yes forms on my lips, and then I remember who I am, what is expected of me.

I wipe my hands on the apron. "It is an amazing opportunity, but I have a job, Mr. Mills. I work full-time at the dead letter office." I hesitate. He should know the truth about me. "My family needs the money I earn. My Pa is ill."

The major takes my hand, despite it being covered in clay. "Miss Ream, don't you worry. I'm sure something can be worked out. To deny you this chance to develop your gift would be criminal."

His words thrill my soul, but I know there is little hope. As much as I'd love to study sculpture, my job at the post office is essential to the well-being of my family. I cannot give it up. Not now.

My salary provides money for those little extras. More meat in the stew pot. A new dress now and then. A fancy hat for Mary. Things that will help my sister attract a well-to-do beau and get over her sadness at losing Boudy. Things that will assuage the guilt that eats at my insides for stealing him from her.

Still, Clark Mills has offered me a chance at fame and fortune. Could I take it without affecting my job?

Chapter 7

NOVEMBER 1863

REAM BOARDING HOUSE, NORTH STREET

All the way home from Mills' studio, I ponder. How can I study with Mills and still hold my job? Will Ma even let me do it? With Pa away, I have lost my strongest advocate. And Mary, she hates being a clerk. What kind of resentment will she have if I am off having what she will see as a childish playtime? We are supposed to be looking for husbands.

Husbands. The idea turns my stomach. No man would tolerate me taking sculpture lessons, except maybe someone like Fisk Mills. I have no interest in him, but would Ma see Fisk as a potential mate for me? Rich people pay well for a likeness, and his father is wealthy enough. But no, Ma would not accept him. I scrub at a smear of clay on my sleeve. The Mills would not be considered gentlemen, despite their financial success—they work with their hands.

By the time the major's rented buggy reaches our place, I have decided, right or wrong, not to mention Mills' grand offer.

Ma is standing on the stoop with a broom and a sour expression. "Where have you been, Vinnie? I've been worried sick."

Rollins tips his hat. "My apologies, Mrs. Ream. I whisked your daughter off to see Clark Mills' studio. I had a medallion to pick up. But it took longer than expected. Vinnie demonstrated exceptional skill—"

"Thank you for the opportunity, Major," I cut him off. "It was a fascinating afternoon. But I must not take up any more of your time." I hasten to alight.

A quick wave and I'm in the house, Ma treading on my heels. She corners me in the hallway.

"What's this all about? I thought you filed papers for the congressman at his office?"

"I do. He was going to Clark Mills' studio and invited me along."

"Did he now? And did you think of how that might appear? A man like that alone with a young, unmarried girl at his side, driving who knows where in the city for all to see?"

"What are you insinuating, Ma? A man like who? Major Rollins is old enough to be my father. His daughters are my age."

Ma takes a deep breath and clasps my hand in hers. She looks me in the eyes. "My dear, naïve child. An eligible man courting you with the intention to marry is one thing, but you must be wary of older men. The major spends months away from his wife, and friend of our family or not, he shows way too much interest in you."

"Of course, he does. He thinks I am talented. He wants me to meet the artists in the city."

"And what about the good people who see him sitting close to you in that buggy with no chaperone?"

"What in the world can happen in an open carriage?"

"Appearance is everything, Vinnie. Something you've never seen fit to learn. You chase after savages, go visit those filthy hospitals, sprint off who knows where the minute my back is turned. Why can't you sit in the parlor and embroider or play your guitar and wait for callers like the lady I have raised you to be? You'll never find a husband acting the way you do. Your sister had to entertain a gentleman from church and his mother by herself this afternoon."

My heart leaps. Has she found someone? "Mary must have been in heaven."

Ma's lips purse. "He is too young for her. Nineteen. The gentleman inquired after you."

"I don't need a husband."

Ma throws up her hands. "You are impossible, child. Of course, you must have a husband. A woman can't support herself alone."

"I have years before I have to think of marriage."

Ma flicks her hand, as if my age can be batted away as easily as a fly. "Your birthday is in two weeks. Eighteen is the perfect age to marry."

"Pa will agree I can wait."

"Your pa will agree with anything you tell him. You're his little angel. Always will be. Spoiled the devil out of you, that man did. Let you think you could do anything you desired, be anything you imagined. Well, you can't." She reaches out and takes my hands. "Listen, you may not fully understand, but many unscrupulous men find young girls especially attractive. You are no longer a child, but you look like one with your tiny stature and boyish figure. If you consort with men alone, rumors will fly across the city. Your father could be fired from his job. Mary could lose any opportunity to marry."

She draws me to her. "I love you and admire your talents. I don't want to thwart you. You have settled well into living here, despite your love of the prairie. But your behavior with men affects the whole family. And from this moment on, you are going to act like it does. You will no longer romp about the city by yourself. You will be accompanied by a chaperone, as is proper for a girl of marriageable age. No more hanging out at Rollins' office or visiting the hospitals alone. Mary, or Pa when he is back, will walk you to the post office and home again. If you have a solo singing engagement or a meeting, one of us will go with you."

I dig my toe into the ingrain carpet. I refuse to be trapped in well-meaning morality when I have done nothing wrong and never would.

My hands tremble, but I answer back. "It won't work, Ma. You are all too busy. Mary has her own job to get to. Pa's schedule is irregular. You have to take care of the boarders' laundry and meals."

I rush on. "But I understand your concern about appearances, and I don't want to harm Mary's chances at a good marriage. From now on, I will take the horse car to and from work, and I promise no more buggy rides alone with men."

Ma is strict, but not unreasonable. The furrows in her brow loosen. She takes my hand in her own. "You are a good girl, Vinnie. You have done so much for the family. I trust you to keep your word on this. All I ask is that you consider how your behavior will appear to others before jumping into things."

I bend my head and stare at our joined hands. Mine small, smooth, unblemished. Hers rough, cracked, worn from years of hard work surviving on the frontier. She wants a better life for Mary and me. I do too, even if we have different ideas of what that future might be. "I promise."

And I really do mean to keep my word. Though how I will be able to do that and still take sculpting lessons from Mills, I have no idea.

The months pass by. Summer turns to bitter winter. Pa returns and agrees with Ma—no unladylike sculpture lessons for me. I tuck my frustration deep inside and focus on landing well-paying music performances and introducing my sister to society women who hopefully have eligible sons who will be taken with my sister's lovely voice and gentle beauty.

But I can't shake my interest in sculpture. Which is why I am standing in the Corcoran mansion and arguing with Mary.

"Just a peek. Please . . . this is a chance to see one of the most famous sculptures in the country."

Mary holds me back. "I understand your love of art, Vinnie, but our audience is waiting." She puts on her big sister don't-be-annoying frown. "You don't have to see every work of art in Washington City, you know."

I really shouldn't force her. Mary hates performing for the wealthy in the city, and it always leaves her in a foul mood. She does it only to please me. But I can't miss this opportunity.

I tug harder. "But this one is special. Come. I'll be quick." I grab her hand and half-drag her into the long gallery at the far end of the Corcoran mansion. "There. In the semi-circular alcove. That's where the cook's boy said it would be. Under the skylight."

Mary's frown deepens. "You trust a cook's boy?"

"He's male. He knows."

"Really? And they keep it shrouded behind curtains?" She pinches her lips together. "What kind of embarrassment have you gotten me into this time?"

I approach the draped work. "It is one of the greatest sculptures in the world. It's been exhibited everywhere. Philadelphia. New Orleans. London."

Mary stops a few feet away, hand fisted beneath her chin. "All right. Let's see this masterpiece."

I set down my guitar case and lift the velvet drape. A white marble figure of a woman appears. "Oh, Mary. It's . . ."

Mary peers over her shoulder at the door. "It doesn't matter what it is. I assume you have an excuse for when they catch us, little sister?"

I'm too in awe to answer. Hiram Powers' statue steals my breath away. Lit by the skylight above, the reality is far more impressive than the engraving in the old New Orleans newspaper I keep folded in my memory album.

Life-size, the smooth curve of the naked woman's hip and breast rises as smooth as my own, mere inches from my fingertips. Her face, turned to the side, wears an expression halfway between resignation and despair. An expression I know well. It is the look my sister is casting at me now.

She's right. We do have to leave. Our paying clients await. Still, I extend my hand those last few inches and brush the chain encircling her wrist. She may be called *The Greek Slave* but, to me, she is all women, enchained by rules and restrictions not of their own making. She is me. She is the kind of work I would create if I were a sculptress.

Mary puts her hand on my arm. "Someone's coming, Vinnie. We must go."

Beneath her touch, chilly bumps race across my skin, and I curse the biting cold of Washington City in November.

I brave a last look at the sculpture. I could make sculptures like this. I know I could. I think again of Clark Mills' studio and wish I were there this exact moment, my hands buried in clay.

"Misses?"

Caught, I drop the drape, lift my shoulders, and face the scowling, white-gloved butler standing in the door.

"I assume you are the Ream sisters? Here to provide the entertainment?"

Mary clutches the music folio against her chest, her chin high, her stance rigid. "We are, sir."

I nod and pick up my guitar case.

"Then move on." He sweeps us through the doorway as if we're marauding rats and points down the corridor to the right. "The salon is in that direction."

I curtsy as I pass by and offer the polite excuse Mary expects of me. "Our apologies. We must have made a wrong turn." And then, because it never hurts to ask, I add, "Mr. Corcoran's art collection is exquisite. Do you think I might come back to study it some more?"

The officious man raises one eyebrow. "My master's art gallery is not open for public viewing, miss."

What he means is that it is not open to paid entertainers like me.

He shuts the double doors with a bang.

My resolve hardens. It won't always be this way. Someday, people will know my name, and doors will open for me.

I tamp down the fury roiling inside me and grab my sister's hand. Time for the Ream sisters' performance. We scurry away from the butler and take off down the long series of opulent rooms leading to the front salon. We might have better dresses than when we arrived, but our cheap shoes scuffle on the polished floor. Our worn flannel petticoats rustle loudly. My battered guitar case bangs against my knee. Everything about us shouts we don't belong.

I survey the crystal chandeliers and gilded ceiling plaster above our heads, admire the French furnishings and the gilt wallpaper. Bile rises in my throat. Only the best for William Wilson Corcoran, banker extraordinaire.

I run my hand along the edge of a delicate table loaded with miniature sculptures. How nice to be so wealthy. Corcoran can dash off to Europe with his Southern leanings, whereas I have had to leave the prairie I love because we are anti-slavery. It's so unfair. I finger a cut-glass bowl.

Mary pulls me away. "Don't touch," she hisses. "You'll break something. Then what will they think of us?"

I shrug. "That I'm clumsy?"

"They'll make us pay, so settle down. The butler already caught us peeking at that naked lady."

"Nude. The proper term is nude."

"Doesn't matter what you call it. That statue was obscene. You could see . . . well . . . everything."

Dear, prudish Mary. I pat her arm. "I didn't think you looked."

"I'm not blind. It was standing right there in front of me."

I puff myself up. "The Greek Slave has toured the country. They let women and children see it. It's a moral statement against slavery."

"Well, I don't think men are thinking of morality when they look at it."

I laugh. "Surely not." My sister might be a prude, but she isn't naïve.

Mary squinches up the side of her mouth. "Ma would have a conniption if she knew what we just did."

The air whooshes out of me. I halt beside a vase of towering palms. "You won't tell her we peeked at a nude sculpture, will you? She's angry enough about the invitation to work under Clark Mills I was lucky to get."

"Lucky you." Mary's lips flatten. "Why is it you who has all the luck? You're the one everyone fawned over at school. You're the one people want to hear sing. You're the one who gets invited to be a sculptress." Her voice turns into a hiss. "You're the one Boudy loves."

"Boudy?" I stare at her. We haven't mentioned him in months, and she brings it up now? The middle of the corridor in Corcoran's mansion is the worst possible place to stir up bitterness. I peer around, but the hall is empty, the butler gone, thank goodness.

"If I can't have him, neither can you. Promise you'll forget about him and marry someone else like everyone's been harping on me to do."

I clutch the handle of my guitar case, the secret kiss a bitter memory, and feign nonchalance. "I'd never." I steal a peek at the small heart etched into the leather of the case right by the lock. The man I love is over a thousand miles away and as unattainable as the frontier life I have lost. He's betrayed my family. Time to toss those hopes away. Forever. If I can.

The words burn, but I force them out. "I promise I will never marry him." I avoid looking at her. "I will never marry any man."

Mary puts her finger on my breastbone. "I don't believe you. I know what went on between you two. You knew I loved him, but you flirted and preened when he was around. Read poetry. Sang duets." Her voice rises to a cutting pitch. "Kissed him. Told him you'd love him forever that night in the barn when you thought no one could hear. You can't deny you stole him from me."

My breath catches. She knows Boudy loves me. Knows about the kiss? No wonder she's been so cold, so unhappy.

I force a shrug. "It just happened."

Tears gather in Mary's eyes. "That makes it worse. He was my beau. You knew that."

I set down my guitar and wrap my arms around her. "I'm so sorry." Hard as I try, I can't wipe the man from my heart, but neither can I bear to see her cry. She's my big sister. My best friend. She's always looked out for me.

I take her hand in mine. "Soon, you will meet some handsome gentleman far nicer than crazy, mixed-up Cornelius Boudinot. You deserve someone who won't abandon you in a hovel on the prairie while he gallivants with his wild buddies."

Mary yanks her hand free. "Vinnie, don't you dare badmouth Boudy. He doesn't live in a hovel. He's a lawyer who cares for his father's people, and I love him with all my heart. I always will." She jerks away. "Besides, his wildest buddy is our own brother."

I am not going to win this argument.

I heft my guitar and head toward the salon. "Like Ma says, there are far better gentlemen here in Washington. You could marry any one of them."

"Saw that in your dreams, did you?"

"No. I see it in how the men look at you. You're beautiful, accomplished, and kind. Who wouldn't want you?"

"Boudy," she hisses.

I rush to cover up my faux pas. "You're wrong about him. He doesn't love me. He only cares about power and politics. He abandoned me to go fight in a stupid war. He put our brother in danger." The words roll off my tongue too easily. I bite the inside of my cheek. As much as I love him, it is the truth of him and why I will never marry him or any man.

Mary huffs. "No, Vinnie, you're the one mistaken. He didn't abandon you. He wanted to marry you."

My stomach drops to my knees. Boudy wanted to marry me?

"Don't act surprised. I overheard him ask Pa for your hand before we left. But Pa said you were too young. Sent him away."

My mouth drops open. "But he never asked me."

Mary's face turns bloodless. "Well, I asked him to marry me. I would have done anything to stay there with him. But he wanted nothing to do with me after . . ." She looks away, then snaps back at me. "He'll come for you one day. He'll ask. You'll see. Promise me you'll refuse him when he does."

What does she mean? After what? But I don't really want to know.

I lift my chin. I'll say anything to drive the despair from her beloved face and the pain from my heart. "If Cornelius Boudinot survives this war and does come, he's going to find us both married to the richest men in Washington City. In the whole country." I babble on, "I can see it now. We'll have a double wedding. Everyone in the government will be there. Even the President. Wearing the finest Italian lace, we'll march down the aisle, cherubic flower girls strewing rose petals at our feet. It will be the biggest wedding ever seen, and all the newspapers will sing the praises of the Ream sisters and their handsome husbands."

Mary's face regains some color. "Oh, Vinnie. What balderdash." She seizes my hand. "Come along. If we don't sing for the high-and-mighty folk waiting for us, you can forget lace and rose petals; we'll be lucky to have a ham hock to put in the stew pot." She squeezes my hand. "And thank you for your promise. It is for the best. You'll see."

The best for her.

Emptiness overwhelms me. I gaze back over my shoulder, toward the gallery, and give myself a shake. I will not be chained to Boudy or any man. I will not break my promise to Mary. There are other things I love. Other things worth fighting for. My gift for sculpture to explore.

Chapter 8

SANITARY FAIR COMMITTEE MEETING

The assembly hall is narrow and full of women wearing the latest hats. Way in the back, Mary sits rigidly beside me. She'd rather be anywhere else than here at the Women for War Relief meeting, acting as my chaperone. Even though I promised to give up Boudy months ago, she doesn't believe me. We barely talk anymore, and when we do, now that the secret is in the open, all her jealousy spews out. Right now, she is quiet, thank goodness, but judging by the tightness in her jaw, I will certainly get an earful when we leave.

Voices rise around us. The committee members might be high society, but they love gossip as much as the rest of us. I haven't been able to make my voice heard since we arrived.

Finally, there is a lull in the bickering, and I wave my hand and yell out, "I have an idea for a booth that will bring in needed money and help the soldiers."

Every woman in the audience turns and stares at me.

Mary jabs her elbow into my ribs. "Now you've done it. You really think these hoity-toity women will listen to you?"

I knock Mary's arm away and spout one of Pa's favorite sayings. "The worst that can happen is they'll say no."

And the grand dames of Washington high society probably will. Still, it can't hurt to try. All my friends at the dead letter office think it's a super idea, and it's a grand way to make inroads into the female side of Washington political life.

I push up from my chair and wend my way to the podium. As I pass, silks rustle, heady perfumes assault my nose, feather-decked hatted heads dip and turn. I know what these influential ladies are thinking: *How did this frumpy child get admitted to their august ranks?*

I nod a thank you to Harriet Voorhees, who is as kind as her congressman husband and has extended the invitation to me. Then I am there, standing before them all. Senators' wives, members of the Cabinet Circle, and noted society hostesses from Fanny Chase to Lizzie Blair Lee, daughter of the postmaster general, at whose salons I have performed.

I grasp the edges of the podium and look out at the faces staring up at me. My throat tightens. Addressing an audience is nothing like singing to a crowd. When I sing, I can disappear into the music. But here, I can't escape into harmony, nor cover up my western twang with song.

For a moment, I falter. While performing for these ladies brought in needed cash, gaining their acceptance is the only way I can think of to attract a well-heeled gentleman to wed Mary.

I stare at her pale face, so devoid of joy, then clear my throat and plunge in. "I'm Miss Vinnie Ream. Some of you may know me from hearing me sing at the hospital fundraisers and at your salons. But I also clerk in the dead letter office, and I understand the workings of the postal system. I propose setting up a post office booth at the Sanitary Fair, where visitors can donate stationery and writing materials for the use of our wounded soldiers."

A familiar woman in a huge hat decorated with green plumes waggles a finger at me. "Donations are fine, but we must bring in funds, too, Miss Ream. Purchasing medical supplies for the troops is our goal. How would your booth make it worth the space it will occupy?"

Oh my. I hadn't expected to do more than gather stationery.

I force myself to smile and think fast. "I am a capable writer. I will write encouraging letters to soldiers in the field, expressing gratitude for their service and sacrifice in return for a donation of one dollar each."

"The idea has merit," Harriet says in support.

But the feathered-hat lady is not satisfied. Her lips clamp together even tighter than Ma's when I told her I was attending this meeting. "How would the soldiers be selected for these missives, Miss Ream? Would they be friends of yours? Your rebel brother, perhaps?"

I grumble under my breath. Pesky news article. The report in the *Washington Chronicle* detailing Ma's desperate search for her rebel son hadn't disguised our identity enough. After all, no other family in the city has a daughter who performs on the guitar for pay.

I steady myself. Not all these ladies are unsympathetic. Many have southern ties as deep as our own.

When I speak, I manage to keep the tremble from my voice. "No, of course not, Madame. The donors will choose from lists prepared by the military and from hospital directories. I will have envelopes and stamps ready. They can insert the letter of their choice and address it themselves."

A woman near the front comes to my defense. "Miss Ream is responsible for organizing the carte de visite display of unidentified soldiers at the General Post Office, and she regularly visits the wounded in the hospitals. She is a most trustworthy individual, devoted to the Union."

Around her, heads nod.

Another woman joins her. "I think the idea is very original. It will certainly attract attendees and the press, as well." She looks over at my critic. "You're probably jealous you didn't think of the idea yourself, Jane. I move that we accept Miss Ream's booth."

A second comes from the back. They sound for all the world like the House Chamber passing a bill, but it is only my small little booth being proposed. My pulse pounds faster.

The chairwoman steps up to the podium and stands beside me. "Now, for the vote on having Miss Ream operate a post office booth at the fair?"

I hold my breath. The ayes ring out, and I exhale. It is done. Now I must make it work.

I shove the tedious task of writing hundreds of letters to the end of my list and focus on introducing my sister to these powerful women. Surely, one of them has an unmarried son or nephew who wants a dutiful wife.

All the way home, Mary fumes at me. Apparently, I have done nothing right.

"I have never been so embarrassed," she says. "How can you fawn all over those highfalutin women?"

"What are you talking about? I presented my idea, and they approved it."

"Standing up there, begging to be allowed to participate in the fair. Couldn't you see the disdain they had for you? And then you had to involve me. That Harriet lady had pity in her eyes."

"She's Congressman Voorhees' wife. They're lovely people. He's a friend of Major Rollins. Her husband came to the opening of the cartes de visite display."

"That has nothing to do with your performance tonight. As far as those women are concerned, we are paid performers, and you are their little backwoods monkey they can show charity to."

Mary has never been so vicious, but it will do me no good to bait her. "I am not," I whisper under my breath, then step out ahead of her so she can't see my tears.

She grabs me by my sleeve. "We have sung in almost every one of those women's parlors. If you think you can get us accepted into Washington high society, then you're a fool. Look at their clothes, the jewels around their necks, the twinkling gems on their fingers. You need to be rich to move in those circles, not paid performers."

"Musicians are respectable."

"Not ones relegated to the back entrance. Not female ones who work for the government."

"What are you talking about?"

"It's in the papers. Haven't you heard what they are saying about the Treasury Department? How girls are selected for their attractiveness, and how everyone knows what the girls have to do to get those jobs?"

"Don't be ridiculous. You know very well how I got my job, how Pa got you the position in the land office. With all the men off fighting, they need women to take their places. There is absolutely no foolishness going on in the dead letter office. If anything, it is the men who ought to be censured in the press."

"You spend too much time with Major Rollins and his friends. Ma says so."

"I have kept my promise and gone everywhere with a chaperone. As you should know, as it is usually yourself."

Mary tosses her head. "So you claim. But your promises are worth nothing. You are going to bring ruin down on the family. I just know it."

Her accusation stabs through me. I expect to hear she's learned that Emma and I have been leaving work early to visit the infirmaries. While Emma seeks information about her fiancé, who went missing after the battle at Lookout Mountain, I ask the rebels brought in if they know anything of Bob.

I grimace. "What promise have I broken?"

Mary stops dead. "You promised to have nothing to do with Boudy."

"Boudy? But I haven't."

"Then how come he's gotten a letter across the lines, *addressed to you*? You wrote him, didn't you, when you were searching for Bob?"

"Don't be silly. I tried to contact our friends in Little Rock and Fort Smith, but never him. Besides, I never heard back from any of them. Don't even know if they received them."

"So you say."

Her jealousy is getting tiresome.

"But the letter? Does it say how Bob is?"

"I don't know. Ma took it before I could open it."

"Well, let's find out." I loop my arm into hers and half-drag her down the street and into our house.

We are met by drawn drapes and profound silence, and my first thought is that Bob is dead. I grip Mary by the wrist and whisper, "Please let Bob be all right."

My sister gasps. "I was so furious I hadn't thought." She jerks free. "Ma's probably out back, hanging up the laundry." She charges through the swinging doors of the dining room and disappears into the kitchen. The last thing I see is her rounded shoulders and twitching fingers. She's scared, too.

I'm suddenly frozen. Maybe the letter isn't about Bob. What if Boudy has sent protestations of love? Repeated the marriage proposal he'd made my parents? Mary will be devastated.

I cover my face and stand, waiting in the foyer for a scream, a yell, a lament.

Then Pa is there. He puts his arms around my waist and swings me around. "He's alive, Vinnie. Bob survived the battle at Vicksburg. He's been paroled and is headed to Indian Territory." He sets me down. "He's well out of it, at last. Finally, Ma can rest easy."

"He can't just leave the Army, can he?"

"It's easy to disappear out there."

I lower my voice. "And Boudy?"

"That young man will always rise to the top. Seems he's the Cherokee delegate to the Confederate Congress. Signs himself Lieutenant Colonel." Pa gathers me close. "And don't worry. He didn't mention you at all."

I give a sigh of relief—or is it regret?—and hug him tighter.

Chapter 9

WASHINGTON CITY

Before I know it, it is summer again, and the battles still rage. Only now, the Rebs are on the edge of the city. Every time a cannon booms to the northeast, a shiver shoots through me.

I move nearer to my father as we dash across the Capitol grounds on the way to work. Would these past three years of exile from all I loved be for nothing? I must see for myself.

"Do we have time for a climb to the top of the dome?" I ask, even though I already know the answer.

Pa shoves back the floppy brim of his hat. He enjoys this diversion as much as I do. We do it often, just not to the accompaniment of cannons. "Sure. Plenty of time." He takes my hand, and we bustle up the steps and hustle into the rotunda. I give the guard a nickel and a smile.

"I'm only doing this because it's you, Miss Vinnie, in gratitude for your kindness in locating my nephew." He points up. "We've got some officers up there, observing the movements of the Confederates. With Early's troops on the outskirts of the city, we have to keep an eye out." He unfastens the chain blocking the entrance. "Stay out of their way."

I tip my head. "Of course."

The chain clanks behind us, and we start up the three hundred steps of the spiral staircase leading to the viewing deck at the base of the pillared tholos, me out front, Pa trudging up behind.

I burst out onto the platform. The view from the dome always restores my inner peace. Up here, the air is clearer, the vista wider, the noise, hubbub, and my worries far below. But not today.

I lean against the railing and watch the first rays of what will be a ferociously hot July sun tip over the Supreme Court Building, gilt its marble walls, then dye the eastern sky yellow. It is beautiful in its own way, but also a reminder of how distant I am from my beloved rolling prairie.

If only I could fly away. Back to the edge of the wilderness. Back to where life was simple and music filled my soul, and not my parents' larder. I stuff the refusal letter I've written to Clark Mills deeper in my pocket.

Since casting the Statue of Freedom, so many commissions from congressmen have poured in that he's set up a studio in the basement of the Capitol. Taking instruction with him no longer means a long buggy ride to Bladensburg. But it is too late for me. I lobbied for months to be allowed to take lessons, but Ma will hear none of it. No way will she let her flightiest child study something as esoteric as sculpture, chaperone or no.

I avoid the north-facing officers with their telescopes trained on Maryland, six miles away, and move to the western side of the balcony. The stub of the unfinished Washington Monument, lit golden, barely touches the horizon, stunted by a lack of money, just as I am.

I turn away. Being an artist was always an impossible dream, anyway.

So is marriage. Mary, at twenty-four, is on the cusp of becoming unmarriageable. Despite my efforts, no well-to-do man gives her a second look. There have been plenty of fine young storekeepers and soldiers come to call on Mary, but she is not ready to give up Boudy for an ordinary man. The fact that he did not mention me in the one letter we received has given her out-of-proportion hope.

A family that runs a boarding house has little chance of entering the upper echelon of society. Money is what we need. Only great riches can raise our status. And I have an idea on how to get it.

I peer over at Pa. He shields his eyes with his hand and squints off toward the forts lining the Potomac. With his leathery tan and crinkled skin, he looks all the world like the intrepid explorer he once was, not the dutiful chaperone he's now pretending to be.

I'm glad of his company. Pa's unruffled calm and slow, deliberate way of talking, so different from my constant movement and unceasing chatter, have carried me through many difficult moments in my life.

A cannon booms from one of the forts. Down below, the city is in turmoil: wounded pouring in, refugees flooding the streets, and all the cowards fleeing north. Maybe they are right.

Puffs of smoke rise like misplaced clouds in the brightening sky. Are Jubal Early's men that close? Is the Capital going to fall?

For a brush of a second, a bolt of panic seizes me. But I'm stronger than that. I don't want to think of what might happen if the city is overrun. I want to think of my future.

I grasp my father's hand and let my newest idea spill out. "Pa, I've made a decision. I'm going to be a cantatrice and give concerts, like Jenny Lind does. You've always said I'm as fine a performer on the guitar as Madame Goni ever was. Too good for haughty ladies' salons. My solos at the Lincoln Hospital Benefit were a grand success. The article in the newspaper praised my rich mezzo-soprano. Even General Grant, who must have far more important things to think about, came over and offered me a compliment."

Pa gives me that are-you-serious look that always makes me feel like I'm three feet tall. "I am not sure your mother would approve of you having any career. She wants you happily married."

"Then you should have said yes when Boudy asked for my hand."

"You know about that?" He swallows. "Ma and I agreed you were too young. And Mary would have been devastated. She loves him."

I ignore the tender way he says Mary's name. I know he speaks the truth, and however much it stings, I made the right decision when I promised Mary I'd give him up.

I gather my courage. "I'm still too young to marry, Pa. Singing is what makes me happy. And singing on stage pays well. Besides the private performances I'm doing, Reverend Hall has offered me one hundred and thirty dollars to sing every Sunday for the rest of the year."

Pa's shoulders sink. "I am so sorry, Vinnie, that you are weighed down by our financial worries when you should be carefree. Going to dances and balls. Enjoying the attentions of the young fellows." He gazes out toward the west. "I have not been the best of fathers. I made a mistake coming east in hopes of a better position. I regret that you have to worry about money. It is not your job to take care of the family. It's mine."

I wrap my arms around his neck and inhale his sunbaked scent, a blend of leather and open spaces. "You are a wonderful father. It is not your fault you came down with the bilious fever when we got here. Let's face it. You being sick has changed everything. You needed a desk job. You are never going to be able to roam the wilderness again."

He pulls away, and I know I have hurt him. But we have always spoken the truth between us.

He steps into the dome's shadow. "I appreciate you taking on the job at the post office. Isn't that enough for you?"

"I love my work. But the war won't go on forever, and you know female clerks like me will lose our positions when the men come flooding back. My boss can't wait to get rid of us. With all the innuendoes about our moral characters, the terrible explosion at the artillery factory last month sealed my fate. All those young girls burned alive have made government officials wary of hiring any more females." I look into his eyes. "I could become a teacher, or a governess, or take in washing like Ma. But it would be a waste of my talents. Singing on stage professionally is my future."

"But Vinnie . . . your mother . . ."

"Please, if you want me to be happy, do what you can to convince Ma. I would be exceedingly respectable and play only the most high-minded songs in the best of venues, like Grover's or Ford's Theater. It is why I am taking harp lessons from the nuns at St. Aloysius. There is no instrument more distinguished."

Pa grunts. "Being a performer sounds grand, but you would not be happy. A life in the public eye, dragging yourself and a harp from town to town, is no life for a woman, especially an unmarried one as small and petite as you."

I never thought I'd have to argue with my father, a man who followed his own dream of exploration, who taught me to ride and shoot, and encouraged me to perform wherever we went. He never once told me I couldn't do something because I was female.

I can't keep the rising anger from my voice. "There is no reason unmarried professional women can't have stellar reputations. The orator, Anna Dickinson, does it. She even travels alone. Yet all of Congress came to hear her when she spoke here in January, even the Lincolns. She makes tons of money, and you saw her. She's no taller than me."

"And the newspapers call her the worst of names."

"*Pah.* Reporters say anything to make news. They also call her America's Joan of Arc."

"She has powerful friends."

"Well, so do I."

"Not like hers. She's supported by the movers and shakers of the abolitionist movement. We only know some Western congressmen, like Major Rollins, who depend on the whims of their voters. Be satisfied with the income from your post office job, sweetheart. When this war ends—if it ever does—you may think differently about what you want to do. Meanwhile, enjoy your harp lessons. It is most kind of the Sisters of Mercy to teach you for free."

Enjoy? When my musical hopes have been crushed by the one person I believed understood me?

I run my hand along the smooth surface of the railing. "It's a thank you for all the hours I put in wiping fevered brows, writing letters home, and singing my heart out in their infirmary."

Pa softens his voice. "You have too big a heart, Vinnie. It's what I have always loved about you. No matter how bad things are, you never stop giving to the family, to the war effort, to anyone who asks for a favor. I wish I could make up for all you have endured these last three years. But when this horrid war ends, you are in the right place to find a fine gentleman to marry and give you children to love."

I close my eyes and squeeze back the tears. My all-powerful father, my childhood hero, sees me as little more than a female to marry off.

The skin beneath my eye quivers. I gather my skirts and head to the staircase. "We'd better leave."

I have three hundred steps to get myself under control. I step into the Rotunda, catch sight of the high-relief portraits of the explorers, and remember my letter to Mills.

I spin around. "There is one thing you can do, Pa. I understand why you and Ma didn't want me traveling out to Clark Mills' Bladensburg studio, but now he's working right here in the Capitol. Ma can have no argument against me taking lessons when it is so close, and I can be easily chaperoned." I squeeze my lips together. Then risk a promise I might not be able to keep. "And I will not mention a career on the musical stage again."

Pa's smile pinches tight, but he nods in agreement. "I'll speak to her, Vin. I promise."

Part 2

1864 to 1868

"I tell girls that question me about how to become an artist that the Divine call, like morning light, comes not at the bidding of the suppliant—that the knowledge of art, like love, comes not by appointment, but springs forth as freely as a mountain spring."

Vinnie Ream

From a speech given in St. Paul, Minnesota, in 1906

Chapter 10

SEPTEMBER 1864

CLARK MILLS' STUDIO, THE CAPITOL

I flatten my ball of clay into the round base of my planned medallion and peer around Mills' studio. The narrow room in the basement of the Capitol is congested with clay works in progress, an array of completed plaster busts, and the living originals of those busts. Every politician, it seems, wants to be made as memorable as Mills' George Washington equestrian sculpture, but without the expensive horse.

Representatives, senators, cabinet members, and political hangers-on stop at the studio at one time or another. All polite, all self-important, all filled with talk of the war and prayers for its rapid end, and all full of compliments for my work.

All but one—my mother.

Ma sits on a stool opposite me, glaring. She hates coming here and chaperoning me.

I turn back to my clay. Using the calipers in the way Mills has demonstrated, I determine my mother's measurements, then sketch out the profile of my mother on the surface of my clay. Dabbing on more clay and ignoring the men creeping up behind me as if I were an unsuspecting partridge hiding in the grass, I quickly add bits of clay to the cheeks and the brow. I must sculpt the whole piece at once, Mills says, if I want to capture the soul of the person and not just a pair of eyes, a nose, and a mouth.

I study my mother's profile. She is a handsome woman, despite the wrinkles of worry around her eyes and lips. Not that I dare do more than hint at them if I want her pleased with my work. That is a lesson Mills does not have to teach me—*always please the vanity of the sitter*.

The huddle of men behind me moves in. Visitors may come to place orders and see their visages emerge from beneath Mills' skilled hands, but they find delight in me. I have just turned nineteen but am so tiny they think me still a child.

"Such talent in one so young," someone says. "A girl of true genius."

"She has a gift," Mills affirms.

Heady words for a beginning sculptor to hear, but the damp clay beckons more. I close my ears and work to my heart's content on a small worktable Mills has set up for me in the farthest corner.

This is my first medallion from life. I glance up at my mother, sitting so demurely on a rickety stool, ostensibly knitting. In reality, she is cataloging the marriageability of every man who enters the studio and casting nasty looks in my direction when I ignore them.

Returning to the profile, I dab a piece of soft clay onto the chin. Being in the seat of power has gone to her head. Somehow, she believes she can wheedle one of these self-important men into giving Pa a fine position in the government, even though Pa's attempts at hanging on to political coattails have always been a failure. But if that falls through, next on her list is marrying Mary to one of them.

And then me, if she can.

But I don't care what she is thinking. Sculpting is what I was meant to do. This is true happiness.

Unfortunately, from her perspective—or fortunately from mine—most of the passers-through are married already. But with wives left back home or wound up in the dreary life of birthing an endless supply of babes, they feel free to flirt outrageously with me. There is always a man hovering nearby, singing my praises.

Right now, it is long-married Senator Nesmith, peering over my shoulder. He is one of my favorites. A twangy-tongued Westerner from Oregon. He understands how Washington society rubs and has been most kind to me and my mother, bringing refreshments, asking after our health.

He bows over my mother's hand. "So fortunate to have such a gifted daughter to capture your beauty."

Ma preens beneath the compliment but does not forget her political manners, honed in the wilds of Wisconsin state government—she knows the best way to influence a man is through their wives.

"Why, thank you, Senator. It is good to see you again. And your wife, Lucinda, have you heard from her? Will she be coming east at all for this session of Congress?"

"She is not one for ship travel, and the children are still young. But I do miss her. Now, if there were a train across the country—"

"I agree," someone shouts.

I gaze up from my clay work. It's Major Rollins, always promoting his cross-continental railroad bill. I give him my brightest smile. He's the one who made it possible for me to be here, studying in Mills' studio.

He nods to Ma and approaches me. "Mrs. Ream, I have wonderful news. Christian Female College has asked for a medallion of your daughter, and Mills has agreed to take the commission."

Overwhelmed and slightly embarrassed, I glance down at my own medallion. Beginner's work, no question.

"I have done nothing worth such an honor."

The major waves a hand, as if to sweep my words away. "But you will, dear girl. You will. They are calling you a wonder in the papers." He pivots. "Nesmith, now about that Northwest Pacific Railroad . . ."

And they are off to formulate how to join the country together, even though we are still fighting a war tearing us apart.

I turn back to the medallion and add on what will become my mother's hair. I use the tip of the clay knife and lose myself in creating each individual curl.

"Don't get lost in the details," Mills warns, coming to stand beside me. I lift the knife. "Remember, show only enough to leave some mystery. Let the viewer fill in what they imagine. That is the way to please a client." He takes the tool from me and smudges away the fancy braids I worked so hard on.

Shame fills me and turns my stomach sour. How could I have forgotten his instruction so quickly?

"There. Like that." He hands back the knife. "Hair is one of the most challenging things to represent well. It must be detailed sufficiently to resemble something soft and fine, but not so much as to draw away from the face. You have a strong affinity for the facial structure, but it is in the handling of the associated elements where you create both the mood and your personal signature. I suggest you visit the local cemeteries and study how light and viewpoint affect what you see in the sculptural works."

"I understand." And I do. I stare down at my forever-changed medallion, my breath heavy in my chest, and fight back tears. He does not think I'm good enough. Despite all those crazy compliments, so easy for artistic dilettantes to toss about, Mills' words are all that truly matter.

"We must go, Vinnie." Ma's voice cuts through the fog I have sunk into. "The boarders will be awaiting their dinner." She gathers up her knitting and shrugs on her shawl.

I glare at my medallion. Then, in a fit of something I don't understand, I crush it between my palms and drop the clay back in the bin.

"Vinnie, why'd you do that? I didn't even get to see it."

"I was merely practicing. The next one will be better."

I rinse the clay dust from my hands, wipe them dry, and then follow my mother out the door. I'm not good enough. Not yet.

But I will be.

I dedicate myself to producing a work that meets Mills' approval, but it isn't easy. Ma's medallion isn't the only one relegated to the clay bin. Day after day, I make the most of the fleeting one to two hours gifted to me by Zevely, who has permitted me to leave early when my allotment of two hundred letters is met. We may not see eye to eye on many things, but in this, he, with perhaps a nudge from his lovely wife, has proven more than kind.

I take out my latest work and set it on the worktable for Mills' perusal.

He turns my medallion of a dying standard bearer to better capture the light. "Melodramatic but appealing to current sensibilities. We will send this to Bladensburg to be cast in plaster. It will be a bestseller."

A bestseller.

Excitement sets me rocking back and forth on my heels. I stop. I must look like a child given a treat. I had not thought my work would please him so soon. Not after a few months of study.

At the worktable, my medallion is already attracting attention from the string of visitors darkening the door. I do a mental calculation. At fifteen dollars apiece, even the sale of four or five will help pay for Pa's expensive doses of quinine. There might even be enough to buy Mary the feathered bonnet she so covets. I wipe my dusty hands on my apron, the canvas rough against my clay-softened palms. Surely, Ma will be pleased. I definitely am. How delightful it is to be paid for doing something I love.

A quick glance tells me my mother is not here yet to see my triumph. But Major Rollins is, and right behind him, the all-important Senator John Sherman, whose general brother has just taken Savannah and is the hero of the city. Beside him, Senator Nesmith of Oregon smiles and winks at me.

I catch the major's eye. "Would you care to be my first client for a portrait medallion?"

Behind my back, I twist my hands together, hoping I have not been too presumptuous. To get commissions, Mills says a successful sculptress needs testimonials from satisfied clients. Who better to start with than my dear friend? And maybe he can help me with Pa's present.

He bows his head. "Of course, my child. I would be most honored to be your first patron."

I jump up and down, no longer caring if I look foolish. "Oh, thank you, Major. I'm merely a beginner and appreciate your confidence in me." I turn to my mentor. "Can you help me handle the details for my first commission? My little medallion will never measure up to the sculpture you made of the major to install at the University of Missouri. Still . . . perhaps his family might appreciate a small remembrance done by me."

It's the right move. Mills beams at Rollins.

I know that the two men consider me an amateur with no real chance at a career in a man's field of endeavor. And for now, that is fine. I'm young. I have time to grow. Time to make my mark. And I have one thing that male sculptors do not—a woman's smile and a child's body. I threaten no one and please everyone—male, that is.

As Mills and Rollins work out a schedule for his sittings, I turn to Sherman and scuff my foot. "My pa's birthday is coming. I wonder if you could help me."

He raises his eyebrows like a puzzled owl.

"My father's hero is President Lincoln. I wish to make a medallion from life for him. Do you think I could meet with the President and do a sketch or two? Take some measurements?"

Sherman grunts. "Really? Model the President? He is completely consumed by this war, young lady. Content yourself with a perusal of the many images and photographs that exist. They should prove sufficient."

His dismissive tone says it all. I have dared too much. Though his rebuff is gentle, and I didn't expect success, the skin on the back of my neck prickles.

Praying my cheeks are not flushed, I add strength to my voice. "I appreciate your advice. I have seen the President on Pennsylvania Avenue, attended some open receptions at the White House, and I am familiar with other artists' works.

However, Mr. Mills has taught me that working from life is the only way to capture a person's true spirit, and I thought—"

"It is a good thought, my dear." Nesmith comes over and pats my shoulder. "I can ask him for you." He casts a sideways look at Sherman. "Perhaps a sweet young face is just what the poor man needs to brighten these dark days. Especially if she's a little Western girl, born in a log cabin, endowed with energy and ambition, and making her own way in this world."

John Sherman scoffs. "She's a mere child."

Nesmith points to my dying standard bearer. "But quite gifted. In fact, I would also like our young sculptress to create a medallion of me."

Two commissions and a hint of hope for a grand possibility, one I will not think too hard on yet. I thank Nesmith with my most elegant curtsey. This is turning out to be one of the best days of my life.

"Vinnie." My mother arrives, her hair falling out of its pins, her mouth pinched too tight. "You must forego your lesson today. We have a special visitor arriving shortly, and I need you to beat the rugs, sweep out the parlor, then run and borrow Maud Wilson's silver tea service."

And just like that, my joy flees. I'm no entitled child of some well-heeled merchant or politician. I'm of ordinary folks, who beg tea sets from their neighbors and do their own sweeping.

Gathering my shawl around my shoulders, I wave a quick adieu, then follow my mother's mud-stained skirts like a puppy on a leash.

All the way home, I rail at my stolen moment of glory and make a promise. I will never turn my back on my family. But neither will I rely on them to help me succeed. I will make my own way in this life, using my wits, my talents, and whatever luck I can create.

I arrive home to discover Mary has found a wealthy suitor all on her own. In anticipation of the arrival of the fine gentleman she met at Mrs. Lance's afternoon tea, she is wearing a brand-new dress of turquoise satin.

I rush to clean the parlor, then help her pile her hair on top of her head in a wreath of curls. Around her neck, I place a sparkly but rather cheap-looking crystal necklace I had to run and borrow from another of Ma's better-off laundry customers.

Mary runs her fingers over it as if it were some fairytale talisman and perches on the settee as if she is a princess fit for a king. Or, at least, a knight in shining armor. In truth, she is waiting for one Perry Fuller of Lawrence, Kansas, who has driven Boudy right out of her head and, hopefully, her heart.

Who the man is, I have no idea. According to Ma, Mr. Fuller saw Mary munching a biscuit, was taken with her, and now is coming to court. I study my sister's glowing face and resolve to help her marry her dream man any way I can.

Someone knocks on the door, and I race to open it. It is not Mr. Fuller.

Mary looks between us. "What's agreed?"

Rollins slips into the high-back wing chair we reserve for honored guests. "Nesmith reported it was touch and go," he says. "The President complained he was tired of sitting so artists could capture his homely likeness."

My sister stops toying with her necklace. "The President?"

I hold up a finger. "Wait, Mary. What happened, Major?"

"Senator Nesmith emphasized the similarity of your backgrounds. He described you as a poor Western pioneer raised in a log cabin. '*Poor*,' Lincoln said. '*Western*? Then send her right up.'" Rollins slaps his knee. "And, my dear Vinnie, Senator Reverdy Johnson misunderstood you only wished to create a medallion. The President has ordered a marble bust."

I jump to my feet and clasp my hands together. "A bust." It's more than I could ever have expected and, perhaps, more than I can deliver.

There's another knock and a bustle in the doorway. A dapper, fair-haired man, clean-shaven, and by his scent, freshly scrubbed, strides into the parlor, a nosegay of violets in his hand. My mother trails behind, all smiles and head bobs.

"Perry Fuller, Esquire," he announces to the room at large.

Rollins rises, all emotion wiped from his face. "Ah, Fuller. You're in town?"

"Doing a roundabout of the political scene." He flicks his fingers. "New business opportunities to promote, a college to fund. You know how it is." They shake hands and move to opposite corners of the room.

Fuller lifts his chin. "Any bills before Congress I should know about?"

Rollins's face flushes. "Been a while since we crossed paths. We will have to catch up later. Condolences on the death of your wife."

"Thank you. The little ones miss her." Fuller drops the nosegay in Mary's lap. She opens her mouth, but he turns his back to her. "What did I just overhear? Are you truly involved in commissioning a bust of Lincoln? Who's to be the sculptor?"

Rollins looks my way. "Why, Vinnie Ream, of course. Protégée of Clark Mills. A rising star."

Fuller gives me the kind of once-over Pa would consider duel-worthy if we were still out West. "So, you're to have the ear of the President, sweetheart? How delightful." He turns to Mary. "You should have said you had such a paragon of a sister." He steps forward and hems me in. The parlor is suddenly too small. Too airless. Too dark.

Wishing I had not listened to Ma, who insisted I spruce up for Mary's suitor, I slink back against the wall. I ought to have worn my hair in braids and my clay-splattered work-a-day gray rather than my petal peach, bare-shouldered performance gown.

Over his shoulder, I spy Mary, frozen in place, her chin trembling, not because she is on the verge of tears, but I suspect because she is furious. And she has a right to be. Her would-be suitor is following in the footsteps of another man—Boudy.

I slide closer and rest my hand on her shoulder. But I can think of nothing to say to either of them. I don't care how wealthy and powerful Perry Fuller is—I don't like him. But I shall not be the one to take the stars out of my sister's eyes.

I catch sight of the wilting bouquet. "I will put these in water for you." I lift the posies from Mary's lap and make my escape to the back garden in search of a vase.

By the time I return, Ma has set up the borrowed tea service, Rollins has taken his leave, and Perry has remembered which sister he is supposed to be courting.

He sits in the wing chair, vacated by Major Rollins, and clasps Mary's hand.

Mary can't wait to fill me in on what I already determined. Perry Fuller, Esquire, is an especially rich man.

She turns to face me. "Besides a mansion in New York City, Mr. Fuller has a huge emporium and a grand home in Lawrence, Kansas, right on Clinton Lake." Mary smiles, her savoir-faire restored. "You remember the lake, Vinnie, where we used to build rafts with Bob?"

I take a sip of my bitter coffee and drop my gaze. I also remember the pro-slavery raids that had us huddling in fear in the cellar and which, in the end, drove us from the Kansas bloodbath to Fort Smith. Lawrence is not a place I hold dear to my heart.

I set my cup back in its saucer. "Lost some good friends of ours there."

Fuller straightens his sleeves. "I must admit that Lawrence has suffered quite a bit from the tides of war. But it will be rebuilt better and more beautiful, I can assure you."

"Your home survived?"

"Fortunately." He slides a silver flask out of his inner breast pocket and raises it. "You don't mind?"

Ma nods, and he spikes his coffee, then sips.

"I have wide influence in the state. Founded three thriving towns—Mineola, Centropolis, and Greenwood. And I'm the federal representative to the Sac and Fox tribes." He looks directly at me. "Though I would give all that up to have a position here in the Capital."

The innuendo passes right over Ma, who can only see the shine of Fuller's gold watch and his real estate holdings, not his roving eye or propensity for drink.

Her hands flutter. "We have found the city to be quite welcoming. There are many lovely homes here."

"I agree." Fuller gives his full attention to the most important member of the Ream family. "In fact, Mrs. Ream, I'm considering purchasing a home here. Perhaps, with your permission, Mary would like to come for a carriage ride and look over some of the properties I'm interested in?"

From someone who has only known my sister for two weeks, it is a blatant offer of marriage, and Mary seizes it, springing from the stool. "How delightful. I will get my hat and wrap. Will you help me, Vinnie?"

I want to scream at her, *Don't be trapped by this snake of a man. He is leading you on.* But how can I with her face filled with joy?

So, I say nothing and pray she comes to her senses sooner rather than later.

Chapter 11

FEBRUARY 1865

THE WHITE HOUSE

The north entrance doors of the White House stand wide open, despite the late February cold. I trace my way across the vestibule carpet, according to the newspapers, one of the First Lady's extravagant purchases, though it is hard to tell its worth as it is currently buried under hundreds of muddy footprints. Holding my breath against the stink of wet woolens and unbathed bodies, I shove my way through the grumbling petitioners snaking up the staircase and along the corridor for their moment with the President.

Back in sixty-two, Ma and I had waited in that line to beg permission to talk to rebel prisoners for word of Bob. But today, I glide past.

I am expected.

John Nicolay, the President's secretary, is waiting at the entrance to Lincoln's workroom.

"He's been poring over the casualty reports from Hatcher's Run," Nicolay whispers in my ear. "He'll be glad to see your pretty face."

I squeeze my lips together and step into an office littered with discarded plans and stacks of maps. A battered table occupies the center of the room. A small fire flickers in the fireplace but does little against the winter chill. The President sits in his rocker, peering out the south window at the Potomac, though I doubt that is what he is seeing at this moment.

Is he picturing the carnage across the way in Virginia or remembering the laughter of his departed son, Willie? He takes no notice of my entrance. His rheumy gaze is somewhere far away.

I remove my sketch pad and charcoal stick from my portfolio. I'm dying to use my calipers to get the proper proportions but dare not. Lincoln is amazingly kind, and I'm sure he would agree if I were to ask. I am fortunate to be allowed into his presence during his thirty-minute respite from the unceasing requests. My task, as I have been told repeatedly, is to provide quiet and ease and ask for nothing.

Perching on the only stool in the room, I rest my back against the edge of a rickety desk, careful not to disturb the teetering mounds of papers and telegrams, and study my subject. Lincoln's massive head has fallen onto his chest, though I can tell he's not asleep—his steepled fingers tap his chin.

Without a word, I set to work. I outline his profile and wish the public could see him like this—with the weight of war and death upon him. But a marble bust calls for a more upright pose. Something heroic. Soldierly. Far-seeing.

Yet, I can't capture him that way. I crumple up my sketch and toss it to the floor.

He turns to face me. "Having trouble, little bird?"

I peer into those large gray eyes, both stormy and sad at the same time. "Sorry to have disturbed you, Mr. President."

"Sometimes a man's thoughts require a bit of disruption." He straightens. "How goes your work?"

I dip my head with a shrug. "I'm a beginner, sir. And a young girl at that. I can only hope to do justice to this honor you have given me."

He leans back in his chair. "Don't let others pigeonhole you. We all start as beginners. Your own determination to succeed is more important than what people say."

"Oh, I'm determined, sir, or I would not be here." I gather my courage. "Would you mind if I brought a small amount of clay with me next time? Before the idea of the bust was presented, my original thought was to make a medallion of you as a gift for my pa's birthday." I scan the untidy space. "Though I fear it will add dust to all these vital papers."

"A little more or less dust will have no effect on the battlefield nor in this windmill mind of mine. Bring your clay." He folds his hands. "My own pa was a hard man. I hope yours is not."

"He's my greatest supporter."

"A rare one then. Tell me about him."

And so, I do.

Being at the White House means sacrificing my time working with Clark Mills, so it is days before I find time for a lesson. When I do, I find only one of my sculptural works is on display, and it is my worst—my first full-body male sculpture, which drew a grunt from Clark and the advice to focus on medallions.

Fisk comes over and whispers in my ear, "Admiring your *Gladiator*?"

I jerk my head up.

"Leave male anatomy to the men. Unless you'd like to do more intimate research." He leans in. "I'd be happy to oblige."

"I think not." It's not his help I want, though I'm sure many a woman would be pleased by his attentions. Fisk is an appealing youth with a profitable future.

Still, he's right. My lack of knowledge of men's bodies is a problem, but unless I accept Fisk's or some other man's offer, gaining that knowledge is impossible.

I look away. I have probably seen more bare male skin than most young ladies, but not enough. Nowhere in the entire United States can a woman artist officially study men's anatomy and maintain her propriety. Only in Rome can a woman work from a nude male model.

Right now, I have something more important to focus on.

With gentle fingers, I wrap the medallion of Lincoln I've made for my father in brown paper and fasten a string around it. Then I head for the door where my mother awaits.

I swallow a laugh. Sculpt nude men? I can't even come to the studio alone. I glance at Ma, her face a study in annoyance. She'd never approve of me going to Rome.

I inhale and feel my breasts press against my corset. I'll just have to confine my sculpture attempts to females.

The day of my father's birthday dawns April-bright and sunny. It is an auspicious day. The war is ending at last. Richmond fell two weeks ago, and Lee surrendered at some place on the Appomattox River. The Confederate government is in flight.

Good news for Lincoln. Good news for the country. Great news for us. Soon, we will be reunited with Bob, and the tight lines at the corners of Ma's eyes will finally loosen. I cross my fingers. Maybe we'll even head back to the West.

I gaze around the dining room table. Pa is at the head. Ma sits opposite. Mary and I face each other, as we have done these past four years. But today is different. My sister's suitor, Perry Fuller, has been invited to this family occasion. He lounges beside my sister, tall, elegant, suave, and grinning with his acceptance by the family members who matter.

I avoid looking at him and stand. "I'm sure you have all been wondering what I have accomplished in my time with the President." I hold up the paper-wrapped medallion. "I have a gift for you, Pa." I set the package by my father's plate, then sit back down.

He gingerly unties the string and folds back the paper.

"I will have it cast in plaster for you as soon as I can. Mills' studio has been in an uproar with the orders piling in."

Pa lifts my medallion with the care he shows his finished maps. "Thank you, my dear child. To think you created this at the feet of the great man himself. Such an honor to our family. To me."

I soak in his honest praise, then wait to hear what I expect will be platitudes from the rest of the gathering.

Instead, Mary rises from her seat and says, "I have an announcement. Perry and I are engaged." She smiles down at the preening man sitting next to her with all the posed innocence and hope of a girl in love. "My darling Perry asked me last night, and I said yes." She withdraws her hand from the folds of her skirt and extends it. The gem-embedded ring is huge, sparkly, and far more earth-shaking than my dull, gray circle of clay.

I force my lips into the expected smile, reach across, and take her hand in mine, adding my murmurs of surprise to those around me.

I peer into her silver-blue eyes, so different from my own dark ones, find my voice, and hopefully say the right things. "That's fantastic, Mary. Congratulations. I wish you much good fortune." I let go gently.

She tugs Perry to his feet.

"The wedding will be in June," he announces.

Ma's head tips up and down. Pa grins.

Am I the only one who sees Perry Fuller for the viper-in-the-grass he is? He is too wealthy, too ambitious. Why has he settled for a poor girl from a floundering family from nowhere?

I search for something safe but unmasking to ask, "Have you determined where you will live?"

Mary wraps her arm around his. "Why, Perry plans to build me a house. On K Street. Near the White House. It will be so much grander than anything available to buy. And you can all reside with us. You will have your own apartment. Just think, no more boarders, Ma. No more cooking and washing. Isn't that right, my dear?"

Perry looks directly at me. "Everyone in the Ream family will be welcome."

"We are most appreciative," Ma assures him. "How can we ever repay you for your kindness to our daughter and to us?"

I imagine passing the snake in a corridor late at night and shudder at how he might want me to show appreciation. His eyes say he wants things from me that I have no intention of giving him.

Perry dabs his mouth with his napkin, then refolds it and sets it by his plate. There is nothing wrong with his manners, just his trustworthiness.

"I do have one request," he says. "Our fellow acquaintance, Edmund Ross, will be arriving to take Kansas's empty Senate seat in the 39th Congress in December. Would you mind taking him on as a boarder?"

Ma pinches up a bit of tablecloth. "Um . . . I would have to ask one of our current residents to leave . . . but, of course, he is welcome. I remember Mr. Ross well from our time in Little Rock. A lovely gentleman."

"Captain Ross, now. Served in the cavalry, Company E, Kansas."

Pa tips his chin. "Well, I am not surprised. He always was a fine horseman and avid hunter. Tell the captain it'll be a pleasure to renew our acquaintance."

Edmund Ross? My memory of the man is foggy. A drinking buddy of Pa and his political friends, perhaps? But I do remember his stern-faced wife and his passel of children. "I played with his daughter, Laura."

"That's right," Pa says. "Somewhere there is a tintype of you, Mary, and Laura sitting on the front porch of his house."

Ma flicks her fingers. "All those photos were lost when we moved east."

Mary laughs. "Just as well. We looked like little Indians with our braids and bare legs."

Perry toys with one of her side curls. "I'd have loved to have seen that."

The tender touch settles my worries a little. Perhaps there is genuine affection between them. Maybe I'm overimagining Fuller's interest in me.

I focus on our upcoming boarder. "Will Captain Ross's family accompany him? I'd love to see his daughters again. Show off the Capital City to them."

Perry taps the tabletop. "His wife is pregnant, and the children are in school, so it will only be Edmund. Easier on you all, I'm sure."

"However," Mary tugs his sleeve, "we do have someone coming to stay with us in a few days."

"My little Alfred," Perry pipes in. "He's only five. Needs a mother's touch." He gives Mary a sappy smile. "He'll be no trouble. A quiet boy. My three other children are in boarding school in New York City."

Mary tucks in her chin. "I don't know if I mentioned that Perry has a house in New York. Since the Washington house will not be finished in time, we will spend our post-nuptials there. It's in a lovely part of Brooklyn."

A five-year-old running underfoot is not my idea of a restful home life, but Ma is clearly excited.

"We will shower that poor, motherless boy with all our love."

"Of course, you will," Perry says. "He will bring some brightness to your home."

My thoughts echo his. I may not like the man, but maybe he will shake things up in the family, not just with his money but his take-command attitude.

Pa's laissez-faire approach to life has never brought us any success. Perhaps a smooth-the-way Perry Fuller and his riches are exactly what our family has needed—what *I* have needed.

My pulse thrums. With Ma, Pa, and Mary being taken care of, I could quit my job at the post office and pursue my art career full-time. I could set up my own studio. I blink. I could go to Rome.

Mary rises to her feet. "It's time to get ready for the theater. Are you sure you don't want to join us, Vinnie?"

"I ought to practice my solos for the three Easter services I'm singing this Sunday." I rise to clear the table. Mary is living her dream. She doesn't want me in the middle of it.

Perry puts a hand under Mary's elbow and brushes past me. He slows. "Oh, by the way, Vinita."

My stomach tightens. Only one person on earth ever called me that, and I don't like it that Perry Fuller knows the nickname.

His voice lowers to a barely audible whisper. "I have a letter for you from a mutual acquaintance. I left it by your guitar."

All my unease returns. Who would trust Fuller to deliver a missive to me?

In no time, everyone is bundled against the spring evening chill and loaded into Perry's hired carriage. Then they're off to hobnob with Washington society at the Grover Theater production of *Aladdin*. It seems the perfect romantic entertainment for a newly engaged couple, even if they are trailed by two unfashionable, out-of-date Westerners. Pa, raw-boned and awkward in an imitation of Lincoln's top hat. Ma, dumpy in her overly ruffled gown of blue taffeta, a supposed copy of one of Mary Todd Lincoln's. Not that they will look any different from the others in the audience.

In the quiet, I wash the dishes, clean the kitchen, dampen the stove, and then head to the parlor. The letter is where Perry said it would be. I recognize the elegantly written *"Vinita"* at once and see why Mary's beau addressed me so. It's from *Boudy*.

I sit in shock as the salon clock ticks and the pounding in my heart slows. Only then do I open the sealed envelope and withdraw his missive.

He is fighting for the rights of the tribes, he writes, and will be in Washington within the month.

He's coming to see me, just as Mary predicted.

My breath seizes. My promise to my sister. How will I ever keep it?

I slap my hands to my chest and concentrate on restoring my breathing. It will be okay. She has a man she loves. She no longer has a reason to deny me mine.

Joy bounces up and down inside me. I picture his handsome face and remember the smell of buckskin and horse he never could shed, even when wearing his lawyering-up suit. But most of all, I relive the brush of his lips, the power of his gaze, and the warmth of his arms about me.

I reread the last line.

He still loves me. Still wants to marry. Once this business with the treaties is done and his tribe secure, he will take me anywhere I wish to go. Do anything I ask of him. As long as I'm at his side, he will be fulfilled.

What more could I desire?

I smile. Perhaps there will be a double wedding, like I foretold those many months ago?

I picture my awkward little statue of the gladiator. When I modeled it, I was thinking of Boudy, imagining it was his warm flesh and not cold clay beneath my fingers. To think that, soon, I might be running my hands, in truth, across that chest, feeling those muscles and limbs pressed against mine.

I ponder his words. He sounds like a changed man. Where has his ambition gone, his loyalty to his tribe? Would he truly be happy living in Washington? Following me to Rome? Watching me sculpt nude men while he mingles with wealthy expatriates?

Has war softened him that much?

Something niggles inside me at the thought of walking down the aisle in a white dress and pledging my body and life to a man, even if it is Boudy, based on promises. How well do I really know him, and what will happen after the vows are said?

Even if framed in love, my Boudy will own me under the law. He could control my career. Or would he treat me as one of his people? Cherokee women wield power over their men. They own their homes and land. They can turn a bad man away and divorce him.

But Cornelius Boudinot is only half-Cherokee. Which half would I be marrying? Do I love him enough to take the chance? Can I trust my artistic future with him?

Do I have to?

I rest my palm on the heart he carved into my guitar case and think—hard.

That is how the news finds me, my heart pulling one way, my dreams the other.

The front door slams open. "They've shot the President," someone says. I think it is Perry. The voice is too calm for the violence of the words.

The guitar case slides from my lap and lands with a *thud* on the rug. "What? What did you say?"

Pa rushes into the room and buries me in his embrace. He holds me tight and repeats the news, "Lincoln's been shot."

I curl into his scent and warmth. "It can't be—aren't there guards?"

Perry tips his hat as if he is already done mourning the man. "No one knows. An attack by the rebels on the leaders of our government. That's all we've heard. They stopped the play. Sent us home."

Denial is the hook to hang one's hopes on. So, I deny with all my strength. "No. No. No. It's an ugly rumor. It must be. Everyone knows not to trust gossip."

I bang my fists against my father's chest. "I saw him just a day ago. I just started my bust."

The pallid faces surrounding me tear at my resolve. The truth gnaws its way in. Nevertheless, I wait through the night, huddled in the parlor, unable to sleep.

By morning, I accept the worst. The yells and cries rising outside the window are too anguished to deny. President Lincoln is gone. The kind, tormented man has passed from the earth and from my life. The shaking begins at my fingertips and rips through me. He is dead. My friend. The country's hero is dead.

"How far along is your bust?" Perry Fuller asks, looking fully awake and ready to take on the town. "Mayhap the press might want to know."

I turn, confused. "The press?"

Perry grins at me, his perfect white teeth macabre in his handsome face. "Vinnie, this is your moment to shine. You met him. You knew him. People will want to hear your remembrances of the President. Buy your bust of him."

Pa smooths down my hair. "It would be a wonderful thing for you to do in his memory."

I gather the swirling grief around me like a blanket and tuck it in deep. Some other part of me answers, "My artwork is nothing special. Clark Mills and his sons did a life mask of Lincoln back in February. And there are all those other grand artists."

Perry Fuller moves closer. "But you spent all that time with him, alone in his office. And you bring a woman's perspective." He gives me a squint-eyed smile. "Do it. It is what you want."

His words tease at something knotted inside me. They sound right. They sound convincing. What better way to honor the President I held so dear? What better way to make a name for myself as a sculptress?

I am still shaking, but I nod my assent.

After they're gone. After I've donned my black dress. After I've mourned at the foot of the catafalque in the East Room. I remember Boudy's letter, the thin, tear-stained paper now buried deep in my purse.

Poor Boudy. His declaration of love arrived on the worst and best day of my life. The day everything changed.

With Perry's influence and the resulting headlines in the newspapers, I'm the Prairie Cinderella who sculpted Lincoln from life. People clamor for my Lincoln medallions. Orders pile in for his bust. I am going to be rich. I am going to be famous. And I will never be unknown again.

I finger Boudy's letter. The man I love promises me my heart's desire, but will his love be strong enough to change my course?

Chapter 12

JUNE 1865

CHURCH OF THE EPIPHANY, WASHINGTON CITY

Mary's wedding day dawns unbearably hot, sticky, and heavy. Black clouds hang low, ominously warning of an impending storm. Washington City can be that way in the late days of June, but it seems more like a bad omen.

In the church foyer, my sister sports yards and yards of creamy satin and rivers and rivers of perspiration. Not that any lady would admit to such a state. I blot her brow and neck dry for the thousandth time with my cambric hanky. Unbelievably, her stylish cats-rats-and-mice hairstyle is holding firm beneath her crown of flowers and veil of Belgian lace. There are surely enough hairpins. Though her updo's survival in this weather is due less to the tightly rolled hair bats than to Ma's liberal application of bandoline gel.

With the few hairpins I could scrounge together, my own hair worn maidenly loose, it is a frizzy mass so tangled a flea couldn't find its way out. Not that it matters. Nobody cares what I look like. This is Mary's day to be the queen. Rightfully so.

"Is he here yet?" she whispers under her breath.

I dab at my brow as I peek through the doorway. The church is full of equally sweaty people gleaned from the stalwart friends and acquaintances brave enough to remain in the city despite the unseasonable heat. Only a few of them are from the top echelons of society or the congressional delegations. Those are long gone to their home states or to the shore.

The ones here are Mary's colleagues, and mine, from work, Pa's acquaintances from the War Department, Perry's hangers-on, and in the back, our neighbors and boarders. Not one of them is a towering blond who thinks he owns the world.

The only Fuller visible is little Alfred, curled against his minder, Celia, the only black woman in the church. She is the one most deserving of being there. She has held our family together these last two months. Caring for a perpetually teary Alfred. Taking over Ma's workload. Fussing over Mary's trousseau. Freeing me to pursue my burgeoning art career.

"Are you sure?" Mary leans forward for a peek.

I hold her back. "Believe me. He's not here yet." I inhale and repeat the mantra I have delivered ever since she abruptly stopped declaring her love for him. "You don't have to marry him. Ma and Pa would understand."

"Of course, I do." Mary's words are forceful, but her lips quiver.

Guilt sits like an iron cannonball in my chest. I don't know what Perry has done to take the stars from her eyes. On the surface, he is all gentlemanly manners and a generous fiancé, everything Mary wanted in a husband. If I have pushed them together here and there, chaperoned poorly, then it is only for the best of reasons. Not because of Boudy's letter. Not because Perry has taken an interest in my career. Not at all.

The weight presses down. I can barely draw breath.

"There are other men," I say with all my love for her.

She spins the gold, rose-cut bracelet on her wrist. "None so rich."

I remember Boudy's lips on mine, the heat rising between us. Have I mistaken her love for Perry?

"Riches aren't everything."

"They aren't? Look who's talking," she hisses. "My money-grubbing sister who's making a fool of herself selling fifteen-dollar *Lincoln* medallions and plaster busts to the mob."

"I'm not. I'm merely following the advice I've been given to gain recognition for my talent."

She whirls on me. "*Bah.* What talent? No lady would grub in the clay like you do." She clutches my hand. "Look at the dirt under your nails. Promise me you will stop this foolishness. There is no need. I have made us rich."

"But Mary . . ."

A door slams, Emma's song dies away, and the congregation of attendees rustles in their seats.

Perry Fuller has arrived to take possession of his bride. It is too late to turn back the future.

Mary does not forget us. In the weeks after the wedding, cards arrive from a New York City hotel. A bolt of fine worsted from Lord and Taylor is delivered for Ma. A long letter addressed to Pa details the newlyweds' outings on trains, ferries, and steamboats. To me comes an invitation to visit them at their Brooklyn residence for July and August. I stare at the Fullers' *At Home Card*, printed on the finest paper.

I should take Ma and go for Mary's sake. I worry about her more than I ever thought I would.

I peer at my guitar. I would have to give up my musical commitments and my harp lessons. I would have to quit my post office job. The day is coming when all the women will be asked to leave to make room for the men returning from battle, but I'm not ready.

I would miss my fellow clerks. I would miss the independence of earning my own income. I would even miss Postmaster Zevely, who has become a strong supporter of my art over the last three years.

But most of all, I would have to give up my work at Clark Mills' studio, where I'm no longer a lowly student but an associate. My medallions and small busts of Lincoln are selling well. My growing list of clients receives their completed commissions with pleasure.

I tap the card against my palm. Family comes first. But the idea of walking willingly into Perry Fuller's domain makes the hairs on my arms stand at attention. Will he broach some new get-rich-sculpting scheme, to Mary's dismay, or demand something from me in return for his helpful advice and financial support?

I relegate the invitation to my pocket and take my guitar from its case, snapping the lid closed and pushing it aside so I cannot dwell on Boudy's etched-in heart. But I can't dismiss the once-upon-a-time memories that overwhelm me.

I strum the opening chords of "Do They Miss Me at Home," hum the melody, then settle into the song, letting the music transport me back to Arkansas nights filled with the whir of cicadas and the chatter of crickets. Overhead, the stars burn bright. We sit on the rickety wooden porch of our Little Rock boarding house and sing our hearts out. Mary and I harmonize the verses. Pa joins in with his deep bass voice. Bob and Boudy and their coterie of buddies tap out the rhythm with dusty boots.

I halt mid-strum. Where are all those men now? Dead on the battlefield? Spread out across the country, like my dear friend, the poet John Rollin Ridge, forging new lives? I am not yet twenty, and I feel ancient.

The parlor door opens, and Ma bustles in. "Look who's here."

I peer over my shoulder and blink. It is my brother, alive and all grown up, with a full black beard, like Pa's, a man's broad shoulders, the bowlegs of a bruising rider, and a woman at his side.

"Bob." I rush into my brother's arms. "We have missed you so. You should have warned us you were coming. I'm afraid, though, Mary is gone. She's in New York City, just married."

"First thing Ma told us." Bob whips his sweat-soaked hair off his brow. "We'd hoped to get here in time for the wedding, but I had a hassle surrendering to the damned Union authorities. The bastards didn't believe I honored my parole. Then some filthy ex-slaves stole our luggage. Thankfully, General Pike showed up and helped us out."

I see Celia peering in from the hallway. I refuse to let my brother offend her. "The war is over, thank goodness."

"And who is this?" I smile at the young girl clinging to his arm.

Bob pats her sleeve. "My wife, Annie."

She bends her head. "It is my pleasure to meet you at last. Cornelius has told me so many stories about you."

From her lace-collared calico to her well-polished shoes, she is everything proper in a lady. Her blue-black braids and her russet skin shout she is of the tribes. I catch the wariness in Bobbie's eyes. He has done a brave thing by bringing her to Washington. But he need not fear her acceptance in the Ream household.

I grasp her hands and squeeze gently. "You are most welcome into our family."

"*Aykpachi.*" That is *thank you* in Chickasaw. She dips her head. "Your family is welcome into mine."

My brother has chosen well. She is strong, gentle, and full of life. I can tell we are going to be best of friends.

"Come," I say. "Let me show you to your room so you can freshen up."

Ignoring everyone else, I take her hand and guide her upstairs to Mary's old room. Everything about my brother's new wife speaks to me of open spaces, clean air, and the freedom to run and ride forever. I hate seeing her hemmed in by the rubbed-bare, flocked-green floral wallpaper and second-hand, dark wood furniture Mary endured while living here. Combined with the July heat, it is like interring a gossamer fairy in a worn-out box.

I rush to pull up the blinds and open the windows. The hot breeze that filters in adds only more humidity to the room.

Annie ignores the heat and examines everything, running the back of her hand over the draperies, across the patchwork quilt on the bed, and along the wallpaper. She tugs on the tassels of the antimacassar covering the chest of drawers and regards the photo of Mary in her plaid taffeta gown.

She holds it up. "Was this her room?"

"Yes, my sister, Mary. She has just married a lawyer, Perry Fuller. They are in New York City."

Her brow furrows. "The Indian agent, Fuller?"

"Yes. For the Sauk and the Fox."

"I have heard he is not . . ." Annie presses her fingers against her mouth. "Forgive me. It is not my place to say. I do not know the man personally."

Every worry I have skitters beneath my skin. "Why? What have you heard about him?"

She shakes her head vigorously. "You must ask your brother. I wish only a blessed life for your sister." She sets the photograph down. "You must miss her so."

"I do. But now you're here. Once you are refreshed and unpacked, we will tour the city. I can't wait to show you the nation's capital. We can go to the top of the Capitol dome, stroll up Pennsylvania Avenue, and visit the White House. With most of the soldiers gone, the city is quieter and safer."

Annie lets out a long breath. "Quiet and safe is good."

Bob enters the room, a carpet bag in each hand, and thumps them onto the bed. "Thank you, Vinnie, for your kindness to my wife, but we can settle ourselves in."

I want to ask about Boudy, but he looks exhausted.

I point toward the back of the house. "The water closet is at the end of the hall. I will tell Celia to bring you plenty of fresh towels."

I slip past.

My brother puts a hand on my arm. "Boudy has plans for you."

I pull away, suddenly chilled despite the heat. "I know."

"He's waited years for you to grow up. Don't disappoint him, Vinnie. Never seen a man so much in love. But he's changed. He'd never say, but the war's been hard on him. He lost many friends and betrayed others. Worse—the tribes are divided, and he and his family represent the losing side. His uncle, Stand Watie, only surrendered a few weeks ago. The last Confederate general to do so. The treaty talks will be long and infuriating for him." Bob takes Annie in his arms. "I would never have survived without my woman's love."

Is my brother right? I know nothing of Boudy's last four years. I didn't think he saw battle. As a delegate to the Confederate Assembly, backroom fighting would have been his milieu. I can't picture the tough, arrogant man I knew, weak and battered by guilt.

I twist my fingers together. Would it make a difference? Change our love?

I return my guitar to my lap and resume the melody of "Annie Laurie."

I hope not.

I peer into the mirror over my vanity, scrunch up my nose, and say the word, "*Chinchokma*?"

Annie giggles. I love the round and bell-like sound of it, rich with the rhythm of her native Chickasaw.

"Too high-pitched," she says. "You sound like a bird being strangled." She runs the brush again and again through my impossible hair. Her touch is far gentler than Mary's ever was.

I try again. "*Chinchokma?*"

She laughs again. "Better. But your man will not be pleased. You should be learning to say, 'How are you?' in Cherokee."

I wink at her in the mirror. "Should I?"

"He is committed to his people and the success of his family. He will not stay unmarried forever."

"He has said he will honor my career."

She grins. "We have plenty of clay in Indian Territory."

I click my tongue. "But not too many commissions for monumental sculptures."

"Is that what you dream of? Making a huge sculpture like that one of that Indian Killer, Andrew Jackson, you showed me?"

"I could memorialize a more honorable man."

"Or woman?" She parts my hair and begins the laborious process of braiding together the frizzy strands that regularly left Mary out of temper.

I am not sure my brother knows what a treasure he's married. Annie is far more astute than most men of my acquaintance.

She pins up the first braid and starts on the other. "What woman would you sculpt? Another *Freedom*, like the one with the silly eagle-head headdress on top of the Capitol?"

I don't know where the idea comes from. It sparks through me like a flash of lightning across a western sky. "How about you? Would you pose for me? I would show the world the pride and beauty of the Indian people, the nation's original inhabitants we have wronged so badly. Women who know their worth and claim it."

Annie stills. "Pose? How?"

"I could model a medallion like the ones I made of Lincoln."

She taps her chin. "Not grand enough."

"Your head and bust?"

She pinches her lips together. "No, you must create a work worthy of our people who once ruled all of the land. Model all of me, a Chickasaw woman, standing tall and proud." She presses her hand to her slightly rounded middle. "A fertile, vibrant being whose offspring will live in this world, embodying two pasts and two futures."

"You're with child." I jump up and hug her tight. "I can try, but I have not yet worked on a full-sized statue."

"Then you will learn. Practice. The opossum walks slowly, as we say, but still gets up the tree."

"But how? Mills' studio is too public, and my brother will not tolerate you modeling for me. He has made it quite clear that he disapproves of my career."

She surveys my bedroom. "How about here? In your room? No one can complain if we claim long naps."

With its one window shaded by the neighboring building, my room is dark and stuffy, the worst one in the house.

I rub my forehead, thinking. "There is not much space, and clay is messy. Ma would never allow it. But maybe I could set something up in the wash shed out back, and we could pray for sunny days when there is plenty of laundry strung on the lines. Celia can be trusted. She will keep what we're doing private."

Annie bites her lip. "If you are sure no one will see. I would not want my husband to discover me exposing myself."

I take Annie's hands in mine. "Thank you for the inspiration and willingness to pose. I will make sure that no one ever finds out that you were my model."

In no time, I'm ready. In the wash shed, behind the rows of sheets, flapping desultorily in the afternoon heat, I have created my own private studio. I take a lump of clay from the wooden bin Fisk has dropped off for me and remove my favorite clay tool from its canvas pouch.

There is a fresh breeze, a sunlit sky, and a work of art that will make my mark. Nothing stands in my way if I choose a woman as a model.

And what a model she is. Annie sits to the side, shielded from view by sheets pinned to a temporary clothesline. I have seen plenty of nude sculptures of women. I know my own body well. But Annie's strong, sturdy limbs and full hips make Hiram Powers' *The Greek Slave* look limp, powerless, and chained to the past.

I daringly bend my wire armature, so my maiden stands slightly turned, as if in mid-step. Unlike Powers' work, my *Indian Maiden* will show movement. One hand shields her eyes as she gazes forward, toward her future, like an explorer or a conqueror. It is a daring position for any statue—the arm in action and unsupported. But for a female one, it is earth-shaking.

It is with lightness of heart that I take up my clay and begin to build the maquette for my full-sized sculpture. I have mastered the calipers, gained proficiency with ratios, and know how to prepare my clay to the perfect consistency.

I render Annie's head quickly. Then I start on the torso, and my fingers slow. I use my eyes to capture the weight of bone and sinew, and the knowledge of my own curves and textures to model the flesh. Slowly, magically, the feminine form blossoms beneath my fingers. The clay flows as if it were alive. The work takes on a reality of its own. This will be my greatest sculpture so far.

Celia crashes through the sheeting. "Vinnie, your brother is coming. I couldn't stop him."

Annie draws on her day robe and leans back into the shed's shadow. But I am too slow covering the sculpture. Bob bee-lines toward me and stops. He stills and stares at the maquette. "I don't believe it. You *are* a trollop. Just like they are saying."

I tremble with anger. "Who says such a thing?"

"*Everyone.* It is bandied about in all the taverns in the city. How you use every female wile to get what you want, like that post office job."

"That is a lie, Bob. Made up by a politician who wanted the jobs to go to his toadies."

"*A lie*?" He points at my model. "Look at this disgraceful thing. A bare-naked woman, suitable only for a Jezebel's boudoir. Or is it a prize to give the next man you want to weasel something from?"

I wrap my arms around the wet clay. "It is a work of art, like *The Greek Slave* or the *Venus de Milo*."

"*Art*? Is that what you call that? I didn't believe Ma when she told me this crazy idea of yours about becoming a sculptor. Well, wipe it from your mind. My sister will not bring disgrace on this family." He looms over me. "And get rid of that."

From the corner of my eye, I can see Annie slowly slipping away. I move in front of my work and put my hands on his chest like I used to when we were children, and I wanted his full attention for some childish request. "Listen, Bob. I am not doing anything wrong. What you're seeing is not finished. It is common practice to sculpt the undressed body before adding the drapery on top. That is how you can make stone or bronze fabric look realistic, as it flows over the limbs and torso."

"It looks plenty real and plenty wrong to me. I'm warning you, little sister, if Boudy sees that, he will abandon you. He's not going to marry a woman with a soiled reputation. And I won't let him."

"*Let him*? What are you talking about? You have no say in the matter."

Clink.

We both turn toward the sound. Annie, in her rush, has tipped over Celia's wash basin. It lies on its side, the water gurgling out, a stain, dark as blood, forming around it.

"Annie?" I can hear the shock in my brother's voice. He glares at me, then turns away. "Pack your bag, wife. We are leaving."

She hurries up the steps and disappears into the house.

"Damn you. I won't be back, sister. Perry will take care of Ma and Pa, and Mary. You . . . you can go to hell, for all I care."

His words strike me like cudgels as he shoves me aside and smashes his fist into my model. The wire armature bends. Clay flies off in every direction. He hits it again and again. Throws it to the ground and stamps on it until nothing is left except wreck and ruin.

He stands there, huffing, then thumps away.

I do not recognize this man as my brother. I do not trust him. But he has lit a fire inside me.

I squat down and untangle the wire. I am going to recreate my *Indian Maiden,* nude and proud, and rise to the top in the art world. I am going to make my brother and all those who denigrate me see me for who I truly am—a world-class artist.

Chapter 13

APRIL 1866

THE CAPITOL, WASHINGTON CITY

But climbing to the peak of the art world will not be easy. Holding back tears, I dash from the committee chamber. What an idiot to think a girl like me would have any chance at gaining a commission for a sculpture of Lincoln. Major Rollins might believe it is possible, but none of those House Committee for Public Buildings and Grounds members do. Only the chair, Representative John Rice, has shown any compassion, and those wagging tongues will say that I have led him on.

Shoulders hunched, I hurry down the corridor to my studio in the Capitol basement. My little Room A—dank, dark, and deep in the bowels of the Capitol—is nothing so grand as Mills' studio was.

But with Clark Mills gone back to Bladensburg to work on larger pieces, I, thanks to Rice's influence, have taken his place as resident sculptress. I'm no longer an associate under Mills. *I'm on my own.*

Arriving at the studio, I pop inside, toss my rejected petition down, then set to work straightening the medallions on display and dusting the Lincoln busts. The studio might be empty at this moment, but it will not stay that way. The isolated location and my congenial presence make it perfect for meet-ups between less-than-friendly congressmen and their hangers-on. Appearances are everything in the art business. I must be ready. Someone could stop in at any time.

I yank my voluminous canvas smock over my head and tie it loosely in the back. The stiff fabric serves as better armor against men's familiarity than any chaperone could. No pinches or pats can penetrate through the rough cloth. I am well protected, even though Ma stopped chaperoning me now that I'm the notorious woman who sculpted the naked *Indian Maiden,* and then dared to display the plaster cast in the window of De Wolf's Jewelers on Pennsylvania Avenue.

Digging out a lump of clay, I toss it on the worktable and give it a good, hard slap. I drive my fist in and smash it again and again, imagining it to be the nasty reporters and nose-in-the-air Washington society ladies who have made me a pariah. I create one nude, no different from Powers' *The Greek Slave,* and I'm an outcast. It isn't fair.

Representative John Rice is such a sweet man, entirely devoted to his wife and children, and he must hate me for how my flirtatious dancing with him at balls and begging for his assistance with my petition will cast aspersions on his morality and mine.

But he is as wise as the owl he resembles with his round glasses and bulging eyes. "Wait till the last days of the congressional session to present my petition," he advises. Meanwhile, I must keep collecting signatures, he insists.

"Ah, this is where you hide out."

I snap my head up. The woman is a stranger, but I can tell she hasn't come to make a purchase or praise my work. Beneath her fashionable hat, adorned with bunches of fake cherries, she wears the nose-pinched expression of someone smelling not the rose petal potpourri discreetly placed around the studio, but the stench of something foul.

She moves along the wall, studying the medallions on display. "These are yours, Miss Ream?" She glares at me. "You *are* Miss Ream, I presume?"

I grab the wet rag hanging on a hook by my work stand and wipe the clay dust from my fingers. "Vinnie Ream, at your service. All the works here are mine. And available for purchase."

She puts on spectacles and peruses my newest work—the bust of a bare-breasted young woman, which I've christened *Violet*.

The woman straightens. "Heard about you. Had to see for myself." She gives me a long stare. "I'm Jane Swisshelm."

A polite greeting sticks in my throat. Everyone has heard of the razor-tongued, overly opinionated journalist who gave her all to the wounded soldiers during the war and had the distinction of being fired by both Horace Greeley and the War Department for being too radical in her news articles.

I curtsy and force out a response. "You are most welcome to my little studio, Mrs. Swisshelm."

"*Little* studio? You're right here in the Capitol. That's an honor deserving of a renowned artist like Clark Mills, not you. You look to be all of fourteen. But buxom enough, I guess. And all that hair. No wonder the men are rapturous about you. Be forewarned: I am not so easily persuaded by a bit of feminine fluff."

She sails across to my bust of Lincoln and places her hand on top of the head as if my most important work is nothing more than a doorpost. "Heard you're claiming the President himself posed for you?"

How dare this woman accuse me of lying? I bite out the words, "*He did*."

"Well, my good friend, Mary Todd, disagrees. Says she's never heard of you."

"My arrangement was with the President and his secretary."

"So you say." She clasps her hands in front of her own less-than-generous bosom. "I'm here to tell you to drop the petition you're circulating. You have no right to make a marble sculpture of him."

I should grovel. Pretend to think about her suggestion. After all, I'm not sure what I am going to do. But I can't. The woman reminds me too much of Ma and her dictates. So, I throw back my shoulders and firm my voice. "You can't tell me how to pursue my career."

She comes closer. "Give up the petition, or I'll spread the rumor that your obscene woman in the shop window is actually you. A self-portrait, shall we say?"

"What? Are you blind? That looks nothing like me. That is a classical pose based on numerous renowned works of art."

"It is unsuitable for you to show such nakedness and an insult to all women. Men do not need their lust stirred by bared breasts."

"It is a most appropriate work to be created by a woman. Why should only men be allowed to sculpt our sex? No one criticizes them for sculpting nude males."

Her lips pinch together. "The only reason to create nudes of either sex is to titillate."

"The human body is beautiful and wondrous. It must be. After all, the Lord has modeled a good many people in the nude."

Swisshelm sneers. "Our good Lord has no place in this den of obscenity or in this discussion. Mark my words. If you continue the course you have set for yourself, you will be rebuffed in society."

"Society, as you call it, doesn't accept me now—an upstart girl from the wild prairie who works with her hands. But people who value excellent artwork support me with their pocketbooks." Poker-hot anger overrides my common sense. "Long after you are gone and your newspaper has turned to dust, Mrs. Swisshelm, my work—nude or dressed—will endure. Do your worst. I'm going to get that commission."

"*Humph.* You're as foolish in your words as in your choice of subjects. You have declared war on me and all women. I will not ignore the gauntlet you have thrown." With a sharp jerk of her finger, she stomps out of my studio like a general in skirts.

I find my clay knife and stab it into my drying lump of clay. I have just made the worst enemy possible.

I stab the clay again and again. That small-minded woman will not bring me down. I am going to get the Lincoln commission by obtaining the signatures of the greatest men in the nation. And I will do what I must to get them.

That is why, an hour later, I find myself standing at the front door of a nicely kept house across the street from the Willard Hotel. I have on my widest-brimmed hat, a simple gray dress, and carry my petition, sketchbook in my workbag, and a posy of pansies. I have put off this visit for weeks, but I can delay no longer. If I can win over Thaddeus Stevens, I can win over anyone.

I lift the knocker. Tap lightly. Then I wait, shifting my weight from foot to foot, hoping he's not home but dreading having to come back.

A woman opens the door. "Yes?"

According to the town gossips, she is Stevens's mulatto mistress, but to me, she looks like a middle-aged woman in a serviceable dress. Tall, self-assured, but with kindness written in the smile lines around her eyes. Someone I could talk to and befriend.

I gather my courage. "I'm here to see Congressman Stevens."

Her dark eyes peer into mine. "And you are?"

"Vinnie Ream, the sculptress."

She laughs and pulls the door open. "Well, this is a first. We've never had a sculptress come to our door before. Come in. Thaddeus could use a reprieve from his political problems."

What a lucky man to have this joyful woman in his life.

I hold out the pansies. "A touch of spring for you."

"How lovely." She takes the stems with their tiny blossoms. The movement spills their scent into the hallway. "I'm Lydia Smith. Thaddeus has told me about you. Follow me."

She leads me to a small combination parlor-office. A wood stove crackles, keeping the room toasty warm on this chilly winter day.

The rug beneath my feet muffles my steps, and when I see Mr. Stevens, I'm glad it has. With his drawn-in cheeks and sallow complexion, he looks far more ill than the last time I saw him, yelling at a fellow congressman in the House of Representatives. His eyes are closed, and his bad foot rests on a low ottoman.

I gather my skirt to keep it from rustling and slip into the nearest chair so he does not have to rise out of gentlemanly politeness. But he is not asleep.

Before I am fully seated, his eyes snap open. "Good day, Miss Ream. I see you have brought your cheerful countenance and outrageous hair directly into my home."

"You don't like my hair?" I tug on one of my curls. "I hear tell it is how I seduce men into doing what I wish."

He adjusts the ridiculous curly, chestnut-brown wig that is in danger of slipping off his pate. "Hair. Having it is a very powerful thing, young lady. Care to lend me some of yours?"

I tuck my curls back behind my ears. "It would be a lost cause."

Stevens harumphs. "If you want a wish fulfilled, you should reconsider that statement."

Mrs. Smith hustles into the room, weighed down with a tray of refreshments and the pansies now in a vase of water.

My mouth waters as the aroma of coffee and gingerbread blends together. It has been a long time since breakfast. My stomach growls. I quickly cover up my embarrassment by gushing, "Oh, that smells delicious."

"Well, you just eat them right up." She sets the vase and the refreshments on a side table and pours me a cup of tea, then one for Stevens.

He points to a chair next to him. "Sit yourself down and take a piece of gingerbread for yourself, Lydia. This young lady has come to seduce me. I need your protection."

Any hesitation I felt coming here dissipates. This is not the angry, acerbic tiger who terrifies the new members of Congress—the one his enemies call a snake.

This is a man, although surely in pain, who's far more relaxed and wittier than I thought him to be.

Lydia takes a sip from her cup. "I'm intrigued. What are you here to seduce Thaddeus into doing?"

Stevens snorts. "I bet you want me to fend off another attack by those ridiculous female journalists. You'd think they'd support another woman trying to make her mark in the world rather than complaining to me."

"Thank you. I did not know you'd been approached."

He flips his hand up. "It was nothing. That Swisshelm woman buttonholed me in the hall the other day. 'How could a girl remain chaste and pure,' she wanted to know, 'with three hundred wretched Congressmen around her?'"

I cover my mouth with my hand, half in shame, half to keep a curse from spilling out.

"Don't you fret, my dear. I stole the breeze from her sails. 'Out of all that three hundred,' I told her, 'No one has done as much harm to Miss Ream as you have with your vicious news articles.'"

"I don't understand why I anger them so." I hold up my hands. "Look at my hands. Working with clay has dried and roughened my skin so they resemble a washerwoman's. Why would I mold clay, use hammer and chisel, and lug heavy bags of plaster around to seduce men? It makes no sense."

"Like I said, must be the hair. You just have too much of it." Stevens grins. "But seriously, I have found that very little makes sense in this life. However, I suspect jealousy is behind the ladies' pokes and jabs."

I draw the petition from my workbag and rest it on my lap. "Well, if I get the Lincoln commission, it will stir up even more jealousy." I chew my lip. Stevens may be teasing me now, but he could turn on me at any minute. My hand trembles. "I'm not sure I should be doing this."

"Nothing wrong with pursuing your dreams. Is that the petition I've heard about?"

I hand it across. "I would be most honored if you would sign. Chairman Rice says I need to get as many signatures as possible, and then present the petition at the last session of Congress."

"Rice has good political savvy." He taps the rolled petition against his thigh. "I've seen the bust you did of Lincoln. There's something softer about it than the other artists' renderings—more humanity, perhaps. Man moved too slowly to free the slaves, and his assassination was a tragedy. Damned Booth stole black folks' chance to be full members of our society, I fear. I never saw eye to eye with Lincoln, but he would surely have done a better job at reconstructing the South than Johnson ever will. Nothing wrong with making a statue of the man." He paused. "So, even though you refuse to share some of that hair, yes, I'll join all these befuddled men of yours and sign. That is, if you agree, Lydia?"

Lydia cups her hands beneath her chin. "Women's causes have always been something you support. I personally think it would be pleasant for all those congressmen to have to look at a statue carved by a woman year after year. How big will it be?"

"I have proposed that it be life-size."

"Excellent." Lydia fetches a lap desk from behind the door.

In seconds, the petition gains another name, a most important one.

My pulse quickens. With Stevens' signature added, I can now approach the Radical Republican faction.

He presses the blotter to dry the ink, then rerolls the document. "I will make sure my colleagues offer their support."

"Thank you. I am overwhelmed by your kindness." I pick up my bag. "Here, let me do something for you in return. May I make a medallion of you?"

"You want to immortalize this ugly face?"

I pull out my pad and charcoal. "It's a wonderful face. With a strong profile. So full of character."

Stevens snorts. "I'm a character, all right."

Lydia puts a hand on his. "I would like a medallion of you."

Whatever their relationship, there is no question that Lydia cares for him.

"There you go. You have the commission." Stevens wags his finger at me. "However, I expect the hair to be as perfect as yours."

Lydia laughs. "I never thought you a vain man, Thaddeus."

Stevens reaffixes his wig. "Well, then. We must order a bust of me as well, but it must have a full head of flowing locks, like yours. It will stand for the ages as a monument to foolish vanity."

My hands fly up to my mouth. A bust? Flowing hair? The man is sick, bald, and a hard taskmaster. How will I ever succeed in pleasing him?

Chapter 14

APRIL 1866

THE MALL, WASHINGTON CITY

It's late afternoon by the time I leave Thaddeus Stevens' home. I should be elated. I have an unexpected order for a bust, as well as for the medallion, which Stevens insists on paying for, despite my protests. Even better, I have two new friends. So, why am I questioning everything?

A vain man. Lydia's words whirl around my brain. Illness-racked, Stevens' appearance has little to commend it. Straight-nosed and hard-mouthed, he has wit and will enough to convince people to do the right thing with words alone. Yet, he is so self-conscious of his baldness that he wears an elaborate wig, most unsuited to his age, that's always falling off.

How am I to sculpt such a man? All my previous sculptures in the round have been idealized. But Thaddeus Stevens is alive and well-known, seen as an angel of justice by the downtrodden or a devil incarnate by the power-hungry. Shall I model a true likeness so future generations can see his debilitation? Or shall I assuage his vanity for the here and now?

Perry Fuller would say not to worry. It is all about the money. He's the paying client, and his wishes should be met. But if I choose to please him, am I truly a fine artist?

I get off the omnibus a stop early and walk across the mall to the Capitol. I halt at the sitting statue of Washington, lit by the setting sun. Many people hate this sculpture because they object to the nude torso. But no one can deny the majesty of the face and pose. Fine sculpture must be more than a copy of a person's visage. A work to last the ages has to capture the inner essence of the sitter. A truly great work lifts the viewers' spirits and gives them a model for how to be in this world.

But am I skilled enough to carry it off? Sculpting a living person is so different from representing a dead hero. People's memories are easily converted by the sculpture before them.

I lean against the wrought-iron railing and close my eyes. Thaddeus Stevens, with his deep-set eyes and long, narrow nose, reminds me of a hawk ready to strike at any injustice he spies. I wrap my hands around one of the uprights. That is how I will show him, looking intensely at the viewer. And if I do a good enough job drawing the viewer's gaze to those eyes, it won't matter if I give him the full head of hair he covets.

I let go of the railing. If I succeed at modeling Thaddeus Stevens, then maybe I will be acknowledged as having the skill to create an Abraham Lincoln statue to last the ages.

I can't wait to get started. So, rather than turning toward home and dinner, I ignore my grumbling stomach and take the walkway to the Capitol, my head overflowing with ideas for Stevens' bust. At this hour, no one will interrupt my work. The congressmen and their compatriots will be at the taverns, wheeling and dealing over their steak and ale.

I bustle down the quiet corridor, step into the studio, then reel back. The tiny space is crowded with men. Clark and Fisk Mills are supervising the delivery of two wooden crates.

Mills approaches. "Your bronze casting was ready, so Fisk and I thought we'd deliver it in person."

One of the workmen crowbars off the top of the box. Fisk and the foundry's right-hand man, Mills' former slave, Phillip Reid, lift the sculpture out and set it on my worktable.

Is this my first full-sized bust? The much-maligned bare-breasted *Violet*?

My fingers tremble as I unwind the thick muslin wrapping and spy the nubile breasts Jane Swisshelm accused of being mine.

Perry Fuller paid for this casting, supposedly as a way to further my career. But his motives concerning me and my role in his plans are always suspect.

My fingers brush the top of the breasts as I untwist the length of linen. Swisshelm's nasty comments in the press have done plenty of damage to my reputation, but I fear more what Mary will do if she learns her husband financed this work.

Fueled by Bob's repudiation of me, she's furious I have not given up what she calls my addled-brained scheme to bring the Ream family down. If she were to learn that her Perry is supporting me in this endeavor, it could destroy our relationship forever. And I love her too much for that.

But, with her in delicate condition, due to deliver her babe any day now, I dare not mention anything about my work. Long before Perry takes ownership, my *Violet* will be shipped off for exhibition in Milwaukee, where it will either bolster my artistic career or destroy it. Though I'm hoping that free-minded Westerners will be less scathing than Washington's prudes and show pride in a native daughter who can create classically styled works.

I pull the cloth completely off, then step back to admire it. My *Violet* is beautiful. The bronze glistens in the gaslight in a way white plaster never can. Her head tips perfectly to the side, far more elegantly than *The Greek Slave*. Her thickly braided hair unfolds down her shoulder. I can't believe my own fingers created this work of art.

Fisk comes up behind me. "So, what do you think?"

"The bronze casting is excellent."

He laughs. "Should be. It's what the foundry does."

Crack.

I spin around. The workmen have ripped open the other crate.

Fisk helps move the lid aside. "I brought you a gift."

He lifts out another cloth-wrapped bust. "Come take a look."

Together, we pull off the wrapping. It falls free from the face.

For a moment, I'm confused. I jerk back. "Who is this?"

"Why, *you*. Major Rollins ordered it for installation at that school you attended. I just finished it."

"You sculpted it?"

"My father assigned me the commission."

Fisk uses his sleeve to wipe away some invisible mark on the cheek. His action gives me a funny feeling, as if he has touched my own face.

"So, what do you think?" He rocks back and forth on his heels.

I don't want to answer. Anything I say will offend him. I study the bust. There is a formality to the face and design of the hair that seems to suck the life from it—from me. Because it is me. Though I do not recognize myself.

I move around the sculpture. I am not a ravishing beauty, and he has not shown me as one. But seeing my face carved in cold stone emphasizes my too-wide-apart eyes, my longish nose, and thin upper lip.

Fisk has stopped rocking and is now tugging on his red-haired chin beard.

I must say something. I fall back on the trite response I hear from so many clients. "Amazing how you captured my likeness." I want to add, *but not my spirit*. But I don't. I need Fisk's help. If I want him to support me as an artist, I must do the same for him.

Running a finger over the extravagant hair that curls from the center like a foaming waterfall, I peer over at him. The smock top he has dressed me in is so thin it looks more like a chemise than the raiment of a reputable woman.

What I really want to ask is if he thought about touching my breasts when he sculpted me, though the idea makes me queasy.

"Do I really have this much hair?" I watch his expression.

"Yes, really."

I see it in his eyes then—desire. He would love to touch my hair. To touch me.

And, for a moment, I reconsider him as a potential husband now that I work with my hands, too. I like Fisk. He is young and energetic, creative, and respects my work. We could form a fantastic sculptor partnership.

I draw my petition from my bag and give Fisk a sideways look. "Would you sign my petition for the Lincoln commission?"

Fisk peers into my eyes. "Of course."

He takes one of the sheets and scribbles his name with the pencil he keeps tucked behind his ear. "I can get all the major artists to sign this for you, Vinnie. Though I fear this is a lost cause. I hear the sculptor, Hiram Powers, is hungry for it."

He moves in, perhaps in hope of a more intimate thank you? The acrid aroma of melted metal that permeates his work clothes assaults my nose. The smell reminds me of chains heated in the sun. Chains are the last thing I want to live with.

And there would be many chains if I married him, far more than becoming his property by law. He has studied at the Royal Academy in Munich. I have only the instruction from his father. If we were partnered, he'd lord his expertise over me—believe himself better. If I earned a commission, he'd be envious. Besides, Fisk doesn't make my heart beat faster the way the thought of Boudy does, even though he fought for the wrong side.

I hold out my hand. "No, I want to collect all the signatures personally. That's something I've learned from your father— everyone is a potential client."

He tries again. "I could accompany you. Make introductions."

I soften my voice and briefly touch his hand. "That is most kind, Fisk, but almost everyone knows me, thanks to Swisshelm and her ilk. Besides, I need to fit my visits in between working here and at the post office. You are so busy at the foundry. Speaking of which, I have another bust to be cast."

Turning to my worktable, I uncover my latest bust and reveal the small boy's head I have just completed. It is of Perry's son, Alfred. The child's face is pure innocence, unlike his father's. Mary will love it. She has become a wonderful mother to the little boy and will soon have her own child to love. In that, I am happy for her.

I run my finger along the intricate flower trellis encircling the base. This work is so much better than Fisk's rigid portrait of me with its formally curved eyebrows and staring eyes.

Maybe I do have talent enough to sculpt Stevens.

After the workmen have gone, after Fisk's last attempt to win my favor, and after the Mills have left for their Washington house, I sit on the floor and study my sketches for Thaddeus Stevens' bust, my confidence renewed.

This will be my best work yet. When it is done, no one, not even my disgruntled sister, will be able to deny my ability to sculpt Lincoln for the country and all posterity.

I clench my fists. I hope.

Chapter 15

JULY 1866

REAM BOARDING HOUSE

I wipe the sweat from my brow and throw open the window in the parlor, not that any fresh air wafts in. It is one of the hottest days so far this summer. It is hard to stir up the resolve to trudge to the Capitol and work. Instead, I set aside my sketchbook and take up my guitar. Without thought, I strum the opening chords to "Annie Laurie." The melody echoes in the empty room and lowers my spirits even more. It has been months since I've played.

With a heavy breath, I let my pick hand drop. Ever since I quit my post office position in January and announced that I was sculpting professionally, I've been banned from singing in all the churches. Nasty biddies. It is a cruel punishment. I miss singing. I didn't do it just for the money. Music makes my spirit soar.

I reposition my guitar and start again.

Thunk. A knock resounds in the still, hot air. Ma, with little Alfred clinging to her apron, hurries to the front door. She is back moments later.

"A visitor for you, Vinnie."

I rise. "Who is it?"

"Mr. Boudinot."

He is here, at last, my Boudy. I struggle to breathe. It is like the air has been sucked from the room.

The man himself looms in the doorway to our parlor, suntanned, long-haired, and impetuous as always, even if he is wearing an elegant day suit. I blink. He hasn't changed a bit.

He rushes forward, swoops me up, guitar and all, and swings me in a wide circle. His scent of prairie grass and leather draws me like nothing else. How could I have ever considered marrying Fisk just a few months ago?

All the worry and anger at his joining the Rebels and dragging my brother into danger whirl away the minute he touches me. The war is over, Bob is safe, and he is here. I wrap my arms around him. My hair tumbles free. My skirts swing out. I'm untethered. Flying. I never want him to put me down.

But happiness that untamed doesn't last forever.

He lowers me to my feet and sets me at arm's length. "You had word I was coming, Vinita?"

I peer into his eyes. "No."

"But you were playing our song."

"I play it often. It's my favorite."

He brushes a finger against my cheek. "And mine."

I gaze up at him, expecting a kiss, and then remember myself. We're not alone. Ma has rushed off to the kitchen to fetch refreshments. Our newly arrived boarder, Senator Ross, is upstairs in his room, unpacking. His shoes thump on the ceiling above us. He'll be coming down shortly to meet with Perry, who's expected at any moment.

Smoothing my skirt, I return to my seat on the piano stool. Boudy pulls one of the side chairs over and perches on it so that our knees touch.

I control my breathing. "Tell me why you are in Washington. I thought the treaties were still being negotiated?"

"Secretary of the Interior, John Harlan, has accepted the Southern Cherokee proposal. I have been promised the position of Indian delegate to Congress."

My heart leaps. "That's wonderful news. It means you will be living here in Washington."

He grins. "Closer to you. And I'm going to be rich. I have a grand plan for the tribe to market our tobacco across the nation. I'll have to go home to set it in motion, but once the tobacco mills are up and running, we can marry." He seizes my hands, his long fingers capturing my own. "You'll wait?"

It is not the most romantic of proposals, but I understand his hurry and his confidence in my answer. Nevertheless, a fission of worry races through me. My promise to Mary to reject him; am I still bound?

I bury the conundrum to think about later and work at sounding calmer than I feel. "It doesn't matter to me if you're rich or not. I love you and always will." I fuss with the binding on the neck of my dress. "I do have something to confess."

He taps the end of my nose. "Let's see. You play the harp like an angel."

I blink. "Who told you that?"

"Your brother."

I turn away. "Oh, then you know what they say about me in the city."

"He shared some thoughts about you with me. But I didn't believe him."

"You didn't?" If anything, I love Boudy more for saying that.

He shrugs. "Men are worse gossips than any woman. And what they say about females who catch men's eyes is always of the nastiest variety. And you, my Vinita, are the type of woman that draws men like honey draws the bear. You're alive, passionate, and appear vulnerable on the outside. But inside, you are steadfast and loyal to a fault. Strong and determined. I trust you to be true."

The words are simple. They reach deep into my heart.

I bare mine in return. "And I trust you. I promise to wait for you."

He laughs low in that deep-throated way I remember so well. "My little Vinita. I've seen your *Violet* on display in that window on Pennsylvania Avenue. I suspect those poor ladies feel they don't measure up." He puts a hand on my knee. "I have a suspicion about who was the model for her." He whispers in my ear, "*You.*"

I give his shoulder a little shove. "How dare you? *Violet* is an idealized classical figure."

"Ha. You think I have no eyes? Or hands?" He runs his palm under my chin, down my neck, and brushes my bosom. My own hand comes to rest against his broad chest. Every inch of me comes alive. My breath comes faster.

I tip my head up. "Oh, Boudy—"

He leans across the narrow space dividing us and kisses me full on the lips. This is nothing like the stolen kiss all those years ago. I have never been kissed so long and so gently. I want it to go on forever.

Instead, I pull back. "We shouldn't."

He laughs. "I caught you young. It's only me you want."

A clatter in the hall reminds me that the parlor door stands open, and we'll soon have company. I sit back and fold my hands in my lap.

Boudy has heard it, too. He straightens and formalizes the tone of his voice. "Tell me more about your art."

So few people ask me that.

"The patriotic medallions and small busts of Lincoln are selling well, and my commissions have tripled in the last months. The *Indian Girl* is popular." I gnaw my lower lip, wondering if I should have mentioned it. I race on. "That part is going well. But ever since I quit my job and put my work on display in public locations, I've been ostracized socially—mainly by women who used to be my supporters—and reviled in the newspapers. It's been hard."

Ma enters with two glasses and a pitcher of lemonade on a tray. "Talk her out of this mad idea of becoming a sculptress, Mr. Boudinot. All this running around, making a fool of herself, hoping for the government to pay her to make a statue of Lincoln. It's sure to come to naught." She wags an eyebrow at Boudy, who has shifted his legs and placed a more decorous distance between us. "I'm relying on you to make my daughter see sense. All this begging for favors from politicians has to stop." She sets the tray on the center table.

"Your daughter, Mrs. Ream, is most remarkable—" He breaks off as Perry Fuller barges in, and my private time to explain more about the Lincoln commission is lost.

"Something terrible . . ." Perry stops mid-sentence. "You've arrived, dear fellow." He puts an arm across Boudy's back.

Their familiarity irritates me. I do not like to think of Boudy being swept up into Fuller's world of bribes, graft, and drink. Nor do I want him to know that Perry has funded my new career.

Ma raises her voice. "What's terrible?"

Perry's arm falls. "Mary sent me. The baby has taken a turn for the worse. Little thing is burning up with fever."

"Heavens." Ma unties her apron. "You must fetch the doctor at once."

He turns to Boudy as if he has all the time in the world. And maybe he does. He's never been terribly concerned about Mary or the baby, who's been sickly since birth. "Heard you were in the city. We have much to discuss." He regards our untouched lemonade. "But you will need something stronger to swallow it down."

Boudy's eyebrows rise. "What's happened?"

"Harlan has betrayed your treaty deal. He's submitted John Ridge's Northern Cherokee proposal to Congress, instead."

Boudy jerks back as if he's been punched. "No. That bastard."

I want to know more, but there's no time. I touch Boudy's arm. "I have to go to my sister. Little Perry is only three months old. We could lose him."

Boudy nods. "I'll go with Perry to fetch the doctor."

My mother grabs our sun hats from the hall tree. "Come, Vinnie. Hurry." She takes me by the elbow and hustles me down the front steps.

We catch a horsecar at the intersection.

"I don't know what you see in that man"—Ma presses her lips tight—"but you have always been moon-eyed around him. So, no girlish foolishness. You will say yes to him this time when he asks for your hand. You have no excuse. Mary is married now. Her husband can afford to take care of us and has offered to do so in style. It is time for you to abandon this idea of being a sculptress and take your rightful role in society as a wife."

A wife. I clasp my hands together. She is right. I have no more excuses . . . unless I win the Lincoln commission.

The afternoon sun of July 27th burns clear and hot. The newspaper headlines announce that the Atlantic telegraph cable has been successfully laid at last. But that is not the news that propels me up and down the halls of the Capitol.

Today is the day the 39th Congress will decide if the Prairie Cinderella, as the papers have dubbed me, is worthy of sculpting President Lincoln. Yesterday, the House of Representatives approved Representative Rice's proposal for my commission with little fanfare. But at this moment, all hangs in precarious balance. Today, the Senate will decide my fate.

I have already listened to the raucous debate over my worthiness as an artist. According to Senator Charles Sumner and his buddies, I am too young, too female, too untrained, and too much a lobbyist. And, more importantly, too American. Apparently, only European-trained artists can sculpt our departed President. A charity case, Sumner called me. No comment could hurt worse.

I peer into an empty office. I do not want charity. I want to be accepted or rejected on my skill alone.

I hustle down to the next office. Senators Nesmith and Conness rose to my defense and declared my model the best likeness of Lincoln of all that have been submitted. Senator Cowan, who doesn't even like me, defended the attacks on my sex as a liability by declaring Sappho's works an example of a woman who was on par with men. But I am not sure their kind words will be enough to pass the resolution. Especially because so many of my supporters have disappeared from the Senate floor.

My heart pounds as I race to the next office. Where are Yates and Wade and everyone else who signed my petition and who were on the floor earlier but have since gone absent?

I open the door—*empty*. They must be in the Senate cloakroom. It's my last hope of finding them, hopefully awake and only semi-drunk. But how? As a woman, I cannot invade the senators' private lounges. I look up and down the corridor. Where is a clerk or messenger boy when you need one?

I stop and listen. There. Footsteps. I gather up my skirts and race around the corner. Thank heavens, it's Yates' clerk. I rush him off with my message, then dash back to the Senate Gallery, praying I haven't missed the vote.

I enter the great rotunda and wish that I could climb to the top of the dome instead of heading toward the stuffy, enclosed Senate Chamber to the right. Will my dreams die on this miserable day?

I halt in the center and stare up at the newly installed circular fresco by the Italian artist, Constantino Brumidi, that lies at the apex of the dome. How arrogant of me to think my novice sculpture belongs beneath such genius.

I drop my head. I should leave and read the bad news in tomorrow's morning editions.

A messenger boy crosses the rotunda and hands me a note. I glance at it. Thaddeus Stevens wants me to meet him in the gallery. The dear man. Ill as he is, barely able to walk, and yet he has come to support me again after his defense yesterday in the House.

I clutch the note, assured of at least one supporter by my side.

House Chair John Sherman approaches. "Have you come alone, Miss Ream?"

I nod. "My parents have accompanied my sister and her husband to his residence in Kansas with the hope of her recovering from the death of her babe."

What I do not add is that I am especially alone because my dear Boudy refused to accompany me here. He has no use for a Congress that has crushed his hopes for a position in Washington, and he questions why I trust them to do well by me. He is ready to dash off to Indian Territory and take me with him. It does not bode well for our potential marriage.

Sherman tips his head. "My condolences, my dear. I wondered why my bright little bird was swathed in funeral black. Though I fear you will be missed in the crowd." He holds up his finger. "I have an idea. I'll be right back. Don't move."

I've been quite happy to be lost in the crowd all through the afternoon debate. But I hesitate to disobey one of the most powerful men in Washington.

He is back in minutes, bringing his brother, General William Sherman, with him. My breath catches. The general sports a thatch of red hair, a bristly beard, and a brass-buttoned uniform. He is rough, tough, and handsome. If he weren't married with nine offspring, he'd have the heart of every miss in Washington. Not that he doesn't try to win them, anyway. He's known as the biggest flirt in the city, and he's flirting with me now.

John Sherman winks. "You know my brother?"

"Of course. We have met at several balls."

The general pins me with his piercing brown eyes, gallantly kisses the back of my hand as if I were some Parisian lady, then loops his arm in mine. "My dear, Miss Ream, let us proceed into the lions' den."

Suddenly, I am no longer unsure or afraid. I'm being escorted by one of the most renowned generals of the war. I toss back my hair and lengthen my stride to match his. Even if the resolution is defeated, I will still have powerful friends. A statue of the general could be almost as impressive as one of Lincoln in establishing my career.

We enter through the center doors to the public gallery. It is a prime location with a direct view of the rostrum. It is also the most closely watched by reporters.

All eyes turn our way. The few ladies in the women's section gasp. Down below, senators turn and applaud. Some wave handkerchiefs.

Thaddeus sits in the balcony seat closest to the door. Despite the heat and humidity in the chamber, he looks a little stronger today.

He calls me over. "Vinnie, I see you have found yourself a champion. I hope he has his sword."

Sherman laughs. The applause continues.

I whisper to Thaddeus, "Look. They are giving the general an ovation."

He seizes my hand. "No, Vinnie. They are giving *you* the ovation. Your *Lincoln* has been accepted."

Chapter 16

AUGUST 1866

REAM BOARDING HOUSE

Ma rushes through the front door, still dusty from the Kansas trip. "Is it true? What they're saying in the papers? You got the Lincoln commission?" She throws her arms around me and envelops me in the cloying, expensive bergamot scent she has adopted since Mary married well. "We never thought . . ."

Pa sets down the valises. "Of course, our Vinnie won. She's our little miracle." He comes forward and deposits a kiss on my forehead. Beads of sweat glisten on his overly pale face. The trip back from Lawrence has been hard on him.

I take him by the hand. "Come sit. I can't wait to tell you."

Celia goes to fetch lemonade, and we settle in the parlor. I give them a quick overview of all that has happened while they were gone.

Ma fingers her collar. "So, your petitioning worked?"

"Yes, despite Representative Butler's objections, the resolution passed twenty-three to nine. They're preparing the contract for me to sign."

"And the amount? Is it as much as the papers say?"

"Ten thousand dollars. Half when the plaster cast is done. The rest, when the marble sculpture is presented to Congress."

"*Ten thousand dollars*. Unbelievable." My mother purses her lips, looking more worried than thrilled. "And you accomplished this how? Perry says—"

"By working hard and being kind and generous," I interrupt, having no desire to hear anything Perry Fuller says. "I made hundreds of medallions and gifted enough candy and cake to feed an army."

"But the rumors say . . ."

"Say what, Mother?"

Pa places his hand over Ma's. "You are tired from the trip, Lavinia. Let's get unpacked and rested. Vinnie can answer your questions over dinner."

Ma huffs out a breath, then rises. "Perry will be here shortly. And Mr. Boudinot. Perry says your beau is leaving for Little Rock at the end of the week. I expect he has something to ask you."

I paste on a half-smile. Boudy is not coming to propose. He's already done that—not that anyone knows. He's coming to ask me to go back to Arkansas with him.

Gnawing my lip, I help my parents get their travel bags upstairs. Then I ask Celia to prepare for dinner guests and take refuge in my bedroom.

I throw myself down on my bed and inhale the cottony scent of the old Prairie Star quilt Ma made for me back when we lived in that Wisconsin log cabin so many years ago. I run my finger along the tiny stitches that crisscross the squares like deer trails in the brush. I love the prairie's wide-open skies, the closeness to nature, the independent inhabitants, and the freedom to be oneself, but I do not want to go back west. At least, not yet. Right now, I have the chance to do something incredible here. Make a mark. Be exceptional. Create a sculpture of Lincoln to last for all time.

I have no idea how long that will take. Boudy says he will live here with me if I ask, but Boudy's heart lies under that bowl of sky. His family is there. His friends. His new tobacco business. It would sap his spirit to stay here in Washington, to escort me to balls, and to face the men who consider him something less because of the color of his skin, and who lie and cheat him because of it.

I can't do that to him. I can't marry him now.

Yet, how will I send him away?

It will break his heart.

It will break mine.

I crush the quilt in my hand. With Celia and Senator Ross as chaperones, we have not shared the intimacies I dream about beneath this quilt. Despite long musical evenings, we have only managed a few stolen kisses.

Most often, he sits in silence in the parlor and listens to me sing. He has started recording my songs in a leather notebook. He says writing down the lyrics keeps the anger away.

But it doesn't. My brother is right. Boudy is a troubled man. His fury at the government's treatment of his people is deep and unrelenting. His resentment over the failed treaty proposal burns hot. Indignation has become his armor, built up thick and impenetrable over the postwar years, and I fear it is what holds him together.

Despite the hopefulness of my parents, there will be no wedding talk while the treaty negotiations go on and on, as the Indians lose more and more, and Boudy spends more time in taverns with Perry Fuller than with me.

But enough worrying about what I will tell Boudy. I must welcome my parents home.

I slip out of bed and rush to get dressed. The pink silk chiffon gown I choose is more daring than I normally wear for dinner at home, especially one with Perry Fuller in attendance. The dress is low on the shoulders and neck, with short, puffed sleeves and rose-patterned ribbon at the waist. It is light and airy, perfect for ballroom dancing and hot, stuffy dining rooms full of blustering men. I smooth the skirt over the cage crinoline and pray Boudy is jealous enough to keep Perry's hands off me.

Downstairs, I give the table a quick once-over. The new plates and silverware I've purchased as a celebratory gift for Ma and Pa stand in sharp contrast to the still drab-colored walls and far-traveled furniture. But men care little for anything but what is on their plates, and I can smell the delicious aroma of the roast Celia has prepared.

A commotion at the front door draws me to the vestibule. Perry and Boudy enter, followed by someone I have not seen in a long time.

"John Rollin Ridge. My Yellowbird." I throw my arms around his neck. At one time, he'd been Boudy's rival for my heart. Now he's the victor for the tribes. It is his treaty that has been accepted.

He hugs me back, then sets me at arm's length. "Why, it's my little Vinnie." He gives me a quick perusal. "Looking mighty fine."

I bounce on my toes. "No one told me you were in the city. I thought you'd moved to California."

Ridge grins at Boudy. "Kept me a secret, did you?"

Boudy scowls, and unease joins the sweat dripping down my neck. He and John have been best friends forever. But a man walking on the edge of anger is sure to be infuriated by the presence of a former rival and current political foe.

I hasten everyone into the dining room and make sure Boudy sits beside me. Ma and Pa sit at the head and the foot. Perry and John take seats on the other side.

Edmund Ross appears in the doorway and is greeted by Perry as the old, beholden friend that he is. Ross shuffles into the seat next to him and shrinks down in his chair.

Ross is no more enamored of Fuller than I. But I have little sympathy. He need not have accepted the vacant Senatorial position and put himself in Fuller's clutches. He's got a fine military record and a wife and seven children back in Kansas, whom he misses and loves dearly.

Celia arrives with the roast and its accompaniments, and for a while, everyone focuses on eating and being complimentary to the cook. I pray it will remain so until we reach the pie. But there is little hope of that.

John Ridge lays down his fork and blots his mouth with his napkin. "So, Cornelius, I see why you have been distracted."

Boudy stops mid-chew. "Distracted?"

"Our little Vinnie is all grown up."

"And a famous sculptress," I hasten to add, not wanting to hear Boudy's answer.

John tips his head toward me. "I regret that I have not been to your studio. From what I've heard, it's been mobbed ever since you received the Lincoln commission. I am pleased to be able to renew our acquaintance in more salubrious surroundings." He nods to the assembled company. "And among good friends."

I look for a safe subject. "I've read your novel, *The Life and Adventures of Joaquin Murieta*."

John clicks his tongue. "So, do you think my bandito is a real person? Many do."

"I think he is a combination of the people you have known, including yourself."

"You have that right, Vinita," Boudy whispers under his breath.

John flashes a look at him. "You think me bloodthirsty, friend?"

Boudy leans back in his chair. "No. Deeply mistaken."

There is a hush around the table. John lifts his bewhiskered chin. He has aged much since I last saw him in Fort Smith. His eyes are sunken, his beard streaked with gray. But I am not sure he has become wiser.

John locks his gaze on me. "You have always seen more than you should, Vinnie. You are made for great things." He reaches beneath his waistcoat. "I have written a new poem. May I share it with you all?"

I still. If it is a love poem, I shall die.

"*The Atlantic Cable*," he begins.

Thank heavens, it is not. I close my eyes and listen.

When the poem ends, we all sigh and clap and congratulate the poet.

"It was a special day for you, too, Vinnie," Perry says. "Was it not?"

Everyone focuses on me.

I tip my head. "You are well informed. That was the day I was awarded the Lincoln commission."

Perry lifts his glass of whiskey. "A toast to my most accomplished sister-in-law."

I dip my head in acknowledgment as everyone adds their cheers. But I do not want to discuss the commission here with these men.

I turn back to John Ridge. "I do think the Atlantic cable far more important than my boon. As you say in the poem, the cable will link land to land and man to man. May it bring us peace."

My brother-in-law raises his glass again. "And so will the railroads link our nation together."

John inserts the poem into his waistcoat pocket. He focuses on Boudy. "Unity is what we must have. We need to bury the cruelty between those who have different viewpoints and embrace the beauty and joy of the world we have been given."

Boudy grasps my hand and holds it up. "And here is the embodiment of that joy and beauty. My Vinita."

More whiskey is poured, and more toasts are given.

I slip my hand free. My decision has been made. I must release him from his vow. His desires lie in the West. Mine in the East. With the Lincoln commission, the future lies open before me with the prospect of money, travel, and renown. But there is no chance to get the words out amidst the hearty compliments.

But later, after Ma's flaky peach pie and a musical interlude, I take Boudy's hand and pull him out into our backyard. The scent of laundry soap, damp linen, and a hint of the neighbor's rose bush fill the stagnant air around us.

I look everywhere but at him. "I can't marry you."

Boudy wraps one of my curls behind my ear. "Not now. I understand. I am not ready, either. I have my tobacco business to take care of." He chucks me under my chin. "We are going to be rich, you and I. Fuller is quite put out that he settled for the other Ream girl."

Despite the heat, a shiver streaks down my spine. "Poor Mary."

"Oh, don't worry about her. Perry is an apt businessman. He'll only keep getting richer and richer. She'll be living in high style. Queen of the City."

"It's not high living, I fear. I don't want my sister hurt. According to the politicians I know, Fuller's a liar and a cheat." I clench my fists behind my back. "He's given me some money for my sculptures. I hope I haven't made a mistake trusting him?"

Boudy shrugs in that annoyingly male way that always makes me feel like a lesser being. "Don't worry. He's okay. Very ambitious, but nothing wrong with that. He knows important people."

The words fly out. "So do I."

He laughs. "I think we can all agree on that. And as long as we keep the wheelers and dealers like Fuller sweet, our stars will rise."

His words clang like warning bells. He is too sure. Too cocky. Too unconcerned about Fuller. I think I like him better jealous.

I tip my chin flirtatiously. "I've had other marriage proposals."

His gaze darkens, the muscles in his cheek quiver. "Have you? From whom?"

"Brigadier General Van Valkenburgh, for one."

Boudy spits on the ground. "Not a friend of my people. Luckily, he wasn't the Indian commissioner for long."

Wrong man to mention.

I turn my back on his anger and stare up at the stars. "I refused him."

"Of course, you did. He's a nasty old man." He whispers in my ear, "And I'm not."

Boudy places a hand on my bare shoulder. Tingles ripple across my skin. He kisses the back of my neck, brushes his lips over my shoulder blades.

I spin around and peer into his dark eyes. He draws me near and lowers his lips to mine. The kiss is warm and soft. I can taste the sweetness of peaches and the sting of whiskey on his breath.

For a long moment, I relish the warmth and closeness, soak in the power of his body, and let all my worries scatter into the night. Then the kitchen door opens, and we jerk apart.

Celia leans out the doorway. "Your mother says the gentlemen are ready to leave."

Boudy steps back and takes my hand. "Come, my Vinita. I must go, too."

All I want is another kiss. And another. Why does love have to be so hard? I shouldn't love this man, but I do. Waiting to marry will be harder than I ever imagined.

Annoyance bubbles up at his hurry to abandon me and go with Perry. My frustration spouts out. "Why must you go? So you can drink and carouse?" Even I hear how petulant I sound.

Boudy runs his finger over my lips, stirring my blood, drawing my attention back to our kiss. "I don't believe the rumors about you. Don't believe the ones about me. Everything I do in this godforsaken city is for our future and the future of my tribe."

"I'm sorry. I just don't want you to leave, especially with Fuller. Did you see how he looked at me at dinner?"

He brushes his palm down my cheek. "Perry looks at lots of women that way. But he won't bother you. He knows you are mine and what I'd do to him if he touched you. But at this moment, with my tribe suffering, I need all the political support I can find, especially Fuller's." He kisses me again. "I would stay if I could, but my tribe's future will be decided in those smoky rooms. Not here."

I trail after him, biting back the promise to go with him to Arkansas and become his wife. He is doing what he must, as am I.

In the foyer, Perry slaps Boudy on the shoulder. The collection of rings on the man's fingers glitter in the lamplight, reminding me that Perry Fuller is an extremely wealthy man. I pray Boudy is right, and that Mary will have a life of good fortune, and that I have made the right decision to trust him.

Then the two of them are out the door, laughing and joking.

John Ridge lingers on the threshold. He halts in front of me. His mouth twitches. "I would like you to have this. Perhaps you could set it to music?" He draws a folded paper from his waistcoat pocket and hands it to me. Thinking it is the Atlantic cable poem, I hesitate—the words are not singable. I look down. It is not the poem he read, but another, scratched out in pencil on a torn bit of paper.

"*I Love Thee?*" I read.

I glance up. Ridge may be Cherokee, but he's the opposite of Boudy. He is more like the old chiefs. He carries himself more calmly, observes more closely, speaks each word after long consideration. His pencil scratches mean more than the words on the page. His whole presence demands respect. I'm ashamed by my disrespect at the table.

I tip my head. "I am most honored to receive a poem from you."

He lowers his voice. "Cornelius is a very lucky man. But know this. My old friend is at a crossroads. He desires money and power too much. He wants to turn our people into whites to acquire it. I fear that if he pursues this course, he will cause deep rifts in our tribe that will be everlasting. I feel sorry for him but rejoice that he has your love."

Before I can respond, he is gone, moving down the street with the long-legged stride that can take a man across a prairie or far from a world he doesn't belong in.

The next morning, Boudy is at the door again. This time alone and clear-headed, thank heavens. He is dressed in traveling clothes and wearing a well-worn, broad-brimmed slouch hat most unsuited for Washington streets.

He kisses me on the cheek. "I have to rush to Arkansas to take care of a problem at the tobacco mill. But before I go, I want you to meet someone. A great man—Albert Pike. He can be a big help to your career."

He lifts my hand to draw me outside, where he has a hired carriage waiting.

I balk in the doorway. I have heard of General Pike. My brother sang his praises. My politician friends, who fought for the Union, detest him.

I slip my hand from his. "I already have a cadre of men ready to help me. I need to get to my studio. The reporters and admirers are sure to have arrived."

"This is important to me, Vinita. Spare an hour. He's a poet, better than Ridge. Perhaps you can put some of his poems to music."

Boudy has asked little of me besides soothing music and magical kisses. I have met many disreputable men. Why worry about one more?

"Then let me bring my guitar."

I rush back inside, pack the guitar in its case, then place my stylish new feather-bedecked hat on my head.

Handsome men like Boudy can escape censure for being less than fashionable, but I cannot. I have a reputation to burnish, and I am not sure befriending the only man condemned as a traitor by both the Union and Confederacy is the best way to help my career.

Chapter 17

SEPTEMBER 1866

THE PIKES', WASHINGTON CITY

I hesitate on the steps of Albert Pike's townhouse. Do I dare visit Pike again? Despite Boudy's enthusiasm for the man, so many friends warn that he is dangerous. Still, if I were to reject every person because they held antithetical views, I would lose half my supporters in Congress. Still, Pike is so notorious for his white superiority that I really shouldn't be here.

Yet, I can't stop myself. After a day of entertaining politicians, tourists, and back-biting journalists, all while trying to complete the next medallion or bust, the peace and calm of Pike's richly decorated home is far more appealing than our rooming house. Especially now with an agitated Edmund Ross and an ever-present Mary, who's relying on Ma to help with her colicky newborn. Though I thank heaven that Mary is smiling again. This second little Perry is strong and healthy, with a curly thatch of Ream-black hair. Not a bit of his father can be discerned. So, with my hat pulled low, I knock.

An unfamiliar woman of my age greets me at the door. Her hair is dark and curly, like mine, her southern accent thick as syrup.

She puts a hand on her hip. "Now, who do we have here?"

I lift my hat brim. "Vinnie Ream."

"The famous sculptress?" She looks me over. "Tiny thing, aren't you, to have earned such a scurrilous reputation?"

"It's not size that counts, but talent."

She winks. "And who you know."

"You have the right of that." We both laugh, and I offer my hand.

She clasps it firmly. "I'm Lillian Pike, by the way. Mama sent me to the city to be my papa's housekeeper. Not that I mind. Quite a fascinating place, this Washington. There is so much to see and learn."

Forthright and curious. I like her already.

Lillian opens the door wide, and I enter.

She taps her chin. "How do you know my father?"

"I've visited before with Cornelius Boudinot. Your father is an impressive man. And we have mutual friends."

"Despite his southern leanings?"

"The war is over. I count many Southerners among my friends and supporters. My brother fought under your father. He spoke well of him."

Lillian laughs. "Then he's the only one. Lost control of his Indians, they say. As if anyone could control such savages."

I bite my tongue. I should expect General Pike's prejudices against those he considers inferior to extend to his daughter, who spent the war in the South. Still, I can't let her comment go unanswered.

I tip up the brim of my hat. "I have lived in harmony with the native peoples out West. Many are *not* savages. Perhaps I should leave?"

Lillian pinches her lips in a crooked grin. "That explains why Colonel Boudinot loves you." She falls back. "Come in. I understand you are an accomplished musician?"

My music has been long neglected, but her question sparks something inside. "Yes. I play piano, guitar, and harp."

She grasps both my hands. "And I play the flute. Perhaps we can practice a duet next time you visit. We could be the next musical success."

"I'm sorry. I no longer perform publicly."

"Then we will entertain Papa. Put some of his poems to music."

My pulse rises. I am hungry for a chance to perform with another woman. I clap my hands together. "That sounds delightful."

"Well, come along then. And please, call me Lilly. I can tell we'll be good friends."

Lilly leads me down the hall to the solarium at the back of the house. She opens the door to the sun-dappled room. Birdsong, feathers, and her father greet me.

Albert Pike puts down the birdcage he's fixing. The vilified man is nothing like I had been led to expect by those who hate him. He is a huge bear of a man, an odd combination of old Southern gentleman and razor-sharp Yankee lawyer with long, flowing white hair and beard. And he has the most wondrous collection of exotic birds I have ever seen.

A turtle dove flutters down on my shoulder.

"See? She likes you." Pike's voice can be powerful when he wishes, but at the moment, it's as gentle as my pa's. "Would you like to have a pair of your own to wow the visitors to your studio?"

I transfer the dove to my wrist the way he showed me when I visited with Boudy and stroke the back of her neck. "Anything that entices reporters to focus on something besides me in their articles would be delightful."

"Then consider it my gift to a marvelous sculptress. Lillian and I will bring them to your Capitol studio tomorrow." He whistles to the macaw on its perch by the window. It whistles back. "Heard from Cornelius?"

I place the dove on the wrought-iron stand beside its mate. "He writes that his tobacco mill is almost completed."

Pike strokes his beard. "Boy has a good idea. Not sure he has taken into account the greed of the Chicago tobacco merchants. Indians selling tax-free tobacco will surely rile them up."

"Anything the Indians do riles people up. I think he's brave and smart."

"That may well be. But you might do better hitching your petticoats to a brighter star."

I resent Pike's scoffing tone. I jab back at him, "Who? *You?*"

He belly-laughs. "You could do worse. I would cherish you more than any other man, my little hummingbird."

I clench my fists. Does he believe the rumors . . . believe me free with my favors?

"I see I've managed to stun you into silence. Come, my dear. I asked Lillian to set out a light repast for us in the parlor."

Relieved, I lead the way out of Birdland and resolve to never visit Pike when Lillian isn't home.

The Pikes' parlor is full of books, Masonic accoutrements, and better cheer. Along with strong coffee and thick ham sandwiches with pickle relish, Lilly shares all the Little Rock gossip.

Pike leans back in his overstuffed leather chair and rests his hand on his well-padded middle. "Have you gotten Lincoln's bloody clothes yet?"

"Yes. Representative Rice intervened. The doorman who was given the garments has graciously sent them to me."

Lilly leans forward. "Oh, my. You have the suit Lincoln wore when he was shot in your possession?"

"I do. Mary Lincoln had forbidden me access. However, the garments are essential for my sculpture. I want to present the man as he was on that fateful day, not as some Greek patriarch in a toga. The Lincoln I knew would never wear such a thing."

Pike lights up his pipe. The rich aroma of Virginia tobacco fills the room. "According to Mrs. Lincoln and her biddies, you never met the man."

"Mary Lincoln is a mean-hearted woman."

He blows out the match. "I would have said small-minded."

I purse my lips. "Or too busy shopping. I went directly to his office to work. Had the permission of his secretaries. I never saw her. She never saw me. She has no right to malign me so."

Pike waves his pipe. "Jealous woman—that Mary Todd Lincoln. I doubt she can countenance the idea of a beautiful girl meeting privately with her husband."

I run my hands down my skirt. I need to curtail Pike's untoward interest in me. "I'm a plain-faced country girl. I don't understand why everyone is suspicious of my morals."

Pike laughs. "It's all that hair."

Lilly rests a hand on my arm. "And definitely not plain." She tilts her head like one of Pike's birds. "I would say unique and most worthy of friendship." She turns toward her father. "I have an idea. Let's hire Vinnie to sculpt your bust. That way, she has to come back again and again."

An hour later, I head back to my studio. Haunting the empty halls of the Capitol is probably not wise nor beneficial to my reputation. But the evening is the only quiet time when I can focus exclusively on the Lincoln sculpture.

Besides, no one is going to stop speculating on my supposed love life, anyway. Boudy believes me, and that is all that matters.

Neither will I stop visiting the Pikes. I already love Lilly. Her inflection is educated and assured. Her southern accent brings back memories. She reminds me of my girlhood friends who are now lost to me. Most fascinating is that she is an inventor. She has designed her own flute and patented it.

I unlock the studio door and slip inside. The vaulted ceiling is cast in deep shadow. The basement dampness pools under my skirt.

I pull my smock over my head and consider my new commission—a bust of Albert Pike. A curl of unease creeps along my skin. Befriending Lilly means being in contact with her father, who has made it plain he lusts after me.

I think my political friends may be right. Albert Pike is a dangerous man.

Chapter 18

SENATE CHAMBER, THE CAPITOL

A year later, I no longer think Pike is the most dangerous man in Washington. That man is Perry Fuller.

I clutch the gallery ticket he has foisted on me. I have no desire to attend the impeachment hearing for President Andrew Johnson. My success is due to the fact that I am politically uncommitted to any one party or person. My friends are both Democrats and Republicans. My Capitol studio is neutral ground.

But in the last weeks, all the bonhomie has become a façade. People either love or hate President Johnson.

I tuck the ticket in my pocket and head to the ladies' section. The last time I sat up here, I was able to hide. No longer.

Women move out of my disreputable way as I take one of the few remaining empty seats. All of Washington is here today, and it smells like it. The feminine stink of powder, hair oil, and perspiration hangs over the close-pressed bevy of chattering society ladies. Across the way, reporters scribble down descriptions of the most outrageous bonnets and skin-baring gowns to ribald in the evening papers.

Having come from my studio, I am plainly dressed with no hoop beneath my skirt, only petticoats. My much-maligned hair is pinned up respectably. Not that it matters. Rapacious newsmen can always find something seductive about my appearance.

My dear friend, Thaddeus Stevens, sits below, his face ghastly pale, his hands atremble. Lydia worries that his serving as House Manager for the impeachment will be too hard on him. So do I.

I draw out my fan and waft it slowly in his direction. Stevens lifts his fingers in response. He's a good man and has been especially kind to me. I would hate for him to think a blackguard like Perry Fuller has any influence over me.

I wave the fan faster. *But he does.*

For days now, Perry has invaded our house and cornered Senator Ross. My brother-in-law, not satisfied with his wealth, wants a plum appointment from Andrew Johnson to the Internal Revenue Service. And by sweet talk or threat, he's going to get it. For Ross's cooperation in casting a negative vote, he has promised the poor man land, riches, and railroad investments.

He has also made a promise to me, though it sounds more like intimidation. When he becomes Commissioner, he will shield Boudy's tobacco enterprise from federal taxation.

I withdraw a handkerchief from my sleeve and blot my brow. All I need do is make sure Ross votes against the impeachment.

I peer down at the seven impeachment managers. I'm sympathetic to their argument. Andrew Johnson is no Lincoln, and he is often a drunken fool. He has made the supporters of reconstruction furious and the former Confederates happy. Albert Pike is totally on his side.

Neither is Johnson a friend to the freed slaves.

When Perry invades the rooming house, Celia has taken to rattling dishes and banging pans. I wouldn't be surprised if she spits in his food.

I twist the handkerchief in my lap. Boudy, in his last letter, says to do what Perry wants.

Can I betray the man I love?

The night before the impeachment vote, I'm still torn. Ma and Pa have begged me to help my brother-in-law. Celia swears she will never talk to me again if Ross votes for impeachment.

My heart begs me to do what I can for Boudy's success. My sense of justice says I should do nothing. It is Ross's decision. He's the one who will have to live with it. But no matter what I decide, so will I.

I sit in the parlor and mindlessly pluck the harp strings. The dissonant sound matches my inner turmoil.

Celia comes in to draw the drapes. "Tomorrow's the vote?"

"Yes."

She presses her lips together. "You're not going to help that foul man, are you?"

I stare up at the ceiling where the crux of the matter lies—Senator Ross—a man with no backbone and a heap of debt. Perry's perfect pawn.

Albert Pike has left Washington on a speaking tour. Lilly has gone home to visit her mother. Ma and Pa are at Mary's grand mansion, where they spend most of their time cuddling their grandbaby. Boudy is in Indian Territory, pursuing his dream of tax-free tobacco. If I were smart, I'd go somewhere, too. But it is too late in the evening to head back to my studio.

Celia is the only person with whom I can share my concerns. "Have you heard the rumors that Butler and his cronies are spreading about me? That Ross is infatuated with me? That we are more than friends?"

"They have been saying nasty things about you forever."

"But now, so are my friends." I drop my hands into my lap. "Congressman George Julien, the kindest of men and my long-time supporter, has asked me to pressure Ross to vote for conviction. Perry and Boudy want me to convince Ross to vote against impeachment.

"Even if I do nothing, tomorrow, I will be accused of taking one side or the other. My clients will flee. My sculpture enterprise will fail." I twist my fingers together. "What should I do?"

Celia straightens and puts a hand on her hip. "Go back home to Arkansas and marry that loving man of yours."

"He won't be so loving if Perry Fuller doesn't get his appointment from Johnson." I run my hands down my face. "No matter what I do, I will be blamed."

And I do get blamed. Ross votes for acquittal, and my career is torn to pieces. I arrive the morning after the vote and find my Capitol studio in turmoil. Workmen carry out my medallions and my busts, my dove cage, and my display pillars. I block their way.

"Move, Miss Ream." An officious clerk waves a paper in my face. "Everything must be removed by order of the Senate."

"The Senate?" I fall back. "I'm being evicted? *Today*?" I peer past the odious little man. Workers are dismantling my displays and tossing medallions, vases, and flowers into crates willy-nilly.

My blood pounds inside my head like a gong. They can't do this.

I race back upstairs. Congressmen who had supported me in my quest for the Lincoln commission turn their backs and hasten away as if I'm plagued. I stop in the middle of the Rotunda and fight back tears. I will never trust these saccharine-tongued politicians again. Never. They only care about themselves.

"Vinnie." Thaddeus Stevens, the one man who has never failed in support of me, waves me over. The two boys carrying his wheelless invalid chair set him down. "I am so sorry about your studio. Bull Butler and his cronies think to punish you for that impeachment debacle."

"But I didn't have anything to do with it—"

He raises his hand. "I know, dear child. My idiot colleagues are using the rumors about you to force you to give up the Lincoln commission. They're pretending they must imprison some scalawag in your little space."

My shoulders sag. "I'd rather they locked *me* and my sculptures in there. There is sure to be breakage if my works are moved."

"Consider this temporary. I'll straighten them out in no time."

I rest my hand on his arm. "But first, you must rest. This trial has worn you out."

"*Bah.*" He removes my hand. "I can rest when I'm dead. Leave the *Lincoln.* And don't worry. I'll get the studio back for you." He signals the boys to lift his chair, waves goodbye, and disappears out the doors.

My *Lincoln!* I have to stop them from moving it.

I rush downstairs, only to see my clay bust of Thadeus tipping precariously in a workman's grip.

"Watch out." I dash forward and, just in time, keep it from crashing to the floor. The worker tightens his hold and carts it off.

The foreman turns to me. "The only sculpture remaining is of Mr. Lincoln." He doffs his cap and wipes his forehead. "Mighty heavy that thing."

I rock back and forth, torn. Will it survive being left to the whims of the politicians who hate me? Will whatever criminal they house here refrain from damaging it? If only I could borrow the cost of moving it from my wealthy brother-in-law. It is his fault this is happening, but why bother asking? He's too drunk from celebrating his assured appointment to care a wit.

I squint at my *Lincoln*, incongruous with his clay head and plaster body, picturing it in gleaming white marble. Will this be the end of my dream of seeing it in the Rotunda? The end of my career?

Knots form in my stomach. Leave it, Thaddeus said. I'll be reinstated. So, despite the quivers in my stomach that something will befall it, I wave the men off, close the door, and pray I will soon be back to dampen my grand work down.

Then, ignoring the side-lookers, I slow-step after the last of the workers like a widow following her child's coffin, my heart in my throat, my back straight.

Congressman Butler and his vicious colleagues may think they have defeated the upstart, Vinnie Ream. They're wrong. All they have done is make me more bitter and a whole lot more determined.

Onlookers line the halls. A Capitol guard hurries me on. I lift my shoulders and walk even slower. Let them all take a good look. This is not a defeat. I'll be back, and I will complete my *Lincoln* and show them all what a woman on a mission can accomplish.

Part 3
1869 to 1872

"She was no fine lady, she was an American girl, who had not attained her rank by birth, or through inherited riches, but had fought for it herself with a talent that had made its way to the surface without early training, through days and nights of industry, and a mixture of enthusiasm and determination."

Georg Morris Cohen Brandes

Recollections of My Childhood and My Youth, 1906

Chapter 19

JUNE 1869

PARIS, FRANCE

I gaze out the window at the wrought iron balconies festooned with flowers. On the street below, passersby converse in French, horses' hooves click on the cobbles, and pigeons coo from the dovecots on the rooftops.

Joy bubbles up, and I laugh. I've done it. Despite nasty congressmen, a lost check for the five-thousand-dollar advance, the hassle of arranging the shipping of the Lincoln model, and the endless complications in selling the boarding house, my parents and I are finally in Paris. I should be out there, exploring the city and pursuing my art, not bent over the hotel's ornate *secrétaire*, writing letters. But I am.

Try as I might, I can't leave my troubles behind. Letters from my admirers and detractors follow me across the ocean. Congressman Sam Marshall sends another marriage proposal. Mary forwards a collection of newspaper articles predicting my failure. And Pike—I crumple up Albert's latest missive and throw it in the wastebasket. It takes a lot to shock me, but old man Pike has succeeded. In lieu of news about Boudy's lawsuit, he sends letter after letter, detailing all the unmentionable ways he plans to touch my body upon my return. Just the thought of the old man putting his hands on me sends ice through my veins.

Tempered by the news of his oldest daughter's death, I dash off a note to him, reminding him that he is married and to never post me such missives again. I blot the ink dry, seal the envelope, and add it to the stack of letters teetering on the corner of the desk.

A cool Parisian evening breeze wafts the curtains and threatens to send the pile flying. I grab them up and tuck them in my purse. I would give anything to never write another.

I get to my feet, straighten my skirt, and rub each shoe tip along the back of my ankles to restore their shine. There is no question that my carefully chosen garments are out of style here in the French seat of fashion—my dresses hang too full in the front and not full enough in the back.

Ma doesn't care, but I hate being thought a dowdy colonial. Wasting my precious funds on any Parisienne fashion irks, but I have made one purchase—a peplum with pagoda sleeves in a soft, creamy-peach silk. I finger the ruched-ribbon trim on my one nod to French fashion. Wearing it instantly transforms whatever I own into something flowingly romantic. I slip it on and tie a colorful sash at the waist. With outstretched arms, I twirl. I love the way it encompasses me like a lightweight artist's smock. Ready to face the stares of the Parisiennes, I step into the adjoining room.

Pa naps on the bed, exhausted by our tour of Versailles. Ma knits a shawl for Mary, adapted from a pattern she found in *Le Follet*.

I touch her on the shoulder. "Let's go, Ma."

She grumbles as she rises out of the elaborately carved chair. "You can't keep doing so much, child. Drawing and French lessons. Touring. Visiting all manner of odd people. Dining out. Sculpting till midnight and beyond. You will collapse from exhaustion before we ever get to Rome."

I give her my most loving smile. "Thank you, Ma, for all you have ever done for me. I know I'm working day and night. But I must. I have only one chance to study in Paris and learn from the masters. And we will need the commissions from the sculptures I'm doing here when we return to the States."

"You should let Perry help with the costs."

I scold myself for upsetting her, then smooth my tone despite wanting to tell her exactly what I think of Perry Fuller, who has turned disobliging since I failed to convince President Johnson to put him in charge of the Internal Revenue Service.

I kiss her cheek and lie. "It's nice to know we have such a generous man to fall back on."

I swallow down the bad taste filling my mouth. What generosity? Perry Fuller has failed in his promise to support my parents in style. He's always ready with some excuse for why they can't move into his empty mansion. And despite his claims of raking in money at his consolation post as director of the Port of New Orleans, he hasn't offered one cent toward our tour, nor allowed Mary to come with us. Amid the grandeur around us, I could have rekindled the loving relationship we had before Perry whisked her away to his domain.

I turn to hide my sour face and head down the spiral stairs to the lobby. He can keep his filthy money. Even if I must dig into the Lincoln Commission's five-thousand-dollar advance, my parents deserve this opportunity to visit the grand places of Europe.

Out on the street, we head toward the small studio I'm renting. Not much bigger than my Capitol studio, it has one great advantage: few to no annoying politicians and no hovering would-be husbands.

Inside, I breathe in the earthen aroma of damp clay. Forget money. Forget Perry. Forget what people say about me. This is where I belong.

I settle Ma and her knitting in the worn but comfy chair in the corner, then hasten to remove my gloves and peplum. I fold it up and don my canvas smock and gaze around the near-empty space. I do not have much work to show yet, only a medallion of General John Fremont and the rough working of a bust of the American ambassador, Eli Washburne. Soon, I will have more, much more.

I uncover the work and wrap my fingers around my clay knife. I will have fame. I will have fortune. I will have proved that a woman should never be underestimated.

Chapter 20

OCTOBER 1869

PARIS, FRANCE

By the time October rolls around, I have several busts completed and a portfolio of sketches for an array of classically inspired statues. Under the pressure of our impending departure for Munich and then Florence and Rome, I rush about my studio, wrapping my sculptures and supervising the crating and loading of them onto the wagon that will take them to the train station. I add my guitar to the load, then turn away.

My stay in Paris has been a great success, but for one thing. If only I could have purchased a harp. The nuns in Washington told me about Érard's seven-pedal innovation, in which pedals replace the levers used on my harp. How can I leave Paris without at least seeing one?

The day before we board the train, I throw caution to the Paris breeze, drag my pa through the door of the showroom, and discover heaven.

It takes merely a few strums, and I'm in love. I explore the pedals, then pluck out "Annie Laurie."

Pa runs his hand down the gilt frame. "That's beautiful, Vinnie. Music of the angels."

My playing draws attention. I rise and curtsy as the proprietor approaches.

"You are interested in *le harpe*?" His French-accented English is guttural and hard to understand.

"*Oui*. I might be. Will you share the price?"

He turns his hands palms up. "*Mon dieu. Mon dieu.* Sixteen hundred francs, *mademoiselle*." He casts one of those condescending Parisienne looks at me. "You have this sum, *petite fille*?"

I bite the inside of my cheek—more than my entire advance. I let my hands fall away and shrug. "I have no desire for such an instrument. I own a far better harp."

"Better, *mademoiselle*? There is no better in the world." With that, the officious man strides off, his goatee tipped higher than his ears.

For my father's sake, I glue on a smile and feign cheery nonchalance. Still, his shoulders droop as we head to the door.

I hug him and blink away my tears. He would buy that harp for me if he could.

I kiss his cheek. "I have chosen sculpture over music, Pa," I whisper. "My harp at home suffices."

But I leave part of my heart behind when I walk out of Érard's.

Packing up my trunks takes the rest of the day. I have just snapped my portmanteau closed when there's a commotion in the next room.

"Come, Vinnie," Pa calls.

I straighten and stretch my aching back. Not another visitor to say goodbye?

I heft the bag atop the trunk, then dash across the way. My long-time supporter, former representative, and now Ambassador Washburne, his gray hair slicked back and his eyes bright, wears a huge grin.

"I received a message that there is a young lady here who desperately wants a harp."

I squint at my father. Has he arranged this? The smile on his face says he has.

Washburne offers his arm. "I've heard that a countess willing to sell hers. I have a carriage waiting."

I lay my hand on his sleeve and, in minutes, am whisked away down Paris's new broad boulevards to a stately mansion, or as my French teacher would say, a *hôtel privé*.

The driver draws the carriage up to the grand front door. Washburne assists me down.

"The lady of the house has her reputation to maintain," he says. "She doesn't want anyone to know she is in such dire straits that she must sell her harp—a gift from her deceased husband. You will be discreet?"

I have the need for discretion as well. The winner of the Lincoln commission cannot be seen purchasing an expensive harp. "Of course. I trust you to be the same."

With a nod, Washburne guides me up the steps.

The lady of the house is ill, we are told. The pompous, poker-faced butler shows the ambassador into a grand salon while a toothy maid, in an over-starched apron, escorts me up the staircase to the lady's private rooms.

The countess is a frail woman with thinning white hair and a tremble in her arthritic hands. Shrouded in blankets, she lies on a blue velvet divan beside a low table, top-heavy with medicine bottles.

"*Viens, ma chérie.*" She waves me over with fingers that barely move. Her voice is low and broken. "*Alors, est-ce que vous veux acheter ma harpe?*"

I struggle to understand her French. I come closer to her. She does not have the smell of an old woman dosed with drugs. Around her wafts the scent of lilacs, lilies of the valley, and a hint of exotic jasmine. The *parfum* is unforgettable.

"*Vous souhaitez acheter ma harpe?*" she repeats.

Using the little French I have learned, I pick out the words *buy* and *harp*. I dip my head. "*Oui, Comtesse.*"

She points to a corner of the room. I turn and gasp. The harp is far grander than the one in the showroom. Obviously custom-made, it is as tall as me, with an elaborately carved pillar and a burnished gilt finish.

Like a butterfly drawn to the most glorious flower, I float across the room and strum the strings. The sound is ethereal.

I peer over my shoulder. The countess's head has fallen back. She lifts a hand and moves her crooked fingers, as if plucking the strings. "*Joue pour moi, s'il te plaît.*"

Her request is unmistakable.

I take position, bend my head, and pluck a few arpeggios, then settle in to play a work she would know. I choose Handel's "Passacaglia."

I glance over when I am done.

She murmurs something else. All I catch is *francs*.

I pull out a pencil and my tiny sketchbook and hold it out to her. "*S'il te plaît?*"—I mime writing—"*Combien?*"

She thumbs through the pad, exclaiming over my quick sketches of people's faces, laughing at the caricatures I have drawn of the local tradesmen. My drawing instructor, Leon Bonnat, says I have only passable talent for drawing, but I'm pleased that my work provides this homebound woman pleasure.

She studies my face with her milky-blue eyes, then scribbles something down and hands me back the notebook. I stare at the number. It is way too low for such an instrument. I shouldn't, but I add a bit more—I can always eat less—and turn it so she can see.

"*Oui.*" Her smile is angelic, making my sacrifice worth it.

She rings a bell, and the maid appears.

I kiss the countess's cheeks, then leave her room happier than I have been in a long time.

Once below, I view the Baroque sculptures decorating the salon while Ambassador Washburne arranges for the harp to be shipped to my Rome studio. Then we return to the hotel at a trot.

There are letters waiting for me: six from Albert, two from Sam, ten or twelve from various supporters. I finger through them for a moment—and none from Boudy. I stash them all in my purse to read later. All those old friends seem far away, a part of some other life.

And Boudy? Is he lost to me?

I scurry my parents out the door.

I don't need the past. I don't need the memories. I don't need the longing. My future lies ahead, in Rome.

Chapter 21

OCTOBER 1869

FLORENCE, ITALY

Cold, damp, and wet, we arrive in Florence under a gray-clouded October sky. I rush my parents into a small hotel off the Via Romana with a view of Ponte Vecchio. Or, at least there would be, if it wasn't pouring.

"Are you sure we need to stop here?" Ma flops into a spindly-legged chair in the hotel lobby and pulls her coat more tightly around her. "I am tired of hollow cathedrals, braying donkeys, and strangers jabbering at me. And the food is inedible—everything tomatoes and garlic. My digestion has been off for days."

Pa rubs her shoulder. "We'll be in Rome soon, Lavinia. Rent our own set of rooms. Cook our own meals."

Ma tosses off his hand. "You mean, *I'll* cook our meals, and *I'll* do the cleaning up after you."

There's no pleasing my mother.

I hand the valet our room key and smile to cover for my mother's petulance. She loves being waited upon but hates the servants with their foreign ways.

Luckily, the rain stops in the morning. Pa and I leave Ma resting in our room and head out to explore the city. But first, I have a visit to make.

I point toward the river. "I think it's this way."

Pa and I follow the map drawn out for us by the concierge. The pavement is still wet, the cobblestones glistening in the sun. Donkey carts full of produce coming in from the country compete with elegant carriages and basket-toting servants. Overhead, women hang out washing on clotheslines spanning the streets. The linens flap in the breeze like welcoming flags.

Church bells ring across the city. Clouds of white doves swoop over the River Arno. I track their flight, remembering my beloved doves left behind in Albert's care. He has written that they are nesting.

For a brief moment, I'm homesick. Then I shake it off and place my feet more firmly. I already love Italy too much. I never want to go back.

I hear Powers' studio before I see it. Chisels tap on marble. Clay slaps against wood battens. We round a corner, and there it is. Statues in classical dress stand outside a large open doorway wide enough for a donkey cart to be unloaded, which is exactly what is happening as we arrive.

The workshop is electric with energy. Muscular men with mops of black curls heft crates and bags. Some chisel away the seams on plaster models. Others mix up huge batches of clay. At the far end, armatures glow in the forge as they are hammered into shape.

Out front, a small boy sweeps the pavement with a ragged broom.

I inhale the familiar scents of damp clay and metal, commingled with male sweat and wet donkey, then approach the keeper of the broom and inquire for Signore Powers. He doffs his hat and points inside.

I tuck up my skirt and wend my way around the cart and through a doorway at the rear. I find myself in an inner courtyard lined with highly polished works in marble—nubile girls, Herculean men.

In the center is the man I've come to see. Near seventy, Hiram Powers stands round-shouldered, in a long canvas smock, his hair grizzled beneath an exotic-looking embroidered cap, his eyes sunk deep into his skull. He is working on a half-size clay model of an athletic young man.

I take a deep breath and step forward. "Mr. Powers?"

He turns slowly, then tips his gaze down to meet mine. His face hardens into a storm of wrinkles. "How did you get in here? This is no place for a female. *Get out.*"

His tone is so unexpectedly high-pitched and unwelcoming that I stumble back.

The workshop falls silent.

I scan the courtyard. What I took for one of the statues is a naked man with the physique of a Greek Adonis. He grins at me and faces forward, showing a row of brilliantly white teeth and everything else.

My face heats, but I do not look away. I can't help imagining modeling that body in clay, my fingers running over the sinewy arms and the strong muscles of the thighs, his manhood far larger than any fig leaf I've ever seen.

Pa nudges me. "Time to skedaddle, Vin."

I wag my head. "I think not. I'm not embarrassed." I hold out my hand to Powers. "Vinnie Ream, sculptress. Winner of the Lincoln Commission."

His mouth twitches at Lincoln's name. He makes no move to take my hand. With a scoff, he huffs himself up and roars in his squeaky voice. "*You? A sculptress? Never.*"

My father tugs harder. "Let's go."

I shake him off and step closer to this man I have set on a pedestal to emulate. I am not afraid of him. He is barely half a foot taller than me, nothing like the size of Albert Pike.

I poke my finger into his chest. "Yes," I say in my most Western twang, "this country bumpkin is a sculptress—a good one. Soon to be a *great* one. It will be my *Lincoln*, the man I knew, that stands in the Rotunda. Not yours."

With a toss of my curls, I spin on my heel and, with my head high, stomp back through the workshop and out onto the street.

My father slips his arm into mine. "Oh, Vinnie. You've made an enemy of that man."

"He was already an enemy, Pa. He can't abide the idea of a young woman outshining him. But outshine him, I will."

I leap from my bed and open the shutters wide. Up and down the street, other shutters slap open. Forget Paris. Forget Munich. Forget Florence and that grumpy old man. I love Rome. The city is everything I dreamed of. Here is where I will shine.

I lean out the window. Below, vendors call out the day's offerings—sweet onions, red apples, golden olive oil, and cheeses from every region of the country. The scent of freshly baked bread and pastries wafts up from Antonio's forno on the corner. My stomach grumbles, and I hurry to dress so I can fetch some of his delicacies for our breakfast.

I throw on my new favorite clothes—white cotton stockings, walking boots of supple Italian leather, a soft linen peasant blouse with embroidered blouson sleeves, and a bright-red merino wool skirt. I lace a black boiled-wool Swiss waist over top and stretch my arms, glad to be free of stiff corsets, bulky hoops, and fashion dictates.

I give a little spin. The skirt flares. The sleeves wing out. I stop in front of the mirror and run a brush through my hair, check the part, and tuck in an ivory comb to either side above my ears. Done.

Simple. Quick. Comfortable.

I wink at the reflection of recreated Vinnie Ream. I have always dressed to please myself but never flouted convention so. But now I am *un'artista*, a member of Hawthorne's "white marmorean flock," the group of American sculptresses who challenge every convention there is for women.

I have no interest in wearing men's pants, as some do. But I love the freedom to dress as I wish.

"Vinnie? You awake?" Ma yells up the stairs.

I flounce my way down, skirt and petticoat held high, and come around the corner. Ma and Pa look up from their daily caffé.

I kiss each on the cheek. "*Buongiorno*. I'll go fetch some pastries from Anton's for our breakfast."

Ma sets down her cup and gives me a good looking over. "You look like a peasant. I can't bear to think of you on the streets dressed like that. Most unsuitable."

"I'm still modeling for George Healy's portrait of me." I throw my shawl over my shoulders. "You'd prefer I change at his studio?"

Pa waves his hand. "Let her be, Lavinia. You've seen the other sculptresses and artists. It's what they wear. Personally, I find the look quite becoming. Never liked those hoop things." He winks at Ma. "Even you are wearing looser clothing."

My mother takes a long sip of her coffee. "Well . . . as they say, when in Rome do as the Romans, so I'm doing."

I love this more mellowed version of my persnickety mother. I give her a hug.

It has taken a ton of effort to get my parents settled in with a servant they adore, food they can digest, and a handful of friends to offer daily conversation. Luckily, the grandfatherly James Hopkins, vice president of the Fourth National Bank of Philadelphia, here in Rome on business, seems to know exactly how to keep them content. It has been worth it, having them here. I've never felt closer to them than I do under the warm Italian sun.

Coins at the ready, I make a quick dash to the bakery and race back with the morning's cornetti. Outside our pension door, an urchin, his feet bare, his face grubby, tugs on my shawl and waves a note at me. "*Signorina*."

I take the note and drop a coin in his palm. Then, with a glance at his thin arms, I add one of the cornetti.

Despite his ragtag appearance, the boy bows as elegantly as the finest lord, then scampers off down the street.

I read the note and run up the steps. I arrive at the breakfast table out of breath. The cornetti tumble from my hands.

Ma draws back. "Vinnie, what's the meaning of this?"

I steady myself. "Colonel Lawrence, the American consul to Florence, is coming to my studio today. He wants to see the *Lincoln*."

Pa butters his pastry. "I'm sure he'll be pleased."

"*Pleased*? I haven't even unwrapped it yet. What if it's cracked or broken? He will be sure to report back to President Grant. And the newsmen will trumpet any damage."

"Then you will fix it." Pa stuffs his roll into his mouth and rises. "Here, I will come with you, and we can unwrap it together."

"But it's broad daylight. The studio will be full of onlookers. I wanted to do it late at night. Just to be safe."

"Calm down. I've never seen you so unsure of yourself," Ma chides. "Keep the studio closed today. It wouldn't be the first time. You close whenever there is an event you want to see. Tell him to come back tomorrow."

I reread the note. "I can't. He's on his way back to Florence. He plans on stopping at the studio on his way out of the city. I'll just have to take a chance." I glance at Pa. "I wish I could have convinced Grant to appoint you consul."

Pa shakes his head. "Grant did me a favor. I would have hated all the pomp and stuffiness. I'm much happier in our little apartment and attending the horse races."

I give him a quick hug. "I know. But you would have done a great job."

Pa plops his straw hat on his head. "In fact, I'm sure this consul could use a break from his duties. Let's go arrange a peasant-style luncheon for him. Lots of bread, cheese, and red wine to take his attention off the unveiling."

"Good idea, Pa. Let's go make it happen."

Together, we hustle down the street. It is only a few blocks to my studio on Via San Basilio in the artist's quarter, but the weight in my chest makes it hard to breathe. I swipe a hand across my forehead. It is not like me to be so worried. I have survived the scandalous attacks at home. I can do the same here.

But it's not the same. Here, I have a fresh start. A chance to be welcomed by my fellow artists and accepted by them as an equal.

I unlock the studio door and stare at the wooden crate that contains my *Lincoln*. Everything depends on the unveiling.

While Pa sets out the luncheon, my sole workman, Guiseppe, pries open the long side of the crate. Inside is a second box. In minutes, it, too, is open. I peer inside, my pulse hammering.

My model rests like a mummy, swaddled in layers and layers of linen.

Giuseppe slowly cuts through the cloth. Bit by bit, it falls back, revealing my *Lincoln* to be whole and uncracked.

Voices sound behind me. I hear the consul's name. I let out a shaky breath, then turn, wearing a smile, just in time to welcome the consul and his entourage into the studio.

He is only the first of many who come to see my much-talked-about and much-maligned *Lincoln*. The plaster model, in perfect condition, is the centerpiece of my studio display. Today, my first visitor is renowned sculptress Harriet Hosmer.

"So, this is your masterpiece." She draws her cape together at the neck and walks around my *Lincoln*. Despite several wool wraps and a blaze in the fireplace, I shiver beneath my smock. She couldn't have chosen a colder November day to visit. Even the Trevi Fountain glitters with icicles. But the chills running through me are less due to the weather and more about what she might say.

Hosmer tucks her hands inside her mantle. She is a small woman of my height, with a broad brow and wise eyes.

"Charlotte Cushman told me I should come and see this." She circles the work again. "I like it. Using the cape as support for the arms and legs is a masterful touch. I'd be worried about the scroll,"—she leans in—"the *Emancipation Proclamation*?"—she glances at me, then resumes her commentary—"protruding as much as you have it. Likely to be knocked off by a drunken congressman. Make it at least three inches shorter."

She comes around and takes a cup of tea from me. She peers into the cup. "Nothing stronger, my dear?"

"I always served tea in my Capitol studio in winter, Miss Hosmer. Everyone commented on how it warmed their hands."

Harriet clasps the cup. "That it does. Just not sure about the insides." She adds a heaping spoonful of sugar and gulps it down.

I fill it again. "I do admit many of the so-called teetotalers came armed with flasks."

She grins. "*Politicians?* Hypocrites—the lot of them. And please, call me Harriet. You are one of us—a rare breed—a woman who sculpts despite those very same hypocrites."

Still holding her cup, Harriet rises and sweeps across to where my three most recent clay works are displayed. She runs a finger along the folds of the drapery that flow over and around the woman playing a tabor inspired by the Biblical Miriam.

She takes a sip of her tea. "You know the female body well."

I nod. In front of this woman, I am not afraid to admit the truth. "How could I not? I know my own body."

"Of course. Have you worked from a male model yet?"

I remember my encounter at Hiram Powers' and my cheeks heat. "I would love to, but I haven't found—"

Harriet flicks her fingers. "Italian men have no shame. I'll send one over." She tips her head toward my mother, plying her knitting needles in the sun by the open door. "You'll need a privacy screen."

"I have access to the rooms above stairs."

She gives me a surprised look. "Do you now?"

I give a sharp shake of my head in an attempt to look more worldly. In America, my respectability is questioned. Here, it is my naivete. "Of course."

Her voice turns motherly. "It is up to you what you want to do. They will criticize your male figures, no matter how much work you do from the model. I have studied every bone and muscle in the male body and can't please my critics. Better to stick to fauns and women and use drapery for the males."

"But your sculpture of Thomas Hart Benton received favorable reviews."

"He was well draped in the classical style."

She looks over her shoulder at my *Lincoln*. "Here's the truth of it. The men know you modeled the President's naked body before you dressed him. The idea titillates them, so they lash back. They will be especially harsh on you for your *Lincoln*. Heaven forbid we should think such a great man had a cock."

I slap my hands to my face and peek through my fingers to make sure my mother hasn't heard. But Ma has buttonholed some passing vendor and is haggling over oranges.

Harriet grins. "You are so young. It is quite endearing."

I don't want to be *endearing*.

I snap back, "I know what men look like. I grew up on the prairie. I have a brother. Everyone skinny-dipped."

"I have seen the male laxness when among their own. That's not what I meant. Your *Lincoln* shows you understand male anatomy perfectly fine. What makes you endearing is your wondrous open-eyed enthusiasm. Where I proclaim and perform and please my buyers, you listen and absorb and learn and still take risks. It is a gift given to the young."

I touch her hand. "You are most kind to say so."

"It's not merely kindness." She faces the *Lincoln* again. "I think there is a little bit of P. T. Barnum in you. It will serve you well. Might even make you the best known of us all."

"Barnum? The showman?"

"Look at that huge American flag and photo placed just so behind the plaster model. The perfect tableau." She grins at me. "You actually thought to bring those with you? No wonder you draw the crowds."

Harriet throws an arm around me and whispers close to my ear, "A piece of advice. Be sure to get a block of marble and tap, tap, tap it with your chisel every day. Doesn't matter what you make. Your admirers need to see you dig into the stone if they would take word back to Washington that your own hands created the finished *Lincoln*, and not one of the hired Italians. Though you and I both know those workers work wonders."

She turns to leave. "You must come to one of my soirées at the studio. Every Friday night. Have you met your fellow sculptresses, Anne Whitney and Edmonia Lewis, yet?"

"No, I have not."

"Do come. We'd love to have you in our flock." She winks. "Which isn't all white. And doesn't serve tea." With that, she kisses me full on the lips and, with a nod to Ma, flounces out into the morning sun.

Ma gets up with a groan and sets her knitting and a pair of oranges down on the chair. "Vinnie, who was that who came so early?"

I offer her a cup of tea. "Harriet Hosmer, a great American sculptress."

She rubs her hands together before taking the cup. "*Sculptress*? That was a woman? What in the world was she wearing?"

"Men's wool trousers, I believe."

"Outrageous."

"But much warmer than these stockings." I kick out a leg. "Maybe I should get a pair?"

"Vinnie. The peasant outfit is odd enough. Tell me you won't put on a man's suit. No man would ever marry you."

"Did you forget? I already have a beau?"

She frowns. "Who? Oh, Cornelius Boudinot? All wind, that man. A regular tumbleweed. Empty promises. Too wild by half for polite society. He should have swept you up and placed a ring on your finger by now."

I play with the new locket around my neck. "Maybe he will." And maybe I won't.

"Isn't he out in Indian Territory? Perry writes he is stirring up trouble over tobacco."

I swallow a snort. Nothing like the trouble Perry is stirring up in the Port of New Orleans, according to Albert. But Ma will hear nothing against Mary's husband, so I don't bother talking about him anymore.

I force my worries about Mary to the side and smile. I do have one thing to share.

"What would you say if I told you Boudy is coming for Christmas?"

Ma's eyebrows shoot up. "Boudinot's coming to Rome?" Puzzlement flits across her face. In her mind, Indians, even educated ones like Boudy, can't cross an ocean or take in the wonders of Rome.

She wrings her hands. "But we have Major Rollins, John Rice, Albert Pulitzer, and Lew Wallace set to visit."

"Well, I don't intend to marry any of them."

"Don't be silly, child. How will we entertain so many?"

"They're coming to see my studio and the *Lincoln*. Perhaps get a marble bust done. We'll hire help. And don't worry. Leave the entertainment of Boudy to me."

Ma glares. "Get that man's ring on your finger and a minister's blessing, and you can entertain him any way you wish."

A commotion fills the doorway. Georg Brandes, the Danish writer I met on the train to Florence, is the first of my friends to arrive. On his face is the sunny smile that signals a grand day ahead, and in his arms, a huge basket of fruit.

Ma rushes over to help him find room among the overflowing table of planters and bouquets from my admirers delivered daily.

I turn back to my *Lincoln*. Do I really want to give up my career and marry Boudy? My head says no. My heart says yes.

Chapter 22

DECEMBER 1869

ROME

The Christmas holidays arrive sooner than expected. The market smells of roasting chestnuts and beeswax candles. I buy panettone and biscotti, dried fruit, a bushel of oranges, and plenty of red wine. I rush around the studio, arranging all my new work to best effect.

Today, Boudy comes.

Bursts of excitement bubble up inside me as I anticipate showing him everything I've accomplished. I can't wait for him to wrap his arms around me and kiss me. While I may not be certain about getting married, one thing is clear: I desire him with the intensity of a woman longing for a man. And perhaps it's time for us to take our relationship beyond just kissing.

After all, this is Rome, where *l'amore* reigns supreme.

By noon, friends, acquaintances, and fellow artists fill the studio. All my fellow sculptresses are present. Harriet Hosmer has brought her companion, Lady Ashburton. My beloved members of the flock—Anne Whitney, Charlotte Cushman,

Emma Stebbins, and Edmonia Lewis—parade in a glorious array of silks and brocades as they sip my mulled wine.

In the far corner, Major Rollins and John Rice, newly arrived in the city, entertain my parents, who are both dressed in rich Italian fashion and looking radiantly happy.

If I have my way, we will stay in Rome forever.

I gaze at the plaster *Lincoln* model set perfectly to catch the light. To fulfill the commission, I must go back to Washington, of course. But once that is complete, nothing will stop me from returning to live here.

I twist my fingers together. I'm sure Boudy would never agree.

"You seem nervous today," Lady Ashburton says as she sips her third glass of mulled wine.

Harriet loops her arm into her dear friend's. "She's expecting a special someone."

"Yes, I am." I perch on tiptoes and look toward the door. "He sent a note to expect him at three."

Harriet turns to Louisa. "Her lover is an American Indian."

The wife of one of the American businessmen Pa has befriended jerks around and stares at me. "A savage?"

The word is like a stab in my heart. I wish my father were not so freewheeling with his tales of adventures on the plains.

"My friend, Cornelius Boudinot, is part Cherokee and a well-known lawyer." I glance at the stairs to the upstairs rooms, *and soon to be my lover—maybe.*

As if they can sense what I am thinking, Louisa takes one of my arms, Harriet the other. "You have brought your harp. Let's hear you sing."

The women escort me to the low platform I have set up in the best-lit corner of the studio. After relying on the goodwill of men for so long, I bask in the joy of having female friends who not only understand my need to sculpt but also see me as a woman worthy of friendship and support.

I pluck a string or two. The crowd quiets. My tension flees. The opening notes of "Silent Night" ring out beneath my fingers. The melody, serene but simple, floats through the air.

My voice melds with the notes. One by one, others join in; some in English, some in Italian, or German. Sunlight pours through the window, highlighting my hands and the gilt on the harp. I let the music flow into other songs of the season, then to the ballad I love most of all—"Annie Laurie."

The song ends. My head and hands drop. The applause starts softly, then crescendos until it is as loud as the roll of thunder across the broad expanse of the plains.

When I raise my head, he is there, standing in the doorway, wide-brimmed hat in hand, hair flowing over his shoulders. His soft, fringed buckskin jacket sets him apart from every other man in the studio—in Rome—in the world.

Boudy.

My savage.

It takes forever for us to find time alone. There are studio hangers-on to urge on their way, my parents and our dinner guests to settle, food to be served, hotel arrangements to be made.

Finally, I grab Boudy's hand and steal him away. We stroll down the narrow streets and come out at the Trevi Fountain. Despite the evening chill, my blood runs hot. I swing our hands back and forth beneath a star-carpeted sky, the moon a sliver of light in the east.

"I love it here so much." I sit on the wall of the pool.

Boudy squeezes my hand. "I can tell. You were alive before. Now you are a firecracker. So, success sits well?"

I slip my hand free and gaze at the fountain. "The commissions are coming in—slowly. But I have only been here two months. The important thing is that I have friends now—other artists and sculptors who are not out to destroy me. And no one cares how I live my private life."

He hovers behind me. "Except your parents. You should have heard your Pa threaten me with his shotgun if I don't treat you right."

"I don't care what my parents think. I'm a grown woman. Besides, Pa didn't bring his shotgun." I spin around and press my lips to his.

"Ah, Vinita," he murmurs. "So sweet." Then his lips claim mine, and I am lost.

His kiss is as I remember it—warm, deep, and all Boudy. His arms enfold me, our bodies press together. Without layers of petticoats and the barriers of hoop and corset, I can feel every part of him flex and tense, then arouse.

I draw back to catch my breath. "I'm so glad you're here."

He flicks the end of my nose. "It was, perhaps, not wise. I have much I dread to tell you." He steps away. "And in the telling, I fear I will lose your love."

I blink. "What's happened?"

"I have—shall I say—a disagreement with the government about whether or not the Cherokee Treaty of sixty-six bans federal taxation in the Indian Territories. I know it does. I wrote that section myself. The federal tax officials disagree."

"So, you're fighting it?"

"I shouldn't have to, but it seems I must. But the thing is, a legal battle costs money, and all my funds are tied up in the tobacco mill and its expansion. I'm heavily in debt. I don't care about the Eastern bankers, but my uncle, Stand Watie, wants his investment back. If I renege on my promise to him, I'll lose all standing in the tribe."

I clasp his hand in mine. "I wish I had the money to give you. But the first half of the commission payment is near gone, and I won't get the remainder till my *Lincoln* graces the Rotunda. But when I do—"

He presses a finger against my lips. "I would never take your money. I am not that kind of man. That is yours to spend on harps and marble and this wonderful life you have here."

I search for an answer to his problems. "Have you asked Perry?"

"Maybe if he were Commissioner of Taxation, all could be smoothed over. But now? His debts are heavier than mine, and he's in trouble over bribes."

"Pike mentioned money troubles in his last letters. So, the rumors are true?"

"Yes. He is in a bad way. But don't worry. Perry is like a prairie dog—always popping up again with a new scheme." He wraps his arms around me. "I came here to escape it all. Perhaps marry you at last. But I can't. I received a telegram this morning upon my arrival. The feds have seized my mill at Wet Prairie and the entire year's store of tobacco. Totally illegally." His cheek quivers. "I'm going to have to go back immediately and take legal action. I will take it all the way to the Supreme Court if I must. If the government gets away with enforcing federal laws on Indian Lands, it will be the death knell of the tribes."

I gasp. If he leaves me again, it will be the death knell for any hope of a future together.

I clasp his hand in mine. "I—I'll come with you. Help you fight this. I love you too much to let you battle alone."

He turns away. "One who truly loves you would not accept such a sacrifice. I have never seen you so happy, Vinita. Stay here. Stay away from the Washington politicians. Away from the rabid American press. My life is in the courtroom and fighting for my tribe. You have blossomed in Rome. Stay. Be the free-spirited artist you were meant to be."

He peers up at the fountain. Moonlight sparkles on the water, illuminating the plunging horses and the struggling tritons. "I have read that these sculptures have been here for over a hundred years. What you create will exist long after we are gone and our love is just a memory." He kisses the backs of my hands. "You must not give your future up for me."

"But Boudy, I want both. I want you."

"Hush." He draws me close. "If the world were just, I would promise to come back and make you mine forever. But there is no justice for Indians. There will be no justice for me."

I cling to hope. "I have important friends."

"No, I will not have you grovel for me. I may lose everything, but never my pride."

Pride. The downfall of men. But I can't take it from him. It is what makes him the man he is.

I look around. No man holds himself the way Boudy does—perfectly balanced, spine loose and flexible. The skin of his shaved face and hands is tinted by the western sun and his ancestors. He belongs on the prairie, not sweeping behind my skirts in a land so foreign.

I can't marry him and trap him in the world I have fallen in love with. I see that now.

I pull a lira from my pocket and turn it in my fingers. I have little belief in superstition. Still, it seems the right thing to do.

"They say if you throw a coin in the Trevi, you will come back to Rome." I place the coin on his palm. "Toss it in. Perhaps it will bring you back to me someday."

He tosses the coin far into the pool. It splashes and sinks below the surface.

I take his hand. "Come. I have fixed up a lovers' nest in the room above the studio. It will be chilly, but I'm sure you know how to warm it up."

He moves toward me, then halts. "No, Vinita. We mustn't."

My stomach drops like the sinking coin. "Why not? There is nothing to stop us. All of Rome is for lovers." I tug hard, but Boudy stands as immovable as the statue of Oceanus peering down at us.

I fold my arms across my chest. "You said you don't believe all those rumors about me."

"I don't."

"Then why? I . . . I saved my virginity for you."

He goes still. "Ah, Vinita, that is a precious gift to bestow on a man. But I would be a dog to take such a gift when I cannot promise forever. Come. Let me take you back to your parents."

Something shrinks inside me. I refuse to hold his hand on the way back.

In the doorway, he kisses my cheek like a mere acquaintance. "Leaving you here is the hardest thing I have ever done, Vinita. No man could ever love you more." He waits a minute for me to say something.

I want to shout that I am not a statue to be set on a pedestal, but a flesh-and-blood woman with desires of my own. But my heart is too bruised. Suddenly chill, I stare at the ground, my body rigid.

He tips my chin up. "I know you hate me at this moment—thwarted desire is a painful thing. But it is better to leave you hungry than have you discover you have given up too much for one night of pleasure." He peers into my eyes. "I promise to never stop loving you. I will make it my life's work to commemorate that love, not through a quick toss under the sheets, but by marking the world so you are never forgotten."

I fight back tears. "I don't care about the world."

"You will." With that, Boudy turns on his heel and sets off down the street, taking my heart with him.

He is right. I do hate him.

"Don't come back!" I shout after him. "Don't you ever, ever, ever come back!"

Chapter 23

FEBRUARY 1870

ROME, ITALY

Rain falls day after day after day. It's as if Boudy stole the Italian sun, along with my joy. So, to the steady drip of the rain, I sculpt until my fingers turn icy and puckered, until the clay is an extension of my hands, until I no longer talk to or visit anyone.

This is how I like it.

Silent. Cold. Unfeeling.

Smash.

The studio door slams open, and Pa barges in. "Come. We've been invited to a concert by Franz Liszt."

I look up from the clay model of Sappho I'm working on. "I can't, Pa. I have too much to do."

I return to my sculpture and smooth the cheek. This will be my best work yet, and I am making it for myself. Senator Cowan's words in Congress, citing Sappho as an example of a woman of great accomplishment, have hung in my memory these last three years.

I pinch my tongue between my teeth and smooth some more, then let my hands fall. But it is a fool's undertaking to work on something that might never sell when I should be working on something already commissioned.

Pa comes further into the studio. "Please, Vinnie. The priest, Don Zeferino, has invited you especially. You can't refuse. He heard your harp playing and knows how much you love music."

I swipe my unkempt hair out of my face. "You and Ma go. I really can't stop right now. The clay is the perfect dampness. It dries too quickly later in the day."

"You need a break, daughter. You're driving yourself too hard."

I frown at him. "Just go."

Pa taps his hat against his thigh. "I will make your excuses to Don Zeferino, then. Though I fear the invitation will not be repeated."

I focus on the curl of Sappho's ear and do not see Pa leave. I scrape away the clay until it is so thin light will pass through the finished marble. But I go too far.

The clay rips. The ear is ruined.

I throw down my tools. Pa is right. I'm pushing myself too hard. But work is my only solace.

For months, I have regretted my last words to Boudy, unable to find pleasure in playing my harp, finding it impossible to sing without tears. Perhaps I do need to get out of the studio.

I wrap Sappho in wet cloths, rinse my hands, and wipe the clay dust from my face. If I hurry, I might still make the performance.

It is not far to the Monastery of Santa Francesca Romana. We've visited the church and touched the basalt stones Saint Peter and Saint Paul once kneeled upon. And I have sketched the statues there.

I take the back streets at a run, dashing between the donkey carts and peddlers, even cutting across the ruins of the Forum. But I am too late. Piano music floats out from the small reception room in the monastery. I halt in the open doorway.

Every seat is taken. Ma and Pa sit enthralled near the front. So many friends and acquaintances fill the room, all dressed in their best. I look down at my clay-splattered skirt and fall back. I do not belong here. But the music . . . I can't tear myself away.

I feel a tug on my sleeve.

Don Zeferino, in his white priestly robe, presses a finger to his lips. "*Come*," he mouths in Italian. He points to an empty chair behind the piano. "*For you.*"

I shake my head, but he is not deterred. He tugs harder until I am nearly unbalanced. The last thing I want is to disturb Liszt's ethereal playing, so all I can do is follow.

The smiling priest leads me around the building and guides me through a side door opening into the assembly. Barely into the room, he stops and waves me forward.

I should retreat, but I have been seen. I cannot back out now.

I slink in, gather my skirt, slip into the seat, and let the sounds wash over me. At first, it dances across my skin like a spring breeze. But soon, the music grows darker. It races and flows, cascading up and down the keyboard.

Liszt's face contorts as he plays. His breath mirrors the rhythm. He is a man in agony, with a heart breaking, just like mine. My love for Boudy swells as the notes fill the air, and then releases. The sorrow locked inside flows free.

Sobs rise from my chest. Tears trickle down my cheeks. A finger wipes them away.

I startle and open my eyes. Liszt has reached across with his right hand while still playing with his left—we are seated that close.

His touch sears me, captures me. Everything falls away. All I can do is stare at this man in monk's robes, collar-length hair tonsured. His intense eyes trap mine.

I do not notice when the music ends. I do not hear the applause. I do not see the people crowding around us. I am frozen in place—bewitched.

Liszt bows and takes me by the arm. "Your tears are all the tribute I require." He pats my hand, and we walk together into the cloisters and share our losses; his, the deaths of his son and daughter, and mine, the disappointment in the man I love.

Come that night, I lean out my bedroom window, gaze at the stars above, and send a message to Boudy far across the sea. *You can't bury a broken heart*, I tell him. *You must free it in order to keep on living.*

Turning my back on music was a mistake—music sustains me. Turning away from my love for Boudy unrooted me from myself.

I brush my hand across the wisteria hanging from the trellises. The sweet scent washes over me.

Yes, Boudy. I will sing again. I will sing for you. The love we have cannot be extinguished. I have tried and failed. You refused my gift, but I will not refuse yours. I will be the best sculptress possible. I will make works that will last as long as the Trevi Fountain . . . no, longer.

And I will start with the *Lincoln*.

Chapter 24

MAY 1870

CARRARA, ITALY

It is time to choose the marble for my *Lincoln*. Armed with directions from sculptor Giuseppe Rossetti on how to choose the best stone—early morning, he says, or evening after a heavy rain—and a huge loan, I pack up the letters of introduction from Italian sculptor Luigi Majoli and dear Harriet and thrust my worries aside.

I have no choice. To get paid for the *Lincoln*, I must produce it in marble.

It is a beautiful day as we set off on the train north. Through the window, I gaze out at the Tyrrhenian Sea. The May sun sparkles on the turquoise water, which shimmers dark and light. Ma basks beneath her broad hat topped with a pink camellia, a gift from Liszt in honor of the trip. Pa's eyes crinkle with delight every time we pass a field of waving grain or horses grazing on spring green grass. He will never be a city man. He needs the space, the air, the joy of nature to be full-hearted.

"Look, Vinnie." He points to a girl in a cone-shaped straw hat, with bare legs and feet, chasing a flock of sheep. Her long black hair swings as she runs. "She could be you as a child."

Ma swats at him. "Vinnie is still that wild child, and I fear she always will be." She turns to me. "You lost Boudy for good, didn't you? What did you do to make him leave so abruptly at Christmas? He didn't even say goodbye. And no letters since?"

I tip my hat back and stare out at the dish of blue extending to the horizon, a sky not unlike the one over the prairie where Boudy is now. "We agreed it was not the right time for us. He left for business."

"So, the non-engagement is off?" The old sharpness tinges her words. I haven't heard that tone for months.

I look away.

"That's what I thought. I hesitated to ask. I'd hoped it was a lover's tiff." She nudges Pa. "Tell her."

My father taps his fingers together. "Hopkins' colleague, Robert Packer, has asked to court you."

I watch the blue-violet hills roll by. "He can join the queue. I will never marry."

Ma's face crunches into a mass of anger. "How selfish of you. Who will take care of you when we're gone? Who will protect your reputation as you gallivant around in places ladies ought not frequent? One of those bizarre women you admire so? I think not. Only a husband can do that. Packer is a wealthy man and a perfect gentleman." She takes Pa's hand in hers. "Marriage isn't easy, but two can face the world's troubles better than one."

There is truth in what she says. But if I can't have Boudy, then I want no one.

I spit out the words. "I can take care of myself."

Ma flounces back against the seat. "You're impossible, child. I can't wait to get home and hold Mary and her children to my bosom again. She did her duty, and she's happy."

My hands clench. I fear my sister will not be happy for long. But I say nothing.

A pall has been cast over the day. We travel on in silence as I stare out the window and try to find my resolve.

We arrive in Carrara at sunset. The quarries are a blaze of creamy white above the town. Steep-terraced vineyards climb the hills below. My father and I leave Ma sitting at a café and walk up the main street to Bowken, Torrey & Company's office.

Pa loops his elbow into the crook of mine. "I knew something was wrong. I could hear the sadness in your music." He presses his hand over mine. "Any chance that Boudy will return?"

I rock my head back and forth. "He's in big trouble with the government and doesn't want to drag me down with him." I press my tongue against the back of my teeth, unsure I should say more, then continue, my voice trembling. "Perry's in trouble, too. His creditors are taking him to court."

Pa tilts his head. "Oh, I wondered what was going on when Mary stopped mentioning him in her letters." He squeezes my hand. "Let's not tell your mother. For all we know, things may straighten out by the time we are back in Washington." He points to the company sign up ahead. "Put it all out of your mind for now. Let's order the marble. Then we can enjoy this beautiful evening."

The owner, Franklin Torrey, is a dapper man with an artist's eye and a tight pocket. A sculptor himself, he calculates the cost for the stone and roughs out my five projects in a few minutes. The amount is more than I imagined and takes the entire two thousand dollars I borrowed from the bankers. Nothing is left of my advance for shipping the finished works back to the States, nor to pay our daily living costs until the *Lincoln* is done.

I think of my *Miriam,* my *Carnival,* my *West*, and my *Sappho* waiting to be carved in marble. This will be my only chance to purchase the finest Carrara stones and bring them to life. I will just have to borrow more money.

I nod yes and open my purse.

Pa casts me a worried look. He knows our finances are dire. "Are you sure, Vinnie?"

All I can do is shrug and be thankful my mother stayed behind. She would be furious to know I don't have enough money left to even pay for tickets to get back home.

"I'll figure something out." I cross my fingers. Surely, once people have seen my *Lincoln*, they will want more of my work so I can pay off my burgeoning debts.

Bill paid, Torrey offers wine and cheerily invites us to visit the quarry and select my stones in the morning.

Despite all my money worries, I awake before dawn, full of anticipation for the day ahead. I gaze up at the mountains. Carrara is where Michelangelo obtained the marble for his greatest works. Today, little me, America's Prairie Cinderella, will be doing the same. But first, I have to get there.

I race down to where Pa waits with an English-speaking guide and the two young boys he's hired to carry our packs for the three-mile hike to the quarry.

Ma waves goodbye from the hotel balcony, and we set out behind a two-wheeled wagon carrying a crew of workmen wearing crumpled hats and disgruntled faces.

The cart creaks and grinds its way up the mountainside, the laborers swaying and grumbling at every bump. The morning is cool. The air fresh with the scent of pine. For a while, we are content to plod slowly through the well-tended fields and vineyards as the rays of dawn gather in the eastern sky and gently brighten. But the road soon narrows and turns steeper, and the cart slows and jerks at every turn as the oxen struggle to find footing. At this rate, we will arrive too late for me to look for flaws in the stones.

I signal the guide. "Is there another way?"

He points to a narrow track off to the left that looks barely wide enough for a goat. I glance at my father, who is huffing slightly. Once, he could have bounded straight up these hillsides. But he is getting old. His health is not the best.

I hesitate. "Should we go this way?"

"Of course." He snickers. "Poor fellows ahead of us are getting their bones shook to pieces in that thing. Never thought much of riding in one of those prairie schooners back home. But that two-wheel contraption has got to be ten times worse. Give me my own two feet, and I can go anywhere."

We set off single file, on foot. The trail turns out to be better than I expected. Slowly, we climb above the town into the cooling pines.

At the top of the hill, I peer over my shoulder. A broad grin illuminates my father's face. I haven't seen him this happy in a long time. This is where he belongs—outdoors, hiking, and exploring.

We start down into the ravine. Soon, I hear men shouting. Chains rattling. Giant thumps shaking the ground. We round a curve, and there they are—the famed quarries of Carrara. Despite the deep morning shadows, the stone gleams shockingly white. I shade my eyes with my hand and survey the marble of legend. Then I plunge forward toward the quarry. I can't wait to select my stones.

At the foot of the rock face, outside the cutting mill, lie the already cut stones ready to be loaded for transport. Order in hand, Torrey's agent, Rolando Bianchi, leads me from stone to stone, taking dimensions, waiting for me to find any flaws, and helping me make my decision.

A clayey knot clogs my throat as I choose five of the best *crestolo*, sign the orders, and then watch the transport of the blocks to the loading ramp.

Pa and I stand to the side as teams of men use sand and gravity to slide the stones from the quarry and onto the bed of a large wagon pulled by a team of six oxen, white as the marble they haul. The animals toss their horned heads, and then, at the snap of a whip, they lunge forward. The oxen's heads lower, and the wagon starts to roll down the steep, rutted track.

Suddenly, the stones shift and tip.

"No—" I scream and run forward, the vision of my precious stones tumbling into the ravine and my burgeoning debt driving away my common sense.

Pa yanks me back as the laden wagon twists and slams into the oxen hitched closest to the driver. The animals go down like tin soldiers, legs and sides heaving. The waggoneer tumbles from his seat. The boy at the front falls, tangled in the harness. The quarry erupts into shouts. Men run from all over, help the man and boy up, and free the stricken animals.

For a moment, I think all is well. Then, as the workmen step away, I see one of the oxen remains lying on its side.

A man approaches with a pointed stick. He raises it above the fallen animal. My blood boils, all my frustration and fury focused on that stick. How dare he hurt that poor creature!

Screaming every Italian word I know, I take off running and leap up to grab onto that wicked pole. "*Non. Non non. Fermo!*" I look up into a heavily bearded face and grimacing teeth. The man looks ready to hit me, but I don't care. I cling on.

"You can't work this ox again. It needs to rest. To heal. Unhitch him at once. And find more oxen. Six, *sei,* is not enough."

The Torrey agent comes up behind me. I don't know what he says in rapid Italian, but before I can yell again, the man with the stick is gone, the injured ox is led away, a replacement is found, and another team of six is unhitched from an empty wagon and added to mine. Compared to the long line of a dozen oxen, my precious stones look small and insignificant, but much safer.

I close my eyes and inhale deeply. They *are* insignificant. At this moment, those five rocks are the only things my parents and I own in the world. Somehow, I am going to have to get more money, or we will be kicked out of our lodgings and onto the street.

I peer over at my father, his face flushed with the exertions of the day. How can I do that to my parents?

"Easy," Ma would say. "Marry a rich man." But I can't. I have sacrificed the man I love to pursue my career, and I will never replace him with another.

Back in Rome, I borrow enough money from dear George Healy to keep our rooms while I search for a lucrative commission. I become the epitome of the hustler everyone believes me to be. No way will I let my parents be humiliated by my poor handling of the money. I never should have purchased the harp or the French fashions, nor taken expensive drawing lessons in Paris.

I set my hat on my head, my cross around my neck, and my art album under my arm. Then I head downstairs, carrying a letter of introduction to the pope's secretary of state, Cardinal Antonelli. A commission from a cardinal, or perhaps through him, the pope, would bring in more commissions, for sure. That is, if I can sway His Eminence.

Cardinal Antonelli is rumored to terrify the bravest men, so I have dressed as innocently as I can in a high-necked, long-sleeved, white gown trimmed with green ribbon. Hopefully, he will be less fierce toward an innocent-looking girl.

Ma waits by the door, ready to leave. "Are you sure about this, Vinnie? I have no idea how one behaves around a cardinal. We're not even Catholic."

"I've spent time with the nuns at St. Aloysius. Let me do the talking and imitate what I do."

My mother tugs down her bodice and pulls on her gloves. "What if he asks us to . . . pray or something?"

"I prefer he ask me to make his bust."

"Oh, Vinnie. Must you always go begging men to pay you money? It's unseemly. Aren't the thousands of dollars you're getting for the statue of Lincoln enough for you?"

Would that it were. But I say nothing. I will not spoil my mother's enjoyment of the elegant life she is living.

I hand her one of the lace-trimmed headkerchiefs we have been advised to wear. "Just think of the prestige I will earn if I can make a bust of the man closest to the pope."

Ma arranges it over her hair and forcibly inserts a hatpin. She gazes at the album in my hand. "Fame will be like dust when you find yourself old and alone with nothing but that scrapbook of yours to console you."

"I have much living to do yet, Ma. Many more sculptures to add to my album."

With that, I hand her the book, grab the handle on the cage holding the trained dove I have borrowed, and head out to the two-wheeled gig I have hired, though we can scarcely afford either.

Twenty minutes later, we enter a long, narrow chamber lined with soaring columns. Cardinal Antonelli sits at the far end in a high, carved-back chair, his satin slipper-encased feet raised daintily on a stool.

I set the dove on my shoulder and approach, my head bent. He extends a beringed hand, and I bestow the required kiss.

With his fingers, he lifts my chin. I gaze into dark eyes impossible to read, inset above a stern, downturned mouth at odds with the cherubic ringlets haloing his face.

He says something.

His secretary bows and translates in Italian-flavored English. "The cardinal welcomes you. He is surprised at your youth and wonders at your reputation as a master sculptress."

"*Grazie mille*. It is a gift from God, Your Eminence."

The cardinal speaks again.

The secretary translates. "He would like to see some of your work."

"His Eminence is welcome to visit my studio anytime. But I have brought some photographs." I signal to my mother, who is frozen, either in shock or in awe of her surroundings, which is understandable—the cardinal's receiving room is richer than any king's. The artwork alone is some of the best in the world. His coat of arms is displayed everywhere.

The secretary offers the album to the cardinal. He thumbs through, then signals me to come closer. He holds up the photograph of Thaddeus Stevens' bust. "*Questo*?"

I know enough Italian to answer. "*Un grand uomo. Un caro amico. Senatore* Thaddeus Stevens." I take a breath. If I have learned nothing else in dealings with men, it is that you have to fawn, and you have to beg. I use my sweetest tone. "*Vorrei scolpire il cardinale per favore?*"

The cardinal nods and hands the album back. He flicks a finger at the Masonic pin Albert Pike gave me. "*Abominio.*"

The secretary whispers, "Remove the pin and step back."

His Eminence speaks privately to the secretary, then faces forward. If possible, his expression is sterner than before.

I stand rigid beside my mother, my breath tangled in my throat, the pin an unwanted weight in my pocket. Thanks to Pike, I have failed.

I coo to the dove and wait to be told to take my leave. Instead, the secretary signals for me to approach again.

This time, I bend my head even lower, ready to be scolded for my insolence.

With a solemn nod, the cardinal lifts a large cameo of Jesus on a braided gold chain. He wafts a finger, and I edge closer, so close I can see the individual gold stitches on his gown.

His secretary stands beside me. "His Eminence wishes to replace the pin. The Masonic order may do good deeds in your country, but not here."

The chain slips over my neck. The cameo settles on my breast. I enthuse my thanks with a low curtsy.

The secretary continues, "He also says he will visit your studio, and if your work is as shown in the album, he will consider a bust by the American angel."

I clasp my hands together, and at my whistle, the dove flutters up in the air above me. She swoops in a graceful arc and alights my outstretched wrist.

Cardinal Antonelli's stern face breaks into a smile. I have won him over. There will be money coming in.

I stroke the dove's head. Crisis averted.

For now.

Chapter 25

NOVEMBER 1871

ROME, ITALY

After two and a half years, it is time to leave Europe and head back to Washington. Gnawing my lip, I wrap up the last of my carving tools, pack them in my valise, then survey the nearly empty studio. So many wonderful memories. So many friends made. So many sculptures of my heart finished.

I write my name in the clay dust coating the worktable and head out to the carriage that will carry us to the station. From there, we'll cross the continent by train to London and board the ship that will ferry us back to the United States.

I'm leaving. But not willingly. If I could, I would hide away in some Italian mountain village, live on olives, bread, and cheese, and create the artworks I choose.

But I can't.

I gaze at my parents as I climb in next to them. They are all smiles. I smile back. Inside, my guts twist and knot. I can never tell them that in order to ship the *Lincoln* home and pay our fares, I have had to take out another huge loan. I will arrive in Washington City penniless and deeply in debt.

I take a last look at the Trevi Fountain as we pass by. One lira sitting on the bottom will never be enough to bring me back. I owe ten thousand dollars at six percent interest. An impossible sum. I may have completed an acclaimed work, but I will be so far in debt that I will be condemned to sculpting old men for the rest of my life.

As we travel north, the weather mirrors my mood. The Mediterranean November breeze, damp with drizzle, turns into icy blasts and bone-chilling snow squalls.

Ma pulls her shawl tighter around her. "I am so happy to be leaving." She pats my knee. "Not that we haven't had a bit of fun, what with counts and cardinals and all, my dear. But I can't wait to get home and see Mary and our little grandsons. Especially now that they are back in Washington."

I swallow a frown. They're back because Pike says Perry is running from the debt collectors.

I dread the answer but still ask, "Have you decided if you will take up Mary's invitation to live with her?"

Ma grins. "Yes. Pa and I agree that it is for the best. I can help Mary with the children, and Pa will not need to work full time anymore."

I glance at my father. He has been so much healthier and happier here. Already, I can see the gloom settling over him the further north we travel. He doesn't want to go back any more than I do. He fears what he will find there, too.

I cross my fingers and pray Mary is okay.

At Portsmouth, we board the *Abyssinia* for our crossing to New York. We leave the port in the teeming rain, our clothes soaked through, the wind icy. I huddle under the covers of my stateroom bed and sink into disturbed sleep. I dream of fetes and carnival, nights of conversation about art with the marmorean sculptresses, the music of Liszt, and the feel of Carrara marble beneath my chisel. All gone. All trapped in a book of clippings, a tiny journal, and a knot of longing.

I wake in the middle of the night. The ship bucks and twists, rolling me side to side in my bunk. It's as if I have been sucked into the craw of an angry beast, and now he is trying to regurgitate me.

Across the way, Ma groans and retches. I should go to her, but I fear to move. My own stomach clamors for the rocking to stop. I curl up into a ball.

Somewhere in the hold of another steamship, my light-hearted *Miriam* and *Spirit of Carnival*, my thoughtful *Sappho*, my ode to the West, and my debt-ridden *Lincoln* shake violently in the same storm. I picture delicate arms broken. Fine-fingered hands shattered. Faces chipped. The stone itself crushed to dust. My career upended and sinking to the bottom of the sea.

The ship jerks perilously to one side. I cry out.

A warm cloth brushes my brow. "There, there." My father, whose digestion has troubled him all his life, seems immune to the wild movement of the ship.

I claw at his hand. "Are we going to sink?"

"No. The captain says it's the tail end of a late tropical storm. We'll soon be in calmer water."

But the waters do not calm. My nightmares do not stop. I disembark in New York, sick and full of foreboding.

Albert Pike meets us at the pier. For once, I'm happy to let someone else take charge and put up with his over-the-top compliments and incessant talking. In desperation, I resort to napping on the train to Washington to escape his voice and my mother's nasty looks.

We arrive at the Washington depot in the dark of night. Pike gets our trunks loaded and settles my parents in a rented conveyance.

I hesitate. After paying for the train tickets, I have nothing left. I bury my distaste and ask Pike to pay the driver.

"Gladly. Taking care of you is my life's dream." Pike gives me that bird-in-the-mouth grin I hate so much and presses a wad of cash into my hand. As soon as we get to Mary's, I will see to it that the money is repaid. But with my parents grumpy and the rain pouring down, I dare not refuse the largess now.

I tip my head in thanks and rush to get into the carriage before he demands a kiss.

"Wait." He motions me aside. "I received this telegram. I suggest you read it in private. I kept it back so as not to distress the old folks."

I nod and slip it into my purse along with a lump of fear.

He comes in for a kiss, and I turn my head quickly, so he barely touches my cheek.

Albert raises an eyebrow. "Stop by when you are settled, my darling. I have written more poems."

Poems? I have a lot more to worry about than an old man's fantasies. I need money, and I need it fast. And the last person I am going to beg it from will be Pike, even if it means I must rely on Perry.

Ma watches him lumber down the platform as the carriage pulls away. "I have never thought ill of that man before, being a friend of Bobbie and all. But his behavior to you is outrageous, what with him married and near old enough to be your grandfather. I wanted to slap him senseless the way he sat so close and fondled your hand on the train."

I give her a wan smile. The wad of borrowed money in my purse irks. "Not to worry. I have no interest in Albert Pike."

Except paying him off.

We arrive at Mary's to find the mansion dark and locked. I stand in the rain and bang the door knocker, but no light comes on. No servant's footsteps hurry to the door. No child cries out.

Ma wrings her hands. "Mary's letter said she'd be here." Already, the old, familiar, on-edge grimace lines her face, the cheeriness of Rome winked out like a candle.

The telegram burns in my pocket. "I'm sure she is fine. Probably delayed in her travels." I survey the overloaded carriage. "Let's find rooms for the night, at least. Then make inquiries in the morning."

Luckily, Ma remembers that the Walkers, who lived across from our rooming house on North B Street, occasionally let rooms. Surely, her good friend would find space for us.

We arrive at their door and find a welcome at last.

After hot tea, a wash, and seeing Ma and Pa settled, I crawl into my narrow cot in the frosty attic storeroom and unfold the telegram. It's from Boudy.

I read the staccato words, each one a world of hurt: *Tobacco suit lost. Face arrest. Gone hunting with Bob and P. Fuller.*

I fold the paper over and over, then wedge it into a crack between the molding and the wall. This is what Boudy hoped to protect me from.

Come morning, I crawl out of bed and wiggle my way back into the travel-weary dress I'd worn yesterday. My Italian frocks are too light for winter, and all my Washington cold-weather wear and everything else we own is locked up in the Fuller mansion.

Downstairs, I join the family at the dining table, butter a piece of toast, and hunch beneath my mother's glare.

Ma's fingers tap the tabletop. "So, where are they?"

I avoid her eyes. "I don't know about Mary, but I do know where Perry is. He's gone hunting in Indian Territory."

She rears back. "Who told you that?"

"Alfred Pike. Yesterday."

"And you didn't say?"

"You were exhausted and wet. I felt getting a roof over our heads more important."

"Do you think he dragged Mary there?"

Pa catches her hand. "I have sent round to Sam Marshall. Remember, he promised to keep an eye on Mary and the children for us."

I blot my mouth on the napkin, thank my hostess, and then rise from the table. The last thing I need is Sam renewing his marriage proposal.

Ma swivels in her chair. "Where are you off to?"

"To check my sculptures. Figure out where to display them. I no longer have a studio."

She slams the table with her palms. "*You selfish little thing. It's always about you. Forget your stupid rocks. Finding my Mary is more important.*"

I blink against the welling tears. Mary has always been her favorite, but to hear it said aloud still hurts. I draw a breath to chide her.

Pa holds up his hands in the Plains hand sign for calm. "Let her go, Lavinia."

I tuck the hurt deep, flee the Walkers', and take the horsecar to the warehouse where my sculptures have been shipped.

The first thing to do is to get the *Lincoln*—if it is still in one piece—delivered to the Rotunda. Next, beg money from anyone I can and rent a place where I can display my classical ladies and perhaps sell one or two to support us.

I gaze at the silent Fuller house as the horsecar passes by. I have a feeling Perry is not going to save my finances nor care for my parents.

I will have to do it myself.

Chapter 26

The morning of January 12th dawns cold and overcast. After the sun of Italy, everything in Washington is gray. The buildings are gray. The sky is gray. My spirit is gray.

I sweep my dreary thoughts away. I am not in Rome anymore. I'm here. Today, I find out if I will be awarded the second half of my commission.

I drag myself up the steps of the Capitol and open the door. It is colder inside than outside. I wrap my coat tightly around me and wish myself back in Carrara, climbing the hillsides under a warm Italian sun. Rolling the shivers off my back, I enter the Rotunda. Arrayed before me are a bevy of congressmen—my jury.

I straighten my shoulders, plaster on a smile, and toss back my hair. My entire career hinges on what happens today. I must look like a conquering Athena, even if I feel like crawling into a hole in the ground.

Behind me traipse Ma and Pa, looking stunned, Mary looking like chiseled marble, and Perry, his face bloated like dough gone bad and smelling like a bottle of rotgut whiskey.

The absolute worst has happened. The Fullers have lost their fine mansion on 12th Street and are now crowded in with us in the small house I've taken on credit and on the good word of Congressman Daniel Voorhees. Our new abode is quite near our old one and equally as dingy, except for the parlor, which I have converted into a display room for my Italian marbles.

All except the *Lincoln*.

I approach the drapery-shrouded crate containing my sculpture and pray it has survived the Atlantic crossing in one piece.

Men rush toward me. I shove my worries somewhere deep inside and turn on the charm. What came naturally just weeks ago now must be plastered together.

I remove my coat, pinch my frozen cheeks, and spread my curled hair artistically across my shoulders. I widen my eyes till they feel like they are popping from my face. Then I fashion my lips into a cute little smile and reach out to shake the hands of the former acquaintances of Lincoln come to judge my work against the man they remember.

Secretary of the Interior Columbus Delano loops his arm in mine and introduces me to some of the new faces while workmen hammer and bang behind the drape.

Every whack reignites my shivers, and I regret removing my coat.

The hammering stops at last. A house usher appears and hands me the pulley rope. Voices hush around me. The movement in the audience stills. I hesitate, my pulse pounding. I really do not want my *Lincoln* exposed to the glare of these eyes. I dread hearing the cries of outrage from all Lincoln's friends.

But, like a relentless ocean wave, the unveiling proceeds. I tug on the rope. The velvet curtain slowly rises. Bit by bit, the base emerges. Then the deeply chiseled name of our lost President. Then the shoes. Then the trousers with their hint of bone and muscle beneath. Then the waistcoat, buttons, shirt placket, and beard.

In some strange act of heaven, rays of sunlight pierce the high-arched windows encircling the dome just as the curtain completes its uplift. Lincoln's face is revealed, his head haloed in the light. P. T. Barnum couldn't have set the stage better.

I hand off the rope, clasp my hands together, and wait for the groans. The insults. The accusations.

Instead, there is silence.

Beside me, my staunchest ally, Pa, claps. Others join in. The applause ripples outward. It isn't thunderous, merely polite. It dies down as does the spot of sun.

The faces around me blur. I wipe my unexpectedly wet eyes. There are too many newsmen here for me to break down. I catch a glimpse of the door, surprised at how close it is. I must leave before I melt into a puddle of tears.

Before I can, someone grabs my hand.

"America's Prairie Sculptress, Vinnie Ream."

This time, the applause drums, bouncing off the walls, filling the space with the clattering sound. I blink up at the man holding my hands—Secretary Delano—and curtsy.

"You have done it," he says. "Captured the true man. Humble. Beneficent. Thoughtful."

Everything inside me realigns. I'm saved. It doesn't matter what any would-be art critic or nasty newsman says. With the secretary who knew Lincoln personally pleased with my work, I'm guaranteed the second half of my ten-thousand-dollar commission.

Now all I need do is find the money to pay off the other half of my loan.

Our celebration dinner should have been full of laughter and good cheer. Instead, we huddle around the battered table Pa has rigged up in the mud-brown dining room and stare at each other.

"There's no money?" Perry asks for the second time.

I jerk my head back and forth. From the tone of his voice, you'd think I drove a chisel through his heart.

"Idiot. How could you have spent it all?"

"As I said, it costs money to buy marble and ship sculptures across the Atlantic."

"And harps, dammit."

"And *harps*." I throw my napkin at my plate and wish it had been Perry's head. "The Lincoln commission money is mine. I do not owe an accounting to you or anybody."

Ma slaps the table. "Vinnie. He's family."

I turn on her. I can't hide his misdeeds any longer. "He's a crook, Ma. Lied and stole all his life. Our fine brother-in-law has millions of dollars of debt. The federal government is charging him with stealing goods at the Port of New Orleans. He's being chased by creditors. So much so, he spent the last month hiding out in Indian Territory."

I turn back to Perry. "I imagine the only reason you came back to Washington at all is to get your hands on my money."

My mother rises to her feet. "Who told you these lies?"

"Albert Pike, Boudy, Sam Marshall, and half the Senate. Everyone knows. Perry's exploits have been in the newspapers."

Pa thumps his whiskey glass down. "Sit, Lavinia. Vinnie is speaking the truth. Many of the letters she received this last year mentioned Perry's growing money troubles. I advised her not to tell you." He looks directly at Perry. "I'd hoped you would have straightened out your financial problems for the sake of Mary and your children by now."

Perry squints at me. "I intend to. Just need a bit to tide Mary and the children over for a while. A small loan. That's all." He folds his hands like a pious schoolboy.

I look across at my sister. She must have known what Perry was doing. But Mary's face is stained with tears, her hands hanging like broken wings.

I will regret my next words, but I can't bear the hurt on my sister's face. "Mary, the children, and the nursemaid can stay with us while you take care of your money problems." I tip my chin at Perry. "But you, brother-in-law, I want you out of this house, right now."

Ma shakes her fist at me. "Vinnie, you have no right to chase Perry from our home. Think of his family."

Mary grabs Perry's hand. "Please listen to Ma. He's sick, Vinnie. You can't put him out in the cold."

Pa's mouth forms a tight smile. "Be kind, Vinnie. It *is* cold out tonight."

Not cold enough. I want to say that I am paying the rent on the house and getting deeper in debt to Pike every day. I want to say that the only sickness Perry has is from the bottom of a liquor bottle. I want to say that if he stays in the house, he will steal what little we have.

I run my hand along the gold chain holding the cardinal's cameo and resolve not to take it off until he's gone.

But I can't fight them all.

I get up from the table and start gathering up the dishes. "Fine. He can stay."

I use my hip to open the door to the kitchen. It will be a long while before we can afford a servant again.

Chapter 27

REAM ROOMING HOUSE, WASHINGTON, D.C.

With those bald truths hanging over us, the family settles in for the night. At the back of the house, Perry and Mary occupy the largest bedroom, Ma and Pa having relegated themselves to what was once a narrow sewing room. It is not the way I would have arranged it, but Ma wouldn't hear of anything different.

My own bedroom lies at the front of the house. Tonight, it is no place of repose. The room is overcrowded with a cobbled-together cot for me and small pallets on the floor for Alfred and little Perry, whom I've taken to calling Perrikin to avoid using his rotten father's name.

Despite my worries and fears, I fall into a dead sleep, only to awaken during the night to find Perrikin nestled against me, sucking his thumb. Outside my door, Perry-the-Crook stumbles down the hall.

I run my fingers over the toddler's baby-fine hair and wait. The back bedroom door opens and shuts, Mary's voice rises and falls, the words indistinguishable, the tone on edge. Perry grunts. Then the house goes silent.

The clatter of a bottle hitting the floor comes just as I'm falling back asleep. I shake myself fully awake. Did I imagine it?

I scan the room. Alfred lies buried under his blanket. Little Perrikin's eyes are closed, a drop of drool in the corner of his open mouth. No sound comes from the back bedroom. All is as it should be.

I curl back under the quilt but can't settle back to sleep. My debts hang over me like the guillotine we saw in Paris. I twist and turn again and again. I sit up. By dawn, I will have worn myself to a nub.

All my life, Ma doused me with heavily sweetened chamomile tea on sleepless nights. I hated it as a child, but now the thought entices.

I slip quietly out from under the covers so as not to disturb Mary's babe, throw on an Italian silk robe, too reminiscent of happier days, and head downstairs.

Halfway down, the shadowy bulk of Perry Fuller suddenly struggles upright in front of me. No longer the trim, self-assured man my sister married, he seesaws back and forth on the steps.

"She . . . she's locked the bedroom door," he wheezes, swilling his foul breath over me.

I smack my hand over my nose and back up a step. "I don't blame her. You're reeking drunk. Go sleep on the kitchen floor, like the thieving cur you are."

"*Cur*?" For a moment, he totters, then catches hold of the railing and hauls himself upright. "You little upstart." Spittle flies from his mouth. "*I* made you what you are. It was my idea to spread that crazy story of a sixteen-year-old who sculpted Lincoln from life. *Sixteen* when you were near twenty. Got you all that fame and fortune. Financed your first bronze works. You owe me." He swings his arm out and seizes my cameo. "Look at this thing. Worth a fortune. Give it over." He yanks hard.

"No." I twine my fingers in the chain and jerk back. There is no strength in him. The cameo slips from his hand.

He swipes wildly at it again. But I'm ready.

"No." I push, and down he goes, flipping and flopping, landing with a *thud* in a silent heap at the bottom of the staircase, his limbs splayed out, froth welling from between his lips.

I scream, but my chest is constricted so tight I can make no sound. I clutch my throat and force out a hoarse whisper. "Perry?"

I tiptoe down the stairs, touch his hand, repeat his name, and am met by silence. Deep, dark, dead silence.

"He's dead?"

I spin around.

Mary stands at the top of the stairs, holding a candle, her face as pale as Carrara marble, her eyes heavily shadowed.

A chill runs through me. Have I killed the man she loves?

"I don't . . ."

Back straight, chin tipped up, a Mary I do not recognize puts a finger to her lips. "Hush."

I draw back against the wall as she glides down the staircase. Her cashmere dressing gown from wealthier times sweeps across my bare feet, sending tendrils of fear snaking through me. Like a ministering angel, she kneels over the body, loosening the collar, straightening his head, smoothing back his hair. She lowers her head to kiss his brow. In the flickering candlelight, his face has a greenish shine.

"May he rest in peace. Now,"—her eyes bore into mine— "Perry Fuller will not bother you anymore. He won't bother anyone anymore." The words clang with bitter finality.

Mary rises. "Now help me get his body upstairs. Grab his feet."

"Upstairs? Feet?" I clasp the cameo to my chest with trembling hands. "He . . . he was drunk. He tugged on my pendant. I barely pushed. He only fell a few steps. How could he be dead?"

"Well, he is. Quite dead." Mary pokes him in the side with her toe. "It's not your fault. I told you he was sick. Deathly sick. I made sure of it."

Little prickles of fear grow inside me. "Mary, what have you done?"

She steeples her hands, reminding me of the sculptures of praying saints I saw in the European cathedrals, and taps her chin with the tips of her pressed-together fingers. "I helped him on his way, and you finished him off. You'll see. It's better this way. For you. For me. For us all."

My heart thumps slowly in my chest as if it's turned to lead. "You . . . *helped*?"

She nods in slow motion. "Perry loved that rat-gut whiskey more than me. So, I knew just what to do. Remember in the old place, how Ma dealt with the rats?"

The fear in my belly spreads outward.

Later, after we have hauled Perry's corpse up the stairs, tucked him into bed, and announced to our parents and the world that he has passed from a heart attack, I look for the bottle. But whatever Mary did with it, it's gone, leaving me with another debt to pay and a secret to carry to my grave.

Twelve days later, Perry Fuller is buried in the ground, and I'm back at the Capitol, putting on the performance of my life. Tonight, January 25th, my *Lincoln* will be revealed to the public, and despite the snow, everyone in the city has come.

I glare at the men pushing past me and tighten my hold on Ma.

She mumbles through her mourning veil, "See, you have nothing to worry about. Your *Lincoln* will be much adored."

She is right about the *Lincoln*, but not about my worries. Not everyone has just helped her sister murder her husband.

Near the west entrance of the Capitol, I veer away from the mobbed steps and head to the entrance usually reserved for senators. Today is my day to be Queen of Washington, even though I would give anything to be little Vinnie Ream, dangling her feet in the Arkansas River.

I force myself to smile and flirt with the dignitaries gathered to honor me. My white Paris over-jacket hides my black mourning well. My white hat, with its one ostrich feather, a loan from my sister, perches jauntily on my head. The recriminating cardinal's cameo adds just the right touch of elegance and piety. Perhaps it will be enough to distract the reporters from the failures of my *Lincoln* and the guilt contorting my face.

We join the other dignitaries entering the Rotunda from the Senate wing and ascend to the platform. Holding my arm, Senator Morrill guides me and my mother to the seats closest to my sculpture. A giant flag, a gift from the French weavers of Lyons, hides the statue from view.

I am barely seated when the doors open. People of all classes and races surge in from the east and west entrances, filling every measure of space. Too many. In minutes, the military guards are forced to slam the doors shut against the surging crowd.

Then, despite the banging and muffled yells of those left outside, the Marine Band begins a slow dirge, the funeral tones a fitting reminder of Lincoln's unwarranted death.

Tears stream down the faces of many in the crowd. Ma wipes her eyes behind her partially lifted veil. My own eyes fill with grief for the kind man with the weight of war on his shoulders and for my sister, who was driven to do the unthinkable. I blink the wetness away.

The music ends, and then Senator Morrill introduces me.

"A little girl from Wisconsin, who occupied a small place in the post office department . . . who had faith she could do something better . . ."

At his signal, Supreme Court Judge Davis pulls the gold-tasseled rope, and the flag rises. *Lincoln* is revealed. This time, there is no hesitation. No need for my missing Pa, lying sick at home, to draw forth accolades with his gentle clapping. The applause that rises around me is *thunderous*.

Lost in grief, I hear little of the rest of the speeches in praise of the statue and in praise of the man. The applause barely registers as I'm brought forward on the platform and displayed to the crowd like some American treasure. I can't even feel the blood trickling through my veins. I am so cold, so sad, so tired.

Accolades over, I shrink back to my seat. A last few words are spoken, and it is done.

My mother crowds next to me, her expression happier than I have seen since her beloved son-in-law's death. Being made much of by President Grant and the most important men in the nation will do that to most anyone, even Ma.

She squeezes my hand. "Those two senators behind us were arguing over whether you belong to Michigan or Wisconsin. Set them straight on that, I did. Wisconsin was where you were born."

Was it? Playing on the porch of a log cabin seems so long ago. My heart says the prairie. My soul says Rome. My business sense says here. But one thing is certain: I don't belong in Wisconsin. I am no longer that barefoot, happy child playing in the mud or racing my pony over the hills.

Ma pokes me in the ribs. "Cheer up. Look at how much they like it."

Delivery boys swarm in and out, burying the base of my *Lincoln* in flowers and wreaths sent by friends and admirers who were not able to attend.

Representative Voorhees, his cherubic wife in tow, comes to whisper in my ear, "Alfred Pike did not come. I'm so relieved."

The last person I'm concerned about at the moment is Albert Pike.

"I didn't notice." I keep my tone sweet.

Voorhees has been a great help to Mary in these last few weeks, untangling Perry's nonexistent assets, helping to sell her belongings, purchasing a cemetery plot, and helping me find a physician to aver that Fuller died of a heart attack.

Voorhees whispers in my ear, "Pike is a poisonous swamp of southern sympathies and belief in the superiority of the white race. You are America's Cinderella now. Look at all the freedmen in the crowd. Keep yourself out of the mess in the South. Avoid that blackguard at all costs."

I give a lackluster wave of my hand. Albert Pike will do as he wishes, as will I . . . once I pay him off.

A man stops in front of me. I look up into familiar brown eyes and a rigid face—General Sherman. My once-upon-a-time knight in shining armor is back.

He bows and kisses the back of my gloved hand. "Miss Ream, may I escort you and your mother home?"

My lips form their first genuine smile of the night. "Oh, yes. Please." I cling to him like a wet piece of clay as we march through the crowd, not stopping for the reporters or slowing to shake the thousands of outstretched hands.

On the way home, I nod off in the carriage. General Sherman carries me in and lays me on the sofa in the parlor. I think he kisses me chastely on the lips. I do not hear him leave, but I do not forget his scent of fresh mint and leather.

Tomorrow, the newsmen and women will take up their cries of fraud, abomination, and failure, and the absurd claim that ten thousand girls could do better.

Tomorrow, I will rise and write a poem to Lincoln, who has given me so much, and then put my hopes and dreams behind me.

I promised to support my parents. Now I must support my sister and her children, as well. Tomorrow, I must figure out how.

Chapter 28

FEBRUARY 1871

REAM ROOMING HOUSE, WASHINGTON, D.C.

All things can be borne, I discover, especially when you keep frantically busy. I fold and slide my poem about Lincoln into my album. I will read it tonight at my first salon, along with the letter from Harriet Hosmer praising my *Lincoln* and countering the charge that I hired an Italian dabbler in sculpture to carve it for me.

But that is for later.

I head downstairs and join the family at the dining table. It is a study in gray and black, the day dark, the people I love most in the world still garbed in black for a man who deserves no remembrance.

Mary, her face swollen, either from weeping or guilt-ridden sleep, sits at the far end of the table in Ma's usual place. Our parents sit on either side.

I hesitate, then take Pa's chair at the opposing end. I press my hands to my temples. When did I become head of the family?

I study my father. He looks worse than before we left on our European tour. His skin has lost its Italian tan. His slicked-back hair reveals a growing bald spot. He looks old and lost.

Mary blots her nose. "I have no idea how I am going to survive." She crushes the hankie in her hand. "According to the documents Daniel Voorhees just delivered, there'll be no money left for me to live on after Perry's debts are paid off."

Pa tips his head. "Surely, the sale of his properties and businesses will provide something?"

"Everything was mortgaged or bought on credit." Her entire body shakes. "The creditors already cleaned out the Lawrence house and our residence in New Orleans, I'm told. Oh, Ma, all my beautiful things are gone—the furniture, my dresses, my jewelry. All I have is what I brought with me when we came here."

Ma pats her hand. "The most beautiful thing in your possession is your child and little Alfred."

"My poor child. You know what Perry's four Keithley offspring have done? Put a lien on the New York house. Their lawyer says any money left in the estate should go to them first, as their inheritance."

Pa clicks his tongue. "Smart move. Can't begrudge them that, Mary. The younger ones are still in school."

"But my child will get nothing. Absolutely nothing. Who will pay for his schooling?"

I hate to see her in distress.

I clear my throat. "I'll make sure things work out for your little Perrikin, Mary."

"How? Are you going to make all the dollars you wasted on stupid sculptures carved by Italian brutes reappear by magic?"

My pulse rises. After what we shared, I did not expect to be attacked so cruelly by my own sister.

I open my mouth to snap back, but Pa interrupts.

"I know you are grieving, Mary, but be kind. Vinnie worked hard on those sculptures. Her *Lincoln* is a masterpiece. I am exceedingly proud of her."

"Fine. I accept that Vinnie is a talented artist, but being a sculptress is no way to make a living. Nothing is left of her commission, and Daniel says she has a mountain of debt."

He waves his hand dismissively. "We won't starve. Ma and I—we have struggled most of our lives. I will reapply for my cartography job at the Department of the Interior. Ma can take in boarders again."

My mother looks at him. "There are only three bedrooms, Robert."

"Mary, Vinnie, and the children can share the back room. We can stay in the small bedroom. That frees the front room."

Ma's mouth twists, then settles. "Pa's right; one boarder or a couple could pay a good part of the rent. I would take in laundry and mending, but my fingers are too stiff for that work. Maybe I can bake pies to sell at one of the shops."

I gaze at my parents' aged faces, embarrassed by their willingness to take up a burden they'd thought lifted. I can't let this happen. I promised to take care of them and give them rest in their old age. And my sister . . . I can't bear to think of the hell she must have been living in that she would be driven to poison her husband.

I clench my hands. If he weren't dead, I'd tear Fuller limb from limb for his crimes.

Mary drags a finger across the tablecloth. "I guess I could go back to clerking. Though I hear it pays half what it did during the war."

Despite my debt to Pike and the bankers, I have to do something. "Maybe the new Corcoran Gallery will buy my Sappho, or one of the other pieces will sell."

"And maybe they won't." Mary gives me a dour look. "They haven't yet."

"I have the cartes de visite. They're doing well."

Ma wags a finger. "And Matthew Brady to pay for them. The bill came yesterday."

The door knocker raps. I rush to escape.

Senator Trumbull looms in the doorway, hat over his breast, his expression as solemn as a pallbearer at a funeral. "I have grave news."

I still, breath trapped in my throat. Who else has died?

"Your *Lincoln* was damaged in moving it to Statuary Hall."

"*My Lincoln?*" The words sink in. I picture shattered marble. Years of work turned to dust. "*Damaged? How?*"

"The scroll with the *Emancipation Proclamation* has broken off."

My muscles tense. I swallow hard. Harriet had warned me about it—I should have listened. "Who ordered it moved without my being there? Wait,"—I slap my hands over my ears—"don't tell me. I am sure he is sorry."

Trumbull nods. "I have a carriage outside if you wish to see what can be done."

"I'll be right there." I grab my shawl, bury the dread that I can do nothing deep inside me, and then dash back into the dining room. "I have to go to the Capitol. They've damaged the *Lincoln.*"

Everyone rises, but it is Mary who pushes past and hugs me tight. In that moment, I know, despite everything, she still loves me.

"I will see if it can be fixed." I gaze at the shocked faces. "And I will ask Congress for more money."

Pa shakes his head. "I don't think—"

"It has to be possible." I twist my hands together. I thought my begging days done. "They gave Clark Mills another five-thousand-dollar bonus for his *Liberty.* And now with the damage—how can they refuse me?"

I throw on a shawl and head to the door. Besides, it's only right that the government bear the true cost of the statue, not my elderly parents and a mourning widow.

So, despite being called a fraud and my *Lincoln* an abomination in the press, I put on my French wrap, my walking shoes, and my courage, and haunt the offices of every congressman I know. And it works. The five-thousand-dollar bonus gifted to me by Congress pays off some of my ever-growing debt and relieves some of the pressure on the family, but not all.

So, when the Corcoran Gallery turns down my *Spirit of the Carnival,* and my nighttime efforts to repair the broken proclamation leave me frustrated and exhausted, I flee Washington.

If I could, I would jump the first steamer going anywhere and forge a new life. But I will not stop until every debt is paid and Ma and Pa can rest again. Instead, I land in New York City in search of rich clients and find one—Ezra Cornell, of Western Union fame.

I hustle into my tiny studio on Broadway, straighten the stacks of cartes de visite—the only thing bringing in a bit of money—and uncover my marbles: *Miriam*, the *Indian Girl*, *Spirit of the Carnival*, and *Sappho*. Then the busts: *Lincoln*, *America*, *Lily*, and the one I am working on—Cornell's.

I spin around, make sure everything is dustless, and then turn the sign on the door to "*Open.*" I feel like some shopkeeper selling shoes, not a grand sculptress that some of the kinder newspapers have dubbed "*America 1871.*"

Cornell arrives just minutes later. I sit him in the client chair and study his face. In his late sixties, Ezra's visage shows the wear and tear of a man who has worked hard all his life. He will be a challenge. I uncover the wet clay armature and begin.

Modeling rich old men—their brows furrowed, their noses and ears elongated by age—is not work I can put much passion into, but listening to them talk about their lives makes up for the lack of inspiration.

I hold up my pencil and take a measure. "Will you be long in the city this time?"

Ezra shrugs. "The construction at the villa in Ithaca has run into some snags. So, hurry up with this bust thing. I need to return home."

"I'm doing my best. Turn a little to the right, please." I scoop up some clay and knead it between my fingers. I have no idea how I will create a unified image for his bust. His grayed hair is long and unruly from constantly running his hands through it. His dark beard, shot with gray, on the other hand, is a mass of tight curls more suited to a wild Viking.

He grunts. "As Ben Franklin said, 'Time is money.'" His beard catches on his collar as he shakes his head. "Speaking of money, I've been looking at the accounts you asked me to peruse. You have no head for finances, young lady."

Isn't that the truth.

I bite the inside of my lip. I should never have given him my accounts. Ezra Cornell is a grandfatherly man with huge ears, good for listening, and a kind smile. But at this moment, he is not the grandfather I want. He's going to give me a hard time about my lack of money.

I lift my tool. "How could I? Schools for young ladies don't teach us about interest on loans, or how it multiplies when you don't pay them off on time." I wave my hand at my display of sculptures, standing clean and white against the black and maroon velvet backdrops. "They did teach me about art."

Ezra snorts. I watch his beard move again and dab on some more clay.

"I looked at what you call account books. Nothing adds up."

I pretend to pout. "I can do my sums."

"Not the sums. I am referring to what you are spending those sums on. You have this studio here in New York, but you just signed a mortgage on a three-story edifice on Pennsylvania Avenue in Washington. You can't afford both. Actually, you can't afford either."

"My parents, my sister, and her boys need a bigger place to live, and it was great luck to find a spot on the main thoroughfare. If we reside nearer to the Capitol, my mother can take in more boarders and charge double." I take a breath. "Besides, after I sell you my *Sappho*, the *Lincoln* bust, and you pay for this grand work of art I'm creating for you, the accounts will look better."

He scrunches up his face. "All right. I'll take the *Lincoln* for the college in Ithaca. But not the *Sappho*, not now. Too classical, I think—need to read about the lady. Instead, I'll organize your finances for you."

"And loan me the money for the first mortgage payment?"

"I am not a bank, Vinnie."

"No. You're Western Union. Good as a bank."

"I'm retired. Just having fun with my last years."

I dab on more clay. "I'm having fun, too."

"Are you? Sometimes, it is hard to tell."

I chew my lower lip. Of all my clients, Ezra understands me the best. I can talk with him and be honest about my feelings and problems. He genuinely cares. He's not overwhelmed with himself despite his multiple successes in life. Unlike every other man I know, he's not out to crush someone less fortunate, and most importantly, he doesn't want or need anything from me. Even with his millions, Ezra Cornell is still the easy-going salesman who hawked plows to farmers across New England. When I'm with him, I am still the girl who grew up running barefoot through prairie grass. We are that good of friends.

I work at taming the hair I've just molded. "I have my worries. And regrets."

"You are too young to have regrets. Save them for the old buzzards like—"

Ding. The shop bell rings.

We both look toward the door. Two men jostle into the studio, laughing and slapping each other's backs.

"There she is, just like I told you," the taller one proclaims, palm out, ready to collect his winnings. "Pay up, Hall."

Ezra turns around completely and narrows his eyes. "Charles Hall?"

The loser doffs his hat. "One and the same."

"I've heard you speak about the Arctic and the Inuit. It's amazing how people survive in such cold."

"Oh my." I wipe my hands on a damp rag and hold out my hand. "You are from the Polaris Expedition heading to the North Pole. Vinnie Ream, how may I help you, gentlemen?"

Charles Hall beams at me. "Had a bet with Bessels here that he couldn't find the most beautiful woman in the city." He drops a kiss on my cheek, then picks up the Matthew Brady photo of me with my hair flowing down my back. "But it was too easy. That portrait in the window is a pretty big clue."

"Charmed." Hall's compatriot kisses my hand. "Dr. Emil Bessels at your service. Would you—"

"Join us for luncheon at Delmonico's," Hall inserts.

Ezra smiles. "Well, Miss Ream, seems you have found some young admirers for your midday repast. I should be going." He rises.

I look at the two explorers. They are the kind I try to avoid—self-satisfied males. The world at their feet. Sucking up air and space. Ready to go make names for themselves that will be remembered through all history. All they see before them is a woman to conquer. A woman to fight over. A woman to leave behind.

I will not be that woman.

"Ezra," I say, "if the gentlemen don't mind, please join us."

Two pairs of eyes narrow.

I bow slightly. "Gentlemen, this is inventor Ezra Cornell. Former president of Western Union, founder of Cornell College, and an explorer in his own way." I slip my arm into his. "Now, let's go learn more about the polar lands."

We step outside and clutch our hats against the furnace-like wind buffeting down Broadway. I ignore the traffic, the people rushing past, the come-hither smiles of the two intrepid explorers, and count off the days until I can go home to Washington to stay.

Part 4
1872 to 1878

"I have worked in my studio not envying kings in their splendor; my mind to me was my kingdom and my work more than diamonds and rubies."

Vinnie Ream

From an address given to the International Council of Women, 1909.

Chapter 29

JANUARY 1872

THE STUDIO, PENNSYLVANIA AVENUE, WASHINGTON,

D.C.

By the beginning of the new year, I'm back in Washington. Still in debt. Still struggling. But hopeful.

Mary rearranges the small models on the fireplace mantel, then steps back and peruses the room. "Vinnie, you've outdone yourself. The studio looks so elegant. But are you sure you can afford such ostentation?"

I can't, but I nod my head in the affirmative. "I have to look successful if I want people to pay the money I am asking now—a thousand dollars for a bust."

My sister's eyes widen. "You plan to charge that much?"

I smooth down my garnet satin dress with its modish train. Mary has the running of the boarding house now. I owe her the truth.

I peer out the window at the carriages passing by, then draw close the heavy velvet draperies. "I've taken a great risk. This house's location is perfect—at the hub of commerce, but near enough to Jouvenal's marble works that the public will find me. But I need to cover the mortgage, and it takes me two months to complete a plaster bust."

Mary wipes her hands on her apron. "I am sorry you've had to support me and the children. I wish I could find more than part-time work at the Interior Department."

We have never spoken of the day Perry died, but we have grown closer over the past year.

I throw my arms around her. "You do plenty. Caring for Ma and Pa. Keeping the house for us. After what you have been through, you shouldn't have to struggle so." I hug her tight. "You're my sister. Sisters take care of each other. I'm just glad that I am able to help. Hopefully, I'll make enough so you won't have to work at all." I kiss her cheek, then take in my new studio showroom.

Mary is right. I have gone overboard. Dear Ezra would not be happy with the way I have spent his money.

Large mirrors reflect the gaslight from the newly installed lamps and give multiple views of my sculptures. Thick Turkey carpets in intricate designs silence footsteps and add to the richness of the maroon velvet draperies.

My piano, guitar, and harp sit invitingly in the corner. George Healy's Italian portrait of me hangs prominently over the mantel. My sculptures peer out from atop fluted columns. Yes, I have spent too much. But the result is breathtaking.

Down the hall lie my other two rooms. Much simpler, the first is for my clients to pose in privacy. The back room is for the muddy, dusty work I spend most of my time doing. The work I love.

I run my hand over my newest, most saleable creation—a lighthearted *Rip Van Winkle*, modeled on the actor Joseph Jefferson. All around me are my busts—Lincoln, of course, but also a group of innocent children—the first, a young girl, *Sensibility*, and the other, the Architect of the Capitol and good friend, Edward Clark's twins, their heads turned toward each other, laughing.

Those sell. Everyone wants me to capture the charm of their little ones.

I glance over at my *Sappho*. They do not want my bare-breasted ladies displayed in their living quarters.

Mary runs a dust cloth over the glass case near the doorway containing the delicately folded hands of Jessie Benton Fremont, completed in Rome. "Are you sure you want him up front?" She points her chin toward my newly finished bust of Captain James Eads, the celebrated engineer who built the ironclads and is in the midst of constructing the first bridge across the Mississippi.

I pat the top of his head. "I agree he is not the handsomest of men, but neither are most of my clients. Besides, I like the challenge of modeling a face that has character."

Mary stops her polishing. "Didn't work out so well with Horace Greeley. He hated your bust of him. Been destroying your reputation in the *Tribune* ever since. What will you do if he becomes president?"

"It was one of my first works, and I admit I didn't do my best. It wasn't his character that was the problem. It was the truth I didn't disguise—I made him too fat. I have made amends. I worked his face in clay at the Institute Fair in New York as one of my demonstrations to prove that all this work is by my own hands. The *Tribune* reporter who'd challenged me was impressed."

Mary gazes around. "So, where's his bust?"

"Back in the clay bin. No one wanted to buy the old owl. If Greeley becomes president, I can remake it as a gift."

I take up the engraved plaque sitting on a side table. All that is left to do is set my sign in the window and wait for the arrivals at my first Wednesday salon.

The door knocker clacks.

"Someone's early. I'll send them away." My sister disappears into the front hall.

Lilly Pike's glowing face appears around the corner. "Welcome home, Vinnie. So glad you're finally back. I brought you a present."

There is movement behind her. For a moment, I'm afraid it is her father. I am in no mood for his overbearing love poems.

She turns her back to me and bends down. "Now, don't be shy." She pushes a young boy of, perhaps, eleven forward. He's bright-eyed with a winsome grin. "This is Zachariah. He's been doing odd jobs for me. But he's as smart as a swamp fox, and I'm thinking he could mind the door for you during your salons. Let visitors in, take their cards. Leave you free to do what you do best—smile, make small talk, and sing. All he needs is a quarter plus the tips."

"What a wonderful idea." I cast a stern look at him. "I am Miss Vinnie Ream, the sculptress. People come from all over the country to see my work. Most will be sightseers. I'm interested in those who will make a purchase. In addition to being my doorkeeper, could you listen to what people say and let me know who might be a client? For everyone who orders a sculpture, I will give you an extra quarter."

The boy squinches up his nose and grins, then doffs his cap and bows. "Of course, miss. I have seen your *Lincoln*. Such a tiny lady to make such a giant wonder. I would be most pleased to assist."

I smile. I can hear Albert's training in his diction.

There's a knock on the door.

I shake his hand. "Well then, I guess you can start immediately."

The first arrival is the one man I don't want to see. Boudy strides into the salon. In town to petition Congress to redress his loss before the Supreme Court, he sucks up the space and the air. He surveys the room as if looking for hidden enemies. Then his gaze lands on me.

We stare at each other. I have no words. A drowned coin and an ocean lie between us. Neither of us is supposed to be here.

He refused me. I refused him.

His face softens for a moment. I turn mine away.

Lilly comes between us and clasps his hand. "Cornelius, you've been a bad boy. Haven't come around to see my papa in weeks." She leads him off, and I can breathe again.

Mary holds up a questioning finger. I signal *later* and rush to greet the next arrival, my dear Will, the imposing General Sherman, in full uniform.

He beams at me and takes my gloved hand in his. The wide smile turns his usually stern expression into something slightly impolite. "So glad you're back in the city, Vinnie. You must come for a carriage ride with me tomorrow."

I catch Boudy's frown out of the corner of my eye and force myself to focus on Sherman's twinkly brown eyes instead. "That would be delightful."

He leads me to the musical instruments. "Now you must sing for me. I have missed that shining voice."

I ignore the guitar and sit on the piano stool, trying not to remember another time I perched on it with a man hovering behind me. I extend my hands over the keys and search my mind for a piece free of memories. But there are none.

I shuffle through the sheet music on top of the piano and find an unfamiliar one. "Here. A new work by Liszt. We met in Rome . . ." My fingers fumble on the keys. I don't want to think about Rome. I play the opening chords too loudly to hide the catch in my throat.

Sheet music is the wrong choice. Boudy turns his back to me and stares at old *Rip van Winkle*. But every time Will leans in to flip the pages, bringing with him the scent of warm wool and horse, I can feel the man I still love flinch.

It's not just jealousy. It is the general's blue uniform. In his heart, Boudy is still a rebel. And that may be the biggest barrier of all.

I get to the end of the piece and bow my head. I don't want this regret to be between us. I arise, foist Sherman off on Mary, and tap Boudy on the shoulder.

He spins around.

I hold out my hand. "I'm sorry. It is good to see you."

He kisses the air above my wrist like some stranger. I let out a breath. He is being noble. Any passion he still retains for me is firmly under control.

His brow creases. "I have done as I promised."

I blink. "Promised?"

He hands me a map. "I have founded a town in your name: Vinitas. It lies near the center of the country in the upper northeastern corner of Indian Territory. It will be a rail hub for the Missouri, Kansas-Texas, and Atlantic-Pacific lines—the crossroads of America. I have put you on the map, my love. Thousands of people will pass through your town every day."

I wince at the "my love" but strain to hide it.

Sherman comes up behind me. Being male. Staking claim. Everyone knows that Boudy and I have a history.

I touch my tongue to my bottom lip. What do you say when someone dedicates a *town* to you?

I settle on formality, despite the longing flooding my body like a summer rain shower or perhaps a prairie thunderstorm.

"I appreciate the honor. Will you be living there?"

He shakes his head. "My interests lie here for now. I have taken a residence in the city. I've a clerkship with the Senate committee on railroads."

I imagine myself encased in cold plaster. "So, we will be seeing each other, I suppose."

"As you wish."

I twist one of my curls and avoid looking into his eyes. I'd prefer to know when we will meet rather than have unexpected encounters.

"Every Wednesday at seven, I will hold a literary and musical salon for my friends." I spin around and smile at Sherman. It is like pulling away from a magnet. "You're invited, too, William."

Lilly pokes my upper arm. "Have you met General George Armstrong Custer and his wife, Elizabeth?"

I turn away from the two men and focus on the famous couple.

"Call me Libby," Custer's wife says, offering her hand.

Elizabeth Custer is wind-chapped, broad-browed, and has a handshake as firm as my own. She brings the relaxed attitude of one who has spent many years in the West among hard men.

I like her and her husband immediately, especially when they giggle together over the possibility of my creating a bust of the general, though both agree to much merriment that it would not do for their temporary quarters in Kentucky.

Custer grins. "One of my wolfhounds would maul it, for sure."

Libby snorts behind her gloved hand. "Those beasts. The bane of Louisville's farmers. Nothing is safe from them. More likely, they'd eat it."

I glance at General Custer. "You have a wolfhound? I have heard they are quite protective."

Libby claps her hands and laughs. "He has over eighty wolfhounds and a stable of all-black thoroughbreds."

Custer twirls his excessive blond mustache. "The horses are reserved for my officers. But the dogs are quite prolific. Want me to send you a pup?"

I spread my hands, encompassing the displays. "Might prove a risk to the artwork."

He grins. "Good guard dog, though. Keeps away the wolves."

"Wolves? She'd escape better on one of those thoroughbreds," Boudy says, coming up beside Custer.

I am struck by the contrast between the two. Custer is shorter, narrow in the shoulders, and quick and neat in his movements. Boudy is expansive and steady, but uneasy beneath his fashionable coat. I wish he had worn his buckskins.

Custer's eyebrows flash up. "So, Miss Ream, among your many talents, you are also a rider?"

"Oh, yes." Boudy laughs. "She is magical atop a horse."

Custer prunes his lips. "Magical?"

"I should know. Taught her to ride bareback. You should see her race across a field. Sitting astride. Wind blowing that hair behind her like a flag. We used to race back in Fort Smith. Bet she could still beat me."

Libby pats my shoulder. "We should go riding sometime."

Boudy turns his open smile on her. "A marvelous idea, Mrs. Custer. We could all go together. There are some lovely spots beyond the city."

Custer leans in. "Any places suitable for racing?"

In a minute, I fear I'm going to find myself in the middle of a horse-racing competition.

I tap Boudy's arm. "That was ten years ago. I haven't been on a horse since coming to Washington."

"You never forget how to ride, Vinnie."

For a moment, I consider it. But no, too many memories would be riding on that horse.

I give Custer my boldest smile and change the subject. "About that offer of a puppy? I think my little nephews would be in heaven to have one of your dogs. And it would make a fine protector." I extend my arms to encompass the display room and the men. "I have much to protect."

Custer dips his head. "Your wish is my command. I'll have one of my men choose the best of the next litter and deliver it to you personally."

I tip my head in thanks and move on to my newest arrivals—a city politician and his wife, potential patrons who deserve my full attention. I shake their hands, guide them to my bust of *Lincoln*, then listen to them extoll its virtues and discuss the cost of a copy.

More of the well-heeled curious arrive. Judging by the crowd, my first salon is a success. Washington society has taken me back in.

So, I do what I do best. I sing some more. I play my harp. I unveil my newest work. I serve Ma's butter jumbles and her famous candied orange peel. I fill cups with tea. Pour glasses of wine. Then I send them all home happy.

Once they have all gone, I turn down the gas, bolt the door, and tap my nails on the table in the hall where the cartes de visite of my sculptures and my Matthew Brady portraits are displayed.

This is it. This is what my life will be—huckstering to the rich, modeling the vain, and sleeping alone.

Chapter 30

APRIL 1872

REAM STUDIO, PENNSYLVANIA AVENUE, WASHINGTON

Spring sunshine dapples the walls of my bedroom. I peer into my mirror and smooth away the tiny wrinkles crossing my brow. Hope for financial solvency has arrived in the form of an open call for submissions for a sculptural monument to Admiral David G. Farragut. Twenty thousand dollars—twice that for the *Lincoln*. Surely, that will be enough to provide for completing the work and paying off my debts.

And I will do everything I can to win it, even act the flirt again.

Mary calls up the stairs, "General Sherman's here."

I grimace and push away from my desk. *The General*. I may be sleeping alone, but I'm not left alone.

"Says he's here to take you to New York."

"He is. Be right there." I bury the stack of overdue bills beneath the mountain of letters from potential suitors awaiting answers and insert one earbob, then the other. The amethyst and spun silver pendants dangle and tickle my neck. They are new and ostentatious—a gift from the general. It is totally inappropriate to have accepted his gift and to wear them, but who will ever know, except the two of us?

And to be honest, I like them too much to keep them hidden.

With a last look in the mirror, I sweep my hair behind my ears, so the earrings are front and center, then pin on my bonnet. Next, I tuck in an extra-long hairpin—always a smart accessory for a woman, but essential when traveling with the general. Sherman is dignified and oh so stern, but his fingers tend to wander more than most men's. I insert it securely. Though I will only use it if words fail me.

Ma stops me in the hall, a solid wall of calico apron scented with the day's baking. She wrings her hands. "Please take Mary with you as a chaperone. I'm happy to watch Perrikin."

I lift my satchel. "Thank you for the offer, but Mary has her hard-won, full-time position at the Interior to hold onto. She can't just take off at a moment's notice after waiting all those months for it. No need to worry. The general is the epitome of a perfect gentleman."

"Don't be a fool. The man's married. Just being seen with him casts dispersions on you. All he desires are your favors, and then he will leave you."

I give her a hug. "I know what the general wants. But he will have to be satisfied with my glowing presence at his side. Nothing more." I pull on my gloves and avoid mentioning my hatpin. "I will be perfectly fine, Ma. We will be in a public car, on a train. In the city, I am staying with Virginia Farragut. She has a lovely row house just off Park Avenue."

Ma flicks a curl off my brow. "I worry about you, Vinnie. You are getting to the age when men no longer see you as marriageable."

I pinch up my lips and give a little wiggle. "Twenty-five?"

My mother squints at me. "That's what the census says, and you look young enough. But we both know you're nearer thirty. If you want children, your time is fleeing."

"I have to go. But I will think on it." I dash down the stairs.

She has a point. There will always be men to marry, but birthing children? Do I want a little Perrikin of my own to kiss and tuck into bed each night?

I love Mary's little boy. There's nothing of his father about him with his Ream-black ringlets and Mary-brown eyes. I love that he is content to sit at my feet and model bits of clay into boats, people, and ponies like I did so long ago.

As I pass by my showroom, I glimpse the two little heads, *Butterfly* and *Morning-Glory*. The infants' marble skin appears flesh-like in the sunlight passing through the burgundy sheers. Aren't these works better than birthing a child with some man? More everlasting?

And solely mine.

I think on it all the way to New York with the off-limits General Sherman sitting too close at my side. I peek up at his grizzled, red-bearded face. He would love me well, I think. He is protective but accepting of my independence. Always solicitous. Outwardly stern, inwardly kind. With a sense of humor and an astute commentary on his fellows, he keeps his thoughts to himself except when we are alone. I doubt he'd turn my salacious invitation down like another man once did.

But he has a Catholic wife and five children he would never abandon. He is that good a husband, and as much as he desires me, a poor choice for a lover.

In New York, we exit the ferry depot and take a hired carriage to the Farragut townhouse located just off Park Avenue. Everywhere, I see mothers and children. Like haunts at a séance, little girls in white pinafores skip into view. Little boys in sailor suits run past. Mothers push buggies or clasp the hands of toddlers feeding pigeons.

I blink the images away. My sculptures are my children. They should be enough. Perhaps if I could have gone back to Rome, joined my sisters-in-art, I would not be feeling these pangs in my chest—this desire to risk all to procreate.

My determination jarred, I'm not ready for the blatant perusal by the handsome man sitting next to Virginia Farragut's son in the gilded parlor. Debonair as any French count, clean-shaven and tidy, Loyall's best friend, Lieutenant Richard Hoxie, an army engineer, casts me one of those nose-down looks I'm too familiar with, flicks the end of his blond mustache, and whips his icy-blue gaze over me.

"You're the sculptress who created the *Lincoln* in the Capitol? A magnificent work. But how? You are a woman. You must have had help to create a work so large."

Woman? The dreaded word used to hinder me all my life.

Heat flushes through my body. I turn away and take a sip of my coffee, letting the bitterness burn away my retort. I need the Farraguts on my side to win the commission being discussed in Congress. Offending the son's best friend would be foolhardy.

Virginia smooths the moment with her warm Norfolk accent. "I am hoping dear Vinnie Ream will create something even more magnificent for us. A memorial to our beloved husband and father. Have you seen her sketches?"

She opens the portfolio I have brought in hopes of gaining her support for the rumored government commission. On top are drawings of the bust I have begun based on the photographs she sent me. She hands them to her son.

"The resemblance is strong." Loyall frowns. "But isn't a full bust too much for his grave? I thought we'd agreed on an obelisk with nautical symbols. Something above the ordinary. I've already ordered it."

Virginia shifts beneath her black mourning and studies her hands. The fingers are long and elegant, like her son's. She curls them over each other. "I would like the bust for here, in the parlor. For me. As a mark of my love for him."

Loyall lays down the portfolio with the precision of a military man. "Then it shall be done." He turns to me. "We will accept your proposal. But I don't want any fussy drapery. I can send his uniform to you if you want to work from it?"

I think of the statue of Minerva I'd much rather create, and the Pittsburgh General George Thomas equestrian commission I hope to win, and clasp my hands together. The stack of bills will not wait for my creative preferences.

"I am most appreciative of any and all help you can give. I plan to be in New York as a featured guest for the King County Industrial Fair in September. The bust should be ready by then."

Now for the part I hate.

I retrieve the invoice from the portfolio. "I usually receive fifty percent as a down payment."

The son bows and steps out of the room.

Sherman takes that moment to broach the subject I'm more concerned about—the one we hashed out on the train.

"Mrs. Farragut. I would like to propose we support Vinnie in winning the sculptural commission for the proposed monument to the Admiral. To be sculpted by the woman who put Lincoln on a pedestal would be the greatest of honors for your beloved husband."

Virginia tips her chin, warning me that she will expect something in exchange, and lays her hand over mine. "I am so predisposed. However, we must get to know you better. I would like you to stay longer than the one day, Vinnie. Perhaps a week? I would have Loyall and his wife, Mary Gertrude, come to dinner one night. And there is no need for you to spend all your time with me. You are too young to be confined to the house and garden." She turns to the strait-laced man I have successfully avoided paying attention to. "I am sure General Sherman and my dear Richard Hoxie will be delighted to escort you around the city. Perhaps to the theater? I hear *Ixion* at the Metropolitan is quite delightful."

I think about the work, and the bills, and the sour faces waiting for me at home. A comedy in the company of this stiff military man is just what I do not need. But Sherman expresses delight at seeing the show. So, off we go, *dainty* me between two towering men with razor-sharp postures and animated conversations about bridges, sewers, and military protocols.

I choke down a breath of the noxious, coal-scented air. As soon as I can, I'll grab a train for home. Meanwhile, I will enjoy the show and play on Virginia Farragut's sympathies. Winning the Farragut commission must take precedence over my own personal desires.

So, as we promenade down Fifth Avenue, I study this new addition to my male vanguard. Lieutenant Richard Leveridge

Hoxie, a man befitting his pretentious name. He is what my mother would call a smart catch—young, handsome, and a war hero, working his way up the ranks. A West Pointer, an army man. An engineer concerned with weights and measures. Not to my taste at all.

I return home, secure in the knowledge I have Virginia Farragut's support.

May blows in unbearable heat and drives away my friends and customers. I put down my clay tool and wipe the sweat from my brow. The Custers are long gone, the general's bust unfinished and unpaid for. Boudy has fled to the prairie for the summer. Sherman has gone home to his wife. The Farraguts and all other sensible people are at the shore, while I remain in the city, slaving over my model of Admiral Farragut.

My orders may have dwindled, but the bills have not. In desperation, my work on the Farragut commission model has become all-consuming, as have my fears. Still, I convinced Congress once. I can do it again. I slap on more clay.

Yap. Yap. Yap. Is that the puppy Elizabeth Custer wrote would be arriving? Shucking my smock, I abandon my grubby studio and discover a grinning cadet holding a puppy.

He holds the leggy pup out. "For you. From General Custer."

"What a darling." I hug the squirming creature to my chest and kiss it on the head. It's a spindly thing with big paws, black patches around each eye, a rough pink tongue, and no expectations of me. I love it already.

My sister peers out the doorway, a pale Madonna enwrapped in black crepe. "I heard barking. It that the puppy?"

I nod.

Mary rustles out onto the front porch and sits next to me on the stoop. She lifts the puppy and settles the wiggly creature on her lap, running her hand rhythmically down the furry back. I almost sigh. Long ago, she used to rub my back like that.

She holds the pup out in front of her. "Such a dear little one. The boys will be back shortly to play with you."

I nudge her with my elbow. "Shall we name it Little General after all the generals that haunt me?"

My sister laughs and rubs his belly. "I doubt this Little General will be little for long." She kisses the black nose, then sets the puppy down.

We watch him stumble about the front yard, sniffing here and there.

Mary puts her hands on her knees. "We have to talk."

"Of course."

I expect to hear about rats, or regret, or another debt. Instead, she passes me a letter.

"Boudy has written me."

My heart squeezes a little. He has sent me none.

I give myself a shake. We are merely friends. A forgotten coin sits at the bottom of the Trevi Fountain to attest to the truth of it. He can write whom he pleases.

Mary's fingers twist. "Bob has been arrested and convicted. He's in prison. We have to do something."

I rest my hand on my heart. I should feel something. I don't.

Mary misinterprets my action. "Just imagining Bob locked up with hardened criminals makes my blood boil, too."

I draw a breath and reject correcting her. "What did he do?"

"Sold whiskey to the Indians."

"That's not a crime. He lives in Indian Territory. Married into the tribe."

"Boudy says"—my sister wraps the chain of the necklace holding the glass pendant containing Perry's hair around her finger—"he brought it in from Arkansas. A lot of it."

My shoulders stiffen. No small offense, then. Just another male playing the system and losing.

I run my palm along the rough boards of the porch. "He's been convicted. What can I do?"

"Someone who hates him gave testimony against him. Ma is preparing to go to Fort Smith. But I thought—you're so famous now—I thought you could ask President Grant . . . to pardon him?"

"I'm famous, but not invincible."

"But you must be close to Grant. You modeled his bust. Surely, he will listen to you."

I watch the puppy lick her wrist. "Modeling someone does not make them my bosom buddy. It makes them a client."

"Well, you can't turn your back on your brother. Ma and Pa would be heartbroken if you did."

I get up. I hoped to remove myself from politics entirely and become an arbiter of the arts and literature—a modern-day Sappho. But I will always be thought a politician, even by my own family.

Mary drops her head. "You don't care, do you? You're not the fount of kindness everyone thinks you are." Her voice trembles. "You should help. After . . . after . . . what happened . . ."

I can see in her eyes that we will never speak of Perry's death or what he did to her. But there's a scar on her neck that wasn't there on her wedding day, and another on the back of her hand. She had reason enough, as did I.

I lift her hand and run my finger over the puckered white line. Her fingers grasp mine. "Okay," I say. "Grant is likelier to listen to his wife, who hates me. However, I will use what influence I can for a pardon."

I scoop up the puppy and stomp inside. Ever since we left Fort Smith, Bob has done nothing for me except cause trouble. Humiliating myself before the President for his sake irks and will do nothing for my reputation. I have never turned my back on my family, but I have never been more tempted.

Pa tumbles through the front door, a laughing Perrikin slung over his shoulder, my nephew dawdling behind. Al, at twelve, is the spitting image of his father—tall, blond, and just as supercilious and indolent. At his age, I was racing horses, drawing maps for my father, and excelling at school. All my nephew will do, despite Mary's tender care all these years, is fail at the academy, run wild around the neighborhood, and accuse her of stealing his father's money.

But it is Perrikin who catches my eye. Swept up in his mother's arms, laughing at the puppy. I love the boy so much.

Unease crosses my shoulders. Will my life be complete if I never marry and have children? I glance at my studio. It doesn't matter what I want. We need money—badly. Winning the Farragut commission is what I must do.

Chapter 31

OCTOBER 1872

WASHINGTON, D.C.

But the decision on the Farragut commission is still two months away. And the bankers will not wait. So that is why, accompanied by my sister, I find myself in an auction house, and I hate it. The room reeks of wet wool and overfed men with too much money. Few women are present.

Mary and I take seats toward the back. On the platform, amid paintings, brass work, and bric-a-brac, stands a cloth-covered figure—my *Spirit of the Carnival.*

I curl my hands in my lap. "Have I done the right thing?"

My sister puts her hand over mine and squeezes. "You have no choice."

I pull the brim of my hat lower. "But what if some tavern owner buys it, or worse—a bordello? No one will take my art seriously then. I couldn't bear it."

Mary surveys the crowd. "They all look like fine gentlemen, Vinnie."

"How can you say that after what that rat Fuller did? He looked the fine gentleman, too."

"I knew what I was getting; he made sure of it."

I turn and stare at her. "You could have called the wedding off."

She mumbles something under her breath.

I lean over. "*Mary*?"

"Oh, Vinnie. Are you so innocent you can't figure it out? He'd already taken a husband's privilege. I might have been with child."

Bang. The auctioneer's gavel comes down, ending our first honest discussion since that terrible night. The tedious wait begins. My glorious *Carnival* is to be last. The star of the show . . . I hope.

But it isn't. The bids do not even reach the two-thousand-dollar minimum I set to cover the cost of the marble and shipping it from Italy, as well as pay the mortgage for the next four months. As it is, it takes almost all my remaining cash to hire carters to haul it home.

Mary and I hasten on ahead. Once home, I follow my sister through the kitchen door. She takes off to round up the boys, who are squabbling loudly in the hall.

I stop at the table where Ma peels peaches for another batch of pies. How many hundreds has she made in the last two years, all because of my failures? I put my arms around her. "Let me do that for you."

She tsks. "You've not dressed fittingly for this work."

"I'm not fit for anything."

She turns and stares at me. "You didn't sell the lady?"

"Nobody bid on her."

"That's what comes of sculpting a naked woman."

"Nudes are perfectly acceptable in classical works."

"Classical, bah. What woman wants a bare-breasted hussy in her parlor?"

My frustration bursts out. "Stop being so prudish. It's a work of fine art. It belongs in the Corcoran Gallery, displayed next to Hiram Powers' *The Greek Slave*."

Ma's lips pinch. "*Powers*? Your father says you acted like a fool in front of him back in Florence."

I jerk back as if she slapped me. "No. Pa would never say that. All I did was introduce myself"—my chest tightens—"and maybe brag a bit about winning the Lincoln commission."

Ma slices the peach and places it in the waiting pie shell. She takes another from the basket. When she speaks, her voice is soft, but her words harsh. "I wish you'd never won that commission, Vinnie. I wish we'd never gone to Europe and spent money like some potentate. We're not aristocrats. You're not a Gilded Age princess. All that Lincoln award has done is give you grandiose ideas while sinking us into poverty. And you've learned nothing. You're doing it again with this Farragut thing. Too much was made of you when you were young. Pride will be your downfall, and I fear you will take the family down with you."

I suck in a breath of air and force the words she wants to hear out. "Well, then. If I don't get the commission, I'll quit."

My mother looks me in the eye. "And marry."

I firm my stance. "No, Ma. Marriage isn't the way to solve problems. It just creates them. Look at what Perry Fuller did to Mary. One of the reasons I have no money is that I support all of you."

Ma raises her hands, dripping with peach juice. "Do you? Seems to me everyone is working hard to keep the family afloat, while you spend money frivolously on clay, castings, and wining and dining strangers at your raucous salons."

"All those expenses bring in the orders that keep the roof over our heads. The busts I make pay the mortgage on this house and the fees for Fuller's brat's private schooling."

"Hush." Ma wags a finger at me. "Alfred is part of this family. You can't blame a child for his father's sins. If you can't afford the mortgage, sell the house and buy something more suitable for a working family. You think we like living amid dust and gawkers?"

I close my eyes and visualize a future without clay or a chisel beneath my hands. "I can't. I'm not ready to give up. Not if there's still a chance I'll get the Farragut commission."

"Do as you must." She turns away and takes up another peach. "You will, anyway."

Someone bangs on the front door.

Moments later, Mary calls back, "The carters are here with your sculpture."

I dash outside and gesture for them to carry the cloth-wrapped marble down the alley and around the back of the house, all the while praying no one important is witnessing my humiliation.

They deposit my *Carnival* in the wash shed. I tip them the last of my coins and send them on their way. Then I untie the rope and remove the canvas cover. My poor *Carnival*—at least Ma's handful of chickens will get to admire it.

I go to recover her, but halt. Attached to her floral garland is the poem I wrote in honor of the work. I read it aloud.

Spirit of the Carnival, reckless, happy, free and gay,
Thou must, like thy blooming garlands, with the season pass
away!
Happy was the thought that caught thee, like a bird upon the
wing,
And in marble reproduced thee, Oh, thou subtle, fleeting
thing!

My breath hitches at the truth of it. Happiness *is* fleeting. Suffering *is* constant.

I run my hand down Carnival's bare arm, the marble cold beneath my palm, and fight back tears. How can I ever give up my art? Oh, Boudy, was this misery what I sacrificed our love for?

The answer comes days later. Six-year-old Perrikin, accompanied by Little General, Custer's oversized puppy, bounds into my workroom.

He waves an envelope at me. "Letter for you."

I lift my clay-covered hands. "Take the dog out of here before he knocks something over, and have your mama put the letter with the rest of my correspondence."

"She said to deliver it directly to you."

I grumble but take the envelope in my clayey fingers and stare at the address. This time, Boudy's letter is addressed to me.

My stomach twists. Has something happened to my poor brother? To everyone's dismay, I failed to save him. But he's served his year in the federal penitentiary and should be back with his wife and children in Indian Territory by now. Surely, after having my request for his pardon turned down, he knows my influence with Grant is nil and will stay out of trouble.

I pinch the letter more tightly between my fingers. Or is Boudy writing about something else? Sherman has been a pleasant distraction, but he doesn't make my heart sing like Boudy still does. I hesitate, then tear the envelope open with my teeth.

It is a long missive in his familiar hand. I plop down on my stool and read. Vinita is thriving, he writes. I can hear the pride in his words as he describes the meeting of the railroads. The burgeoning town. The modern amenities. He hopes I might visit this summer to see what he has accomplished. He has put forth a proposal to the Cherokee tribe for a bust of Sequoyah to be modeled by me.

I set the letter down. Trevi Fountain in Rome is a long way away. My hurt feelings seem so childish now. Boudy loves me. He knows me better than anyone else on earth. He allowed me to pursue my desires, and I am glad he is doing well.

But my career is stumbling, and I'm so tired.

I survey my messy model for the Farragut commission. I feel like a rag doll being pulled in too many directions. An economic malaise hangs over the country. Orders have been slim to nothing. A few copies of Lincoln's bust, and the purchase by Ezra Cornell of Peter Cooper's bust, have been the only sales in the last month.

Meanwhile, my debts continue to pile up. Ma and Pa are in poor health. Mary shoulders the work of the boarding house as well as her job at the Interior, while I play with plaster and clay.

I could swallow my pride, abandon my family, and marry Boudy. Or I can remain firm, capitalize on Sherman's sympathies, and win the Farragut commission.

Twenty thousand dollars. I'd be smart this time. No flamboyant trips or purchases. The money left over from the casting would go a long way to making Ma and Pa's last years more comfortable. It is my only choice.

As much as I love him, marrying Boudy would mean abandoning them and my sister to a hard-scrabble future.

I set the letter down. The Farragut decision isn't until January. Can I bear Sherman's constant pressure to consummate our relationship, and his perchance to sit too close and speak too familiarly in public for four more months?

Mary pops her head into the studio. "Sherman's here. *Again.* Wasn't his barging in on our breakfast enough? Ma's ready to put a sign on the door: No Generals Allowed."

A deep-throated laugh fills the hallway.

Besides, the general is becoming a pain.

I wipe my hands clean, then unwrap my turban, freeing my hair. That's as much prettying up I plan on doing for his second visit of the day.

Will appears in the doorway. "You work too hard, Vinnie."

I scowl at him. "You know I don't like to be disturbed when I'm in the workroom."

The crease between his eyes deepens. "My dear girl, scolding doesn't become you. You are all smiles for the tourists. It pierces my heart to be rebuked."

"They rarely find their way back here. It's filthy." I point down at his polished boots. "Look at the plaster dust on your boot tips. The orderly who put that shine on them will be quite upset."

"Worth it to get some time alone with you." He walks around my model, then halts behind me. "You've made a lot of progress." He slips his hands around my waist. The heat of his body is like a furnace—so hot I have no idea whether I want to get closer or further away. All I know is I must keep him sweet until the Farragut commission is decided.

I lift his hands off me. "I *was* making progress."

He returns his hands to rest on my shoulders. He nuzzles his face in my hair and presses against me. "Come have dinner with me, sweetheart."

I can feel his excitement through my canvas smock.

A shiver runs over me and leaves the hairs on my arms erect. I pull away. "I haven't time. Albert Pike is coming at five to read his poems to me."

"Dirty old man. Why you and your family tolerate him, I have no idea."

"Because he has been kind to us over the years. And his Masonic connections have been extremely helpful in my career." More importantly, even in his dotage, he scares away men like the general.

Will rubs his chin. "Well, I have no use for the Masons. All that secrecy."

I rise on tiptoes and peck him on the cheek. "I like secrecy. So do you. Do we not destroy each other's letters? Now, go find some other willing partner to share dinner with so the gossip about us is shown to be merely rumors." I give him my little girl *moue* that women hate and men respond to with aplomb. I add in a womanly caress across the back of his hand. "And put in a good word about my Farragut model to the Secretary of the Navy, Robeson, for me."

Will bows. "Your wish is my command." And he is gone—happily. And I am left alone with my clay and honor intact. This time.

I shape a lump of clay into a facsimile of Will's rugged face, then smash it hard beneath my fist.

Oh, Boudy. If I fail to get this commission, I swear I will marry you and move to this Vinita you write so glowingly about.

Chapter 32

WASHINGTON, D.C.

The last day of January 1873 dawns gray and bitter cold. I hold my breath as the workmen load my precious plaster model of Farragut into the cart I have hired for the short trip to the Capitol. The seven-foot-tall sculpture wobbles.

"Al," I shout at my pseudo-nephew, who stands gawking on the porch. "Get up in the cart and hold the model steady." I offer a quarter, money being the only thing that gets his attention these days. He seizes it and jumps aboard.

The wobbling cart takes off, splashing through the icy January mud, my heart tagging after and jumping at every tip and wobble. I run inside to grab a shawl, then dash after them.

Shouting up ahead makes me forget decorum. I hike up my skirt and take off at a run. I arrive at the Capitol steps to see my model lying in the mud, pieces strewn everywhere. My body turns colder than the wintry gusts swirling around me. My pounding heart freezes mid-beat.

Seven months of my life destroyed in a moment.

I swipe away tears. "What happened?"

"It was intentional," some onlooker says. "The boy pushed it."

I whirl around and let anger dry my tears. Alfred may not be my favorite person, but I will not let anyone blame a mere boy for my inability to afford a better conveyance.

Another bystander points to the workmen. "Wasn't the boy's fault. He'd already scrambled down. The cartwheel sank into the mud. It tilted too far."

I bend down, retrieve an arm, and lay it gently on a nearby snowdrift. It is like picking up my own limb. It takes all my effort to rise and peer blurrily at the men I hired. "You should have secured it more firmly to start."

They shrug and fade into the crowd, leaving a pit of fear in my stomach. Has someone purposely tried to sabotage me?

I clench my teeth so hard pain ricochets through my head. There is nothing more I can do but make repairs.

But should I, or am I doomed to disaster?

I survey the damage. Farragut's head lies smashed, the nose missing. Both arms are broken off, and his spyglass sits half-sunk in a puddle so black I fear my destiny lies there with it.

The dear ushers from the Capitol hurry to me, all kindness and solicitation. They help carry my destroyed model into a lower vestibule where they set up a screen behind which I can work.

There is no time to rail at fate. As much as I want to turn away and call it quits forever, I cannot give up now, not with everyone depending on me. My family needs the money. I need the satisfaction of proving the naysayers wrong again.

I find a messenger and send him off to Robeson with a request for an extension. I order another to fetch fresh plaster and wet cloths.

Then, despite the gnawing in the back of my brain warning this is a mistake, I sweep up my smashed hopes and try to put them together again.

I get a week's extension and a head cold. The general shows up to offer sympathy and hot coffee.

Adorned in buckskins and braids, Boudy arrives in the city only to face taunts of "Redman" in the street and rumors of a liaison with me in the papers. He ignores it all and, shivering against the cold, holds the pieces in place so I can plaster them back on.

I am thrilled to see him and have him here, despite Will's propriety condescension. But I'm angry, too, because he came in answer to a letter from Mary.

But the two hovering men are angels compared to the throngs surging around me, arguing over whether I can fix it in time, their hands reaching out to touch the wet plaster. Some even take bets in front of me.

Worst is the crowd of naval officers who knew the admiral and offer pointed comments every time I make a change. But at least I know what they're thinking. It is the quiet army man in the back, Richard Hoxie, who worries me. He is the eyes and ears of Virginia Farragut. What he reports to her matters most.

Cowed, I say nothing to him, and he says nothing to me. Under his gaze, I toil day and night and finish an hour before the deadline—only for the committee to be deadlocked.

Then I wait. The news, when it comes, is disastrous. The Farragut project has been tabled until next year. Meanwhile, there's no income coming in, and the bills keep piling up. I finish a letter to Ezra Cornell, urging him to buy my *Lincoln* and my *Sappho* and add it to the growing pile of beggarly requests and applications to every sculpture exhibition I can find. If I don't have an influx of money soon, we will have to sell this house. Then, where will I hold my salons and display my sculptures?

And it is my own pride that is to blame. Mark Twain is right to have mocked my *Lincoln* in his newly released novel *The Gilded Age.* My sculpture doesn't depict a heroic leader, he says, but a man holding a folded napkin and contemplating the washing.

If I truly had talent, if I could truly capture the human spirit, all my Italian marbles would have sold by now. But nobody wants my *Spirit of the Carnival* or my *Miriam.* The Corcoran Gallery even refused to display my *Sappho*—the best of them all.

I knock the pile of letters to the floor and cover my face with my hands. Ma is right. All that effort and early success have only brought me and my family pain.

"Vinnie." Ma stands in the doorway. "There's a young man downstairs asking to see you."

I wipe away a tear and lift my head. "A young man? Who?"

"An officer in uniform. Lieutenant Richard Hoxie."

"*Ugh.*" I grit my teeth. "Send him away. Tell him I'm indisposed."

"You know him?"

"We met in New York." Thanks to Virginia Farragut and her matchmaking wiles.

Ma hustles into the room and shuts the door. She grasps me by the shoulders and gives me a shake. "This isn't like you, Vinnie. Pull yourself together and get dressed this minute. If you want him to leave, you must tell him yourself. Though I think you foolish to do so."

She is right, if for the wrong reason. It would be unreasonable to turn him away as long as the Farragut commission is still possible. The model is done, Farragut's widow is disposed to me, and the next Congress may be more amenable than this last. Though success is a feeble hope.

I force myself to rise. Ma helps me into a velvet dress too fancy for an afternoon visit. I allow her to brush my hair and gather it up with the ivory combs I purchased in Rome. The same combs I wore the night Boudy left me. Then I settle for my cameo from the cardinal around my neck to remind myself how persuasive I can be.

By the time I enter the salon, Lieutenant Hoxie has settled on the loveseat, neatly nibbling a slice of Ma's apple pie and sipping a steaming cup of coffee.

Resentment fills me. It should be Boudy sitting there, not this rigid-backed soldier who looks like he belongs in a way Boudy never could.

But Boudy is gone, returned to Fort Smith, to lawyer and publish the Cherokee language newspaper his father founded so many years ago, and it is I who did not open my heart and follow him—again.

Richard Hoxie sets the cup on the saucer and rises. Tall and slender, he towers over me. "Miss Ream."

I offer my hand. He bows at the waist and delivers a kiss, his lips softer and warmer on my skin than expected. I tuck my hand away and move to the piano stool.

"You play?"

"I do."

And to avert more small talk, I face the keyboard and play one of my more recent compositions. My fingers dance over the keys, my voice carries the refrain, and the tightness in my chest loosens as the music wraps around me. I barely notice when Hoxie joins in.

And then I do. His voice harmonizes perfectly with mine.

We reach the end, and I spin around. "I have never sung with a man who has such a fine tenor."

"I love music." A broad smile transforms his long face from military stern to slightly boyish. "You based that on Joaquin Miller's 'The Ship.' What else have you composed?"

I hesitate, shuffle through the sheets until I find my composition of John Rollin Ridge's "I Love Thee" and hand it to him. "John asked me to set his poem to music."

"Let's sing it." He leans over to place the music on the stand, and I catch a whiff of cedar and something spicy, so different from the politicians who reek of whiskey and tobacco, and totally unlike Boudy, who carries the scent of the prairie in his very being.

We sing, and, as always, music works its magic. My muscles loosen as our voices meld. My frustrations, my money troubles, and apprehensions about the Farragut commission fly away to be worried about another day.

Chapter 33

MARCH 1874

THE FARRAGUT RESIDENCE, 113 EAST 36TH STREET, NEW

YORK CITY

With the Farragut decision delayed, I put all my effort into convincing the committee of the worth of my entry. Which is why I find myself peering up at Richard Hoxie in the doorway of the Farragut house.

He escorts me and General Sherman into Virginia Farragut's parlor and guides me to the loveseat. He sits beside me, leaving the general standing. Will grunts and takes a seat opposite us, his stern face more dour than normal. Does he suspect why I've brought him here?

Under Will's glare, Richard slides nearer to me. I can feel the heat of his body against mine. My pulse speeds up. My fingers clench. It is one thing to flirt. It is another to lead two men on for my personal benefit.

Virginia enters the parlor in a swish of ruffle-bedecked, black moiré silk and wearing a pressed-lip smile, the kind that hides a shared secret. She has read my letter professing an attraction to Hoxie—I glance out of the corner of my eye at the man sitting too close—and shared it with Richard. The cold-fish lieutenant believes a few musical interludes have won me over, and she thinks her matchmaking dreams are coming true.

I wallow in guilt through the perfunctory coffee and sticky-sweet bonbons and wait for Virginia to make the proposal she and I have cooked up.

"I've an idea." Virginia Farragut claps her hands. "I will name General Sherman to the Farragut committee, and Vinnie will get the commission."

Richard opens his mouth, then closes it, thinks for a minute, then opens it again. "Mrs. Farragut, this sounds a bit underhanded to me. I can understand why you may want to have the general help select the sculptor you prefer, but it seems a bit unethical to get around the Secretary of the Navy by stacking the committee. Surely, Miss Ream can win the commission outright."

Virginia sets down her coffee cup with a *clink*. "But why chance it? It's a three-person committee, and we all know how much Secretary Robeson hates our Vinnie. He blames her for the deaths of Hall and Bessel on his pet Polaris Expedition. Says they fought each other over her. With that in his craw, he won't vote based on the merits of her work."

She rises and moves to my finished bust of Farragut on the mantel, resting her hand on the base. "Look at this marvelous artwork. It is the very image of my David. Why should I allow a prejudiced man to select some hack sculptor over Vinnie? How is that fair?"

Richard turns toward me. "What do you think of this proposal?"

I gaze at the bust and search for the right words. "I am honored that Virginia admires my work so much and wishes me to create this monument to her husband." I adjust the napkin on my lap and brush Richard's thigh with my gloved hand in the process. A touch I hope Will does not see. I tuck my hand back in my lap.

I have sunk incredibly low indeed. I have become exactly what the nastiest of reporters claim—a woman manipulating men for monetary gain. But I am willing to do anything to win the Farragut commission and save my family.

Will shifts in his chair to look at Virginia. "I am not sure I can find the time."

She bestows a well-perfected smile. "It won't take any time at all. I told Robeson I don't want to be running back and forth to Washington. Surely, you can attend a few meetings to make certain my David receives the monument he deserves?"

Will hesitates, then nods. "Of course." He taps his booted foot.

He hates politics and has just been manipulated into doing something he hates even more—being at the beck and call of a government committee. He'd be even more furious if he knew Virginia and I planned this together, and that Richard Hoxie now thinks I welcome his pursuit. Men and their foolish possessiveness.

I want to stamp my feet. Instead, I smile. We should all be happy. I have worked magic. With Secretary Robeson outnumbered two to one, I'm guaranteed to earn the commission. *Twenty thousand dollars*. I will be able to pay off all my debts and give my parents the years of leisure they deserve.

As for myself—I glance between the two—I want neither man. But until the commission is approved by Congress, I am stuck with them both.

Despite Secretary Robeson's dawdling, it works. Three months later, I am voted the commission over Horatio Stone, and Congress approves it.

Bubbling with the news, I stop in the middle of the Rotunda. I want to shout. I want to dance. But neither would be fitting in this august place. Instead, I dash outside into the June sunshine, intending to head for the intersection of K Street and Connecticut Avenue, the place where my grand monument will stand for all time.

The reporters stop me before I'm halfway down the Capitol steps. Richard is not the only one to protest the unseemly appointment of the general to the committee. The newsmen are in an uproar. But none of them are brave enough to assail Will, the great hero of the Civil War and the serving Commander General of the Army.

But me? A woman? I'm fair game.

I toss my hair back, hold my head high, and stride through the press of men.

"How did you get the general named to the committee?" one of the newsmen asks. "Everyone knows he's sweet on you."

I call over my shoulder, "I had nothing to do with it. Mrs. Farragut requested him because he knew the admiral well."

"All you've ever done is work in marble. What do you know about bronze casting?" another cries.

I wave my arm toward the Capitol Dome. "I studied under Clark Mills, who cast the bronze Statue of Freedom."

"Will you use Clark Mills' foundry?"

I falter. I have no idea how I will cast the statue. I must figure out how to make the ten-foot model first.

A man in uniform approaches. Ah, Richard Hoxie to the rescue. For once, I'm glad to see him.

He tips his head in formal military style. "Thank you, gentlemen. Miss Ream will keep you informed of her progress. Now, please, make way." Dressed in his officer-blue, double-breasted jacket with its rows of gold buttons, he barely has to raise his voice to send the rabble fleeing.

One of the most aggressive stands firm. "How is a five-foot woman going to make a bronze sculpture twice her height? The idea is ridiculous."

I glance away. It does sound impossible. I can imagine the cartoon that will appear in the next edition of his newspaper.

Hoxie loops his arm in mine. "Miss Ream will have an engineer by her side every step of the way—me." Then he whisks me around and heads down Pennsylvania Avenue toward the Ream rooming house.

It takes all my willpower not to yank my arm back. I should be grateful. Hoxie has dispersed the reporters who would have dogged me all the way to the square, but I don't want Richard Hoxie dogging after me, either.

Still, I can't help asking, "So, Mr. Engineer, how do you suggest I model a statue twice as tall as me?"

"I will build you whatever lift mechanism you need."

I tip my head and study him. "You would have time for such a project? Aren't you still in the Naval Corps of Engineers?"

He nods. "That I am, and that's where I intend to stay. The work I do is important. It makes a difference in people's lives."

I suddenly realize I know nothing of this man, besides his singing voice and his over-the-top sense of fairness.

"What do you do for the Corps?"

"I am helping to redesign Washington's sewer system."

I lift my head and sniff loudly. "There's a *sewer system*?"

He laughs. "Not really, but there will be. But never fear, there will be plenty of time for me to assist you. I plan to forego spending the summer at my home in Iowa City."

Surprise shoots through me. "You have a house in Iowa?"

He smooths his already too-smoothed back hair. "My father was an importer, and my family lived in France and Italy until I was eight. Then, when my parents died, I was sent to stay with my aunt on the Iowa prairie."

I hear only one word. "*Prairie*? You grew up on the prairie?"

He chuckles. "Still own her house. It's nothing fancy, merely a clapboard farmhouse with no conveniences, but I love it. I usually spend my summers there."

The scent of wildflowers and the sound of the wind tickling the tall grass wash over me.

I burst out, "I love the prairie. I grew up there, too."

"I know. Your father told me all about your childhood."

"I'm sure he did." Imagining the crazy tales my pa has surely shared helps me tear myself from dreams of my longed-for prairie and focus on the work ahead. "So, my first step is to build the armature and make the ten-foot clay model of the admiral." I turn and stare at the house. "Oh. That's higher than the ceiling in my studio." My stomach cramps. Blinded by the fame and the money, I'd paid no attention to the major task I'd taken on.

"What do you suggest I do?"

"You could rent a warehouse."

I smack my lips together. "No, I need to be here to deal with my potential clients."

He taps his chin. "You could build an addition onto the back of the house. It wouldn't have to be fancy. I'd be happy to design it and scrounge up the lumber for you."

"That's it. Let's go around to the back, and I will show you the space."

He seizes my hand. "Let's."

Is this excitement over helping me model a ten-foot sculpture, or is he flirting with me?

I peer up at him. Most women would deem Richard Hoxie a fine-looking man with his razor-straight nose, neat mustache, and arctic blue eyes. His short, slicked-back pale hair matches his stiff West Point posture. There is nothing soft about him except his warm hand in mine. And that is what bothers me.

Is this outwardly stuffed uniform the real man, or is there someone else beneath that perfectly fitted navy-blue coat? Someone who is kind, gentle, and passionate?

I tug him down the side alley and into the backyard with its old privy, a dilapidated wash shed, and clotheslines full of sheets. Dropping his hand, I recapture my thoughts.

"So, is there enough room to build an extension?"

Dodging flapping linens, he paces off a rectangle in line with my back-of-the-house studio. "I think so. It is helpful there is already an exterior door from the studio—you won't need to tear into the existing wall. The shed will have to go. But it's seen better days, anyway. The addition could become the new wash shed when the *Farragut* is done. Or you could dismantle it and resell the lumber."

I draw in a breath. "And you will help me build it?"

Richard lifts my hand. "For you, Miss Ream, I will do anything." He deposits a kiss, then strides away.

I watch him go, my thoughts awhirl. Lieutenant Hoxie is just one more man to have fallen for my charms. Another man to add to my long list of besotted men.

But this time, it feels different.

This time, I can't shake the feeling that he won't go away as easily.

And he doesn't. The months go by. The Farragut workshop rises in the yard under Hoxie's watchful eye. He arrives daily. My mother stuffs him with food, my sister treats him like royalty, and Pa spends hours debating the slope of the roof and what crops he should plant in Iowa.

Me? I escape the house and take refuge in the Capitol.

I hear her footsteps before I see her. Lilly Pike stops opposite me.

"I heard you were on display here, like some treasured artifact."

I peek around the bust I am working on. "I needed a place to work while the construction of my new studio is ongoing, and the Library of Congress agreed to let me use this space."

Lilly looks up and down the empty west wing corridor of the Capitol. "More like you've hidden yourself away. Not a reporter or lovelorn suitor in sight."

"Just the way I like it." I smooth the clay chin.

Lilly comes up behind me and tips her head. "Is that who I think it is?"

"Probably not. It's no one you've ever met."

"Not Boudinot?"

Up to this moment, it was. It's all my fingers want to sculpt. Time to stop dreaming.

I take a deep breath and impress a cleft into the center of the chin. Then I swoop up globs of clay and add bags beneath the eyes, high cheekbones, and wrinkles at the corners of the mouth.

Lilly lets out a huff. "Okay. Who is it?"

"Sequoyah."

"Huh? Who's he?"

"The man who invented the Cherokee alphabet and turned his people more literate than us whites. Cornelius's newspaper,

The Phoenix, is written in it." I wipe my hands on the ever-present wet rag and study the changed face. "Boudy is working to get the Cherokee chiefs to commission a statue of him. I'm hoping this will help sway them."

Lilly grins. "Despite what I heard, I guess you're still in love with Boudinot, aren't you?"

I grimace. "I see I'll get no more work done today." I wrap damp cloths around the bust. "So, what have you heard?"

"Papa Pike says you will be marrying that army lieutenant who follows you everywhere like a puppy"—she glances about again—"except here, it seems."

I glare at her. "I'm not marrying anyone. Richard Hoxie is just helping with the addition."

"Oh, he's helping all right—helping his suit. When I stopped by your place, looking for you, he was standing in the kitchen, drinking a glass of lemonade and hobnobbing with your mother—in his shirt sleeves."

I dip my head to hide my heated cheeks. "What can I say? He's been coming every day and laboring beside the hired construction crew. Out of uniform, he's a different person. He's clever and hard-working. My parents like him."

What I don't add is that when I see him with his hair in disarray and his shirt sweat-stuck to his lithe, muscular body, I find him more and more irresistible, and my longing for Boudy more and more faint.

Lilly taps her finger to her lips. "It's not just your parents who like him. I'm going to tell Papa he's right. You'll be abandoning him soon."

I spin around. "Forget Richard Hoxie. I have other things to worry about. The Philadelphia Centennial Commission had the gall to put my sculptures in the women's exhibit. I am as good an artist as any man, and I deserve to be in the main sculpture hall."

"You *are* a woman, Vinnie." Lilly wraps an arm over my shoulders. "You've lived long enough to know it's a man's world and always will be."

I let out a harsh sigh. "That it is. I've had my successes, but always at the price of my reputation. Men like Horace Greeley call me an 'audacious little humbug' because I dared win a government commission. Mark Twain calls me Congress's Pet. I should have listened to Elizabeth Stanton when the woman approached me all those years ago and asked me to support her fight against the politicians. But I was young and stupid. Turned her away. Now, I have to play the sweet coquette with the centennial chairman, Daniel Morell, to get my work moved. That's all I have over men, Lilly—feminine wiles. What power would I have if I were married?"

"Your husband's. So choose wisely, Vinnie. Choose wisely." Then she waves goodbye and swirls her way down the corridor.

I turn back to my bust and dampen down the cloth wrapping. Is this sculpture, done gratis, enough to assuage my guilt over giving up my first and only true love?

I gather up my scrapers and fettling knife. Boudy is still being threatened by the law and under death threats from members of his own tribe. He has written, rescinding his invitation, warning me not to come, not even to visit.

I take off my smock and tuck it into the chest beside my tools. If Albert Pike has figured out I'm about to be swept up into another man's arms, the rest of the world, including Boudy, will know soon, too.

But marriage? It's so final. And it means giving up Boudy forever.

But, as Ma says, I'm getting older, and I do want children.

I pat the top of Sequoyah's head. Once, I thought creating amazing sculptures would be legacy enough, but only in Rome did I have the freedom to sculpt what I wanted without worrying if it would sell or not. Now, every work must be marketable. Every work must please a buyer.

I slip on my shawl as I head toward the door. My mother is right. It is time for me to dampen my pride, tuck my love for Boudy away, and marry.

But who? All signs point to Richard Hoxie. But is he the wise choice Lily says I should be searching for?

Chapter 34

APRIL 1876

REAM STUDIO EXTENSION, WASHINGTON, D.C.

I walk around the plaster armature again, peering up until my neck creaks. Of all the sculptures I have made, the Farragut commission is the hardest. I have always worked human-sized, but this colossus of a man is twice that. His eyes alone are more than a hand-span apart.

With a huff, I circle again. People will view this masterwork not face-to-face but on its pedestal from twenty feet below where I'm standing.

I re-climb the scaffolding and scrape away at the eyes again.

Ma enters the barn of a building where I have spent almost every day for the last year. She calls up, "Lieutenant Hoxie has brought news."

"I'm working. Send him out here." I return to the eyeball I'm modeling.

"I will do no such thing. You look like a ragamuffin in that washed-out calico smock and your hair scrunched under whatever that gray rag is. Come down, clean the dust off your face, and put on something decent."

"I must finish these eyes before I lose the light."

"If the lieutenant sees you looking like that, you'll lose the man. And you don't want that. He's the best of the bunch."

The bunch. I wipe my hands on the rag hanging from the scaffold. He *is* the best of my fawning suitors. Especially now that my protective escort, Will, has left Washington and gone back to his family. But he can be so annoying, showing up during my best working time after the gawkers have departed but before the sun sets.

"She won't lose me." Richard strides into the studio addition. "Vinnie's dedication to her art is what I love most about her."

My mother slaps her hand over her mouth. It is the first time Richard has professed his love openly. She will never stop pestering me to marry him now.

Richard gazes up at me. "Forgive me for interrupting you, but please, wrap up the head and come down. I have some bad news to share with you."

His commanding voice is softer than normal, and my chest tightens. It must be truly horrible.

Richard hands me up a bucket of water, then waits below while it takes me several minutes to apply the damp rags to the oversized head. Then I am down the scaffold and facing him.

He clears his throat. "This hasn't been made public yet, but I thought you should know and be prepared."

I swallow hard. "What? What's happened?"

"General Custer's been killed in a battle with the Sioux."

"George? Dead? But he was just here, at my salon, a few weeks ago, tussling with Little General and singing along with me and Libby. Oh, his poor wife." I can't stop the tears; they well up and stream down my cheeks. "They were so in love. She wanted him to pose for his bust, but he insisted there'd be plenty of time later."

Despite my being covered from head to toe in plaster dust, Richard pulls me against his chest and rubs my back. His tenderness wrings the sobs out of me.

I snuggle into his solid warmth. "Now there will be no later."

He rocks me gently. "No one knows what life holds for them. He died doing his duty."

I twitch at his military tone. "But George hated it. He told me he didn't want to go fight the Indians."

"But in the end, he did, and he will be remembered for it."

I sniff. "He told me my victories are lasting, unlike his, purchased at the expense of the lifeblood of fellow creatures." I struggle to regain control. "I hate this conflict our government is waging on the Indians. We take their land away. Persecute them. The tribes just want to live their lives like we do, but we won't let them." I toy with one of the gold buttons on his uniform. "Remember how, back in April, Pleasant Porter and David Hodge of the Creeks met Custer and talked about all the underhanded dealing going on by government officials?"

Richard hugs me tight. "That's another thing I love about you, Vinnie. You see the good in everyone. Custer, with his defiant attitude and self-importance, was no perfect man. And yes, the Indians have been treated ill. However, they have also ravaged and slaughtered."

Richard's fair-mindedness restarts my tears.

Oh, Boudy. I am here in this man's arms because of how the government treats Indians, even well-educated ones. And that will never change. It will always keep us divided as people. It has divided Boudy and me.

I snuggle deeper into this near-stranger's arms. I had my chance all those years ago. I could have stayed behind in Fort Smith, like my brother, and married Boudy. But I didn't have the courage to abandon my family and pierce my sister's heart. Now it is too late for him and me. Maybe it has always been too late.

Richard draws me against him, and all I want to do is let him take over my life and my responsibilities. I am oh-so-tired of being denigrated and maligned by corrupt politicians merely because I've crossed the boundary of what is acceptable for an unmarried woman. Tired of supporting my family while trying to make my mark in the art world. Tired of aching for a man's arms around me.

I peer into Richard's eyes and surrender to the inevitable. This is the man I will marry. He's seen me at my worst and still loves me. Now all that is left is to learn to love him back.

By February, the full-size model is ready.

Richard paces around the towering figure that even makes him look small. "So, it's been accepted?"

I nod. "Robeson tried to block it again, but since I had the general and Virginia's votes, the Congress is set to approve it tomorrow. If all goes well, I will get the next five thousand dollars."

"That's good news."

I wring my hands. "Yes, but, Richard, I'm afraid."

He moves closer. "Of what?"

"Of failure. I have no idea how to cast this monster in bronze without landing in debt again. Clark Mills and his foundry assistant, Phillip Reid, have both passed in the last two years. When I applied for the commission, I was relying on getting their assistance. But now . . . where can I have it cast and not spend a fortune?"

I shake the plaster dust from my skirt. "I've thought of Paris. They just cast a huge sculpture, *La Défense de Paris*." A shiver runs over me, and I turn to look at him. "But I have no desire to ever cross the Atlantic Ocean again or trust a work of art to the unpredictable seas."

Ignoring the polish on his boots, Richard walks back and forth, a habit he has when thinking. Little General, my constant companion now that both boys are away at school, follows at his heels.

He stops suddenly. "I have an idea. You could use the foundry at the Navy Yard."

"Robeson would never allow it."

Richard grins. "Ah, but he's on his way out. He's being charged with bribery and profiteering on shipbuilding contracts."

I study the plaster-dusted toes of my school-girlish shoes with their rubber soles. "And the man had the nerve to accuse *me* of being an underhanded criminal?" I look up at Richard's kind face and rest my hand on his arm. "I'm glad you're not a politician. I hate all those weaselly worms who are only out for themselves. You are the true patriot. You answered the Union's call and fought to end slavery. Now you're making life better for everyone with your expertise. You're a wonderful man."

I gather my courage.

"I love you, Richard, with all my heart."

There, I said it. There will be no going back.

With Richard by my side and the approval of Thompson, the new Secretary of the Navy, I invade the Dahlgren ordinance building at the Navy Yard with my model. The barn-like foundry is awash in ear-numbing noise and acrid smoke.

The foreman in charge of casting guides me to the cordoned-off area where workmen unwrap my *Farragut* from its packing. The admiral's strong visage appears.

He stares up. "This will be the largest thing we've ever cast here at the foundry. It will have to be done in sections."

That part of the casting process, I understand from watching Mills and Reid.

"Yes. And the cuts in the mold will need to be carefully placed so they are hidden from view." I draw out the plan Richard and I have made and trace the cut lines on the model. "I'm thinking of six sections: the head and shoulders, each arm, the sword, the telescope, and the lower body and plinth."

The foreman nods in agreement, then goes over the next steps—the tedious coating and recoating of the plaster in gelatin, and then with wax in preparation for creating the mold for the bronze.

"We can provide a team to do the gel coating. But I advise you to hire an expert to do the wax layer. The more accurate it is, the less finishing will need to be done. We only have a few men we can spare for this project."

I raise my voice and interrupt. "I intend to do all the finish work myself."

The foreman frowns. "But this is not a place for a woman. There is always the risk of an explosion." He looks up. "And the size alone—"

I hold up my hand. "I'm no wallflower. I created that model. Besides, I happen to know that women have worked here since the early 1800s and still do. I saw several on my way in."

"But they only do menial tasks or secretarial work."

Richard takes my hand. "If Miss Ream says she will do the work, then she will."

He might be wearing the wrong uniform, but there's fortitude in his voice. His words bring acquiescence from the workmen—I tighten my grip on his hand—and make me respect him more.

The men doff their caps. "Of course, sir."

I pull the other plan from my bag. "Once it is waxed, I will need a platform I can raise and lower." I roll up the sheet and hand it to them. "Perhaps you can construct this for me?"

"And the bronze?"

"The Secretary of the Navy has given permission to melt down the propellers from Admiral Farragut's flagship, the USS Hartford." I hand him Thompson's order.

Minutes later, we are back in the carriage and heading home.

I turn and pat Richard's hand. "Thank you for supporting me. Not many men would have."

"I'm not many men. I am the man who loves and honors you above all things. I want to be more. Much more. I want to be your protector and your helpmeet. I want to be at your side from now until death takes me. I want you to be my wife. Miss Vinnie Ream, will you marry me?"

I peer into his eyes and say the words I have avoided all these years. "I will."

"My dearest Vinnie, you have made me the happiest of men." He removes a small velvet bag from his inner jacket pocket and draws out a ring. He offers it to me on his palm. "I wish you to wear this trinket to symbolize our promise."

The large diamond surrounded by rose gold filigree is worth a fortune.

"That's no trinket. It must have cost way more than you can afford on an army engineer's salary."

Richard laughs, the sound of a lighthearted man. "Didn't you know? I'm rich, Vinnie. Remember my aunt in Iowa? She was an astute woman and used my inheritance to buy up land around Iowa City. Made a grand profit as the city grew. I still own hundreds of acres of prairie, just waiting for development."

I search his face. "But you don't live like a wealthy man. All you have is a room over on G Street and a horse."

"That's because I didn't need anything more from life until I met you. Now I have dreams. I have hopes. I have you to spend my fortune on."

My pulse rises. "Oh, Richard."

He slips the ring on my finger. The diamond gleams in the sunlight. My chest tightens. In exchange for my yes and this ring, he will have ownership over me. Yes, he will inherit my debts and my family. But in return, he will possess my body for the rest of my life.

Have I chosen wisely?

I lean over and tentatively press my lips to his. His lips do not press back. I twinge. It's been a long time since I was last kissed by a man, but I know enough to recognize a lack of ardor.

I straighten up and stare down at the sparkling gem on my finger. Have I made a mistake? Does he think I'm impure, like the rumors insinuate? I go to slip it off.

"Vinnie." Richard lifts my chin with his finger and turns my face to his. "Your kiss was a treasure, my love." He gazes at the people strolling up and down Pennsylvania Avenue. "But this is not the time nor place for the outward show of our affections. You are too well-known, and I'm too jealous of other men's eyes. For now, know that I love you and will do anything for you."

He's right, but his level of control irks.

"Anything?" I take a breath. "Would you forego the money and keep your prairie land in Iowa wild and undeveloped for as long as I live?" It's a question designed to poke the truth from him, I hope. I watch his face carefully. Does he truly love me, or does he value money more than a wife, like most men?

His expression brightens. "Of course. I'm loath to sell it myself. As soon as we marry, I will take you there for our honeymoon."

I touch my lips, not sure if he has said enough to convince me.

"Ah." He leans in and whispers in my ear, "Don't you know how much I want you? I can see you now, lying in a field of wildflowers, under a clear blue sky, your hair spread out like a raven's feathers. And when I kiss you, I will feel your heart flutter and your breath brush my skin. That is when we will truly consummate this marriage with all the passion poets write about."

The words are lovely. The romance enticing. All I need do is believe him.

Chapter 35

SEPTEMBER 1877

THE REAMS, WASHINGTON, D.C.

Pa stares at me. "Richard living here with us makes perfect sense, Vinnie. The room is vacant, and he spends half his time here or at the foundry with you, anyway."

I hate to give Pa a hard time, but everything is closing in on me. The idea of Richard boarding here, seeing him every morning over the breakfast table, and every evening on the way to bed, is more frightening than the upcoming bronze pouring of the head of the *Farragut* sculpture.

Pa taps a finger on the arm of the chair. "It will save him money not having to rent those rooms of his."

I rise from the loveseat and kiss Pa on his balding head. "He has plenty of money. Owns acres of land out in Iowa City."

Pa harumphs. "Land is not money in the bank. Too many men have lost money in land speculation. Besides, the taxes will eat you up."

I bite my tongue. My father should know. After all, it wasn't just the war that chased us from Fort Smith; it was his losses in real estate that impelled us to Washington all those years ago.

"He has money in the bank," I counter. At least, I hope he does. It is not something we have discussed. I glance at the diamond-encrusted gold bracelet I'm wearing. Though he seems to be able to purchase plenty of lavish gifts.

"And just think, he'd be closer to you." Pa winks. "You *are* engaged."

And that is the crux. I don't want him closer. I don't want to be driven to wed him. Not yet. Marriage is inevitable, but I refuse to give up my freedom or my body sooner than I need to.

Little General bursts into the salon, barking wildly, followed by Perrikin and the man in question. At ten going on eleven, my sister's boy is taller than me, but still full of childish excitement.

"Uncle Richard's brought his horses and is taking me horseback riding over in Rock Creek. Can Little General come, too?"

The dog circles, then plops at Richard's feet. That is the other problem. Richard has managed to win over everyone in the family, even my dog.

I peck him on the cheek. "Morning, Richard."

"Morning, my love. I hope you don't mind if I take the boy. I need to check out the area for the sewer commission."

"You must ask your mother."

Perrikin runs to fetch Mary.

Richard tips his head. "Also . . . I have news from the foundry. They've poured the head. They said it went well."

An angry little fire starts deep inside me. How dare they inform him before me? Having a man by my side might get me more respect in the world of men, but it also means I'm treated as his appendage.

Pa waves his hand. "Sit, Richard. We were just discussing your possible move here. The front-room boarder has ventured on, and we'd love to have you."

At that moment, Mary and Ma arrive, carrying a steaming cup of coffee and a slice of peach pie.

Ma beams at him. "Of course, you must come live here. You're family now."

Mary nods her agreement and hands Richard the pie.

He forks up a bite, swallows, then looks at me. "How do you feel about me taking up residence, Vinnie?"

I want to scream, *No, I'm not ready*. I haven't even told Boudy yet of my impending marriage. But ever since we announced our engagement, I have been swept up in a current of frenetic energy, forcing me closer and closer to that ultimate wedding day.

The burning in my stomach turns from anger to despair. "I have no issue with you moving in. But I would like to make it clear to everyone,"—I gaze around the room—"that Richard and I have agreed the wedding will not take place until the *Farragut* monument is done, so we can honeymoon at his home in Iowa."

"*Done*?" My mother clasps her head with her hands. "Oh, Vinnie. That thing will never be done. What's it been now? Four years? How much longer must you wait before settling down with this man who adores you?"

I can't keep the brittle edge from my voice. "*Settle down*? Is that what you think I'll do once I'm hitched to Richard? Well, you're mistaken, Ma. Creating art is my life's work. And I don't plan on stopping just because I marry."

Everyone stills.

Richard puts an arm around my waist, pulls me against him, and kisses me on the cheek. "We will set the date when we are ready." He removes his arm. "Now, if you have your mother's permission, Perry, let's go for our ride."

Dog, boy, and man flee the scene, leaving me to face a furious mother, a perplexed father, and a stiff-faced Mary.

Ma stomps toward me and waggles her finger in my face. "You are going on thirty. You don't have years to waste doing men's work. I hear you coughing in bed at night every time you come back from that hellhole. All your clothes stink of smoke. But it's the cuts and blisters on your hands that pain me the most. Look at these hands." She holds her roughened palms in front of me. "I've hard-scrabbled all my life. I wanted better for my daughters." She glances at Mary. "It did not work out for your sister, but you . . . somehow . . . you have attracted a wonderful man who loves you and will protect you. I will not let your insufferable pride drive him away."

My face heats. My skin crawls. "Pride? You think I've done all this"—I wave at the marble sculptures surrounding us—"because of pride? I've done it for *you*."

"*For us*? So you can lord it over us and act the suffering benefactor? We've put up with your self-glorification for years, because we love you. But I've told you before—we're simple people. We don't need this fancy house nor servants underfoot. We don't need extravagant clothing or beef on the table every day. I like cooking and cleaning. I like taking care of my boarders. It's what I have done all my life. When I think of all the money you've wasted on rocks, clay, mortgage interest, uncomfortable furniture, and galivants with questionable men, I could weep."

But it is not my mother who is crying. I am.

Tears roll down my cheeks and drip onto my new rose-silk day dress.

Pa takes Ma's hands and pulls them back. "Vinnie knows what she needs to do. Come, Lavinia. It's a beautiful day for a walk on the Capitol grounds." He leads her away.

Mary calls after them, "I'll come, too." She casts me a worried look, then hurries after them.

My sobs are too loud in the silence that fills the room.

I run upstairs to my bedroom and slam the door. Has everything I've done in my life been for nothing? Sobs rack through me, over and over. My chest heaves futilely against the garments caging me in.

I tear at the dress, not caring if I rip it to pieces, discard the bustle, and shuck off the corset. Freed at last, I fall to the floor, curl up in a tight ball, and sob myself to sleep.

When I wake, I know what I must do.

I sit at my vanity and start the goodbye letter to Boudy that I have put off for years.

I will be getting married, I tell him.

And it won't be to him.

The wedding is set for May 28th, 1878. The invitations go out on the same day the last section of the *Farragut* bronze is cast. For the next several months, the workers at the foundry will unmold the pieces and weld them together. When we return from our honeymoon in Iowa, the statue will be ready for my finishing touches. Hopefully, our marriage will be welded together, too.

"Are you ready?" Richard stands in the doorway, his hat in his hand. "I have found the perfect location for the house."

I slip on my newest beribboned straw, stride out the door with him, and ascend into the elegant two-seater buggy Richard has bought to ferry us about town. I would prefer to walk, but I know he wants to show off the woman he has netted to all those erstwhile fellow suitors. So, I imagine myself a lucky lady and sit with my head held high and my eyes on him.

"So, where is this perfect piece of land?"

"We are almost there."

We cross the Presidential Park in front of the White House and start up 17th Street. I survey the area. Ahead is the intersection of K Street and Connecticut Avenue.

A fission of joy punctures my respectable pose, and I clap my hands. "This is where the *Farragut* monument will be. The house plot is close by?"

He grins. "Our house will be right over there on the corner. The front window will have a full view of the monument. Our children can play in the park."

Our children. However this marriage turns out, I will have children to love.

I lean against him. "It's wonderful, Richard. But such a prime location. Can you sign a deal before someone else scoops it up?"

"I already have. It's ours, Vinnie, and I can't wait to show you the plans I've had drawn up."

The joy swirling inside me settles into a tangled knot in my stomach. "You bought it before asking me? And the plans are drawn up?"

"You have enough to deal with, with all the wedding plans, those last-minute orders you are finishing up, and the *Farragut*. I knew you'd love it. You'll love the house plan, too. All brick, three stories, with tall windows and plenty of light. And every convenience—six bedrooms, gas lights in every room, filtered water, and a water closet on every floor."

"And my studio? Where will that be?"

"Just think, Vinnie. Will you really need a studio?"

I open my mouth to say, *Of course, who would Vinnie Ream be without her art?* But he puts a finger over my lips.

"Listen, my love. You will no longer have to worry about selling your work to pay your debts. I have plenty of wealth to support you in the grand style befitting my wife. You'll even be able to give your family the entire Farragut commission award, as you wish to do." He runs his finger down my lips and over my chin, sending shivers down my spine. "Besides, you will soon be busy running a household and caring for our children and me."

How can I argue with that? I've watched my mother. I've watched Mary. That is what marriage is all about. Time to stop hustling and turn my energy into love for this man.

I gaze up into his face. Richard loves me. That's all that matters.

I rest my hand over his. "I can't wait."

Chapter 36

FEBRUARY 1878

THE PIKES, WASHINGTON, D.C.

I knock on the Pikes' door. Behind me, Richard shifts his weight from foot to foot. This is the last place he wants to be. He hates Albert Pike, as most former Union soldiers do, for being a Northerner who supported the Confederacy during the war. Even more, he detests our reason for being here.

Lilly opens the door, wearing a red-and-green plaid frock with a fashionable, slender silhouette and a slight train that makes my ruffle-bedecked, cashmere walking dress look dowdy. For the first time ever, she doesn't smile when she sees me.

"Papa's waiting for you in the aviary."

I clasp Richard's hand tighter and hope he doesn't realize Albert is showing disdain for my choice of husband by entertaining us in the befeathered solarium rather than the parlor.

A subdued Lilly glides before us through the hall and opens the double doors to the sunny, bird-filled room. A din of cheeps and coos greets us. A parrot squawks a piercing, *"Throw the politicians out."*

With a wave, Lilly ushers us in, then backs out. The door snaps shut with a *click*.

Opposite us, Albert, wearing a work smock stained with bird droppings, his pet macaw perched on his shoulder, confers a look so grim you'd have thought someone died. And maybe my upcoming wedding is like a funeral for him. It will be the death of his hopes for ever possessing me. A time for him to bury his futile love.

I smile with all the bridal anticipation I can manage. "This is Lieutenant Richard Hoxie, my fiancé."

"Is he, my love?"

Richard twitches at *my love* yet maintains his military composure. He bows at the waist. "Mr. Pike."

Albert licks his lips. "Grand Master Pike."

"I am not a Mason, sir."

"Vinnie is. Eighth degree."

"Miss Ream is many things." Richard takes me by the arm. "Including being the woman who has agreed to be my wife."

"I believe we've met at one of Vinnie's Wednesday salons. Heard you sing. A pleasant tenor." Albert moves closer, sucking up all the space around us. He stops in front of Richard. At sixty-eight, he is twice Richard's age and twice his size, standing half a head taller with broader shoulders and lion-size hands.

Albert looks him up and down. "So, this is the man you've chosen over me, my love."

Richard lets go of my arm, fists his hands, and spreads his stance, as if to wipe those words from Albert's mouth.

For a moment, I fear there will be fisticuffs. I can't let Albert bully my future husband.

I lift my chin. "Yes, he is, and we have come to ask a favor." I look to Richard.

Albert quirks an eyebrow. "Have you?"

Richard nods. "We have moved the date of our wedding to this May. I would like you to be the best man."

Albert slowly turns his head and frowns at me. "And this is what you want, my love?"

"Yes, Richard and I are agreed that we do not want to wait until the Farragut project is completed. There have been too many delays. So, it would be a great honor to have you as part of our wedding party."

Out of the corner of my eye, I can see Richard's jaw twitching. He will explode if we don't conclude this meeting shortly.

I clasp both Albert's hands. "I want you there on the most important day in my life." I throw in something I know will entice him. "And if you agree, I would love you to write a poem for the occasion that I can set to music and have sung in the church. Please say yes." I let go and wait.

He runs a finger up and down the macaw's throat and side-eyes Richard. "For you, my dear Vinnie, I would do anything, even help you make the biggest mistake of your life. Yes, I will be there."

"Thank you." Richard reaches out to shake his hand. At the same time, the macaw lifts into the air, its wings smacking his face and whacking off his officer's cap. Feathers fly. Richard shouts and bats at the bird, all the while backing up until he's pressed against the door. The parrot swoops around the room in a flash of blue, and then, with a proud tilt of its head, settles back on Albert's shoulder.

"No harm done." I swoop up the hat and set it back on Richard's head while sending a grinning Albert a stern shake of my head.

He shrugs and reaches out his own hand. "I'm so sorry, Lieutenant. These birds can be quite unpredictable at times." He utters a short laugh. "I think he was after the gold insignia on your hat."

Both he and I know better. The macaw is well-trained.

I loop my arm into the seething man's beside me and thank Pike again. Richard bows, and I hustle my fuming fiancé out of the house and into the street.

Richard helps me into the buggy, slides in on the other side, and takes up the reins. "Despicable man." He gazes down at me. "Vinnie, I want you to have the most amazing wedding, one that will live long in our memories. If you want Pike to be the best man, then he will be. But once the wedding is over, I refuse to socialize with Albert Pike ever again."

I peck him on the cheek. "Relax, my dear. There's no reason you will have to. He's my friend, not yours."

"Not the kind of friend I want my wife to have." His tone has an edge.

I draw back. "I've known Albert Pike far longer than I have known you. He has stood up for me and shown me great kindness. You may think him a traitor to our country, and I agree, but that war is long over. And yes, I find his views on race abominable. But I refuse to give up my friendship with him. I don't care what the world thinks. To me, he will always be the grandfather I never had."

"*Grandfather*?" Richard's jaw clenches. "I think not. The man insulted and humiliated me because he wants you."

I pat his arm. "Albert? Well, I agree he's not happy I'm getting married."

"Albert Pike is a lustful old man who has no business being an intimate acquaintance with another man's wife. In the future, you may visit him in the company of others, but once this wedding is over, you are never to invite him to our home."

I hear only one word. "What do you mean *intimate*? I'll have you know that no man has ever touched me that way."

Silence answers me.

Is Pike right? Have I chosen wrongly?

I chew my lip. "*Richard?* Do you believe those rumors about me?"

He turns to look at me. "It doesn't matter what anyone says. I love *you*. I love your brightness. I love your openhearted joy. I love that you see only the good in people. Even me. And in a few months, all the wonder that is you will be mine."

I let out the breath I was holding.

He faces forward and concentrates on maneuvering the buggy through the vehicle traffic. Anyone looking at us would question what I see in this cold, dictatorial-sounding soldier. My mother sees wealth and grandchildren. My Pa sees someone to watch over me when he's gone. Mary sees me achieving what she once dreamed of. General Sherman and all my other suitors see a successful rival. But I see a man who is passionate and desperate for love—my love.

And I *will* love him.

We pull into the drive beside the house. Hidden from view, I rest my head on Richard's shoulder and breathe in his scent of horse and earth. He does not draw away this time. He gathers me closer and lowers his lips. Desire uncurls.

I remember Boudy's loving refusal of my virginity. I am finally glad that he did.

I kiss Richard long and lovingly. I can't wait for our wedding night.

Chapter 37

THE REAM'S BOARDING HOUSE, PENNSYLVANIA AVENUE

My wedding day arrives sooner than expected. I glance around the bedroom. Why had I thought this was to be *my* wedding? There is barely room for me, the gown, and the four women gathered around me, every one of whom has an opinion on what I should do or wear.

Virginia Farragut, here from New York to revel in the success of her matchmaking, picks up the fan I plan to carry. "Are you sure you don't want to carry a more traditional bouquet?"

"A fan is more practical. I refuse to stand at the altar with sweat dripping down my forehead."

Ma drapes my veil over the chair back. "Well, then. How about a wreath of flowers in place of the head wrap?"

"It's a turban, and it will keep my hair under control in this humidity. I want to see Richard when he says, *I do*." I turn back to the mirror and finish powdering my face and shoulders. "Besides, there will be plenty of flowers at the church."

Perrikin pops into the room, Little General at his heels. "Aunt Vinnie, have you seen the newspapers?"

The dog romps toward me and paws at my petticoat. Mary and Lilly shriek, grab the gown and veil, and back up.

I rub his head and hug him tight. "I'm going to miss you in Iowa."

Virginia clicks her tongue. "I doubt that."

This wedding has brought out a whole different side of the staid widow. She's even taken me aside and told me what I should expect, and what I should demand, from my soon-to-be husband.

I frown at her. "I'd love to take him with us. Wolfhounds shouldn't be kept in a city, but free to race across the prairie, chasing jackrabbits."

"Well, he certainly doesn't belong here." Mary grabs the newspaper from Perrikin and scoots both boy and dog out of the room. Then she turns and smooths down the satin skirt of the all-important gown with its rows of braiding running from hem to bodice. "Thank heavens you weren't dressed yet. And don't worry. The boys will give that dog plenty of exercise."

Ma comes behind me. "Now, let's get you ready. Brides can be a bit late, but not so late the flowers wilt."

She combs and separates my hair into twisted coils and wraps them around my head to give me height. I have no need for hair rats. My thick, wavy hair has always been my glory.

As she works, I wave to Mary. "What's so exciting in the newspaper?"

She shakes it open. "Oh my. There are hundreds of letters from your admirers wishing you and Richard the best."

She hands me the paper, and I spread it open on the desk. Names both great and ordinary fill the pages. I spy old friends and new. Dear Major Rollins, now serving on the board of the University of Missouri, has not forgotten me, nor have so many who have passed through Congress.

A moment of sadness washes over me. Despite these overflowing pages, there remain so many who are not here, especially my mentors, Thaddeus Stevens and Ezra Cornell, and then there are those who loved me—Sam Marshall and Boudy, who know by now the path I have chosen. And, of course, Abraham Lincoln, who gave a girl the chance of a lifetime.

I flip the pages again. There are more accolades here than I have ever received for my sculptures. The thought cuts deep, but I push it away.

This is the happiest day of my life, and I will let nothing spoil it.

The Church of the Ascension antechamber smells like a botanical garden. I peek through the doors. Red roses, orange blossoms, and violets bedeck the aisles. All of the Washington elite, the top levels of government, and the military brass fill the pews, as do the ambassadors from Japan and Denmark. Even my brother, Bob, but not his wife, has come east to witness my wedding day.

Over it all, four male voices sing the beautiful poem Albert has written for us.

General Sherman approaches. "It is time."

I finger the lily-of-the-valley spray affixed to my bodice and fight back tears. I take his proffered arm. "Thank you for filling in at the last minute."

"I am sorry your father has taken ill on this important day."

I swallow a sob and nod. "Richard and I will say our vows again in his presence when we get back to the house."

"That is what I love about you, Vinnie. You have always put your family first."

"As have you."

He squeezes his eyes shut. "I have treated you ill all these years, my dear. And while I wish I were the one standing at the altar, waiting for you, I want you to know you could not be marrying a more upright man, nor he a better woman."

The doors open. My bridesmaids, led by Mary, proceed down the red carpet. The organist plays the lyrical melody that Franz Liszt has written especially for the occasion.

Trembling, I grasp Will's arm and hold my head high. After flaunting society all my life, I am finally doing the right thing.

At the altar, Richard's face breaks into that boyish smile I love so much. I have made my choice, and whatever the future holds, I will embrace it with all the love I have inside.

Two days later, we arrive in Iowa City. Richard assists me off the train, and I clasp my husband's hand as we cross the platform, then wait patiently while he hires a conveyance for us and our trunks. I can't believe we are truly married, nor that I am back on my beloved prairie at last. I can't wait to run free across the rolling grassland that whizzed by our train window. But first, we must consummate our marriage.

Inside, my stomach clenches, and my pulse thrums. I smile up at him. Soon. Soon, I will discover the joys of wedded bliss.

His aunt's clapboard house is as plain and old-fashioned as Richard claimed, with sun-faded calico curtains on the windows and well-washed quilts on the beds. But it's clean and airy, and I love it.

Sunlight streams into the bedroom as I remove my too-fancy hat, unpin my hair, and shuck off the confining traveling dress with its annoying corset and bustle. Freed of society's expectations, I lean on the windowsill and breathe in the scent of wildflowers and grasses. My lungs fill with memories, and I feel like a girl again. All I need is my pony, and I would be off, thundering across the fields stretching out before me as far as my eyes can see.

The door opens behind me, and Richard enters. He's a different man from the one who stood at the altar, sat rigidly beside me on the train, and who just carried me over the threshold. With his jacket gone, his sleeves rolled up, and his shoulders relaxed, the man before me, sucking a stalk of hay, has the ease of a Midwestern farmer. Most delightfully, he is barefoot.

He moves further into the room. "The farmer brought over my horses. Just got them settled in the stable. I know how anxious you are to get out there and race across the fields. I think the mare will suit you. She's spirited, like you. But first . . ."

First? I peer out the window. It is the perfect time to ride.

I turn back to urge him on and freeze. Richard's fingers move down the front of his shirt, slowly pressing each tiny pearl button through its hole. Then he slips it off, and I draw in a breath.

He is more beautiful than any marble sculpture I have ever seen, and he is mine.

He takes me in his arms, then slips my chemise off my shoulders and down. Our bare skin meets. His mouth claims mine, and I am glad we did not consummate our marriage in the stuffy hotel room we stopped at in Chicago.

This is the perfect place for two lovers. Crickets chirp. Birds warble. The curtains waft in the breeze.

We sink onto the bed, and I discover his passion, and he releases mine.

A well-satisfied woman, I spread my arms, spin around, then throw myself into the grass. I am in heaven. Above me, the sky is as blue as my husband's eyes are when he gazes at me on awakening. Below me, the warm earth cups my body like his warm hands when we lie down to sleep at night. For the first time in years, I am truly happy. I have wed the best of men.

I flatten my hand against my pocket and listen to the paper crinkle. Boudy's letter, delivered the day of the wedding, has weighed heavily across the miles. Do I dare read it? I don't even want to think of him in this moment.

I pull it out and wave it in the gusty breeze. I toy with letting go, but I can't. I remember him coming to my aid when the Farragut model broke and braving the catcalls and disparagement for wearing his Cherokee heritage with pride. I can be that brave, too.

I rip the envelope open and find no hard words, only loving goodwill. He has sent congratulations and joyful wishes. I kiss his signature, wish him equal joy, and then tear the letter into tiny pieces. Holding the scraps on my palm, I blow them into the wind and let them fly free.

I follow the whirling white bits with my eyes and finally see what my pride and selfishness have blinded me to all these years. Not all love is of the flesh, as delightful as it is. The greater love is sacrificing your heart, your energy, and your desires for those you love. Boudy did that for me all those years ago, and for that, I will always hold him in my heart.

Some people are lucky to find one person to love them in a lifetime. I have found two.

I carry that thought with me after we settle in Washington, and I resume work on the *Farragut* project. Assembled and on its temporary plinth, my bronze colossus towers over me. I have no desire to climb up on the pulley-rigged platform Richard has designed for me, to do the tedious work of filing down the seams to near invisibility and smoothing the surfaces so they catch the light. I want to watch our future home emerge from the ground. I want to return to Iowa and spend my days running free and my nights curled up by his side.

But it doesn't matter what I want. When finished, this sculpture, and the plaza it will be erected in, will not only support my family but immortalize an honorable man who helped win the war, repay his wife, Virginia, for the joy she has brought me in Richard, and stand for the ages as a monument to what one dedicated woman, with two pair of hands and boundless creativity, can accomplish in the world of men.

The End

Author's Note

"Just think when we are all dead and gone, someone will write a novel about you, and another will write a play. Your studio in the Capitol will be the grand tableau in the play. Bingham and Butler will be in the play, and there will be spoons and broken statues . . . and Thaddeus Stevens will be one of the heroes."

Robert Lee Ream

Letter to Vinnie Ream from her father, 1868

Well, I have written that novel, and although the artist George Caleb Bingham does not play a major role, many other people of note do. I hope you have enjoyed this foray into the Washington society during and after the Civil War—the period ridiculed in Mark Twain's novel, *The Gilded Age*.

In many ways, Vinnie Ream's life mirrors the best and worst of the second half of the nineteenth century, when people willing to game the system could get rich overnight and go broke in a heartbeat. From railroads to land schemes, it was a period of little government regulation and unlimited corporate and personal greed.

At the same time, the turmoil of the Civil War created new career paths for women to pursue. With the men at war, women could find work as nurses, journalists, or government workers, such as Vinnie did at the post office. Orator Anna Dickinson, the subject of the first book in this series, was not only one of the first women hired by the U.S. Mint but also the first to address Congress. It was a time when a woman might consider a career other than marriage and be successful in the male-dominated society.

Despite her frontier background, there is no question that American sculptor Vinnie Ream did exactly this. In an era when young girls were sheltered, she haunted the seat of government in pursuit of fame and fortune. Her story is peppered with grand undertakings, amazing accomplishments, and associations with most of the major political and artistic figures of her day. When I created my character list, I was shocked to discover that almost every single person she interacted with was notable in some way.

Vinnie's ten-thousand-dollar Lincoln sculpture commission ($250,000 in today's dollars) was a fantastical amount of money for a young, untried sculptor, but also her undoing as a creative artist. With limited experience handling finances and in striving to live a lifestyle more appropriate to the wealthy than her lower-middle-class roots, she sank her family into debt. Compounded by her sister's disastrous marriage, it took winning the Farragut commission by underhanded means to alleviate it.

After her marriage to Richard Hoxie, money was no longer an issue. However, Richard expected her to be a conventional wife and serve as a hostess to further his career. Still in the military, he was stationed around the country, taking her away from her beloved Washington and the art world.

In 1883, after the birth of her son, who suffered a brain injury affecting his mental development, she slowly withdrew from her art. Only after a heart attack in 1903 did she return to sculpture, creating the statue of Samuel Jordan Kirkwood for Iowa and that of Sequoyah for the Oklahoma Cherokee, both in the Hall of Statuary in the Capitol.

HOW AUTHENTIC IS *PRAIRIE CINDERELLA*?

Often, in a biographical historical novel, it is necessary to change some events for dramatic purposes. In *Prairie*

Cinderella, I have made few changes—Vinnie's life was dramatic enough. My fictional version of Vinnie Ream's life is based on the timeline as presented in the numerous letters, diary entries, contemporary news articles, and several biographies about her. The characters, almost all drawn from the historical record, are represented as accurately as possible, based on my research. Where I have let my fancy fly is in depicting Vinnie's motivations and desires.

Many questions remain about how Vinnie Ream accomplished what she did as a woman to obtain her government commissions. During her lifetime, she was accused of being a hussy and offering sexual favors to politicians in return for their votes. Even today, noted male historians wink when they talk about her. On the other hand, many who knew her, such as Georg Brandes and Franz Liszt, saw her as a girlish creature whose naivete and enthusiasm brought joy wherever she went. In her own writings, she claims she used smiles, posies, and gifts of candy to win favor with her political friends.

I believe her true persona lies somewhere in between. I have chosen to depict her as a self-promoter who used both feminine wiles and showmanship to gain wealth and recognition for herself and her family at a time when women were more often treated as second-class citizens.

At the same time, I have drawn on my own background as a professional artist to imbue her with the frustration that comes from the financial pressure to produce art that will sell to support oneself and one's family, as opposed to creating the artistic dreams in one's heart.

One other instance of my imagination at work is the idea that Perry Fuller was murdered by his wife with Vinnie's help. His death, on the same day the Lincoln statue was unveiled, while attributed to a heart attack, was never fully explained. It seemed fitting to me that, in my story, Mary should take revenge on the man who'd hoodwinked her and ruined her life.

SOME HISTORICAL NOTES

Vinnie's age. No one knows exactly when Vinnie Ream was born. Not because no birthdate is recorded, but because so many different ones are. Small-framed, dainty, and savvy, she played up her youth and "lost" years in each succeeding census. I have chosen to make her sixteen at the start of the story, even though, based on the 1847 date on her tombstone, she would have been fourteen. This is a compromise on my part. It is quite possible she was older.

The census in 1850 lists her age as nine and that in 1860 as eighteen. However, ten years later, in the 1870 census, she loses five years and is listed as twenty-three. This date change, which fits the 1847 birthdate, played well when marketing herself as a child prodigy during her campaign to win the Lincoln Commission.

Christian Female College. Founded in 1851, this was a two-year women's academy in Columbia, Missouri. It evolved into a four-year, co-educational institution, and in 1970, it changed its name to Columbia College. Vinnie's painting of Martha Washington still hangs there.

Winnebago. This name, meaning "people of the dirty water," was given by white explorers to the agricultural Native American tribe occupying Wisconsin in the 1600s. Despite its connotation, I have chosen to use this name, as it would have been during Vinnie Ream's time. But the correct name for this tribe is Ho-Chunk, meaning "people of the big voice."

Indian Territory. This was an evolving area set aside in 1834 for the relocation of Native Americans removed from their tribal homes. This area became smaller and smaller as white settlers infringed on the tribal lands. In Vinnie Ream's time, Indian Territory occupied mostly Oklahoma.

The West. Throughout the novel, I have used the term "The West" to describe the central part of the United States, now known as the Midwest. For the people of the time, anything west of the Mississippi was the West.

REFERENCES

To learn more about Vinnie Ream

"Vinnie Ream" Historic Missourians.
    https://historicmissourians.shsmo.org/vinnie-ream/
Labor of Love: The Life & Art of Vinnie Ream by Glenn
    Sherwood, Sunshine Press, 1977.
Vinnie Ream: An American Sculptor by Edward S. Cooper,
    Academy Chicago Publishers, 2004.
Vinnie Ream: The Story of the Girl Who Sculpted Lincoln by
    Gordon Langley, Hall, Holt, Rinehart, and Winston, 1963.
The *Vinnie Ream and R. L. Hoxie Papers* are available at the
    Library of Congress.
To learn more about 19th-century women sculptors:
*A Sisterhood of Sculptors: American Artists in Nineteenth-
    Century Rome* by Melissa Dubakis, 2014.
"The White Marmorean Flock: 19th Century Lady Sculptors in
    Rome" by Lindsay Lynch https://the-
    toast.net/2014/11/21/white-marmorean-flock-19th-
    century-lady-sculptors-rome/

**To learn more about the Cherokee and Cornelius
Boudinot**

Elias Cornelius Boudinot: A Life on the Cherokee Border by
    James W. Parins, University of Nebraska Press, 2006.

To learn more about the Gilded Age

The Gilded Age: A Tale of Today by Mark Twain, 1873.
*The Republic for Which It Stands: The United States During
    Reconstruction and the Gilded Age 1865-1896* by Richard
    White, 2017.

WHERE TO SEE WORKS BY VINNIE REAM

Abraham Lincoln, U.S. Capitol, Washington, D.C.

Abraham Lincoln bust, Cornell University, Ithaca, New York.

Abraham Lincoln medallion, Ford Theater Collection, National Park Service.

Albert Pike bust, House of the Temple, Washington, D.C.

America, State Historical Society of Iowa, Iowa City.

Admiral Farragut, Farragut Square, Washington, D.C.

Idleness, State Historical Society of Wisconsin at Madison.

John Wentworth, Chicago Historical Society, Chicago, Illinois.

Kirkwood, U.S. Capitol, Washington, D.C.

Martha Washington oil painting, Columbia College, Columbia, Missouri.

Morning Glory, National League of Pen Women, Washington, D.C.

Passion Flower, State Historical Society of Wisconsin at Madison.

Samuel Powell bust, Brooklyn Borough Hall, Brooklyn, New York.

Sappho, Grave of Lavinia Ream Hoxie, Arlington National Cemetery, Washington, D.C.

Sappho, National Museum of American Art, Smithsonian, Washington, D.C.

Sequoyah, U.S. Capitol, Washington, D.C.

Spirit of the Carnival, State Historical Society of Wisconsin at Madison.

Susan B. Anthony Medallion, Oklahoma Historical Society, Oklahoma City.

The Violet, National League of Pen Women, Washington, D.C.

The West, Wisconsin State Capitol at Madison.

William Seward bust, Louis E. Warren Lincoln Library and Museum, Fort Wayne, Indiana.

Historic Personages

Note: Almost every character in this novel is based on an actual person. Here are the personal details for many of them.

THE REAM-HOXIE FAMILY

Hoxie, Lavinia "Vinnie" Ellen Ream (1847-1914): Born in Madison, Wisconsin, Vinnie was a gifted child in music and art. She attended St. Joseph Female Academy and Christian Female College in Columbia, Missouri, where she attracted attention for her artistic and musical gifts.

Hoxie, Richard "Richie" (1883-1936): The only child of Vinnie Ream and Richard Hoxie, a childhood injury, possibly an accidental pellet shot in the head, affected his mental development. He lived with his parents until Vinnie's death, then resided until his passing at Still-Hildreth Sanatorium in Macon, Missouri.

Hoxie, Richard Leveridge (1844-1931): Born in New York City to well-to-do parents, he spent his early years in Europe. Upon their deaths in Italy, he was sent to live with his aunt in Iowa. He attended Iowa State University and West Point, serving in the First Iowa Cavalry during the American Civil War. Then, as an army engineer, he worked on designing the Washington, D.C. water and sewer systems and Rock Park.

Ream, Lavinia "Ma" McDonald (1809-1893): Born in Brookfield, Ohio, she ran a series of boarding houses, starting with the log cabin, "Madison House," on the banks of Lake Mendota, Madison, Wisconsin, as well as in

Lawrence, Kansas; Columbus, Missouri; and Little Rock and Fort Smith, Arkansas.

Ream, Robert "Bob" (1838-1887): Vinnie's brother served in the 1st Battalion Arkansas Cavalry, Company H, which fought in the Battle of Pea Ridge. Paroled, he settled in Indian Territory (Oklahoma) and married Annie Guy, a member of the Chickasaw Nation.

Ream, Robert "Pa" Lee (1809-1885): Born in Centre County, Pennsylvania, Vinnie's father was a government land surveyor and explorer. He drew the earliest maps of Nebraska, Iowa, Kansas, and Missouri.

THE FULLER FAMILY

Fuller, Alfred (1861-?): Perry Fuller's youngest son by his first wife.

Fuller, Cynthia "Mary" Ann Ream (1844-1917): Vinnie's older sister was born in Madison, Wisconsin, and attended St. Joseph Female Academy and Columbia College in Columbia, Missouri. She was called Mary by her family. She married Perry Fuller and had one child. After her husband died, leaving her destitute, she worked as a clerk in the Department of the Interior. She never remarried.

Fuller, Perry (1821-1871): Politician, Indian agent, businessman, and hustler, Fuller served as Indian agent to the Sac and Fox tribe, where he defrauded them out of their government stipends, hawked tainted liquor, and sold off part of their reservation. Pursuing real estate deals, he founded the Kansas towns of Centropolis, Minneola, and Greenwood and ran a large mercantile store in Lawrence, Kansas. As thanks for his help during his impeachment trial, Andrew Johnson named him Customs Inspector for the Port of New Orleans. There, he was accused of stealing goods from the port and brought up on federal charges. He was deeply in debt when he died of mysterious causes, possibly pneumonia or a heart attack.

Fuller, Perry "Perrikin" (1867-1933): Mary and Perry's only surviving child.

THE CHEROKEES

Boudinot, Elias "Boudy" Cornelius (1835-1890): Politician, lawyer, and editor, he was the Eastern-educated son of Chief Elias Boudinot, who was assassinated by fellow tribesmen for signing the treaty that led to the Trail of Tears. Boudinot was editor of the *Cherokee Phoenix*, the first Cherokee language newspaper, and co-founder of *The Arkansan*. He served as a Lieutenant Colonel in the Confederate Army and was the Cherokee delegate to the Confederate Congress. He was the first Native American lawyer to try a case before the Supreme Court. He worked to establish Oklahoma as a state and founded the town of Vinita, named after Vinnie Ream, located where the Missouri, Kansas, and Texas Railway and the Atlantic and Pacific Railroad intersected. On his deathbed, his last words were reportedly, "Tell Vinnie Ream I love her."

Ridge, John "Yellow Bird" Rollin (1827-1867): Cherokee poet and author. First Native American to write and publish a popular novel in English, *The Life and Adventures of Joaquin Murieta.*

Watie, Stand (1806-1871): Politician and second chief of the Cherokee Nation from 1862 to 1866 and the last Confederate General to surrender.

VINNIE'S FRIENDS & ACQUAINTANCES

Bessels, Emil (1847-1888): A German Arctic explorer, zoologist, and physician, Bessels accompanied Charles Hall on the Polaris Expedition to the North Pole, serving as physician and head of the scientific team. Circumstantial evidence indicates that he murdered Charles Hall by arsenic poisoning due to jealousy over the attentions of Vinnie Ream, as detailed in the book, *May We Be Spared to Meet on Earth* by Russell A. Potter, et al. https://visionsnorth.blogspot.com/2019/01/emil-bessels-serial-poisoner.html

Blair, Montgomery (1813-1883): A Maryland lawyer, he served as U.S. District Attorney and Common Pleas judge before being appointed by Abraham Lincoln as Postmaster General, serving from 1861 to 1864.

Clark, Edward (1822-1902): He served as Architect of the Capitol from 1865 to 1902.

Corcoran, William Wilson (1878-1898): An American banker, Corcoran was one of the wealthiest men in the United States and an ardent collector of American artworks. In 1874, his collection became the Corcoran Gallery of Art, now part of the Smithsonian. He also established the Oak Hill Cemetery in Washington, D.C.

Cornell, Ezra (1807-1884): Inventor, businessman, and philanthropist, he founded Western Union and Cornell University.

Custer, Elizabeth "Libby" Bacon (1842-1933): After the death of her husband, George Custer, Elizabeth spent the rest of her life speaking and writing about her husband's exploits.

Custer, George Armstrong (1839-1876): Graduating last in his class at West Point, Custer served as a cavalry officer during the Civil War. He died at the Battle of the Little Bighorn.

Farragut, Loyall (1844-1916): Son of David and Virginia Farragut, he was raised aboard his father's ship. In 1868, he graduated from West Point and served in the army for three years. He married in 1869.

Farragut, Virginia Dorcas Loyall (1824-1884): Widow of Admiral David Glasgow Farragut, who captured New Orleans during the Civil War.

Hall, Charles Francis (c.1821-1871): An acclaimed Arctic explorer, Hall received a $50,000 commission from the U.S. government to launch the Polaris Expedition to the North Pole. While in the Arctic, Hall became violently ill and accused the ship's doctor, Emil Bessell, of poisoning him. He died in 1873 and was buried in Greenland. In 1963, his body was exhumed and found to be laced with a lethal amount of arsenic. Affectionate letters and gifts to him from Vinnie Ream, and the suspicious death of Bessell's fiancée on their wedding day, have lent credence to the hypothesis that Hall was murdered by the doctor.

Pike, Albert (1809-1891): Author, poet, lawyer, judge, and Freemason, Pike served as a Brigadier General in the Confederate Army and held the distinction of being named a traitor by both the South and the North. He spoke several Native American languages and often represented the tribes in court. He served as Grand Commander of the Scottish Rite of Freemasonry, Southern Division. Known for his racist views, he may have supported the development of the Ku Klux Klan.

Pike, Lillian (1843-1919): Lillian was the sixth child of Albert Pike and the one who took care of him in his elder years, only marrying William Oscar Roome in 1898 after her father's death. She is credited with inventing and patenting a part for the flute.

Swisshelm, Jane Grey (1815-1884): A supporter of abolition and women's rights, Swisshelm was the first female American syndicated journalist. During the Civil War, she served as a nurse. She was known for her fiery temper, which led to her being fired by Horace Greeley of the *NY Tribune*.

Zevely, Alexander Nathaniel (1813-1888): Zevely held the position of Third Postmaster General from 1859 to 1869. He was in charge of the dead letter office and is credited with the idea of displaying the soldiers' cartes de viste in the General Post Office, a practice that was then taken up by post offices all over the country.

THE POLITICIANS

Browning, Orville Hickman (1806-1881): A Republican senator from Illinois from 1861 to 1863 and a close friend of Abraham Lincoln. He was Secretary of the Interior under Andrew Johnson from 1866 to 1869.

Butler, Benjamin "Bull" Franklin (1818-1893): An abolitionist, Civil War general, and politician, he served in the U.S. House of Representatives from Massachusetts from 1867 to 1879.

Conness, John (1821-1909): Conness served as U.S. Senator from California from 1863 to 1869. He established Yosemite Park.

Delano, Columbus (1809-1896): Delano served in the House of Representatives from Ohio from 1845 to 1847, from 1865 to 1869, and as Secretary of the Interior from 1870 to 1875. He was responsible for the establishment of Yellowstone Park, but also for the slaughter of the bison and the policy of forcing Native American tribes onto reservations.

Harlan, John (1820-1899): He served as U.S. Senator from Iowa intermittently from 1855 to 1873 and was Secretary of the Interior under Andrew Johnson from 1865 to 1866.

Johnson, Reverdy (1796-1876): The defense lawyer in the Dred Scott case, he served as Attorney General under Zachary Taylor and as senator from Maryland from 1849 to 1868. From 1868 to 1869, he was U.S. Minister to Great Britain.

Julien, George Washington (1817-1899): Julien served in the U.S. House of Representatives for Indiana from 1861 to 1871. He was a strong supporter of equal rights and introduced a women's suffrage bill to Congress in 1865.

Lincoln, Abraham (1809-1865): 16th President of the United States, assassinated April 15, 1865.

Marshall, Samuel (1821-1890): He served as a U.S. Representative from Illinois from 1855 to 1859 and from 1865 to 1875.

Nesmith, James Willis (1820-1885): Nesmith was the U.S. Senator from Oregon from 1861 to 1867 and the Oregon Representative at-large from 1873 to 1875.

Nicolay, John George (1832-1901): Author and diplomat, he served as secretary to Abraham Lincoln from 1861 to 1865.

Rice, John Hovey (1816-1911): Rice served in the U.S. House of Representatives for the state of Maine from 1861 to 1867 and was a member of the Lincoln sculpture commission.

Rollins, James Sidney "Major" (1812-1888): Founder of the University of Missouri, he served in the House of Representatives for Missouri from 1861 to 1865. He initiated the bills establishing the transcontinental railway and state agricultural colleges. He played a key role in the passage of the Thirteenth Amendment.

Ross, Edmund Gibson (1826-1907): A journeyman printer and ardent abolitionist, he served in the 11th Kansas Volunteer Cavalry. In 1869, with the help of Perry Fuller, he filled the vacant senatorial seat for Kansas. During his tenure, he boarded with the Ream family. He is best known for his vote against impeaching President Andrew Johnson.

Sherman, John (1823-1900): The younger brother of General William Sherman, he served in the House of Representatives for Ohio from 1855 to 1861 and the Senate from 1861 to 1877 and 1881 to 1897. From 1877 to 1881, he was Secretary of the Treasury.

Sherman, William "Will" Tecumseh (1820-1891): A graduate of West Point, he is best known for his exploits as the commander of the Western Division of the Union Army during the Civil War. After being Secretary of War in 1869, he served as Commanding General of the U.S. Army until 1883.

Stevens, Thaddeus (1792-1862): A lawyer, politician, and abolitionist, he served as a member of the U.S. House of Representatives from 1842 to 1868. He was the leader of the Radical Republicans during the Civil War.

Sumner, Charles (1811-1874): U.S. Senator from Massachusetts from 1851 to 1874.

Thompson, Richard Wigginton (1808-1900): Thompson served in the U.S. House of Representatives between 1841 and 1849 for Indiana. He then served as a circuit court judge and played an active role in several political parties, eventually supporting Lincoln for President. In 1877, President Rutherford B. Hayes named him Secretary of the Navy.

Trumbull, Lyman (1813-1896): From 1855 to 1873, Trumbull was a United States Senator from Illinois and key political ally of President Lincoln.

Voorhees, Daniel Wolsey (1827-1897): Voorhees served as a member of the U.S. House of Representatives from 1869 to 1873 for Indiana and U.S. Senator from 1877 to 1897. His wife, Harriet, was a strong supporter of Vinnie Ream.

Wade, Benjamin Franklin (1800-1878): A senator from Ohio, he served from 1851 to 1869 and was President of the Senate from 1867 to 1869.

Washburne, Elihu Benjamin (1816-1887): Washburne was a member of the U.S. House of Representatives for Illinois from 1853 to 1869. As Ambassador to France, from 1869 to 1877, he heroically stayed in Paris during the Franco-Prussian War, where he helped American and German citizens trapped in Paris to escape.

Yates, Richard (1815-1873): Following positions as a U.S. Representative from Illinois and Governor of the state, he served in the Senate from 1865 to 1871. He was a close friend of President Lincoln.

IN ROME

Brandes, Georges Morris Cohen (1842-1912): A noted Danish author and literary critic, Brandes met Vinnie Ream on the train from Vienna to Rome and spent seventeen days with her. He was so fascinated by her that he devoted eight pages to her in his memoir, *Recollections of My Childhood and My Youth*, characterizing her as "a mind akin with my own."

Liszt, Franz (1811-1886): Liszt was a gifted Hungarian composer, pianist, and teacher, who was a superstar of his time, subjected to what was called at the time Lisztmania, with women mobbing him for a piece of his clothing or a cigar butt. When Vinnie met him in Rome in 1870, he was at a low point in life and had withdrawn from most public appearances. His son and daughter had recently died, and his planned marriage had been scuttled.

Pulitzer, Albert (1851-1909): The younger brother of the publisher Joseph Pulitzer, Albert was a star reporter for the *New York Herald*, later serving as their Washington and foreign correspondent. He founded the *New York Morning Journal* in 1886.

Torrey, Franklin (1830-1912): Torrey was the younger partner in the Boston firm, Bowker, Torrey & Co., the largest marble works in the United States. They also owned one of the best Carrara quarries. He served as American Consul to Genoa.

Wallace, Lew (1827-1905): An American lawyer, diplomat, inventor, and author, after fighting in the Mexican-American War, Wallace served as a major general during the Civil War. After the war, he ran unsuccessfully for Congress but was named Governor of the Mexican territories by President Hayes. He is best known as the author of *Ben-Hur: A Tale of the Christ*.

THE ARTISTS

Bingham, George Caleb (1811-1879): Artist, Civil War soldier, and antislavery politician, Bingham served in a variety of political positions in Missouri during his lifetime. Mainly self-taught, Bingham traveled the country painting portraits. A close friend of Major James Rollins, he met Vinnie Ream during a visit to Washington and became enamored of her, much to his wife's displeasure. His 1876 portrait of her shows her in her artist smock with a clay tool in her hand, the bust of Lincoln in the background.

Healey, George Peter Alexander (1813-1894): A popular painter of the nineteenth century, he was well-known for his portraits of eminent people. During Vinnie's stay in Rome, Healy painted her portrait with her dressed as an Italian peasant girl.

Hosmer, Harriet (1830-1908): Hosmer is considered the first and most eminent of nineteenth-century sculptors. She was a prominent member of the colony of American artists and writers working in Rome that included Nathaniel Hawthorne, William Thackeray, George Eliot, and the sculptors who flocked around Vinnie. She worked in a neoclassical style and is credited with inventing a process to turn limestone into marble.

Lewis, Edmonia (1824-1907): Of mixed Native American and African American ancestry, she gained fame for sculpting abolitionists in Boston, earning enough to pay her way to Rome. Her style was neoclassical, but her subjects represented Native American and African themes.

Majoli, Luigi (1819-1897): A sculptor from Ravenna, Italy, he shared a studio in Florence with Enrico Pazzi. He is the sculptor of the bust of *Giuseppe Valadier* on the Pincian Hill in Rome.

Mills, Clark (1810-1883): A self-taught American sculptor, Mills is best known for his sculpture of Andrew Jackson on horseback. With the horse rearing on its two hind legs, it was considered the best equestrian statue of its time. His Bladensburg, Maryland, foundry cast the *Statue of Freedom*, which sits atop the Capitol dome.

Mills, Theophilus "Fisk" (1840-1916): Clark Mills' second son. He and his older brother, Theodore Augustus, studied at the Royal Academy of Art in Munich, Germany. They both became well-known sculptors.

Powers, Hiram (1805-1873): A neoclassical sculptor, he was one of the first American sculptors to gain international recognition. His most famous work was *The Greek Slave*, which was adopted by the abolitionists as a symbol of their cause.

Stebbins, Emma (1815-1882): Daughter of a wealthy New York banker, she was encouraged to go to Rome to pursue her interest in sculpture. There, she met Harriet Hosmer's mentor, the actress Charlotte Cushman, who helped her get commissions. Most of Stebbins' work was small-scale and delicate. Her most famous work is *Angel of the Waters* in Central Park, New York City. When Cushman was diagnosed with breast cancer, Stebbins gave up her art to nurse her and later write her biography.

Stone, Horatio (1808-1886): To learn anatomy, Stone attended medical school before establishing himself as a sculptor in New York and Washington. In 1856, he was named Chair of the National Arts Council and was instrumental in founding the National Gallery of Art in 1860. During the Civil War, he worked as a surgeon. He was one of Vinnie's stiffest competitors. He received a number of sculpture commissions from Congress, including *John Hancock, Alexander Hamilton*, and *Edward Dickinson Baker*, all located in the Capitol.

Whitney, Anne (1821-1915): A member of the group of female sculptresses in Rome, she was a prominent and popular sculptress during the late nineteenth century. Her work focused on historic figures and, as a supporter of abolition and women's rights, on women in the movement.

Thank You for Reading

If you enjoyed learning about a forgotten woman who played a major role in the arts and politics of the Gilded Age, I would love to hear from you. Honest reviews on Goodreads, BookBub, and all online booksellers are always appreciated.

To learn about other amazing women, check out the other standalone books in the series: *That Dickinson Girl* and *Censored Angel*. To know when the next book in the *Forgotten Women* series is available, sign up for my newsletter, Historical Tidbits at joankoster.com to get book news, articles about forgotten women, old recipes, and more.

Thank you!

Joan

Book Club Questions

1. Mark Twain coined the term the "Gilded Age" to describe the period of railroad building, rapid industrialization, and political corruption, starting in the early 1870s and extending to the late 1890s. How does Vinnie Ream's life exemplify this period?

2. Do you think Vinnie Ream made the right choice in marrying Richard Hoxie instead of Cornelius Boudinot?

3. Would you agree with Mark Twain that Vinnie Ream was "the smartest politician of them all?"

4. One of the hallmarks of the Gilded Age was the high level of corruption in government. Were you surprised at the underhanded dealings, including manipulating the impeachment vote for Andrew Johnson, that allowed Perry Fuller to wheel-and-deal his way from crooked Indian agent to Customs Inspector of the Port of New Orleans while piling up billions of dollars in debt?

5. Why do you think Mary Todd Lincoln insisted that Vinnie Ream never met her husband?

6. Were you surprised to learn that Vinnie Ream was part of a large group of American female sculptresses, most of whom lived and worked in Rome? Have you heard of any of them or seen their works?

7. When Elizabeth Cady Stanton approached Vinnie Ream about signing a petition titled, "A Plan to Move on the World of Man, the Monster," Vinnie

refused, citing the support shown by men, many of whom were listed on the petition, versus the jealousy and nastiness of society women and women reporters, such as Swisshelm, toward her work. Do you think she made the right decision not to join the women's movement?

8. Like many women who accomplished major firsts in their lives, and despite the fact that her *Abraham Lincoln* sits in the Capitol Rotunda, and her two works, *Sequoyah* and *Kirkwood,* are in Statuary Hall where they are viewed by three million people yearly, Vinnie Ream is little known. What factors do you think explain this?

9. What do you think is the purpose of public sculpture? Should the government spend taxpayers' dollars to fund major works as it did on Vinnie's *Lincoln* and *Farragut*?

Forgotten Women Series

Biographical Historical Fiction based on Real Women's Lives

All proceeds from this series are donated to the Freedom to Read Foundation.

Book 1

That Dickinson Girl: A Novel of the Civil War

CHANTICLEER LARAMIE AWARD FINALIST ~ BEST HISTORICAL FICTION COFFEE POT BOOK CLUB ~ BOOK OF THE YEAR BOOK HEAVEN

Eighteen-year-old Quaker abolitionist Anna Dickinson is nothing like the women around her, and she knows it. Gifted with a powerful voice, a razor-sharp wit, and unbounded energy, the five-foot-tall, curly-headed girl sets out to outperform the men of her day as she speaks out against slavery and for women's rights. There are only two things that can bring her downfall: the entangling love she has for her devoted companion, Julia, and an assassin's bullet.

Forced by poverty and false accusations to accompany the fiery orator on her speaking tour of New England, Julia Pennington fights her growing attraction to Anna while protecting her from the onslaught of the press, and one newsman in particular: Floyd Burns. Blocked from becoming Anna's promoter, the traitor sets out to assassinate the young orator. Can Julia save the woman she loves before his bullet flies?

Loosely based on the life of forgotten orator and feminist Anna Dickinson, *That Dickinson Girl* is the story of one woman's rise to fame and fortune at the expense of love during the political and social turmoil of the American Civil War.

Book 2

Censored Angel: Anthony Comstock's Nemesis

FIRST PLACE WINNER: THE BOOK FEST ~ SHORT-LISTED FOR THE CHANTICLEER GOETHE AWARD

Brilliant, corseted, and haunted by spirits from the Borderlands, Ida Craddock, the only surviving daughter of a well-to-do Philadelphia Quaker patent medicine purveyor and the serving girl he married, is outraged by unmarried women's lack of knowledge about what happens in the marriage bed.

Turning her back on the tight constrictions of Victorian society, Ida strikes out on her own and sets up as a marriage counselor. Eager to share what she views as essential knowledge, she runs afoul of Anthony Comstock, the nation's Anti-Obscenity Postal Inspector. Infuriated by her article recommending belly dancing as preparation for marriage, the

Inquisitor of Smut sets out to destroy her work and silence her forever.

With prison hanging over her head, Ida and her guardian angels must prepare for a battle they may not be able to win.

Based on the life of mystic marriage counselor and First Amendment defender Ida C. Craddock, this is the twisted tale of the woman who helped bring down Anthony Comstock, of Comstock Law fame, and whose defense led to the formation of the Free Speech League, antecedent of the ACLU.

About the Author

Dr. Joan Bouza Koster is an award-winning author of fiction and nonfiction works in the fields of ethnography, education, anti-racism, and the arts.

She blogs about women who should not be forgotten at JoanKoster.com, about daily life during the Civil War at AmericanCivilWarVoice.org, about romance at ZaraWestRomance.com, and about ways to write better at Zara West's Journal (zarawest.me). She also teaches numerous online writing courses. Find her current teaching schedule on her website, joankoster.com.

Other Books by Joan Koster

Historical Fiction

The Forgotten Women Series
That Dickinson Girl
Censored Angel: Anthony Comstock's Nemesis

Romantic Suspense
(Under the Pen Name Zara West)

The Skin Quartet
Beneath the Skin
Close to the Skin
Within the Skin
Under the Skin

Tide Harbor Suspense
Concealed by the Tide
Lost Beneath the Tide

The Write for Success Series

Fast Draft Your Manuscript and Get It Done Now
Revise Your Draft and Make Your Writing Shine

Joan Koster

Research Your Subject and Validate Your Writing
Power Charge Your Language and Make Your Writing Sing

Tidal Waters Press

303

9 781959 318187